# Damaged Goods

Alexandra Allred

# DEDICATION

Thank you to my friends and family for taking part in this story and this journey with me.

"We do not inherit this earth from our ancestors. We borrow it for our children."

- Anonymous

# HISTORY OF THIS BOOK

In a small town in Texas, when no one was really watching, air quality had become a very real problem as local industry began emitting hazardous pollution into the air. Some of the state's biggest polluters were given immunity for previous violations for the benefit of big business but to the detriment of its citizens. By the year 2000, as upper respiratory diseases, asthma, unusual/rare cancers reared up, this small town was exposed to 1,502,123 pounds of Chromium, lead, manganese, mercury, and sulfuric acid – to name a few. Dioxin, the worst of the cancer-causing agents, was the cherry on top of the toxic sundae.

But rather than draw great alarm, local politicians and industry circled the wagons and fought to keep 'business as usual.' In 2005, Erin Brokovich would visit that very town and in a secret meeting at a Dairy Queen, one brave resident would sign on to become the necessary client for the infamous law firm of Masry & Vititoe, the firm responsible for the largest settlement ever paid in a direct-action lawsuit in U.S. history, to have cause to investigate.

***Damaged Goods***, though fictitious, is based on many of the ridiculous, the absurd, the shocking, the unethical and disturbing, and the oft hilarious antics of life under the cement plant umbrella.

# ACKNOWLEDGMENTS

Very real and wonderful people were the inspiration behind this book. Therefore, I would like to thank  the brave members of Downwinders at Risk (www.downwindersatrisk.org), Earthjustice in Washington D.C., all the grassroots' programs around the US who fight for clean air, water, and soil, and fight for the future of our children. I would like to thank those US Senators and Congressmen and women who have listened to reason and morality over corporate dollars. You know who you are. Thank you for putting personal time, families, and finances on hold to fight for the world around you!

# 1

It was the most outrageous, most appalling thing Joanna Lucas had ever done in her life. It was so beneath her, yet so absolutely appropriate, that she would wince and smile at the memory of it for the rest of her life. It was shocking, horrific, and disgusting that her single action of rebellion had reached legendary status before the ink had dried on her divorce papers.

In one pivotal moment, she had gone from lady to rebel. The audible gasps still rang in her ears. The gaping mouths and widened eyes were empowering, but it was the look on her soon-to-be ex-husband's face that was forever etched in her brain. That was her moment of true liberation.

Her story was no different from most of the women in the Hamptons. She had been a trophy wife. Her husband was a successful, uptight snob who would never have amounted to much had the family fortune not been dropped in his lap. She, too, had been caught up in the lavish lifestyle. It had been hard to resist the country clubs, yachts, expensive cars, whirlwind trips around the globe, designer clothing, and expensive jewelry.

Maybe that was when she had lost herself. Maybe that was

why she had tolerated his name-calling and infidelity.

But the drive to the Fuller's wedding had been the deal breaker.

She'd been wearing a Vera Wang dress made of a light yellow fabric. It was sheer, elegant, and almost transparent. Then she had started her period. More specifically, she had not anticipated the heaviness of her flow and was in dire need of a tampon change.

"We have to pull over," she said to her husband. But he was on yet another phone call and waved an agitated hand at her. She was to sit prettily, say nothing. She shifted in the seat, crossed her legs, and stared out the window.

"We really need to pull over." She tried again after a few minutes. The situation was moving into a critical stage. Soon her dress would be ruined.

"Hold on," he said, and at first, she wasn't sure if he was speaking to her or the person on the phone. She stared at him expectantly and he glowered. "Can you just hold on!" It was not a question but a command. "We're almost there."

"When?" she asked.

She wanted to scream at him. She could feel unpleasant things happening and knew if she didn't make it to a bathroom in a few minutes, the result would be disastrous.

He groaned, rolling his eyes. "Ten minutes. Can you just wait ten minutes?" He shook his head and laughed into the phone, trying to make light of it all. "It's like raising a little kid . . . Yeah, don't I know it."

Joanna looked out the window again. He was such an ass. She couldn't believe she'd ever loved him or thought she had. Everyone, in his view, was of lesser value than he was. She shifted again, feeling the growing warmth in her panty liner.

"Clayton," she pleaded. "We need to—"

"Holy shit! Would you shut up? Damn, just hold it!" he yelled and waved an arm as though he might backhand her.

She made a huffing noise and grabbed a small tissue box. She

pulled three or four out and stuffed the wad down her panties
Clayton swerved from their lane, then readjusted with an overreaction. "What the hell are you doing?"

Then he shook his head. "No, man. Not you. My crazy wife is doing . . . I don't know what the hell she's doing."
He looked at Joanna. "What are you doing?"

"I told you, I need to change—"

"Hold it. Can't you just hold it? Quit acting like a spoiled child and just—"

"It's not something you can hold." She shot him a dark look *What did he think?* She adjusted in her seat again, pondering what she'd just said. "Because if it were, if women could just turn their period on and off, your grandfather would not have been able to amass the fortune he did!"

She made an excellent point. The Lucas family owed their fortune to women. Clayton Lucas Sr. was the father of feminine hygiene products. His grandson, Clayton Lucas III, was also involved in the family business, yet he knew nothing about the actual products. Or about women, for that matter. He was such an ass. He didn't know one thing about women's issues. He knew what he needed to know, which was money makes some women easy.

"Look, I gotta go," he said into the phone. "I'll call you later." He disconnected and sneered at his wife. "You're like a cow. A simple-minded cow. You're just going to have to hold it."

Those words cut her like a knife. She knew he meant it. She knew he looked at her in this manner, and she had no one to blame but herself.

He was an arrogant, lying, cheating, horrible person who, based on the success of his grandfather, believed himself better than other people. His words raged within her. Even as they arrived at the church, as she hurried to the women's bathroom, as she prepared herself to do what she planned to do.

Pure rage drove her. She was so tired of his cruelty, his

faithlessness, and his condescending manner. When he had called her a cow, she'd bristled. Something powerful arose in her that she'd never known she possessed.

She exited the women's bathroom and strode across the lobby of the historical church. The interior was exquisite, but Joanna hardly noticed. She focused on Clayton as he chuckled and schmoozed with fellow Hamptonites.

The small group parted as she approached, some smiling at her arrival. But smiles faded into curiosity and then horror as she extended her hand toward Clayton. In response, he also extended his, ready to accept whatever it was she'd intended to pass off to him.

There was no smile on her face. No tension. No hesitation. No embarrassment. She was a woman on a mission.

As Clayton's hand opened, Joanna plopped the warm, heavy object into his palm.

"Why don't *you* hold it for a while."

The crowd gasped as she turned and walked away. Clayton Lucas III held a fully saturated, bloody tampon.

* * * *

Joanna Lucas was the typical client for Marcus Watkins. She was striking, and in many ways, she was the typical Hampton socialite—slender, athletic, blond, well-manicured, and immaculately dressed. But unlike most of the Hampton ladies who sported sun-kissed tans from either tennis or golf, Joanna was neither tan nor the outdoorsy type.

Clayton had set Joanna up with her own trendy yoga studio where clients could expect overpriced classes that were nothing more than social get-togethers. With designer yoga outfits in the gift shop, overpriced smoothies and organic health bars in the snack bar area, and expensive membership fees the norm, no one batted an eyelash.

When Clayton Lucas had established it as the place women needed to go, it was an overnight success. Everyone who was anyone belonged. The ironic thing was Joanna never wanted to be there. She liked yoga and she was a good instructor, but she was an artist of a different sort. She'd fantasized about owning her own art studio since she was a child—her own sculptor's studio. But Clayton had said that was a ridiculous dream.

"You're not getting the studio. You know that, don't you?" Marcus's voice was deep.

She glanced up. An old client at the studio—one who had taken her lying, cheating bastard of a husband to the cleaners—had given her his name, and Marcus Watkins had cleaned house. But Clayton Lucas had been through the wringer before. The Lucas men were known for their use and abuse of women, but he'd been far more discreet about his affairs. Material things replaced love and loyalty. This included the yoga studio.

Marcus shook his head. "It's a hard sale for me . . . posing you as the victim when you threw a . . . bloody tampon at your husband . . . in a church!" He could hardly say the words, and she rolled her eyes.

"I didn't throw it. In fact, I very politely handed it to him. Is it my fault he stuck out his hand?" She placed her hand to her chest. They both sat back in their chairs, each one studying the other, and Joanna noted how Marcus struggled not to smile.

"Sweetheart," he said, lacing his fingers together, "I don't know what you hoped to accomplish by doing that. Do you know that I was eating lunch the other day when an old associate of mine came up and asked if it was true I was representing the woman who threw a bloody tampon at her husband in a church?" She shrugged.

"A bloody tampon . . ." There was another chuckle. "You can't write that kind of stuff . . . and don't you know the tabloids are loving it."

"Poetic justice." She smiled.

Marcus was a large man in stature, but too many afternoon cocktails and high-calorie power lunches had caught up with him.

He looked more bloated than overweight. His fair complexion was blotchy with patches of broken blood vessels. He spent too many hours indoors, neglecting both fun and exercise. But he knew his clients, the array of judges on rotation, and how the law worked. And Joanna liked him. He was one of the few people she felt she could trust. He was honest, if not aggressively so.

Poetic justice or not, she would be lucky to walk away with anything after the Lucas family was done with her. Both Marcus and Joanna knew it.

"We can fight this, tell your side of the stor—"

She raised her hand. She knew the reality of the situation. She had taken a bloody, clotted, used-up tampon and placed it in her husband's hand. Though wrapped in tissue, it was clear what it was. Blood saturated the tissue and part of the string was exposed. And she had done this in front of witnesses. In a church. Before a wedding ceremony. Her days at the studio were over, but she'd never really had any friends there. She'd never wanted a yoga studio anyway. Everything in the Hamptons had been false. She had no real friends, no connections, and no sense of belonging. There wasn't anything worth fighting for.

"I want to cut and run." She was tired and embarrassed.

As she spoke, Marcus looked at a list of properties, ranging from beach homes and condos to dilapidated farm houses and cotton fields. He pushed the papers across the desk, letting her peruse them.

A penthouse in New York caught her attention and she held her breath. She considered it for a moment. Clayton used that place for his multiple affairs, and she imagined the kind of women he had paraded through those doors over the years. Certainly it would be an annoyance to him if she claimed this property. But how could she stand to stay in such a place?

She let out a sigh and continued to scan the paper. She smiled at a name, looking up.

"Marcus, Texas. They named a town after you?" A smile crept

along her lips.

"What can I say? I'm legendary."

"What are the odds of that?" She laughed, though she liked the sound of it for no better reason than it shared the same name as this man, her one friend.

"If memory serves," he said, leaning forward and reaching for the listing, "it's a fixer-upper. Eighty-five acres in a small farming community outside of Dallas."

He nodded and typed a website on his keyboard, and after a few more clicks, he gestured to the screen. It was a fixer-upper, but the place also held a certain elegance.
She stared at the old farmhouse with an oversized, wraparound porch, three gables, and a sweeping landscape that begged for horses. She felt a pang in her heart.

"No chance of me ever bumping into anyone from here in Marcus, Texas."

"You can count on that," he said and laughed at the thought.

"I'd never have to worry about ever laying eyes on Clayton again," she mumbled to herself.

"We could stipulate that if you take this property off his hands, he's responsible for all home improvements until it meets our satisfaction," Marcus said, not missing a beat. "All transactions can be done through this office."

"I'd never have to talk to him again," she said and then sighed.

"Not if I can help it." He reassured her.

She turned and smiled.

"That's a big job. Construction could go on for months and months . . ."
"I'm sure that it could," he said.

# 2

When I was twenty-three years old, I almost lost my life. Instead, while I lay almost bleeding to death, the doctor explained to me that I would make it, but I would have to say good-bye to my left leg. Gnawed beyond repair, there'd be no fixing it, so it had to go. Mind you, while I was plenty displeased about this, I was less angry at the wild beast that did it and more mad at my brother.

Two years my senior, Simon could mess up a fight. He couldn't do one thing right. If you'd said, *Simon, I'm about fed up with this life of mine, c'mon over here and help me end it—just shoot me,* he'd forget the gun and bring you flowers. So, while it should have been no surprise to me or anyone else that he'd forgotten to properly latch and lock the gate, I still found myself asking the same question over and over throughout the years. *How could you forget to lock up a tiger?*

Knowing I had a brother who was unreliable, I suppose I had no one to blame but myself for that fateful evening. I'd come home late and the cats were hungry.

At the time, we'd had two tigers, two lions, a cougar, and a bobcat.

Now before anyone goes off about how cruel it is to cage

animals or how wild cats should never be locked up or how I had it coming to me because, after all, wild cats are wild, let me emphatically state that I rescued big cats that were found by animal control or turned over to authorities after someone said, *Hey, these cats are wild.* There was always some jackass who thought his precious wee-wee would grow a few more inches if he owned an exotic animal or ferocious dog that caused others to say, *Damn, you own that?* Wait a few months and that same jackass would either get mauled or begin abusing the animal when he couldn't bend it to his will.

Not to be fooled by his name, Tony the Tiger was the most ferocious of the big cats we'd had at the time. He was not one to suffer well when his tummy growled, and he was not one to share his food. So, at mealtimes it was Simon's responsibility to lure one of the cats into the adjoining pen and close a drop gate between them. While Tony was fond of Queenie, they still had to be separated during dinner.

By the time I'd gotten there, dragging two hundred fifty pounds of meat in my meat wagon—actually it was an old Radio Flyer wagon, but we called it the meat wagon—the cats were in an uproar. Tony the Tiger was surly. He ripped through his food, snarling and carrying on until the last of the food was gone. Simon released the gate again and watched Tony step through to join Queenie. While the cats cleaned each other, Simon dropped the gate again, cleaned out the water pool, and left. But not before he opened the drop gate again, forgetting to lock the gate behind him.

That evening, I made the last of the rounds, making sure all were secure and content—a habit I'd begun when Lawrence of Arabia, our sixteen-year-old lion, had begun crying at imaginary figures in the night. I'd go out, set up the lantern—his nightlight— and reassure him once more. As always, Tony would pace alongside me inside his cage, growling softly. I'd learned from his first day never to walk too close to the cage or he'd take gigantic-pawed swipes at me. The laws of wild cats are easy enough to understand. Don't get too close and don't ever trust them because they're wild. The laws of Tony were even simpler. He loved Queenie and hated everyone else. It wasn't personal. It just was what it was.

But it was pretty personal as I passed his gate, and to my horror, I recognized a familiar sound—the soft creak of the gate opening. Even more horrifying was the second realization that his low growling was not beside me, but rather, behind me.

They say your brain protects you from the horrible things in life by causing selective amnesia. I've heard about guys who had terrible motorcycle accidents and couldn't remember the entire day leading up to the accident. The same is true with me. That low growl was my last clear memory of anything to do with the attack, including Simon's screams when he found me and the life-flight helicopter that rushed me to Dallas. The way the story goes, it was harder than it should have been to rescue me because Tony was missing for almost three hours. Everyone was afraid of an ambush, so my now-late father, Luther, dragged me out to the front of our property by while Simon waved a fire torch into the darkness.

I made national news, and for months my brush with death and myths of a still-missing tiger were all anyone talked about in Marcus, Texas and in nearby counties. I like to say I helped put Marcus on the map.

For the record, once Tony was tired of running around our fenced compound, my daddy said he strutted right back into his pen to rejoin Queenie and, I'm sure, had a good laugh about what a gamey thing I was. Never did I cry so hard as when I buried that leg-stealing bastard. He was wild, but he was a good cat.

After he died, Marcus returned to its normal state: boring, dusty and rural. I couldn't imagine that our mortality rates were any different from any other town, but it did seem that we lost a few too many good folks to illness from time to time.

That was when Ms. Redmond had begun to plant her trees. It had started when she lost Mary Hekking, her good friend. In her name, I believe, Ms. Redmond planted a red oak. It was a popular tree around Marcus that seemed to grow really well. When another friend and the grandchild of yet another friend both died, she planted two more. Within five years, it seemed more disturbing than beautiful that thriving red oaks lined an entire side of her long driveway.

When she lined the other side of her driveway with more tree memorials, local folks called her driveway the "tree cemetery." But Ms. Redmond hadn't liked that and began to refer to her home as "The Shady Land." It sounded nice, but we all knew what the shade represented.

The town held its collective breath when Ms. Redmond's boy, Bradley, died of pneumonia. *Would she plant a tree? Where would she plant the tree? Would she plant it alongside all the others?*

She never did. Her grief was unbearable. You could see it on her face. She never got over it, and I imagine she knew that planting a tree wasn't going to help her pain one bit.

I had thought about planting a red oak when the Redmonds died, but I never got to it, and I regret that. Ms. Redmond succumbed to a viral infection. But I don't know about any viral infection that stays with you for almost two years and has you up all night, hacking your head off. Six months later, Mr. Redmond was dead, too. Back then no one talked much about cancers or environmental issues. If you died, you died.

However they died, they were good, decent folks and mighty fine neighbors. They never complained about my big cats or the fly problems we sometimes had as the cats liked to gnaw on dead deer carcasses. And later, when I got horses, they never complained about the manure smells.

Before the Redmonds had died, their place had been somewhat of a gathering place for the community, and a source of pride for the citizens of Marcus.

Anyone traveling along the country road FM 875 would find one of the most beautiful spreads in all the state, with its majestic entrance to the long driveway lined by trees and forest green pipe fencing that led toward the brick home, it was more mansion than house. The intricate pattern of the brick and bay windows showcased the wide oak doors with old cast-iron framework. It was a house that held promise for Joanna's new life but hosted ghosts of the past. It was modern living meets rustic farmhouse. Behind the house lay wonders yet to be discovered by any passersby: a rolling creek, a stock pond, and a back pasture complete with over eighty acres of open pasture. There was a tree house, complete with matching iron moldings and bay windows.

But that was before John and Ellen Redmond got sick, before their son got sick and died, before the feral hogs tore up the ground so badly you couldn't drive, much less walk, through the back pastures. That was before kids with inattentive parents had broken all the windows in the house, before weather and neglect had taken care of the frame and paint.

Now the house—like the land—was uninhabitable.

As it turned out, The Shady Land was built on nothing more than confusion, despair, suffering, and longing. Although none of us knew or understood that yet. We thought it was all just horrible luck.

Too often, I'd look out across the land where our two properties met and wonder about the past. What might I have done differently? Who's to know? Maybe it was why I was so distrustful of Joanna when she first arrived. I didn't want to be hurt again. Then again, maybe it was why I began to care too much. I wanted things to be right this time around, I wanted someone to be able to make things right. What I do know is that the day she moved in, nothing would ever be the same in Marcus, Texas again.

* * * *

Word was that she was an uptight snot from somewhere up north, come to play Texan while she licked her wounds. Her name was, as reported by Eva Tobey, Joanna Lucas. She'd nosed around Marcus for two days before she'd found Eva in her real estate office and completed the paperwork on the old Redmond place. According to Eva, Joanna Lucas was given full ownership of the land. Eva had tried in vain to learn how a woman from New York might have acquired the deed to the Redmond estate, but Joanna Lucas had been tightlipped and prissy. When Eva told the Yankee about all the extensive work that needed to be done on the estate, the woman hadn't batted an eyelash. Not one eyelash.

So, there was sort of an unofficial welcome committee at the Redmond place when Ms. Lucas rolled into town because everyone wanted to take a peek at the artsy-fartsy yoga instructor from New York who had breezed in to take residence in such a place, feral hogs and all.

I saw the entourage and smiled. A large moving van, towing a fancy red Jeep, followed a girl driving a canary yellow Volkswagen with a large daisy on the side. In the land of pickup trucks and old beaters, this automotive parade could only belong to the New Yorker. With visions of being the first Marcus resident to greet her, I hustled out the door to my golf cart. More than anything else, I was intrigued by the name. There was a rumor that the Redmond place had been owned by some feminine hygiene corporation, and I don't mind saying that no sooner did the word get out that douche and tampon money had been used to purchase that land, there was a renewed interest in that place as intense as the time my own cat gnawed off my leg. I didn't yet know who this Joanna Lucas woman was, but I'd found a certain delight in knowing she would soon be earning herself a nickname in this town. I'd gotten mine, like it or not, after Tony ate my leg. Slow. That was my nickname. Slow. Apparently, someone thought it funny to call a woman who had had her leg ripped off by a tiger slow. But what, oh, what would the townsfolk of Marcus call a lady who bought a house with feminine hygiene money? I could not contain myself.

My name is Suzette Lee, and while some might tag me as being eccentric, the actual word should be invested. I am, and have always been, invested in my community, my neighbors, our future, and the day-to-day activities that somehow involve me, however indirectly. A tampon queen outsider certainly involved me.

I climbed into my old golf cart and rattled down the driveway to meet the girls leaning against the post dividing our properties. Even with pedal to the metal, the old golf cart would not exceed ten miles per hour, and I watched the other Marcus residents beat me to the driveway as Joanna Lucas pulled in.

By the time I'd circled out of my driveway and into hers, a small crowd had formed with Eva, Dixie Quigley, Brianna Smart, and Ruthie Emory already set in the honorary welcome-to-Marcus pose: arms crossed, smiles in place, and ready for judgment.

"Damn it!" I jerked back and forth in the golf cart, urging it a little faster. By the time I arrived, the Lucas party was already unloading.

"That's her," Eva Tobey said and pointed, "right there."

In unison, we looked.

Joanna Lucas was a sweet little thing, looking more like a California surfer girl than a snooty New Yorker. Long blond hair with golden sun streaks billowed around her lean, athletic frame. She was fair-skinned enough, and we discerned she would burn quickly in the Texas sun.

She was a hard worker—ignoring the locals, moving between house and truck, unloading boxes as fast as her legs could carry her, and working as hard as the moving crew.

"She's what you'd call a cool drink of water," Dixie Quigley said with certain approval.

"Honey," Eva said with a snort, "she's cool, all right. And I'll tell ya this; I don't think she's footin' the bill. I think she's got herself a sugar daddy."

I'd had enough of the idle curiosity of the Lucas move-in. I needed a closer look and set my cart in motion again.

In my day, I moved about quite frequently. But in recent years, acute bronchitis and emphysema—not to mention being short a leg—prevented me from too much activity. But I could not complain. The poor health of Franklin, my darling husband, had put things in perspective for me. He was such a dear, sweet man.

He never complained, never took the Lord's name in vain, and as he carried on, so did I.

Not only had we once rescued big cats, but we'd owned a successful horse-breeding ranch. Of course, these were at different times. I enjoy excitement as much as the next gal, but lions and Arabians do not mix. When we'd owned the horses, we'd employed many locals, and regaled in a reputation that brought lots of top-notch horse buyers from out of state. At one time, ours was *the* place to come for a champion Arabian. But like all things, times changed, and unexpected circumstances altered our lives. We were no exception to this little rule of life. It was cry or get a golf cart and move on. I got the golf cart.

As my cart zipped down the long, driveway leading to the old Redmond house, I managed to kick up enough dust to catch the attention of Joanna Lucas and her moving crew so that by the time I reached the front porch, the city girl was waiting.

Joanna Lucas cocked her head to the side in a curious manner, wondering, no doubt, why she was being visited by a golf-cart-driving woman. Or, wondering what a one-legged woman driving a golf cart might have to say.

Whatever she was thinking, I did what needed to be done. I gathered as much information as I could about that woman and gave her a history of Marcus that would set her brain spinning.

# 3

Beyond the gratitude she felt toward Marcus Watkins, Joanna felt sadness. It was burdensome and weighed her down, slowing everything around her. She wasn't the one who'd cheated in the marriage. She hadn't changed or been deceptive, yet she couldn't quite shake the feeling that she'd somehow failed. That, she reasoned, was why it took her so long to act. That weight had immobilized her from taking action for herself, her dignity, and her happiness. It was why she became so entrenched in her yoga. After countless hours attending classes to relieve stress and express herself, it seemed natural to take the next step. In truth, she just needed some direction. She'd wanted to be an artist, but Clayton hadn't liked the idea of her working with messy clay. Yoga, he'd said, was more dignified. So, she'd worked hard to become a certified instructor.

Silly as it sounded, it was the yoga that allowed her to place that tampon in Clayton's hand. It was the yoga that allowed her to take the final deep breath and exhale all the crap, all the derogatory comments and release it like flushing toxins from her body.

Clayton agreed to her terms and was more than happy to be rid of her so that he could turn the studio over to some young woman named Charity, who didn't know a snot's worth about yoga. No doubt, Charity was the new flavor.

*Why did that bother her? He was a bastard. Why should she care?*

Clayton, however awful, however rotten, was not expected to change. He was not the one who would have to uproot his life, pack his bags, and slink away. He remained in the Hamptons with his family, his money, and his supposed friends—laughing at his ill-advised marriage to Joanna. And she could just hear all her old clients and friends reassuring Clayton. *You're better off without her. She was never one of us. Where did you meet her anyway?*

Joanna sank back against the pillar on the front porch, drinking in the ambiance of her new home. It was hers. It was all hers. And if she kept her back to the house, blocking out just how much time and effort had to be put into its remodeling and focused on the front property, she had hope.

The house was something out of a dream. On the surface, it needed a lot of help. Described as a country farmhouse, it was more of a mansion with five bedrooms, a three-car garage, a huge eat-in kitchen, three bathrooms, and a library complete with floor-to-ceiling bookshelves and a rolling ladder. The house sat on lovely wooded, fenced eighty-five acres with a creek, a stock pond, and a five-stall horse barn. Joanna knew at the time that it was too good to be true.

But then, she'd been in denial about so many things for so many years. With the dream home came fifty-year-old plumbing, well water, faulty wiring, broken windows and stairs, and countless cracked and broken boards, plaster, and concrete throughout the entire property.

"Ever see *The Money Pit?*" the local real estate agent had asked Joanna when she first arrived in Marcus to look the place over.

It was a question she would be asked three more times before she moved. No one seemed to think that Joanna Lucas could stand on her own two feet.

"What? Are you daring me?" she had asked a mutual friend of hers and Clayton's. You don't think I can do this?"

"I don't think Clayton thinks you can do this," the friend had said. Clayton had made sure that all their friends knew she was crazy to move away, to give up everything for a rundown piece of property. Oh, he'd been so sweet in their agreement over the property and then turned on her with snide remarks and predictions of doom.

"This has nothing to do with him." That had been one of Joanna's last promises before she packed up and moved away.

But it did. Money had been one of the biggest contentions of their divorce. She wouldn't make it. Along with the house came the budget to repair it, but she was on a deadline. She had to make things work with enough time to set up a house and find a job before all the money was gone. She wouldn't last six months before she went under financially, he'd said. She was a disaster when it came to finances. It was a point he had pounded into her brain since their first year of marriage.

So much so that she'd sometimes believed it to be true. Still, there was a small whisper that kept humming in Joanna's ear. The whisper was full of promise and excitement. "Can you imagine what that place could look like once you've finished the landscaping? The way you want to do it? No holding back. Can you imagine?" And beyond that, everything else melted away.

Yes. She could imagine. She had fantasized about the big, white farmhouse with a wraparound porch, huge bay windows, hanging plants, vast array of shrubbery and flowers lining the walk and surrounding the house, and a canopy of ivy hanging over an old-fashioned swing. She could see it perfectly.

And for months, she had built up the image of how the house would look so that she had almost believed it would be complete when she drove up the long driveway. With every task complete—the signing of bank papers, the last box packed and loaded, the final good-bye to old neighbors—Joanna had become more optimistic about the move. Then, Marcus, Texas was no longer a dot on a map. It was real, it was here, and she felt her heartbeat quicken as she'd pulled off the highway to her new life.

*What had she done?*

Civilization was behind her, some twenty-three miles back. Marcus—population: fifty-seven hundred—sported a Dairy Queen, a prerequisite for any small Texas town; a small grocery store; three gas stations; a CVS; and a post office. While she couldn't see them, there were police and fire stations on Main Street, an elementary school and small high school.

She'd slowed to turn onto FM 875 at the Dairy Queen, making sure the moving truck following her made the turn as well. The silence was deafening. She'd looked at sprawling ranches with cattle, long horns, horses, pastures with hay, and dried grass. She'd seen the countryside of Kansas and Nebraska. While flat, the fields were beautiful. Green grass bent and whirled in the wind, feeding a varied wildlife. And the terrain in Colorado, Montana, and Wyoming was rolling, filled with trees, rock, and color. This had none of that. It was flat, brown, and almost lifeless but for the livestock, which was careful not to move too much under the scorching midday sun. Then, just over the crest of a hill, the scenery changed. Trees, sparse at first, filled out the skyline. Joanna had remembered the trees as a landmark. Two miles beyond, she slowed, turned left onto a driveway, and stopped.

Two trees marked the entrance, each standing proudly on either side of the driveway. Beyond the trees were crumbled rocks where pillars once stood. Immediately, Joanna noticed the iron fencing that had broken or rotted away from a beam, leaving a huge gap at the entrance. Far away, sitting alone and abandoned, was her dream house. Broken windows, broken stairs, and faded, peeling paint shattered her fantasy. This was her new home.

*What had she done*? She'd only thought about money. It hadn't mattered that it was Clayton's. She was looking at a giant money pit. All she could think about was how much it would cost to fix the problems, and Clayton's condescending voice crept into her head.

Marcus, the cement capital of Texas.

*Don't piss people off. Don't ask too many questions.*

That voice was not Clayton's but that of the strange woman on a golf cart. Joanna squinted, trying to recall the woman's name. Suzette Lee.

Before she'd even introduced herself by name, Ms. Lee was barking out the Ten Commandments of Marcus.

*Don't ever get alone with Tallulah Walker, and don't look at my leg.*

Joanna hadn't looked at Ms. Lee's leg until she'd mentioned it. Sure enough, there was nothing but a stump resting on the seat of the golf cart. Joanna opened her mouth to speak.

"And don't *ask* about my leg. I'll just tell ya before someone else does. I got it torn off by a tiger. One of my tigers to be exact. But don't worry. That tiger's dead and gone." She'd paused, and Joanna had thrown a cautious look around anyway.

"The tiger I got now is not a leg eater."

Joanna's eyebrows shot up.

If it weren't so horrifying, it might be funny. While Joanna stood stupefied, Ms. Lee went on to explain that she possessed four wild cats: two lions, one tiger, and one rare snow leopard. She also owned a llama and an emu.

Joanna wiped the sweat that continued to roll down the side of her face and sting her eyes. Without electricity, her house had become an oven. She looked around, hoping for a drink of water from her water bottle, however warm. It would be refreshing against her dry throat and maybe act as a mild distraction to the one thought that drummed through her brain.

*What have I done?*

Again, the voice of Suzette Lee nagged her. There were ten Marcus commandments. Joanna, however, was so tired and had been so surprised by the woman, it was hard to recall the rest of the strange rules. Don't ask questions. Don't talk to someone named Talada, Tawanda, Tallulah. Don't piss people off.

She sighed and stared out across the horizon. The sun, which had morphed into a giant orange ball, slid behind the trees and offered the last light Joanna would see again until morning. It would be a long night without electricity, and her closest neighbor was a one-legged woman in a golf cart.

Then Joanna remembered another commandment:

*Don't drink the water . . . it'll kill ya.*

Joanna suddenly looked down at her bottle, holding a mouthful of water in her mouth.

# 4

They moved silently, picking through the heavy brush and debris, eyes scanning the vast territory. It was the dead of the night, pitch black and isolated, but they knew there was a very good chance eyes were already upon them. They needed to move quickly, set up the equipment, and get out.

They'd rehearsed their moves many times, making sure they worked as a team. But they had been besieged with problems from the start. They hadn't been able to park where they'd planned, adding an unanticipated twenty minutes to their hike. The third leg to the metal tripod would not lock, and a canister would not open.

"We're running out of time." The voice was a whisper. Indeed, they had exceeded the plan already by more than thirty minutes. It would only be a matter of time before their car was discovered.

"We need to head back," another whisper rang out.

Even in the dark, they could sense each other's nods. It was time to abort. There would be another time. There would have to be another time.

* * * *

Paul stooped and inspected the soil. He pursed his lips and

blew out. Behind him, Frank stepped forward.

"The question is, what were they doing here?" Frank asked.
Paul stood again, sifting the dirt between his fingers. He was rail thin with a thick mass of brown hair, making him look like a human mop. This look was exaggerated by his passion for skintight Wranglers, pressed and starched.

He was in his mid-thirties, born and raised in Marcus, and couldn't imagine life beyond the town's borders. Everything he wanted or needed was within the town. Anything beyond was convoluted trouble created by liberals and heathens.

"Teenagers, I suppose." Paul's drawl was slow and deliberate as he studied the tracks on the ground.

Frank shook his head, unsatisfied. He'd gone to school with Paul. They'd grown up three houses from one another. They shared childhood memories, booze, girlfriends, and their loyalty to Future Foundations. But Frank was one thing Paul was not. He was a realist. Paul chose to believe that everyone living in Marcus loved the town. Frank knew better. There were always people trying to cause trouble. There was always a group that needed to bitch and moan about something. And given the direction Future Foundations was moving, the very last thing they needed was a group of troublemakers.

"Maybe." Frank scanned the terrain.

Together, he and Paul surveyed the property of Future Foundations Industries. It was more than four hundred acres of flat, barren land that had been home to FFI for forty years. But last year, the Simmons family had sold out to an international company. It was a deal made in the middle of the night and took the residents of Marcus by surprise. No one saw it coming, and there were some bitter feelings.

But John Simmons had made a few stipulations that had smoothed some of the ruffled feathers, including those of the Marcus Chamber of Commerce: FFI couldn't be moved. The name of the company must remain Future Foundations. No one could be replaced or demoted. FFI had always been about family and community. Even if it had sold out to an international corporation, it was about family.

Still, tensions had been high until the bigwigs came in. A team of Austrians had arrived, complete with suit-and-tie lawyers, two scientists, the corporate heads, and a massive human who had to be some kind of bodyguard. They were a sight to behold, leaving tongues wagging for some time after as to why a bodyguard was needed. But whatever animosity the locals felt was squelched as Mr. Gustoff Mattias met with team leaders.

Mattias's English had been top-notch with an Arnold Schwarzenegger accent that only endeared him to the crowd. Within minutes, he had offered outstanding bonus and incentive packages that equaled more money than anyone could ever have imagined. Both Frank Wolan and Paul Cowell, local football stars and town sweethearts, were promoted. Before the hour-long meeting was over, Marcus residents had settled happily into a new relationship with the Austrians and touted themselves as the adopted sons and daughters of Austria.

Later, behind closed doors, a handful of FFI employees would understand the mission of their newly owned company. It was, they were told, a move for the future and their families.

This was Frank's company. He worked it inside and out. He knew every inch of it and he loved it.

He frowned at the ground and then looked at his friend. "But I don't like it. There's too much goin' on right now to have a bunch of teenagers or . . . whoever to be nosin' around here."
Paul shrugged. "We'll post a few more signs and restring the restrictive cables."

"Hell, Paulie, we've got no trespassing signs all up and down the road. If it's a bunch of kids, they don't give a damn 'bout that. We need to post some guards out here."

"Guards?" Paul said with a laugh. "For a bunch of kids?"
Frank scowled and swatted at his legs. "Damned chiggers!" He

stomped back toward the truck, stepping high over the weeds and rocks.

Paul's laugh followed him.

"This is what I'm sayin'! Who'd want to come out here to get tore up by chiggers?" Paul followed Frank's tracks back to the truck to avoid any hitchhikers. "I'll tell ya what happened. A bunch of boneheaded kids came out here, stayed for two minutes before the chiggers got 'em, and then hightailed it out of here."

"Still," Frank said over his shoulder, "if it's all the same to you, I'm gonna have security double their rounds out here."

"It's just a bunch of kids. Who else would come out here?" Paul muttered to himself, brushing vigorously at his legs before he climbed into the truck.

"Damned chiggers. Things'll eat you alive."

* * * *

"Which would you prefer," Jeanie Archer asked with some urgency, "for pee to come out of your mouth or your nose?" RuthAnn Emory spit up her coffee, gagging and causing such a commotion, Jeanie's question was temporarily forgotten.

"Lordy, Ruthie," Brianna Smart said and patted Ruthie on her back. "You okay?"

Tears rolled down Ruthie's cheeks as she fought for composure, giving a little wheeze as she steadied her breath again. Jeanie leaned back in her seat, sipped her coffee, and smiled.

"You're just going to sit there until you get your answer, aren't you?" Brianna scowled at Jeanie.

Since the day Jeanie had moved to town in the second grade, she'd been posing questions like that to the girls. Now, more than four decades later, Jeanie never ceased to shock and dismay. She was outlandish without an ounce of modesty, and her wild-child streak had been tempered only mildly as she aged.

In her late forties, Jeanie's hair was still blond, though now short and unruly and representative of its owner. She was lean, attractive and womanly, but her brutish behavior was sometimes off-putting to the more feminine set of Marcus. Her laugh was boisterous, most often followed by a hard punch to an innocent person's shoulder. Man, woman, or child. It did not matter to Jeanie. She was an equal opportunist in her raucous humor.

When Jeanie had punched Caroline McCutchin in the mouth in the second grade, she'd become a bona fide sister to the girls. Brianna, Eva, and Ruthie had all been victims of Caroline for years. In fact, Caroline's reign of terror had begun in preschool, and the girls were under the grand delusion that she was all powerful and could not be stopped. But Jeanie saw things differently. When Caroline cut off Brianna's braid with a pair of scissors during art class, Jeanie said she was going to tell the teacher. Caroline told her she better not or else, and she proceeded to do the most horrifying thing. She'd balled up her fist and showed them all "what else" meant.

But Jeanie had not understood the power that Caroline possessed. She didn't know that even the second- and third-grade boys were afraid of Caroline. So, when Caroline began to raise her fist again to illustrate her power, Jeanie slugged her in the mouth. Caroline dropped to the floor like wet cement, her blood flowing across the art room floor, and a legend was born. From that moment on, two things were permanent. Jeanie was one of "the girls," and she was allowed to say whatever she wanted, whenever she wanted.

Ruthie drew in a full breath then sighed. "Why does urine have to come out of my nose or my mouth? Why can't it just come out where it's always been coming out?"

"I've had pee in my mouth before," Merilee said, and all heads turned. Merilee Chambers was the manager of Quigley's Down Under and didn't have much to say most days. But from time to time, she would have the urge to share.

"I mean, indirectly, of course. Clyde Bishop whipped out his wee-wee when we were on a Slip 'n Slide, you know, as kids. When us kids was comin' down the slide, he showered us. I was laughing and got it right in my mouth. I'll never forget that. I don't know why he did that. It ruined the day." And she went back to preparing sandwiches.

For a moment, Ruthie and Jeanie stared at her, slack-jawed.

"Oh, for hell's sake," Brianna said with a snort, rising from the table. She caught Merilee's eye and waved her coffee cup for a refill as she walked away from the table.

Jeanie huffed.

The girls knew it was Brianna's habit to walk away from anything she considered unpleasant. Any activity that required sweating, any recipe that was too complicated, any politics that caused debate, any important topics like contemplating pee coming out of your mouth were all walk-aways. It had been true since Brianna was in the second grade, when the girls became friends. Her name was Brianna Keller, and she had allowed herself to be bullied even then. Brianna and Jeanie became friends after the hair cutting incident with Caroline.  Jeanie figured she needed a protector and that was that. Later, she'd married and become Brianna Smart. Different name, same gal. She'd married Terry Smart, a one-time stud who'd mistreated her as a teenage sweetheart and continued to do so into their forties. Together, the girls had commiserated over what a low-down, cheating rat he was, but Brianna stayed with him, always refusing their offers of support—both emotional and financial.

When she'd licked her wounds and gotten over whatever it was Terry had done to hurt her, Brianna would turn on the girls. She would rebuff their pleas to get out of her dead-end marriage with insults of her own, always carefully identifying problems in the lives of others. If nothing else, Brianna was a brilliant strategist in turning the tables and shutting people down.

"Out my nose," Ruthie said with some thought.

Jeanie jerked her head back toward her friend. "Ha! I knew it!" She nodded. "Me, too. I would much rather have urine come out my nose."

Brianna half turned, mouth poised for a tongue-lashing when she stopped and smiled toward the door.

"Oh, thank you for coming! You wouldn't believe the conversation they are having," Brianna said and pointed an accusatory finger toward Jeanie and Ruthie.

The woman at the door stopped, cocked her head, and flashed a brilliant smile. She was short but shapely. A blonde bombshell. Marcus's own version of Dolly Parton, though not quite as endowed. Dixie Quigley was the owner of Quigley's Down Under and a loyal fan of actor Tom Selleck, who starred in the film *Quigley Down Under*. She was loyal enough to forgive him for that particular movie and still name her establishment after it.

Dixie always loved a grand entrance. "What have I missed?" She made sure everyone present focused on her.

"Oh, get over yourself," Jeanie said, directing her wrath to Brianna. "I'm just asking a question, is all. Geez!"

Dixie's smile widened. A former stripper who had married her favorite patron and best tipper, Dixie had converted to Mormonism but never lost her lust for dirty stories or Jeanie's inane questions.

"Hit me," she said, throwing a defiant glance at Jeanie. "I've had a crap day and need something to jump-start me in the right direction. Whatcha got?"

"Would you rather have pee come out your nose or your mouth?" Jeanie asked without missing a beat. Even Merilee stopped from behind the counter, looked up, and awaited Dixie's reply.

Dixie's mouth opened for a moment. Then, she broke into a gleeful cackle. And she would have answered had it not been for a new customer entering the café.

The sight of Joanna Lucas caused instantaneous silence in Quigley's Down Under. Even Dixie herself was caught off guard for just a moment.

*It was her! It was her! The Yankee!*

An excited aura wrapped in deafening quiet seized the room.

All eyes were on Joanna as she stepped in, halted abruptly, and looked around the room.

"I'm sorry," she said with some caution. "Did I . . . Am I interrupting something? I can always come . . ." Joanna made a motion back toward the door to indicate she could or would leave.

"Oh, honey," Dixie said with renewed focus. In typical Dixie fashion, she latched on to Joanna and yanked her forward. "My goodness, no. We were just gabbing. C'mon on in here."

Joanna stumbled forward, half-dragged, half-walked. Before she could catch her balance, Dixie plopped her onto a stool and hurried around the counter, tying on an apron.

"Now, what can I do ya for?" she asked with a drawl for effect and flashed one of her most dazzling smiles. Joanna Lucas would be eaten for lunch. At their own table, Ruthie winked at Jeanie and eased over to the counter. But the Yankee lived up to her reputation, offering only the most basic of details to each and every question Dixie spooned out. She offered no new insight, and much to Jeanie's frustrations, Dixie politely danced around the big one: Had the Redmond place been bought with tampon money?

Yes, Joanna was polite, but noncommittal in answering, she had once married. No, she had no children. Yes, she was renovating the Redmond place. No, she'd never been to Marcus before. Yes, she was living out there all alone. No, she hadn't thought about what she was going to do once the place was fixed up. Yes, she used to be a yoga instructor. No, she had no plans of starting a studio in Marcus. Yes, she was ordering food because she didn't have electricity yet, but with luck that would change by the end of the day. Yes, she had finally gotten water. And no, she wasn't drinking it.

In the time she'd answered all those questions, she'd placed an order and allowed Dixie to prepare a club sandwich and chicken enchilada soup to go.

But Jeanie couldn't handle it any longer and rose from her seat. "Is it true—that it was tampon money that bought that old place?"

Joanna was slow to turn in her seat, missing how hard Ruthie slapped Jeanie on the arm. When she did turn, she found Jeanie holding her arm and scowling as Ruthie, stricken with embarrassment, stood next to her.

There was a long pause before Joanna managed a smile. There was an eerie calm in her demeanor—one that all the women noticed.

"You could say that tampons definitely led me here." She turned, paid her bill, murmured a thank-you, and gathered up the bag of food.

Everyone stood in wonder. Dixie managed a nod and smiled back.

"You come again, ya hear?"

As she walked out, the girls eyed one another behind Joanna's back. *What the hell was that supposed to mean?*

Not surprisingly, it was Dixie who regained her composure first and turned to Jeanie.

"In my mouth," she said.

"What?" Jeanie asked, her eyes still trained on the back of Joanna Lucas.

"My mouth. I would rather pee come out my mouth."

"Oh, my heavens!" Brianna said, clasping her hands over her ears.

"Ha!" Jeanie was elated. "That's disgusting! Why in the world would you—"

"Oh, come on." Dixie threw a hand on her hip and grinned so mischievously that Brianna braced herself for what was to come next. She'd known Dixie long enough to know that look. "You, of all people, Jeanie. With a trash mouth like yours, I wouldn't think a little urine would be so bad tasting."

Jeanie's smile widened. It was pure adoration. Jeanie, too, could feel the big one coming.

"And I know you've had worse things in your mouth than a little urine."

Brianna cried out, covering her ears, and everyone smiled.

# 5

Joanna leaned against the doorjamb, watching the man. She had water and soon, she had hoped, she'd have electricity. But her joy had been short lived.

"I'm gonna have to come back," Doug Mitchell said.

Joanna had called Mitchell Electric on her realtor's advice.

"If it's anything electric," Eva Tobey had said, "Doug Mitchell's your man."

But he wasn't her man. Not today. Joanna thought she might cry.

"I'm going have to bring power in," he said and Joanna slumped.

"How long is that going to take?" She sounded whiny.

"Mmm, couldn't say exactly." He rubbed his chin. "At least another day or so. I'm gonna have to call Jimmy, downtown, you know . . . set up a few things."

"I don't understand." She could feel a scream welling up in her throat. If Clayton could see her now, he'd be enjoying this. And it was no one's fault but her own. She'd taken on this project to be a smartass. She wanted to show everyone how independent she was, but she'd also wanted to take something of Clayton's and make it ten times better.

She'd been fooling herself.

She sighed, looking around the structure that surrounded them. There was so much work to be done.

"Why can't you just flip a switch or something? That's how it's always been done before."

He smiled at her as a man would smile at a little girl who had just declared that the Easter Bunny was real. He looked as though he might pat her head.

"No, ma'am," he said, suppressing a smile. "The wiring in this house . . . well, the whole place is going to have to be rewired. We have to bring in a new cable, bring in new circuits."

She continued to stare at him.

"Which means we have to dig a trench, you know, to bury the cable . . . and that's going to take a little time to set up. Things don't move quite a fast as I'm supposin' you're used to."

Joanna ran her hands through her hair and then wished she hadn't. She was filthy. Her hands were filthy. She was covered in sweat and grime and who knew what else.

She was dirty, beat down, and tired. Besides everything else that was going on, she'd not been sleeping well. Throughout the night, the roars of a lion had awakened her. This was not something she'd experienced living in the Hamptons.

She managed a smile and nodded.

"No. It's okay. I understand. Just . . . if you could make things go as fast as they can, well, I'd just appreciate it. I know this house is a mess." She offered a smile, however pathetic. "I'd just like to be able to take a shower—a hot shower—and then cook a meal."

"Well, you're welcome to come to my house," he said.

*Was he kidding? Was he serious? Or, was he making the moves on her?* His expression never changed, and she decided that the offer was genuine, an example of Southern hospitality she was not accustomed to.

He was all cowboy. Short and thick with a barrel chest and

solid, meaty forearms. He looked like he could a wrestle a bear and win. And, she noticed with some relief, he sported a wedding band.

"Oh, no . . . what's another day?" she said with a sigh. "I'm kind of getting used to my own stench now."

"Well, if this is your worst, I can't imagine how pretty you look when you're all cleaned up," he said, pushing his ball cap back a little on his head. She froze. "If you don't mind me sayin' so?" He started to smile but turned his head at the sound of a horn. Eva Tobey was barreling down the driveway at great speed, kicking up dust and rocks as far back as the highway.

"Well, I'll get back to ya," he murmured and sauntered off the front porch and back to his truck. He paused just long enough to give a wave to Eva as she screeched to a halt.

Eva was just as Joanna remembered her from their first meeting. She wore a peasant skirt with a flowing blouse, large and expensive turquoise jewelry, and big Texas hair that was back-combed, hair-sprayed, and volumized to the extreme. It was hard not to smile. In every respect, Eva was an icon, a throwback to the big-hair eighties. But she ruled the town, so she wore what she wanted and no one dared say a word.

"Don't you be gettin' too close to that one," Eva said as she moved around the car without so much as a *hello* or *how's it going?* She was all business, and it seemed item number one on that list was setting Joanna Lucas straight on Doug Mitchell.

"You want something taken care of in your house, he's the one to call. But if it's not about your house, don't listen to anything that comes out of that man's mouth. He's a regular Romeo, complete with accent and tight britches, only the accent's not Italian and what he has to say is definitely not clean or all that suave, if you ask me."

Joanna's mouth fell open. She dared not laugh out loud. Eva kept right on talking, hustling around Joanna and up the front steps.

"So, how's it comin'?"

She disappeared into the house, leaving Joanna standing on the bottom step.

"Just great," Joanna mumbled and shrugged. "Just frickin' great."

She turned and saw Eva in the doorway, peering down at her with her hands on her hips.

"You don't have electricity." It wasn't a question. It was a news bulletin.

With a hand on the railing and one foot already on the next step, Joanna dropped her head in utter defeat. "No. I don't have electricity. I don't have hot water. I don't have crap," she said, talking to her feet.

"You've been here for . . . for almost a week!"

"And seventeen hours, twelve minutes, and counting the seconds."

"Well, Good Lord. This is unacceptable!" Eva pulled out her cell phone.

Joanna managed a weak smile, trudged up the stairs, and plopped down beside Eva's feet. The truth was she hadn't liked Eva when she met her. There was too much Hampton in her. Joanna sensed that no sooner had she left Eva's office than the woman had been on the phone, talking to every citizen of Marcus. Eva had a way about her when she asked questions. She cocked her head and listened, much as a parrot would. But now, as Eva threatened Doug Mitchell with loss of wages and reputation, Joanna felt a sudden affection for her.

After her stand against her horrible soon-to-be-ex, Joanna had come to think of herself as strong, but now she was broken down, dirty, and exhausted. She'd hauled more lumber, pulled more weeds, and carried out more trash than she ever could have imagined. What was most defeating, however, was she'd hardly put a dent in the work that needed to be done.

She'd been told by a tiger-loving, golf cart-driving crazy lady not to drink the water or to look at her leg, and the only normal-looking women in town had been having some inane conversation about having pee in their mouths.

Joanna pulled her feet up on a higher step so that her knees drew even with her chin, and she rested her head there. She closed her eyes for a moment and listened to Eva.

"I don't give a rat's shit about code. She's got no electricity, Doug! I would think you would be just a little more inclined to show some proper Southern hospitality." Eva paced across the porch, causing boards to creak and groan. "Uh-huh. Well, let's try this on for size. I'm going to hang up, and I'm going to call your father, and I'm willing to bet . . . Well, now, that's much better, Douglas. I would appreciate that, as I'm sure Ms. Lucas here would, as well."

Joanna opened her eyes. With her head still resting on her knees and too heavy to lift, she rolled it to one side and peered up at Eva, who gave her a thumbs-up sign and a wink to clinch the feeling of good will.

Joanna smiled, allowing her head to roll forward again, and she closed her eyes. Eva's appearance could not have been better timed. Before Eva arrived, Joanna had been contemplating calling Marcus Watkins and telling him that she wanted to come home.
She had wanted to quit. She'd become so disillusioned with her act of defiance that she'd been rethinking just how awful Clayton was. Another day without electricity and hot water had felt like the final blow. But Eva's well-timed intervention had enabled Joanna to push back the feeling of hopelessness.

"C'mon, honey," Eva said, appearing beside Joanna and bouncing down the steps. "You've got to take care of a few things, and I can see that you need some help."

"What? Where are we going?" Joanna picked up her head. The last thing she wanted to do was go out or be seen.

"We're going to the money tree. You need some help." Eva shifted her gaze over toward the house and then returned it to Joanna. "I thought you said you were going to hire help?"

"Well, I was . . . but, well . . . I wanted to, you know, get electricity, water, and all that set up before I had people in and out of here. I'm just trying to get—"

"No," Eva said and shook her head. "No, that's not how you do it. You need help now."

"The money tree? As in," Joanna asked, shaking her head, "the bank?"

"Ha. That's funny," Eva said with little humor. "Lordy, girlie, you *are* new here. No, the money tree or *árbol dinero*," she said in perfect Spanish. "It's where all the illegals stand to get picked up for day labor."

Joanna squinted at her.

"They call it the money tree."

"Isn't that . . . illegal?" Joanna was instantly sorry she'd asked.

Eva rolled her eyes to the heavens, making loud noises of annoyance. "Please! They're already here. They work much harder than any of the local idiots and for much cheaper wages."

Again, it was a news bulletin.

"But first," Eva said, wagging a finger. "You're coming to my house to take a shower."

"No," Joanna said with a soft laugh. "That's sweet of you, but I—"

"Honey, I'm not asking you, I'm tellin' you. You stink. You really do. You smell worse than some of those fellas I had working on my roof!"

Joanna looked down at herself, as though the source of smell might be identified by one stain on her shirt. She brushed self-consciously at her clothing and frowned.

"Oh, yeah, you stink," Eva said with a laugh.

Joanna went inside and gathered a clean outfit, and then the two of them left. Just as she'd driven onto Joanna's property, Eva peeled out, spewing dust and rocks from beneath her car before they hit the highway and drove into town.

They only managed snippets of conversation between Eva's

constant stream of cell phone calls. It reminded Joanna of Clayton as she settled back into the passenger's seat and stared at the scenery flying by.

"No, John," Eva said into the phone. "I'm not endorsing anything. But I have a vested interest in this town as well. Don't you forget that. I don't want to be rude about it, but you sold out, not the other way around. I still got a business to run, a living to make here in Marcus."

In the distance, Joanna could see a traffic light. There were just four in town, and this one marked the intersection where the Dairy Queen and Exxon stood.

"I'm just going to listen, John. Just to listen," Eva said.

As they pulled up to the red light, Eva motioned with her hand—opening and closing it like a mouth. She rolled her eyes at Joanna.

"Well, I didn't plan on wearing a billboard. I thought I might just take a seat in the back." There was a pause and a final nod. "Fine, then. I'll be looking for you." She shut off the phone.

"That was John Simmons," Eva said, and when Joanna raised her eyebrows, Eva pounced. "Girl, this is going to be a day of education for you, I can see that now. If you're going to live in this town, there are a few things you need to know."
Joanna smiled.

"You want something done cheap, you go to the money tree. You want good food, you go to Quigley's Down Under. You want good gossip, you go to Quigley's Down Under," Eva said, laughing at her own joke. "You want to know what's really going on in town, well, now, that's a subject for debate. Fact and gossip aren't always the same thing but they aren't always separate, either!"

The light changed, and Eva turned left on to Main Street.

"Some might tell you I'm the source of information," she said with feigned modesty. "Maybe, maybe not. But others will tell you that John is your go-to guy. The old coot. He's got his thumb down on just about everything that goes on around here."

"I know that name," Joanna said.

"You should. He used to own what's now called FFI. You know, Future Foundations Industries."

Joanna nodded.

"The old cement plant. But he sold it off to some Austrian outfit, got money coming out of his ears now, so he turned around and bought up half the property in this town."

Joanna nodded. This was hitting closer to home than Eva realized. Joanna had come from a world where one family owned a town, yet it was hard to imagine anyone from Marcus, Texas possessing the same qualities, or lack thereof, as the Lucas family.

"And because of that, he has, in his oh-so-delusional state, come to believe that he can tell me what to do." Eva snorted to herself. "I don't think so." She eased to a stop, slipped the car into park, and turned to Joanna.

"Ta-da. Be it ever so humble." She extended a hand toward the passenger side of the car, and Joanna turned. The two-story gingerbread-style house was painted pale blue with white trim. Manicured shrubs dotted a perfectly manicured lawn. It reminded Joanna of a dollhouse she'd spent hours playing with as a child. It was the most delicate, perfect home and so well matched to Eva Tobey, Marcus's own Zsa Zsa Gabor of the real estate world.

* * * *

Fifty minutes prior, Joanna would have refused to step out of the car. She'd never been a big fan of approaching entire groups of strange men, particularly when she didn't speak the same language. Not an hour before, she'd been encrusted in dried sweat and grime. But Eva's vintage fifties-style bathroom had been a welcome sight. Joanna was invigorated.

At the house, they'd laid out the plan. Eva would do all the talking. After being assured that Clayton Lucas would be footing the bill for the renovations, Eva was sure they could get the deal of the century from the men at the money tree.

"I know the best man," she insisted.

As promised, there was a large group of men standing under a single large tree. The money tree. The small patch of land surrounding the tree sported an official sign: Simmons Park. Two park benches and an eight-foot stretch of sidewalk were all that encompassed the park.

"As in John Simmons?" Joanna grinned.

"Yeah. Look at that." She laughed as she stepped out of the car. "It's the size of my backyard, but John buys it up so he can put a sign on the land and call it his park." She rolled her eyes.

Joanna followed Eva's lead and climbed out of the car. Their movement caused a sudden interest among the men standing at the money tree.

"Why not buy some actual land for a real park?" Joanna asked. Eva stopped in her tracks and placed a hand of her hip. "Because, my dear, this little patch of land is right smack in the middle of town for everyone to see his name." She swept out her hand along an imaginary skyline. "John Simmons Park." She let her hand drop back to her side and smiled.

"*¿Qué hubo?*"

"Ah," Eva said as she turned to the man walking toward them. He was, Joanna guessed, Mexican. He was short, thick, and callused. Although his gait was stiffened from hard labor and injury, his swagger was one of confidence. He was in his early forties, powerful as though he hadn't missed many meals. His work shirt and jeans were faded but clean.

As he approached, he pulled a straw cowboy hat from his head and flashed a grin. Offset by his dark skin, his teeth were a dazzling white.

"Allo, Ms. Tobey."

"Manuel!" Eva came forward, giving her hand to him as though she were the queen of England. He took it in good spirits but uncertain what he was to do with it, gave it a half-pump half-squeeze.

"This is Joanna Lucas," Eva said, pointing back to Joanna. "She bought the old Redmond place."

"Oh, the Redmond," he said as he pondered the new information.

"She needs about six men, and someone's got to speak English because she doesn't speak a lick of Spanish."

*"Si,"* he said with a nod.

"Pays ten dollars an hour, comes with lunch, you provide the transportation. This is a big project, Manuel. I'd say at least one month. Monday to Friday, all day. Can you handle that?"
Manuel shook his head. "Hmm, we need rides."

"I can handle that," Joanna said before Eva could say another word.

He smiled at Joanna. "Then, yes."

"What are you up to, Ms. Tobey?" A voice rang out from the side of the road. Eva turned to see who it was, but Manuel turned back toward the men at the money tree. The recruiting had begun.

"Drumming up some business, fixing to take care of the business you couldn't, Doug," Eva said. Her smile was as wide as the road.

"Aw, now, c'mon, Ms. Tobey. You know I'm going to take care of everything. I just needed to—"

"Oh, quit it, Douglas. I'm just giving you a hard time. I expect you'll take care of her electricity by tomorrow, right?" Eva gave a little nod and pointed behind her, not waiting for an answer. "Meantime, we've got to get the house in shape. We're talking lawn, mending, remodeling—the works." She gave a little wave, took Joanna by the elbow, and led her back toward the car, calling back over her shoulder toward Manuel.

"Manuel, we'll be seein' you in the morning, first thing, you hear?"

*"Si,* Ms. Tobey."

Before Joanna could speak, Eva was shoving her into the

passenger seat. Behind her, Doug and his friend looked on, scowling at the men from the money tree.

* * * *

They watched as the women popped into Eva's little sports car and roared off.

"That's a good-lookin' woman," Todd Hawkins said and Doug nodded.

"I told ya. A body that don't quit . . . built for speed, that one."

He smiled, and Todd smiled back.

Together, they'd shared many things, and this, they both knew, was something they would very much like to share. Since grade school, everyone in town knew that the Hawkins boy and the Mitchell boy ran around together, found trouble together, and shared the same girls. When they were lucky, all in the same night. Though they'd both filled out, settled down with families, and were less inclined to cruise up and down the streets as they did as teens, the thrill of the hunt was still alive.

"It's a shame. A woman like that living all alone," Todd said. Doug chuckled. "In the dark. She still don't have any electricity."

* * * *

Joanna had wanted to be home sooner but Eva would not be put off. She'd insisted on driving Joanna all over Marcus, pointing out various landmarks, the homes of outstanding citizens, and all the you've-got-to-see-this sites. All the while, she was pumping Joanna for more personal information. She'd been as subtle as a stampeding rhino.

As Eva sped away, Joanna looked at her house. *The last night,* she thought. *The last night without electricity. She'd be so overjoyed to have actual lights,* she thought as she climbed the porch steps. She might turn on every light and keep them on for a week. She planned to watch CNN around the clock with a few *Law and Order* reruns mixed in. But for now, she would have to settle for her little portable radio and hover over a book with her flashlight.

As soon as she placed her hand on the doorknob, she sensed it. Something was wrong. She paused, listening to her house.

Behind her, the breeze was gentle. Crickets were just gearing up for a night of singing, but for the moment, it was quiet outside.
She hesitated.
Nothing.
She cracked the door, pressing her ear to the opening, and listened harder. Nothing.
*Calm down*, she said to herself.
As she stepped over the threshold, she cursed. She'd been so frustrated about the electrical problems and left in such a rush with Eva that she'd forgotten to shut the back door. Mosquitoes, she was sure, had taken refuge in her home in great multitudes. Or even worse, snakes. Rodents. She froze.
There was a scratching noise and . . .
She raised her hand to her nose. There was an odd odor. She squinted into the growing darkness.
*What the hell was it?*

Her heart began to pound, and a voice rose in her head. *Get out! Get out! Get out!*

A noise came again and she began to ease backward, careful to move without sound. As she did, the scratching noise sounded to her right. There was little time to react. It moved toward her, bursting forward from the shadows. Joanna screamed, throwing her hands up to her face.

# 6

I found Joanna Lucas laid out on her front porch, a cool cloth on her face, fanning herself like she was up for the remake of a Scarlett O'Hara movie. For a Yankee, she had a serious Southern belle thing going.

She appeared to be saying something to herself, and I would have liked to know what it was but the curse of the golf cart made reconnaissance impossible. She rolled to one side, pulled the towel from her face, and eyed me hard.

"You screamed," I said. There didn't seem much point in asking her if she screamed. She knew she screamed. I knew she screamed. Hell, half the town heard her scream.

"What? That horrified, throat-wrenching, gut-reaction to pure terror?" she asked in a deadpan tone, pulling herself up into a sitting position. It sounded like an attempt at embarrassed humor.

"We just call it a scream around here. Makes things less complicated," I said with a shrug, and she eyed me again, trying to decide what to make of me.

I have to admit the look was just long enough that she made me a bit uncomfortable.

"Does that thing belong to you?"

"That thing is Eduardo. He's an emu," I told her.

Another long stare.

"Okay." She drew in a long breath. "And what was Eduardo the emu doing in my house?"

That was easy enough to explain. After John and Ellen Redmond passed on, the Redmond house had remained vacant. It was a nice enough house, but no one in town wanted any part of it. The long row of red oaks, each representing a death, was a bit too eerie for most folks. So, it just sat empty. But it hadn't taken long for it to become a playhouse for the local teenagers. They partied there, made up stories of ghosts forever walking The Shady Land, and the boys brought dates there to do whatever they needed to do to impress the girls with acts of bravery and whatnot.

We all knew what they were doing, but the house was far enough off the road that people just didn't care. Truth was, most people were just happy to have a place where they knew the kids went rather than driving to who knows where and wrapping their trucks around a tree.

Only my precious Franklin had argued about this new teen hangout, as they tended to discard their beer cans all over the property—including our adjoining property—and drive Eduardo crazy with beer-calling taunts.

While the Redmond house had sat empty, their back property had been used for years as a grazing pasture for different herds. Over the years, I'd say a good five or six families used that land for their goats, horses, and cows. There was a community effort to keep the barn up and running to store hay and bring in the livestock in bad weather. Then Hollis Duncan changed all that. He got drunk one night and showed up to the Redmond house looking for a party. Leastways, this was all any of us could figure. But there weren't any kids around that night, so he wandered his drunken self out to the barn and found Lewis Urlche's seven-month-old filly in the barn.

The bastard tipped over a bucket, climbed atop, and attempted an unspeakable act upon the filly that then kicked him, knocked him off the bucket, and injured him.

Folks say there isn't any more sexual perversion than there used to be, that it's just more widely reported, but I can tell you that even before young folks could download and fixate upon the naked, I never heard of a boy standing atop of an overturned bucket to do unnatural things to a seven-month-old horse. It just wasn't done. The result of that incident, besides Hollis being so drunk that he explained in full detail what had happened, was that local farmers started taking turns staying out at the Redmond place. We'd been in the middle of a drought and the grass that surrounded Redmond Lake was far too valuable to just give up to a bunch of animal-humping teenagers.

If memory serves, it was John Simmons, Nate Blauncett, Tim Davis, and Randy Cross who worked in shifts, protecting their livestock from perverts. It put a stop to the teenage loitering but brought in a new problem. The men took to late-night poker games and such, which included beer and pizza, and the lure was too much for Eduardo.

Ever since he'd been put on a diet by Dr. Hendricks, Eduardo had become a bona fide buzzard, a regular scavenger. Feed and worms weren't enough. Eduardo took to streaking across the properties to fish around for pizza crust and, eventually, droplets of beer.

I don't believe, nor does Dr. Hendricks, that Eduardo had developed any kind of dependency on the beer. It was just a liquid of a different taste, and I'm sure it made him feel good. Although it had been months and months since the last poker party, Eduardo would still scavenge the property every morning. No sooner than I would open up his pen in the morning, he would dart across the fence line and search around for pizza and beer.

"He wasn't attacking you," I said to her. "He was just looking for some beer."

There was that long stare again.

"You understand that, of course." The last thing I wanted was for her to call the police and report any trouble about Eduardo. He wasn't a bad bird. He just had a few peculiarities, was all. "At least it wasn't one of the cats, right?" I asked with a laugh.

She started to smile.

"So . . . this is going to be a daily occurrence? Your . . . your five-foot-tall pet bird, Eduardo, is going to come into my house looking for beer and pizza?"

"You could lock your doors. That would help."

She nodded and then looked around. "Where is it . . . Eduardo now?"

"You scared him off when you screamed." I'd just come out the back door, ready to call him into his pen when I heard her scream. Seconds later, there was a loud bang, and Eduardo was running for his life. In fact, I could not remember the last time I saw him run like that. He'd made it out and around the house, across the driveway and over the fence in about twenty steps. His strides were so long, he looked more ostrich than emu.

It was a wonder that she didn't give him a heart attack. "You didn't need to scream like that," I said. Screaming never soothes an already agitated animal. He was looking for beer, not to peck her eyes out.

She smirked. "Yeah, well, I just wasn't prepared for house guests. The house is a mess."

"All right, then," I said and began to turn around the cart. There was no need to get smart. "I just wanted to be sure you were okay."

"Thank you," Joanna said, rising to her feet. "I'm supposed to get my electricity turned on in the next few days. You be sure to tell Eduardo I'll have cold beer soon."

In hindsight, I should have known right then and there that she was going to fit in fine with the girls.

* * * *

I had been talking to Franklin, sitting with my precious and telling him about the progress at The Shady Land. He would have been so happy to know Joanna was working on a garden and giving new life to the old place. I had also been discussing the seriousness of our cat situation. Every month, there was another call from an animal control officer somewhere in the state, looking to house a big cat. Until new laws were set in place to stop the importation and breeding of exotic animals, we would continue to get those calls. But the truth was we couldn't take on anymore. We didn't have the money, and I did not have the strength or energy anymore. And it made me sick. It made me sick to think what would happen to those beautiful, abused animals. They were victims in all this.

I'd been telling my precious about everything that was going on when we heard the boom. The medications streaming into Franklin's veins created little more than a twitch but he never woke, never moved. All the same, I knew he'd heard it, too, and it was reassuring to me to know that he was still, in some way, a part of this world.

Then, the power went out.

"Well, I'll be damned." For I knew I was. Everyone in this town was damned. Just damned. So many were getting sick, but everyone was denying what was happening, and now we were sitting in the dark. Oh, the irony.

I watched as the pretty little lights that keep my dear, sweet Franklin's breathing apparatus working flickered out. I knew just how much time I had before he would start to struggle.

I cursed under my breath, picked up the landline, and made two phone calls.

"That jackass Jack Frawley just blew out the circuits," I said to Mary Ryan. "Why on earth did you all hire that guy?"

"Don't you think I know that, Suzette?" She was snippy.

Mary Ryan was the city's secretary. She was secretary to the mayor's office, chamber of commerce, and to the planning and zoning committee. This meant any time Jack, the wonder city employee, blew out a circuit, Mary got all the calls.

"Don't get snippy with me," I said to her. "I got less than two minutes before things start to get real ugly here for Franklin! I don't care who, what, where, or when, but you get someone out here to set things right."

I hung up. Then, after thinking on it, I knew I needed to call back.

"Yes, Suzette," she said without even the standard, "Marcus Chamber. What can I do ya for?" They always said that and thought it was real cute.

"Because if you don't get someone out here—"

"I know. You'll sue the town. I know, I know." And she hung up this time. I felt a panic growing inside of me. *Who was there to call?*

Then I heard voices and raced to the window.

It was the Spanish Armada, of sorts. Three cars, a pickup truck, and Joanna's Jeep had pulled into Joanna's driveway and circled around to park in front of the house. It looked as though Ms. Joanna had hired herself every free man from the money tree, and there were Mexicans piling out of the cars, ready to work. There were able-bodied men everywhere. I hobbled over to my cart and took off.

Doug's work truck was parked alongside Jack's truck at the crest of the driveway. The two stood gaping at the power box hoisted some twenty feet in the air.

"What have you two boneheads done?" I asked as I skittered by them.

"Oh, hush up, Ms. Lee," Doug said in an abrupt tone.

Ass.

I could hear Jack feebly explaining himself as I tottered on. "I was tyin' the circuit into the grid and the damn thing just blows up."

As my trusty golf cart whined and jumped over the driveway, I saw Joanna step down from the front porch. She had been talking to the man who had driven her Jeep but stopped when she saw me.

Dust and rocks shot out from behind me, and I was moving as quickly as the little cart would allow. She waved a finger at the man, silencing him for a minute, and walked toward me.
It was funny how in a moment of crisis, a near stranger can feel like such a friend. And how dear and sweet Joanna looked to me at that moment. So young and strong. I knew she would help me.

"The power has gone out!" I shouted. "My dear Franklin! His breathing machine is shut down, and I can't move the generator by myself!"

"Oh!" Joanna sprang to life.

Before I could even turn the cart around, she'd yelled to a few of the workers and was off and running. Like Eduardo, she was a sight to see, leaping over the fence line and charging toward my front door.

As I neared the highway to double back to my driveway, she and the men had already disappeared into my house. Oh, how my heart pounded as I urged my cart forward. I'd lost track of the minutes without electricity to Franklin's machine. I almost lost my composure and surrendered to frightening and powerless thoughts when she emerged again. She waved at me.

"I think I did it right, but you need to come check. The machine's . . . working," she said, struggling to breathe. And beautiful. I swear there was a halo about her head that day. "You need to come see if we did it right."

They had. But when I tried to thank her, she waved me off, staring down at Franklin.

"What's wrong with him . . . I mean," she said, almost apologetically. "If you don't mind me asking."

"This town," I said but backed off. She wasn't ready for the truth. Hell, the entire town wasn't ready for the truth. It was like that line from *A Few Good Men* when Jack Nicholson yelled, "You can't handle the truth!" That line should have been the theme song for this town.

Joanna snapped up her head and drew her eyebrows together. I smiled and shook my head.

"I'm sorry. I'm just . . . it's complicated. He's got CMT. It's Charcot-Marie-Tooth Syndrome. It's a rare form of muscular dystrophy."

"Char—" she said then stopped. "That's a mouthful. Never heard of it."

"I know it." I never liked the name. They should have given it something people could better remember, but it was named after the three neurologists who discovered and identified it.

I sighed and looked down at my husband. He was such a dear, sweet man. "Basically it causes severe muscle fatigue and immobilizes the arms, hands, feet, legs. It just paralyzes you."

"How awful," Joanna said, still staring at Franklin.

His breathing had improved again. Even in his deep slumber, he'd detected trouble and had begun laboring for breath. His hands were knotted into fists, just another side effect of the disease, and he looked brittle, as if he might break at any moment. I'd been so used to how he looked; I'd forgotten how he must look to others who'd not seen him. As Franklin's state had worsened, we'd become shut-ins.

Franklin hadn't been able to go anywhere for almost a year. He hadn't been able to walk for the last several years, but the CMT had progressed so much that he wasn't even able to use a scooter or wheelchair anymore, which only made him worse. It was a bitter pill to swallow, for when he became completely inactive, other ailments cropped up.

Emphysema, upper respiratory infections, and diabetes. They just continued to pile up.

"Well, what's the prognosis? Is there any cure or hope for rehabilitation?" Joanna asked slowly.

I smiled. It was silly, but I liked to hear some optimism from someone.

"No. No cure." I sighed and looked down at my husband again. "This is pretty much it."

A voice from behind us caused us both to turn. " 'S'cuse, please, Señora Lucas."

Hat in hand, the young man dipped his head to both of us. I gave a nod. I'd seen him around before—always at the money tree.

"What you want us to do? We . . . we ready," he asked, waving a hand behind him, indicating to the men waiting for direction.

"Oh, yeah, right," Joanna said, stepped away from the bed. She cleared her throat. "Are you okay? I mean, I need to . . ." She, too, made a vague hand wave, and I nodded.

"I appreciate your help, Joanna. It means a lot."

"I guess it would help if I gave you my new phone number," she said with a smile and searched the room for a pen and paper. When she spotted such on Franklin's old dresser, she jotted it down and pressed it into my hand. "You know, the next time something like this happens, you just call and I'll run right over."

# 7

There was no question that Doug Mitchell was moving slower than molasses. As Joanna worked in the barn, she squinted toward his truck. Sweat slid down from her temples, traveling in perfect unison on either side of her jaw, down her neck, and into her cleavage. The latter sensation made for a cooling effect each time she bent forward to drop another pile of lumber on to the ground. She paused, squatting in the blistering sun. Doug, on the other hand, had to be content. Parked along the tree line of her shady driveway, he sat eating a sandwich and watching the show. He had a perfect view down the side of the house toward the back of the property to where her barn sat.

She could feel him scrutinizing her as she worked alongside Manuel and Marcos in the barn.

Manuel had not hesitated when she informed him she wanted to clear out the old barn and turn it into a studio for her art. He'd simply asked, "What kind of art? Painting?"

When she told him clay, he offered a thoughtful expression, turned to Marcos, and they were off. She could have said she wanted to start a yoga studio for all he cared. But to hear her own words, to hear herself say that she was a sculptor—out loud—to another human being had been huge. In that moment, her heart had leapt. It was sensational. It was strangely victorious.

For hours, they hauled out old lumber, farm equipment, and countless empty crates. Manuel promised they would have a huge bonfire later. Joanna could see past the junk and envisioned a great working studio. It was something she'd wanted all her life, and now she was going to have it.

As the days passed, Doug had made no bones about his feelings about the money tree men working The Shady Land. He didn't care what she was doing, he just didn't like who she was working with.

"You shouldn't have them working here," Doug had warned Joanna several times. The word *them* had a particular bite to it.

"You're way too pretty to be alone," he'd said again and again. In fact, Joanna was not quite sure which she had objected to the most, the constant reference to her living alone or her appearance.

Doug had made sure of several things. His work never seemed to be done, he was always present, he was always commenting on her clothing and appearance, and he was always watching her workers.

But there appeared to be no one she could complain to about this situation. While Eva rolled her eyes and warned about Doug's lascivious ways, she also insisted there was no one else. Since a city employee had blown out the transformer on the highway, Doug had managed to park in her driveway permanently.

The interest he held for Joanna was equaled by his intense dislike for the illegals. And his feelings had not gone unnoticed.

"Why does he stay here?" Manuel asked. Joanna turned, sliding around on her knee and peered up at him.

"I don't know."

"I don't like it."

"Neither do I," Joanna said with a nod. She was careful not to look down the driveway, but Manuel had no such worries. As he chewed thoughtfully on a straw, he pushed his cowboy hat back and stared at Doug's truck.

"You want come see what is done in back?" he asked, still staring down the driveway.

She stood, dusting off her knees and managed a peek to the side. Doug was glowering.

She was equal in height to Manuel. But where her muscles were long and lean, Manuel possessed the power and build of a pit bull. He extended a hand, allowing Joanna to go first. As he fell in step behind her, Joanna could see Doug staring at Manuel. She looked over her shoulder and saw Manuel stiffen, lock eyes with Doug, and offer a nod. If Doug thought he could intimidate Manuel Vergara, he'd chosen the wrong man. As soon as Joanna came around the side of the house, she halted. She was stunned by the dramatic change.

"Wow." She smiled.

The once barren, dusty back steps to the house had been transformed. Bright turquoise and brown Spanish tile covered a twenty–by-thirty-foot area with a twelve-inch-tall stone wall surrounding it. In a most perfect and precise pattern, turquoise tile was placed into the wall, each several feet apart from the other. At three points around the patio, seven-foot-tall iron hooks stood.

"You put, hang . . . flowers," Manuel said, waving his arms to illustrate how hanging pots would decorate the patio, and Joanna nodded.

"Oh, yeah, yeah." She could hardly keep from clapping her hands.

"Not so much we do in the house. No electricity. But this," he said, sweeping an arm over the patio again. "We do this for you."
She stopped and looked around at the group of men, all of whom were smiling at her.

They had not been with her long, but she'd come to know them all both by name and personality.

Rolando Costilla was perched on the edge of the wall, arms

crossed and thumbs tucked under the opposite armpits. He was quiet, but mischievously content, as though he had a fantastic secret. Like his brother, Roberto, he was handsome. Just under six feet, both brothers were classically handsome with straight, strong noses and high cheekbones.

Despite herself, she couldn't help but watch them. From a physical sense, they were perfect men, with thick, round shoulders and lean waists. On more than one occasion, Joanna had admired the sweat-soaked T-shirts clinging to their bodies. They were distractingly chiseled. So often, men who lifted weights neglected their legs, leaving them underdeveloped, but the Costilla brothers were buff by way of genetics and hard labor. Their legs were strong, rounded, and muscular, and Joanna found herself watching Roberto in particular.

He knew this. He'd caught her one too many times looking his way, and he smiled openly each time, almost laughing at her. To her great consternation, she could not get a read on this smile. Was he laughing at her? Flirting with her? And she couldn't just ask. Never mind the language barrier, it was too embarrassing.

Marcos Arai was the youngest of the group. Joanna was sure he was a teenager from various comments Manuel had made. He was willowy and short on endurance compared to the others— something he was teased about. What she did know was that he was a hard worker who was saving money for school.

Of the lot, his English was the best, though he was careful not to engage in any lengthy conversations with Joanna, despite her efforts. Each time they began to talk, Manuel had a reason to pull him away.

Joanna smiled back at Rolando and then forced herself to find Manuel again.

"I can't believe you've done all this. It's gorgeous!"

Manuel smiled and stepped forward, pointing to the fire pit in the middle. Joanna gasped. It was perfect. A large pit was centered in the middle of the patio, lined with cast iron molding. Extra tiling had been broken and fitted to decorate a two-foot ledge above the floor, allowing cups, plates, or candles to rest on it. Joanna could imagine herself barbecuing at the pit.

"It was Roberto," Gerardo said. He flashed his most winning smile, and Joanna froze. She knew from talking and listening to the others that Gerardo was considered a ladies' man. Or he considered himself as such. He had an oversized mustache—a compensation, she was sure, for other shortcomings. He was the stereotypical cartoon image of the macho Latino, complete with a large belly. He was the kind of man who winked at women, believing he was smooth, but he didn't try this with Joanna. His smile was teasing—a joke.

Joanna felt herself flush.

The others knew of her secret crush on Roberto.

She forced herself to smile and find Roberto in the crowd.

"It's beautiful," she said, locking eyes with him. He was perfect. Perfect teeth, nose, eyes, hair, body. Perfect. A Latino Brad Pitt.

*"De nada,"* he whispered. Smooth as silk.

"You talk to Doug Mitchell?" asked Andres Velasca. Seated on the back steps to the house, he'd been watching her from behind. "How long he going to take?"

"I don't know," Joanna said, deflated. It was the truth.

"He taking too long, you know, because he . . . more money. I don't like him." As Andres spoke, he rubbed his fingers together to gesture Doug Mitchell's desire for money. His accent was so thick it was almost unintelligible.

Joanna had discovered that Andres, Manuel, and Carlos Garza had been regulars at the money tree for decades, traveling back and forth between the small Texas town and their homes in Mexico. Both Manuel and Andres were grandfathers, and all three were dedicated husbands trying to send money back home. They were well versed in traveling visas, immigration laws, and local opinions of their status, though not all had a visa. All the men were certain of Doug's true intent. As long as they were there, Doug had no interest in completing his job.

"I don't like him, either," Joanna said, moving around Andres on the steps. Inside the house, she found her purse and pulled out cash for the day's wages. Outside, she could hear the men speaking in Spanish.

"You see this?" Manuel stepped into the kitchen, pointing to the dining room hall behind her.

Using natural daylight, the men had done as much as they could, spackling and painting the walls and tearing out carpet and rotted wood. She could see that the railing to the stairway had been removed and the center bathroom was gutted.

"I can't believe how fast you guys work," she said with a laugh and handed the money to Manuel. She would have him count it and distribute the money among his men. While there had never been an official appointment, Manuel was the foreman. He had found more men for Joanna, including a work truck they could pile into.

He accepted the money with a nod but didn't bother to count it. Joanna stood in her freshly painted kitchen. The color was called peanut butter, and it had a warm, Mediterranean feel to it. With the help of the men, she would make this house something to be proud of. And one day, she thought, she would be able to send a picture to the Hamptons. Maybe the picture would arrive by chance at the yoga studio or at some public function, and the jerk-off ex would see her beautiful home. He would see that she'd made it on her own, after all.

The voices of the men faded then, disappearing around the side of the house and leaving her alone again.

She rubbed her eyes and pictured Roberto's beautiful smile.

Why she was thinking about another man, much less a probable illegal alien, was beyond ridiculous. It was stupid. Still, she could not help herself.

A knock at the front door jerked her from her thoughts.

It was Doug.

"Ms. Lucas," he said. As Joanna opened the door, he bulled his way into the house. He was angry. "Should have your problem taken care of late tomorrow or Thursday mornin'." There was an undeniable edge to his voice.

As he spoke, he looked around the inside of the house, not bothering to make eye contact with her.

"Tomorrow? That's great," she said, trying to sound enthusiastic, but she wasn't. She didn't believe him, and she was tired of his antics.

"Yes 'm, should be."

He nodded at her. She nodded back. Both stood in uncomfortable silence.

"When are them beaners gonna be done?"

"Beaners?" Joanna cocked her head to the side. She wanted to laugh; this guy was disgusting. She tried to look as innocent and clueless as possible.

"Those Mexicans." He sighed heavily to indicate he was trying to be patient. "I'm tellin' ya, Ms. Lucas. You don't need 'em 'round. Ever'day in the news there are stories about Mexicans comin' into a woman's home, beating and raping her." He looked around the house for a moment. "You're here all alone. One of 'em comes here at night . . . what are you goin' to do? You got a gun?"

She blinked. Naïveté and common sense were having a debate in her head.

"I have a gun," she lied.

He nodded. "You know how to use it?"

"I'm a lot meaner than you think I am," she said, rising up to full height. It only made him smile.

"I hope to see that," he said, leaving Joanna perplexed.

*What was that supposed to mean?*

She took an involuntarily step backward. "Well, I look forward to getting electricity tomorrow, Mr. Mitchell."

"Doug."

"Doug," she said politely just to get him the hell out of her house. He nodded and turned. She wasn't quiet when she threw the latch behind him. Then, she moved quickly through the house, checking and locking each window.

For more than four hours after Doug left, Joanna had kept the radio off, wanting to hear any and every noise outside her house. But by dusk, she'd settled down again.

"I'm gonna get a dog," she said out loud. The sound of her voice was reassuring. She just wanted to relax. She was so tired of being tired. She was so tired of looking over her shoulder and worrying about what could be behind her.

Gathering up a variety of candles, she made her way outside and lined them around the fire pit. It was lovely, and with the candles lit, it created a very pleasant mood. Inevitably, her mind wandered to its creator, Roberto.

The image of Clayton Lucas seeing her with the likes of Roberto Costilla made her smile, and she chuckled until she felt a presence behind her and froze.

He was back.

He had said he would like to see her be mean.

Her heart began to pound as she decided what to do.

He would be too fast and too strong for her. She knew this. Her mind reeled, searching for some kind of effective strategy.

He felt huge, lumbering behind her, and she reached forward casually as though she were inspecting her candle. She would smash it in his face.

He moved, and she jerked to the side and reared back.

She screamed.

He moved in, darting around her.

She tried to throw the candle but wound up splashing herself with wax instead. Then, in extreme agitation, she screamed again. "Eduardo! Go home!"

# 8

The blanket of darkness was misleading and made it easy to think no one could see them, that they were invisible—invincible. But someone would be watching.

They'd made too many runs to FFI's property. Someone would be waiting and watching. The question was, when and where?

Barbed wire and thick mesquite bushes hampered the trek from the roadside to their point of set up. Already, the long, poisonous thorns had scratched several from the party. But whatever discomfort they felt after this adventure was well worth it.

They were on constant alert for any lights or movement, and once they reached their destination, they would need an additional ten minutes. They had practiced this same run over and over, each time requiring ten full minutes to set up their gear and clear out.

Nothing moved. No breeze. No light. No activity. Even so, they stayed perfectly still for several more moments, watching and waiting. Given the cost of this mission, they did not want to be caught setting up.

The silence was more painful for some.

"It's good . . . it's good," a voice in the darkness rang out.

"Let's do it," said another.

More waiting. More silence.

No one came. On this night, no one waited for them.

The signal came, readying the group for set up. They had ten minutes.

* * * *

For the briefest of moments, the sound had terrorized her. It had sounded demonic. The location of the house, so far off the beaten path, the trees, her strange new surroundings and the noises were beginning to take a toll on Joanna. She was getting jumpy. More than ever, she craved lights, electricity and the company of another person.

*Tap. Tap. Tap.*

With a baseball bat and cell phone in her hand, ready to call Marcus's finest, Joanna moved toward the kitchen. She could only get reception on one side of the house—the side from where the noise came. With phone to ear, she saw him.

Eduardo. "Dammit!" she cried out. Enough was enough.

"You should be home." She flung the back door open. "Why aren't you . . . Argh! You should be in your pen."

As she stepped out, Eduardo stepped back, flapping his wings. He hopped around the fire pit a few times, impatiently waiting for Joanna to give him something. Instead, Joanna looked toward the Lee house.

Suzette was diligent about putting up all her animals at night for fear of coyotes. That was one thing she knew about the country living.

"C'mon, you stupid bird," she said and walked toward her neighbor's house. Not two weeks ago, the idea of an oversized, hungry, beer-loving bird would have terrified her. Now, she was just annoyed. As they walked, she heard Eduardo scratching and kicking at the ground behind her.

She stopped at the fence line, threw one leg over, and looked at the property behind Suzette's house. Martha the llama was wondering about.

Something was wrong.

She knocked on the front door. When she heard a strange

noise, she tried the doorknob.

"Ms. Lee?" Joanna called out as she leaned into the house. It was dark. A single light shone from the back of the house.

"Ms. Lee? It's me. Joanna Lucas."

Nothing.

"You okay?"

There was a small noise. She licked her lips and moved into the house a little more.

"Eduardo is . . . he was knocking on my back door, and I thought . . . Ms. Lee? Are you in here? Are you okay?"

She heard something that sounded like someone had called back, and she stepped inside.

"I'm coming in," she said, although common sense was telling her to run. She followed the light, and when she saw Suzette sitting on the edge of her bed, instant relief filled Joanna's heart.

"Ms. Lee, I called for you—" There was something about the way Suzette was sitting. Deflated. Dejected. Broken.

Joanna looked at Franklin lying in the bed, and she knew. Suzette's husband of almost fifty years was dead.

"Oh." She looked back to Suzette. "Ms. Lee. I'm so sorry." Her voice was a whisper. "Do you . . . should I call someone?"

"He's gone. He just couldn't do it anymore," she said at last. Joanna stood still, unsure of what she was supposed to say.

"I thought maybe he was just sleepin' funny. I thought maybe . . . but as soon as I touched him, I knew. He was just gone," Suzette cried.

* * * *

"All I'm asking is that you just behave yourself while we're in there." Brianna gave Jeanie a stern look.

Jeanie looked insulted. "Why me? Why do you always look to me? I'm just sitting here." Jeanie pressed her hand against her chest.

"Because you're the sicko who likes caskets," Dixie whispered.

"It's not like I lick 'em or anything. I just think they're interesting." Jeanie huffed, pretending annoyance. Secretly, she was giddy. She'd once considered going into the funeral business, and this was an opportunity to check out caskets, see Franklin Lee, *and* upset the girls.

"Well, you're not walking around lookin' at all the caskets, Jeanie. We're going straight into the receiving room and that's it." Brianna scolded her with a maternal tone, and Jeanie pretended to cringe in terror.

Both Brianna and Dixie had dressed in black, but that was the only commonality. While Brianna's dress was oversized and frumpy, Dixie's dress was a full size too small. She'd cinched her belt so tight she looked as if she'd been cut in half and stuck back together again. Spiked heels, teased hair, and black stockings with a seam line creeping up an inappropriately short dress completed her outfit. Be it a funeral, wedding, or party, Dixie always appeared to inspire wonder.

As Ruthie charged into the funeral parlor, breathless and hurried, she gave a quick appraisal of her friends. Neither Brianna nor Dixie surprised her. Instead, she turned on Jeanie.

"That's it? That's what you decided to wear?" she asked.

"Why is everyone always picking on me?" Jeanie asked with a squeaky voice.

"Because, of all the clothes in your wardrobe, of everything that I know you could've picked from, you chose that," she said and pointed to the pink and purple flowered peasant dress that swallowed Jeanie.

Jeanie peered down at herself and frowned.

"Hey, I didn't want to wear this, but you told me I wasn't allowed to wear pants."

"So you wore a muumuu?" Ruthie put a hand on her

hip.

Brianna snickered.

"It's the only dress I have. I don't wear dresses. You said—"

Ruthie waved her off. "Okay, okay. I don't care. We're here. Let's all go in, pay our respects, and see Suzette."

"It's not a muumuu." Jeanie sulked.

Inside, the entire town of Marcus had turned out to pay respects to Franklin. For the last several years, Franklin had been living as a hermit, so there had been stories. He had a rare exotic bird disease from the emu. He'd had a leg taken off like his wife, but Suzette didn't want anyone to know that Tony the Tiger still lived.

People were intrigued. All these years later, Suzette was still a celebrity of sorts. But there was an added interest. The queen of the tampon industry was the first to help Suzette with Franklin. The tampon heiress was said to be standing guard over Franklin's body. That alone brought in people from all over the county.

"He looks like a stuffed sausage," Jeanie whispered.

There was an instant gasp, and both Dixie and Ruthie scowled at her.

Dixie raised her hand, showing her forefinger and thumb. "I will pinch you if you don't shut up."

Jeanie knew the signal, but she was in her element, a funeral.

"He looks uncomfortable," she said, giving Ruthie a nudge to take another gander at Franklin.

"I don't think dead people can be uncomfortable." Ruthie sniffed and rolled her eyes.

"Why not?"

"Because, they're dead. If you're dead, you're dead. How are you going to be uncomfortable if you're dead?"

"Well, if you believe in the afterlife like you're always

sayin' you do, then you better believe he needs to be comfortable right now before he launches . . . you know, to the afterlife." Jeanie looked around, her voice lowered. When she looked back to Ruthie, she nodded. It made perfect sense.

Franklin was dressed in a black velvet suit with a scarf wrapped around his neck rather than the traditional tie. The effect did make him look bloated and puffy.

Beside his casket, Suzette was parked in her chair. It was tragically comic. She also wore a scarf around her neck, making her look equally overstuffed. She was drawn, pale, and subdued.

"She doesn't have her usual spit and vinegar," Jeanie leaned over and whispered in Ruthie's ear.

"Her husband just died."

"She knew it was comin'."

Brianna leaned forward and slapped Jeanie's arm. "Would you kindly shut up? We are here to pay our—"

"Oh, right, like y'all don't know what I'm talkin' about. I'm not sayin' she has to be jumping up and down for joy but . . . I don't know. I thought she might look a little more chipper or somethin'." Jeanie scanned the room until she spotted the buffet table laid out with goodies. She sniffed and lifted her chin.

"Ah. Now that's what I'm talkin' about." She turned on her heel and marched toward the food.

Jeanie knew the girls disapproved of this, but she also knew they wished they could do the same thing. How many funerals had they attended together over the years? How many women their age had suddenly gotten a brain tumor or some kind of weird upper respiratory disease that killed them? The big fat elephant was in the room, and no one wanted to talk about it.

The problem with the elephant was it wasn't something everyone could see. Some people got sick, others didn't. If there was something in the air or the water, why wouldn't everyone get sick? In fact, this was the very point many second, third, and fourth generation Marcus residents always made. "My family's been here since my great-grandfather, and none of us have been sick."

They had all heard that a lot. What was interesting was who got sick. Newcomers or little ones. While the other girls were all third generation Marcusites, both Dixie and Jeanie were transplants.

Statistically speaking, Jeanie bet on the odds that she would get sick. Both she and Dixie had talked about it quite a bit. All she could figure was that those who were born and raised had built up some kind of immunity to the pollution. But every now and then, someone like Franklin Lee would get sick and make some of the most hard-nosed residents pause to think.

Maybe they couldn't see the elephant in the room, but they could damned sure see the pollution-belching gorilla of a cement plant hovering in the corner.

She'd once read that in an editorial. The Marcus cement plant depicted as a pollution-belching gorilla. And Jeanie Archer was not afraid to call a gorilla a gorilla.

"That's why you got to live in the moment," Jeanie said as she surveyed the table of food and smiled.

Brianna was always harping on the fact that Jeanie had no manners and that one day, Jeanie's ill temper and bad behavior were going to catch up with her. But Jeanie knew something else. When you live your life honestly, good things happen. Like, for instance, standing at the food table was the Yankee-Doodle tampon princess herself.

"I thought you were guarding Franklin's body," Jeanie

said with a smile. She was careful not to show too many teeth.

"What?" Joanna knitted her brows together.

"Or something." Jeanie shrugged. "Didn't you find his body?"

"Him," Joanna said politely. "And yes, I found Franklin in his room, but Suzette was already with him."

But Jeanie was undeterred. "Nah. It was his body you saw. Franklin, the person, was gone a long time ago. Trust me, the Franklin we all knew wouldn't have just laid around like that, developing bedsores. The real Franklin was gone a long time ago." Her hand hovered over some pigs in a blanket. "Ooh. I bet you Myra Thompson brought these." She looked to Joanna. "I'm tellin' ya what. Around here, funerals and Myra's pigs in a blanket go hand in hand."

* * * *

Joanna watched in stunned silence as Jeanie piled half a dozen pastry-wrapped weenies on a plate, snarfing down just as many as she did so.

With her mouth half-filled with food, Jeanie chomped happily away as she talked on. After a moment, Joanna refocused on the table, not wishing to see any more than she already had.

"I guess this is your first funeral." *Chomp. Chomp.* "It won't be your last. You learn that real quick around here."

"You say that like there's something in the air," she said and almost laughed.

Jeanie stopped mid-chew and looked at her. The two stared at each other until Jeanie managed a hard swallow, pushing down whatever chunks of food were still in her mouth. She gritted her teeth and swallowed again.

"Not just the air. The water, the soil, everything. What

goes up must come down." She shook her head for a minute. "It amazes me that no one seems to get that."

Again, Joanna found herself studying Jeanie's face, looking for some kind of smile. There was nothing.

"I'm sorry?" It was Joanna's turn to smile.

"Oh, come on. Don't tell you don't know anything about this." Jeanie grimaced. It was a look of astonishment, as though she were waiting for Joanna to confess she was only kidding. Again, they studied each other for a moment.

"The Redmonds?" Jeanie spread out her hands, dodging her head from side to side.

Joanna shook her head. Dread filled her heart. Vaguely, she knew there had been references to the Redmond home and something that had gone wrong there. There had been repeated comments about bad things happening, but she hadn't paid attention. She'd written the comments off as people just being dramatic. These were people who didn't even have dial-up for crying out loud.

"I don't know what you're talking about," Joanna said finally.

Jeanie plopped down her paper plate in disgust. Shaking her head, she reached for a napkin and wiped her hands. She was searching for the right thing to say. Then, as though she were having a private conversation with herself, she shook her head again. She sighed and looked up at Joanna.

"They all died because of the water, Ms. Lucas. Right out there on your property. And I'll tell you how it all happened. John and Ellen Redmond . . . good folks. They'd been tryin' to have babies for years. Couldn't. Or they did, and each one was a stillborn. You know, dead." She shook her head. "It was so sad. All 'em funerals for all those little babies. Then, when they had little John, people started talking 'cause that boy wasn't right. He had some . . ." She made little circle motions with her index finger by the side of her head. "Not so much crazy as just . . . off. And I'll tell ya, when he died, it was the beginning of the end for Mrs. Redmond."

"'Bout that same time, Suzette's horses started dyin'." Jeanie munched on her pig in a blanket for a moment. "She didn't have the exotic animals then, just the horses, and they were getting sick. Just fallin' over, dead in the pasture. No reason, just dead. One after the other, and the weird thing was . . . the thing that no one could get was that it wasn't always the same thing that killed 'em. I mean, you could see how if ever' time a horse died and it looked just the same, why, you'd go get an expert and see what it was all about. But in the case of her horses, one had some kind of funky skin problem and it just . . . itched itself to death. Then, one died of cancer and another of some kind of breathing problems.

"It got so that people weren't payin' too much attention because Suzette's always been a little out there with her pets, if you know what I mean."

Joanna nodded. "I've got an emu who likes to come over to have a beer."

Jeanie didn't bat an eyelash. Instead, she waved a finger. "That's it exactly. You and me don't think it's normal for an emu to be drinking beer, but for Suzette, it's just another day at the house."

Jeanie looked around, lowering her voice. "Then, the babies started dyin' . . . the horse babies, I mean. Suzette had these . . ." She eyed Joanna. "I don't know if you heard this, but the Lees used to be a big name in the equine world. They had major horses, like with some kind of champion bloodline that folks from all over the United States would come for. Top dollar, too. Then, just all in one spring, her babies started dyin'. The ones that weren't dead were . . . majorly deformed.

"She went to Dr. Hendricks and had him check into it. He ran all kinds of tests, and when something didn't look right to him, he did the right thing. He alerted the EPA, told 'em he thought there was something wrong here in the soil or the water."

She stopped, popped a small pastry into her mouth, and chewed on it for a few moments.

Joanna's mouth fell open. She almost laughed. When she saw that Jeanie would not be hurried, she waved a hand at her. "And?"

As Jeanie swallowed, Brianna, Ruthie and Dixie sauntered up, first eyeing Jeanie with some suspicion and then turning to Joanna.

"I don't know if you remember me. I'm Dixie Quigley. I own the Quigley's Down Under." She thrust out a hand over the food display, taking hold of Joanna's hand and pumping it.

Joanna nodded. "Sure, I—"

"Yeah, yeah, and that's Ruthie, Brianna, and I'm Jeanie."

"What have you all been talking about?" Brianna asked with a weak, shaky smile.

"The Redmond house and the poisoning of our nice, little town." There was no emotion in Joanna's voice. But Brianna gasped. Dixie shook her head.

"Jeanie Archer! You don't need to be . . ." She flapped her hands against her body. "Of all the times and places."

"Oh, what? Like I'm sayin' anything that's not true?" She turned back toward Joanna. "I'll tell you what happened. The old cement plant got shut down. It was on the south side of town, and its winds and all the shit that came with it—you know, the emissions—came down our way. Suzette and 'em were downwind of it all. That's how Redmond Lake got to be so contaminated. The old plant got shut down and a new one was built.

"Future Foundations Industries. Everyone said it was crisis averted—no harm, no foul. Except for all the dead animals and the Redmonds, it was business as usual. But the EPA came back and found that something wasn't right around here. Oops. Another crisis. Then our country got a new president who likes business more than babies, and all of a sudden, just clear out of the blue, Dr. Hendricks has got a brand-new clinic with all that state-of-the-art equipment and wouldn't you know it? Dr. Hendricks suddenly doesn't know anything about Suzette's horses and the EPA doesn't think anything is wrong. They can't explain what is making everyone sick. Just like that."

Joanna watched the other women, expecting them to reprimand Jeanie for outlandish statements or horrible mistruths. Instead, they all stared at their feet.

"Are you serious?" she asked, looking at each of them.

Jeanie shrugged. "Same year the state awarded FFI a big hazardous waste permit, livestock started getting sick and babies 'round here started getting born with all kinds of skin problems, cancers, asthma, whatever . . . you name it."

"You're serious?" Joanna turned to Dixie, the woman who seemed to shoot from the hip.

"Well, honey, I hate to say it but . . ." Dixie made a clicking noise with her mouth. "Yeah, that's about right. I woulda figured you already knew that, buyin' the Redmond house and all."

Joanna was stunned, and the silence grew uncomfortable.

"Oh, but don't worry about it. Like Jeanie says, that old plant was shut down." Dixie tried to pat Joanna on the arm to make her feel better.

"Didn't Eva Tobey ever talk to you about that?" Ruthie asked.

"Uh, no." Joanna raised her eyebrows as she choked out a bitter laugh. "No, she managed to forget that part." She politely excused herself.

* * * *

"We should have invited her to that burning permit meeting up at the community center," Jeanie said loudly.

"You should have maybe given her a little more time here before you dropped such a big bomb on her," Ruthie said, frowning.

The girls watched Joanna make her way through the crowd to Suzette. Joanna leaned over, whispering in Suzette's ear and then glided out the back door.

"You think she believed us?" Brianna wore a worried expression on her face.

"I think she's gonna go rip Eva a new one," Dixie said with a wicked little smile.

"I think she's gonna pack her bags and run," Jeanie said.

"I think, if we play this right, she might be the one who can help," Ruthie said in a quiet voice.

They all considered this for a moment.

"That is, if she doesn't get scared off by certain people," Jeanie said, picking up the plate of pigs in a blanket again.

"Those Myra's?" Ruthie reached for one.

"Well, then," Dixie said with a heavy sigh, "that's where we come in. We make sure no one scares her off."

"When Suzette's feeling up to it again, we need to get her to bring Joanna to that meeting so that she can see what's going on firsthand," Ruthie said.

They all nodded. Joanna Lucas had to be in attendance at the upcoming meeting with the Texas Commission on Environmental Quality. There was no doubt about that.

# 9

"This wasn't teenagers." Frank squatted on the ground, inspecting the canister. He lifted it gingerly, releasing it from the two posts that had been wedged into the ground to guarantee its support. "No, definitely not teenagers," he said again, more to himself than anything else,

Paul stood by, mopping sweat from the side of his face. "It's hotter 'n Africa out here. Who else but teenagers would come out here?"

"The same person who'd use one of these." Frank stood and showed the canister to Paul.

"Who'd do that?" Paul asked incredulously, looking around. The land was barren. Beyond the mesquite, sparse Texas brush, and the occasional jackrabbit, there was nothing.

"Someone who wants trouble." Frank sighed. "And trouble they're gonna get."

Frank tucked the canister under his arm and began his trek back to the truck. Paul followed—both men high stepping over cactus and mesquite.

"I don't know how much more you want to do," Paul shouted, not taking his eyes from the rough terrain. "We got security 24-7."

"Well, it ain't workin'," Frank hollered back over his shoulder. Behind them, FFI billowed great clouds of smoke.

"So, what do you have in mind?" Paul huffed. He was losing his breath. Man, but he hated this heat.

"I got some ideas," Frank said. As they neared the fence line, the mesquite thinned out, and he resumed a normal gate. "I got some traps."

Paul stopped in his tracks and watched the back of his friend for a moment.

"What?" he shouted at Frank's back.

Frank turned. "Traps. I got some traps."

"Your bear traps? Those iron-clamp things?" Paul laughed out loud. It was absurd. Insane. But Frank wasn't laughing.

Paul took a few more steps, then stopped.

"Frank. Have you lost your mind? You can't set traps for . . . for humans."

Frank reached his truck and opened the driver's side, placing the canister inside. "I'm not setting anything for humans." Frank's voice was almost a whisper. "That would be irresponsible and illegal. I'm setting traps for the wild boars that've been tearing up FFI's land."

Paul picked his way through the rest of the mesquite and circled around the truck. He wasn't interested in any more conversation until he could climb into the cab, crank the air-conditioning, and catch his breath.

"You're crazier 'n hell." Paul hefted himself into the seat and groaned as he leaned back, closed his eyes, and drew in a deep breath. "You can't go settin' traps for anything out here."

"Why not? This is private property, and I got no reason to believe there are humans out here. I got wild hog troubles. That's it. And I'm going to set my traps."

As Frank turned the key in the ignition, Paul rolled his head to the side and looked at his friend. He almost believed Frank would do it.

* * * *

Marcus Watkins was silent.

"So, eventually, they just stopped breeding altogether. They sold off all the horses and just quit the business. About three months later, her husband was diagnosed with this . . . this CMT thing and now he's dead." Joanna was nearing a full-fledged rant.

"And he's not the only one, Marcus," she said into the phone, pacing back and forth on her beloved new patio and being careful where she walked. Marcus would fade in and out on her cell phone, depending on where she stood. "I'm finding out that there have been quite a few deaths around here with people in their thirties and younger, dying of brain tumors. What the hell? Is that normal? I mean, is that normal for a small town to have so many brain tumor deaths and rare cancers and . . . and things like CMT? Or am I wrong?"

She paused for the first time, allowing Marcus to talk. Instead, he said nothing.

"Hello . . . Hello? Damn it!" She was sure she'd lost him again, but then he spoke.

"I'm here."

"Oh. Well, hell, Marcus. Say something."

"I don't know what to say. I mean, do you know if this is true? Could be small town rumors."

"It's not." There was doom in her voice. From what she'd seen, she had a sinking feeling that the truth was not good.

Marcus said nothing.

"Geez, I can't believe this." Outside on her perfect, beautiful patio created by the perfect, beautiful Roberto, Joanna stopped pacing and gazed out over the back of her property. From the back of the house, there was a slight, gradual slope that led down to her barn—her new studio. Beyond the barn was the remaining eighty acres of open pastures and a huge lake in the center.

The angle of the sun was such that it cast an orange beam across the lake. It was picturesque, and Joanna realized that that view alone would have sold her on this land.

The Shady Land.

The trees, the lake, the antique cast-iron fence, the wraparound porch, this patio. It was all that she'd ever wanted. And it was very possibly toxic.

"Please tell me Clayton doesn't know about this." It was important to Joanna that the Lucas family knew nothing of the pollution problem.

"How could they?" Marcus was hesitant. "I haven't talked to anyone in weeks, Joanna."

"But what if they already knew? Maybe that's the reason they never did anything with this property. I mean, why the hell did they have this in the first place? You ever think about that? Do they have any relation to the Redmonds?" Joanna was keenly aware of the fact that she was nearly shrieking.

"The Redmonds? Who are the Redmonds?" Marcus asked.

"The Redmonds! The Redmonds!" she yelled as though it would clarify everything. "The people who lived here before me. The people who owned this house and then just died. The people who lined their driveway with red oaks to honor all the people who had died before them. Geez, Marcus, I'm living in some kind of death house!"

"Okay, look, honey. Settle down. You're getting yourself all worked up over something you don't even know is true. It may just be some kind of... of folklore. Just give me some time to investigate this."

"Yeah. Right. Sure," Joanna said. She tried to settle herself, but she couldn't. What if the Lucas family knew about this land, this town? What if they had been laughing the entire time? Hell, she'd been so damned concerned about not being able to finish the house and looking like an idiot for traveling all this way for a money pit that she'd never entertained the idea that Clayton Lucas was just waiting for her to die from toxic poisoning.

As she closed her cell phone, she plopped down on the stone

wall. She could feel her chest tightening. Without exception, without one single stinking exception, her life was nothing but a series of messed up, mixed up mistakes. One right after the other. Each time she thought she had caught a break, it was nothing but a giant disaster.

She'd left home, hadn't even sent a card when she met Clayton, hadn't invited her family to her wedding. She'd spent her entire childhood living with alcoholics, cleaning up their messes, covering for them at work, paying bills, and holding the household together. She'd done that pretty well. As an adult, however, she couldn't get one thing right.

When they were kids, she and her brothers had been united. Together, they made sure their drunken parents made it to bed, and were clean and cared for. The term "functioning alcoholics" hadn't made the airwaves when Joanna was a child. It wasn't something people talked about. All she and her brothers knew was somehow their parents managed to work through the day, hold steady jobs, and bring home paychecks. But by seven o'clock every evening, the challenge was to get them to bed before they hurt themselves. If they weren't fighting, they were in danger of falling down stairs, breaking bones, or setting the house on fire.

As children, she and her brothers were the Three Musketeers. United they stood.

Dillon was the first to fall. By high school he had changed. His friends, clothing, attitude, and, finally, devotion to his parents were completely altered. Joanna watched as he came home later and later. Sometimes, he never came home. Dillon knew no one was watching. No one, that is, but Joanna.

When she was a senior in high school, it was clear that there was no longer a family. Dillon had moved out and had become a drifter of sorts. Only when he needed money did he come around. Joanna's little brother, Nick, was smoking marijuana by his sophomore year.

There was no sense in talking to anyone about anything. The

thing about functioning alcoholics is they are treading water—always treading water. It wasn't that they didn't care or didn't have the interest. They just couldn't afford to invest themselves emotionally because they were just making it through each day, and to recognize and stop the destructive behavior of another person meant they had to recognize and accept their own problems. What Joanna had not been prepared for was the backlash. When she tried to save her younger brother, when she tried to convince her parents that he needed counseling or rehab, they turned on her. And then she was the problem. Suddenly, she was the bad guy.

Still, she hung on, believing that it would all turn out all right. She had also believed that her presence and constant pressure on the situation would eventually turn things around. The truth, she'd maintained, would set them all free.

It was a farce.

On her twenty-second birthday, she'd walked out and never looked back. Earlier that day, her mother had lured her from work, teasing her about her present. She was going to love it, her mother had said. It was something very special, she'd promised. But before the presents could be opened, Nicky arrived home stoned out of his mind. Already tipsy, her parents didn't want to discuss the matter on her birthday. But, she'd pointed out, there was always an excuse not to talk about it.

Enough was enough. She'd been exhausted, fed up, and scared. So she'd thrown down her final card.

"I still love you, but I won't live like this. Call me when you're ready to get help."

They never called.

* * * *

The roar of the lion drew her attention. Or was it the snow leopard? Joanna wasn't sure but it pulled her from the patio and into Suzette's backyard.

The lion Suzette called Joshua puffed his lips as Joanna approached. He was, in a word, gorgeous. He watched her with large, golden, almond-shaped eyes. He was picture-perfect with a golden mane framing his massive head. His fawn-colored body was thick, muscled, and well groomed. He appeared to be the king of the animal world.

Wooden railroad ties had been stacked toward the back of his pen, making a deep, three-step tier, and the king was perched on top, looking down on Joanna. Just the tip of his tail moved, swishing back and forth. It was a mild effort to keep the flies away.

"It's just an illusion." The sound of Suzette's voice caused Joanna to jump.

"What's that?" Joanna asked and smiled at her neighbor. It was good to see her out and about. In the evening, she could always hear the big cats calling out for dinner but she never actually saw Suzette feed them. It occurred to her that she could, and should, help.

"His tail." Suzette poked at chin toward Joshua. "He'd have you believe he's bored with you." Both women looked back at the gorgeous cat. Indeed, he looked bored by his visitors. "Trust me, he's watching your every move and just waiting for you to step inside the pen"—Suzette moved a little closer to the fence—"and then he'll have himself a new toy."

"Good to know," Joanna said.
Joshua continued to look bored.

"So what are you doing here?" Suzette asked pleasantly. "You want a tour?" And with a nod from Joanna, Suzette introduced her. Each cat had his or her own story—one that Suzette was unable to turn away from. The animals had been abused and by virtue of their size, temperament and abusive background, had no other place to go.

"But why you?" Joanna asked.

"Why not me?"

"Well, I mean, let's see . . . this place is toxic, for one," Joanna said, deciding not to mention that Suzette was already down one leg because of a tiger.

Suzette sighed. "I know that. Yes, I do know that. But where are these cats going to go? I'm the last stop. There's not a whole lot of cat sanctuaries around, you know? Cats, their upkeep . . . it's expensive."

She looked at the snow leopard named Molly. "She's the only one a zoo was interested in, and you know why they wanted her? Because she could have babies. But I got two problems with that. One, many of the exotics have babies with birth defects when they're in captivity. Not because she's here in Marcus. This is a real problem among wild animals kept in captivity. It's a horrible thing. But no one wants to talk about that. No one wants to have to . . . ahh," she said and waved a hand as she wiped her nose.
Joanna had taken a seat on an old saddle rack next to Suzette, and together they watched the cats. The large animals never moved, but the women were transfixed all the same. The cats were so beautiful, Joanna could have stared at them all day.

"The other is, this one has already had enough. I won't sell her or send her off just so she can be used as a baby-making machine." Molly didn't look real to Joanna. The cat's spotted white fur, long ears, and exotic features made her look like a stuffed animal Joanna had once had as a child. Molly hissed at Joanna after several minutes of an unofficial staring contest, reminding her that Molly was real.

"Isn't she pretty?"
Joanna nodded. Exquisite.
Suzette shook her head. "The wrong kind of person wanted her for all the wrong reasons, so I took her. I hope for the right ones. I won't sell her or use her or abuse her. She doesn't trust me. Hell, I don't think she likes me but . . ." she said with a shrug. "That's okay. I didn't take her so we could become friends."

She turned to Joanna.

"I hope one day you'll get to know that feeling. I hope one day you'll get a call where, if someone needs help or maybe they got a stray, you can step in and help. You won't do it because it makes you popular or liked. You just do it because it's the thing to do." She looked back to Molly and smiled.

* * * *

"So, exactly how does a pole dancer become a Mormon?" Jeanie asked. She'd been watching Dixie chop onions and celery, preparing deli items for the noon rush.

Dixie stopped mid-chop and looked up.

Jeanie had on her lopsided grin, the one that promised at least twenty more minutes of nonsense, trying to get someone—anyone—riled up for her own secret pleasure of watching a person's blood pressure rise.

"The same way someone decides they want to turn their life around and join any church," Dixie said, her voice unemotional.

"But what a jump! Pole dancing to Mormonism. What triggered that?" she asked, still pushing.

"I don't understand the question." Dixie did but she wasn't going to play along.

"So . . . you're swinging on a pole, gyrating and wiggling. You're wearin' next to nothing and dancing on a metal rod just to excite a bunch of men, and suddenly, your mind wanders to religion and you say, 'Hey, I think I'll become a Mormon.' How does that work, exactly?"

"Let me ask you something first, Jeanie," Dixie said and scooped the fixings into a large container. "What do you believe? Do you believe in God?"

"Maybe."

"Maybe. Maybe yes? Maybe no? You can't say *maybe* to the God question."

"Who says?" Jeanie asked as she looked around the room for support.

"There are some questions in life that demand a yes or a no. This is one of 'em. You either are or you aren't pregnant. You can wish you are or hope you're not. But in the end, you either are or you aren't. Same with religion. You either believe or you don't."

Dixie wiped her hands on her apron and looked up.

"What happens if I say I don't?" Jeanie stood from her table and walked over to the counter where Dixie was working.

"Then," Dixie said with a shrug, "you don't."

"And if I said I did?" Jeanie asked.

Dixie smiled. "Then you do."

Jeanie stared at her friend for a moment. "That's it?" She leaned over the counter, reaching for some samples, and Dixie slapped her hand.

"No. If you decide you do, then you have a responsibility. The question becomes what are you going to do about it? You can't just decide you believe in God and then not do anything."

"Says who?" Jeanie looked indignant.

"Uh, says the Bible, for one."

"Is that your Mormon Bible or the Christian Bible?" Jeanie smiled.

"Ah, geez . . . here we go," Dixie said and offered a mock grimace. In truth, she enjoyed this open forum. Since announcing her religion, most folks in town just pretended not to know. Jeanie was one of the few people who would share her true feelings. Even the other girls had some kind of unspoken agreement to never discuss Dixie's religion. But Jeanie had missed that girls meeting.

"Hey, you're the weirdo, not me," Jeanie said defensively.

"Okay, first, thank you. I appreciate being called a weirdo. Although it loses some of its punch coming from the person who asked me which would be worse, licking cat poop or a toilet seat."

"Cat poop, definitely."

"The Book of Mormon, as it's called, is Christian. We are Christian. But then, you know that."

"I'm just repeating what I hear." Jeanie spread out her hands and smiled.

"I'm sure," Dixie said, smiling brilliantly, and Jeanie knew that Dixie was still playing along. No hurt feelings. So, she pushed a little more.

"Then, if you're Christian, why add another Bible?"

"Because," Dixie said with a sigh, "we are the Latter-day Saints . . . you know, latter day, meaning there is more work to be done, more word to be spread."

"But Myra Thompson said that it's blasphemy because the Bible is a complete and final book. It is perfect, and to add on to it is an insult and a lie."

"Ah, yes, Myra Thompson. The Bible also says it's not good to be glutinous or a sloth, yet there she is, making plate after plate of pigs in a blanket and inhaling most of them."

"Ooh, you are green-eyed jealous because everyone in town loves those piggies of hers, and you can't stand it." Jeanie snickered.

Merilee walked into Quigley's Down Under, a happy smile on her face. She opened her mouth to say hi, but then she stopped. She sensed that Dixie and Jeanie were at it. Again.

"What are we talking about today, girls?" she asked.

"How it came to be that Dixie here traded in her stripper pole for the Mormon Church."

"Aiyee." Merilee winced, pretending to shield her eyes from the women. She ducked her head and charged toward the kitchen. "I don't want to hear nothing! I don't want to hear nothing from you two today."

Together, Jeanie and Dixie watched Merilee disappear, both grinning. As soon as Merilee was out of sight, Dixie's smile faded.

"I'm not jealous. Not of that cow. But I am sick and tired of people talkin' trash about something they know nothing about."
"Mmm-hmm." Jeanie feigned empathy. "Is it true you wear magical underwear?"

Dixie raised a single eyebrow. It was a warning, and Jeanie started to back off.

"Mormons have sacred undergarments," Dixie said, her voice flat. "They're not magical or anything weird like that. The idea is that the underwear is . . . like a reminder of your commitment, your belief, your faith to the church. That's all." Dixie grabbed a third container of vegetables and began pulling out the choice pieces to be sliced and diced. "And, no, I don't wear that underwear."

"Because you don't wear underwear. Yes, I would imagine that would make it difficult to wear your magical underwear unless it was invisible magical underwear." Jeanie began to laugh.

"Little FYI here." Dixie paused from cutting her green peppers and held her knife high so that Jeanie could see it. Jeanie smiled. "However disappointing this may be to you, I do not live a wild life anymore. There are no late nights, whoopin' it up, drinking, or carrying on. I do actually wear underwear, I attend church regularly, I read the Holy Bible, I pray to God, I give thanks to my Savior, Jesus Christ, and more than ever in my life, I appreciate the importance of family and honor and integrity."

"Geez," Jeanie said, pretending to be insulted. "I just wanted to know if you wore magical underwear."

"I'll keep you posted," Dixie said and began chopping green peppers again.

"I also heard that—" Jeanie could tell by Dixie's expression that her patience had run out. Jeanie shrugged. "I'm just tellin' ya what I've heard so you can know what people are sayin'."

"Yes, I appreciate that. I'd also appreciate it if the next time you're attending one of your damned Druid meetings, you'd pass on to your high priestess that what I wear and what I believe are my business. And that," she said, poking her chopping blade toward Jeanie, "is the very foundation of religion in this country. Freedom of religion. If I was Muslim, it'd be the same danged thing. It's my choice and my belief."

She nodded and went back to chopping. Jeanie opened her mouth to respond but was saved by Ruthie.

"Girls," she said as she rushed forward. She looked excited. Most mornings, Ruthie was dressed in her Capri sweats, zip-up jacket, and walking shoes. She'd taken to walking the three and a half miles from her home to Quigley's Down Under so that she could flop herself down and stay for the next two hours, drinking high-calorie cappuccinos and gabbing. Instead, today she was dressed in office attire.

"Well, now, don't you look nice," Jeanie said, whirling around on her stool.

"Just came from the mayor's office." She breathed heavily. She was excited. She hustled up to the counter, peered over to see what Dixie was making, and then continued—probably because it was not chocolate. "It's on. It's on. The TCEQ, local EPA office, reps from FFI, and some press are coming to the meeting." She clapped her hands together.

Dixie nodded and smiled. "It's about time."

"Where's Brianna?" asked Jeanie. It was a question that deflated Ruthie.

"Tried to call her all morning," she said. Both Dixie and Jeanie knew what was to come next, and both sighed in unison. "She was supposed to come with me. She was supposed to pick me up . . . I came by to see if one of you wanted to come with me. I don't want to go over there alone."

Jeanie, somber, slid off her stool. "I'll go," she said, her voice so quiet that Dixie stopped what she was doing and watched her friend.

"Y'all be careful. If you see his truck there, maybe you should just call Stan," Dixie said.

But even as she said the words, they all knew it was a difficult call. To call the chief of police might just make matters worse. Brianna had made the decision long ago to stay with her husband. On the one hand, she might really need their help. They had all watched too many shows, heard too many stories, and read too many news items about women who might have been saved had someone just made a phone call. But on the other hand, if they called Stan and then it turned out that Brianna just wasn't answering the phone, Terry would be furious. There was no telling how he would react to that kind of embarrassment.

Neither Jeanie nor Ruthie answered. As Jeanie gathered up her bag, Dixie offered her a boost.

"I never answered your question," she said and Jeanie turned, looking confused.

"How's that?"

"Why I stopped stripping and became a Mormon," she said. Jeanie perked up. "He was one of my regulars." As Dixie spoke, Jeanie's expression lightened. "He was also a Mormon!"

Jeanie shook her head, chuckling. "I appreciate that, Dix," she said and headed out the door.

# 10

Joanna parked outside Tobey Realty. It was an office she knew well. Located in the center of town, Eva had told her that when she purchased the building it was at the center point of the business community. Her sprawling office allowed her to look out on Main Street and further to the highway that ran through town. While most of the downtown offices had smaller windows, Tobey Realty had huge bay windows that made the office look open and inviting.

Joanna could see Eva from her car. She was wearing a bright orange, red, and blue blouse over a red skirt and Frye riding boots. On anyone else, this ensemble would have been a disaster. On Eva, it worked. Nicely, at that. But Joanna was in no mood for paying compliments. As she stepped out of her car, she trained her eye on that bright outfit.

Had she wanted to creep up on Eva, her plan was ruined by a passing 18-wheeler. Its driver laid on the horn as Joanna stepped onto the sidewalk. She jumped and then grunted. The 18-wheeler, hauling crushed cars, was not an uncommon sight in Granby. *But why? Where in the hell were all the crushed cars coming from?*

Eva was talking to a tall man, waving her arms around with fluid, exaggerated movements. As Joanna walked into the office, setting off a door chime that beeped loudly, Eva winked at her.

"Just a minute, hon," she said, refocusing on the man before her.

"You can't let 'em use it, Eva. You're every bit a part of the problem if you do," the man said as Joanna found a seat near the front window.

There was no doubt that Eva had decorated the office herself. The bright colors, rich fabrics, and creative flair all screamed Eva. Joanna picked up an *Architect's Digest* and thumbed through it as she continued to watch the goings-on of the office.

As Eva and the man bickered over the use of some building, Joanna spied Tommy Tobey. Both of Eva's grown children worked in her office with her. Tommy and Tiffany Tobey. It was too cute. Too Eva.

But they appeared to be good kids. Both had earned their real estate and broker licenses by the age of twenty. Both already had a plethora of listings under their names and were already in the business of restoration or, as they called it, flipping houses. In the corner of the office, Tiffany Tobey was tapping away on her keyboard, checking on a listing while talking on the phone. But Tommy moved toward Joanna.

"Ms. Lucas," he said, his drawl slow and easy. He extended a hand. "You still enjoying your house?"

"It's a work in progress." Joanna offered a smile. She didn't want to include Tommy in her woes and not in front of another person. She eyed Eva again.

"Look, John," Eva said, tapping her foot, "I'm not offering up anything. They called. They needed the space, and I assure you, this meeting is taking place with or without my building."

"But why cater to 'em, is all I'm sayin'." His voice was almost a whine.

"I've been meaning to come by and take a look around,"

Tommy said, distracting Joanna. She smiled back at him. "That is, if you don't mind. I'd love to see what you've done to the place."

"Sure," Joanna said. "Anytime."

"I always said that house had great potential." He was like a giant Opie Taylor, just not quite so red. He was young, clear-eyed, pale, and covered with freckles. His arms and legs were lanky, and Joanna had a sense that he'd not yet grown into himself.
Joanna nodded with another smile.

"We got to be smart about this," the man was saying. "We have a lot to lose. You should know that better than anyone else. If people start talkin' or decide there's something gone afoul, it'll cost us money."

"Don't you think I know that?" Eva asked. With that, she took hold of his arm and led him to the door as she continued to smooth talk him. "But don't you also think it's better business to stay on top of what's going on here?"

"Well, I—"

"Trust me, John, I'm keeping an eye on this situation." They both stopped at the door to look at each other. Eva smiled up at him, but he was more tentative.

"I surely do hope so, Eva. I hope so."

She patted his shoulder. "You and I need to have open communication. We just need to talk to each other but always keep an ear to the ground. It's the best way to protect our investments, if you know what I mean." She gave him a final pat, and he opened the door. He only seemed to relax with her final words. "Trust me, John. I've been here too long to let anything bad happen. You can trust me on that."

He nodded and walked out.

The office was suddenly very quiet as Eva watched him walk to his truck.

"Uh, Mom," Tommy said, interrupting his mother's thoughts. "Ms. Lucas has invited me to go out and take a look at the progress."

Eva turned. The smile was brilliant. The consummate saleswoman.

"Joanna! What brings you into town?"

Joanna threw a cautionary look toward Tommy, and he excused himself. Eva's smile flickered.

"Is something wrong?"

"You didn't tell me about this town." Joanna's voice was low, almost growling.

"What?" Eva cocked her head, sitting down next to Joanna.

"This town . . . why didn't you tell me when I came to see the house? Why didn't you tell me about the Redmonds?" Joanna asked.

"Tell you . . . " Eva's voice trailed off, annoying Joanna. She didn't want to play games. Eva's stalling tactic frustrated Joanna further.

"Oh, come on. It didn't occur to you that you should tell me that the former owners died of some kind of toxic poisoning? That their only child was born with some kind of abnormality? That the Lees' animals all died?" Joanna had to work to keep her voice calm and quiet with Tiffany still clicking away at the computer in the corner and Tommy somewhere in the back.

"No, Joanna, it didn't." Eva's sweetness was gone. Her voice had a hard edge to it, challenging. "You may recall that when you first phoned me, I asked you what made you decide to look here in Marcus, and you told me in no uncertain terms that you knew all about it here, that you'd come into some property and wanted to settle down here." She paused, and Joanna drew in her breath.

It was true, Joanna realized. She hadn't wanted anyone to know she'd *inherited* the land through a nasty divorce. So she'd made sure to shoot down any questions a nosey, small-town real estate agent might have had.

Now, like everything else in her life, it'd come back to bite her in the ass.

"I had no call to tell you about the Redmonds as I assumed you already knew. That's how you made it sound."

Joanna focused on breathing.

"As for the other business, Joanna. You have to be careful. Be sure to get the right information. This is a town divided. You got some people who have worked for FFI for decades—"

"Future Foundations Industries," Joanna said and sighed. The bread and butter of Marcus.

"Yeah," Eva said. "We got folks who are third- and fourth-generation employees of that company, and the last thing they want to hear is people saying that their own bread and butter is harming folks. Then you've got the other group making claims about two-headed cows, and every time someone gets sick, they blame the air or the water."

Joanna opened her mouth to speak, but Eva lifted her hand, silencing her.

"I'm not saying anything one way or the other. I'm just saying before you go charging off in one direction, get all your facts. That's all. Just . . . get all your facts."

* * * *

Jeanie raised her hand to knock on the front door when it was yanked open, surprising her. All three women jumped and then laughed nervously. No one was sure what to say. As usual, Jeanie charged in.

"What the hell?"

"I was just going out," Brianna said. She looked flushed and embarrassed.

She pulled the front door closed behind her, crowding forward and forcing Jeanie and Ruthie to step back.

"You were supposed to pick me up this morning," Ruthie said. The three women stood huddled on the tiny front step of the Smart home.

"I'm sorry." Brianna managed a weak smile. "I was going to call you, but I just . . . I didn't. I'm sorry."

More silence.

"Well," Ruthie said and stepped forward, squeezing Brianna's shoulder. "Are you okay?"

"What? Oh." She waved a hand at them, forcing a laugh. "Oh, yeah, I'm okay. It's no big deal."

"We were a little worried," Ruthie whispered.

"Well, don't be. I'm a big girl. I can take care of myself." Her eyes darted back and forth between her friends.

Jeanie scowled. "I'm a bigger girl. Maybe I should just go on in there and stomp the shit out of him."

"Shh," Brianna whispered and began shoving Ruthie and Jeanie off the front porch. "Are you crazy? Don't go saying things like that, Jeanie. Land sakes!" Brianna did not stop pushing until she had effectively walked them all to the street and the parked cars.

"Why don't you—"

"Jeanie Archer, just hush. I don't need your help. I'm just fine. I'm fine!" But even as she scolded her friends, she was whispering. Jeanie and Ruthie exchanged glances.

"We were just worried, that's all," Ruthie said. "So, if everything's okay then . . . come on." She stepped around Brianna to get into her car. "We got things to take care of."

* * * *

"Shit."

He looked at the blood and groaned. He couldn't say he was surprised. He hadn't been feeling well. Although, it was a tough ailment to describe. He didn't have the flu or anything like that. He just felt off-center, tired, a little weak. But there was no specific symptom like a fever or headache.

You can't call in sick at work because you feel off.

He stared into the toilet. Blood.

There were two common ground rules at work. Periodically check your stools for blood and report it if you got it.

"Shit."

He had it.

Hands on hips, he stared down into the toilet for several seconds more. *Blood in my own damned shit.* He reached forward, hesitated a moment longer, then flushed it down into the septic system. Blood.

It was tempting not to report it. After all, who would know?

* * * *

John Simmons sat at his desk, brooding.

He was a large man, grizzled by hard labor and hard living. Although he had been the primary owner of Future Foundations Industries for almost two decades before selling, he liked to be in the mix of things. For this reason, he was respected both at work and in the community. Marcus was a blue-collar town that celebrated its laborers as much as its owners.

He was also known to tip back a few with employees as well. To his face, he was considered friendly, honest, hardworking, and intelligent. Behind his back, he was all these things, but there was wide speculation about how he got into his cups. One was never enough. More often than not, his eyes were bloodshot and his speech slurred. And there was something else. There was a quiet but growing concern that he'd begun to buy up too much land. His aggressive entrepreneurialism broke from the blue-collar ranks, and he was making a few people nervous.

What John knew, however, was that land was for sale and he had the money. But a group of citizens and their continued protests against pollution had renewed interest with the EPA, and that was a concern. He had to treat it as a challenge, nothing more. If he showed undue concern or alarm, it would cause people to talk. The straight facts were: He'd lived in Marcus all his life, and there wasn't a damned thing wrong with him. The same could be said of his father and grandfather. No one ever thought anything of people getting sick. It was sad, but it wasn't something to be blamed on the air or on local industry. Getting sick and dying was a sad part of living. No one questioned Matt Carlson's death. No one worried too much when Charles Holden got sick, or when Virginia Black got cancer. Then a bunch of horses get sick and people go nuts. Suzette Lee and her big mouth. It was years ago, yet she just couldn't let it drop.

John could not have been more invested in the town. He was a fifth generation Marcusite. He had three sons and a grandbaby on the way—all living in Marcus.

It was absurd to think he would stay if he believed there was anything foul or dangerous going on in the town. The fact was, no sooner had he sold out to the Austrians than he'd pumped the money right back into Marcus. Almost every cent went back into purchasing land, and what had not gone into the market had gone into his private fund. It had been his intention, for many years, to run for state representative. His pockets were deep, and he had friends with even deeper pockets and political connections.

He'd never once in his life had the desire to leave Marcus, and he would be damned if he was going to let some asinine tree huggers, jumping on the global-warming bandwagon, take it from him.

This was his town. Literally and figuratively. No one was going to screw with his plans.

# 11

It would have been brilliant timing to have the results of the canister analysis, to be able to present the evidence at the big meeting and quiet the doubters and deniers. But there were scheduling conflicts. Once again, industry had ruled the meeting time and place. With a pro-business administration at both the state and national level, the Environmental Protection Agency and Texas Commission on Environmental Quality were just two little kids to be kicked around. Memos and in-house meetings had made it clear to the current agents: play nice with business and everyone wins.

They would have to go back for the canister later and save those results for another time.

The meeting was Tuesday evening at the Marcus Community Center. The truth of it was the town had no real community center. Any time there was a wedding, funeral or fundraiser, Tobey Realty let the townspeople use the old building. It had once been an old office supply store, but no more. Like so many businesses in Marcus, it had folded within a decade and moved on.

Officially, there was no sign outside marking it as such, but to everyone in town it was the community center.

The purpose of the meeting was listed as a permit hearing. FFI had applied for a permit to burn tires in its cement kilns. By law, citizens had to be given a chance to appeal and gather more information. Thus, it was also seen as an opportunity for the industry to better explain their plans and relieve some concerns.

There was cause to be concerned. While small in population, Marcus held the largest hazardous waste burning permit in the United States. According to the EPA, it burned and released a remarkable 11,000 pounds of chromium, 2,000 pounds of butadiene, 7,000 pounds of benzene, 2,550 pounds of methyl ethyl ketone, 3,000 pounds of toluene, 750 pounds of xylene, and 2,500 pounds of cyclohexane per year. While emitting "probable carcinogens" such as benzene, butadiene, and chromium, FFI also released toxic heavy metals including arsenic and mercury. But, unbeknownst to most Marcus residents, FFI had been exempted by Texas law from adhering to the current environmental regulations.

It had long been a common argument that the pollution couldn't be all bad if the government allowed it. No one had stopped to consider that the government had turned a blind eye.

Almost no one. Some were paying attention, and they would be the watchdogs for the small community whether the citizens liked it or not.

* * * *

Joanna smiled. A little. She had walked into Quigley's Down Under with the hope of getting lunch for her men and was now involved in yet another ridiculous conversation. She had deluded herself into thinking she needed no one. She'd been so used to the women of the Hamptons treating her rudely; she had forgotten how much fun it was to have female friends.

*Friends.* She felt an emotional tug. She had nothing in common with these women. They were crazy. Insane.

"That's ridiculous." Brianna craned her neck around the coffeemaker to look at Jeanie. She stood at the café bar, playing barista for the day. "I'm not even going to dignify that with an answer.”

“I would say—” Ruthie started.

“Careful. Remember that your answer will be very telling,” Jeanie said to her, plopping her feet on a chair from the next table. Ruthie snapped her mouth shut again and pondered this. “What do you mean?”

“Well, the kind of woman you’d have sex with says a lot about you,” Jeanie said, and Brianna snorted from behind the bar.

“That’s disgusting,” she said.

“You’re telling me you’ve never found another woman attractive?” Jeanie asked. “Please. I see you lookin’ at Dixie.” Jeanie winked at her but Brianna had no sense of humor.

“Not like that!” Brianna glared at Jeanie. She turned to Ruthie, who was seated next to Jeanie and lost in thought about her perfect fantasy female lover. “And you should not answer that, Ruthie. This is disgusting and just another Jeanie-ism to get me upset.” She turned her attention to the coffee machine and began pushing buttons.

“Probably an athlete,” Ruthie said.

“Do tell!” Jeanie fixed an elbow on the table, grinning.

“Well, she’d need to be more butch. I definitely like being the female in a couple.”

Dixie laughed out loud.

“So, what are we talkin’ here? Like a Billie Jean King or a speed skater?” Jeanie asked.

“Speed skaters are not butch! They just have big legs.” Dixie looked up from her station at the deli counter and shook her head at Jeanie.

“Why are we having this conversation?” Brianna asked.

“I was talking more about size. They’re big girls. Powerful.” Jeanie winked at Ruthie. “I thought maybe she’d like to be tossed around a little."

Brianna gasped and Ruthie giggled.

"It is true. I do like to be tossed around." Ruthie beamed at her own little joke. Jeanie had opened her mouth but snapped it shut and marveled at her Ruthie—small boned, petite, soft-spoken, demure Ruthie.

"Why, Ruth Emory, I do declare," Jeanie said and put her hand to her chest.

"More like a basketball player, I guess. Billie Jean King is too little. I like 'em bigger than me, please."

"Maybe an Ann Wolfe," Jeanie said.

"Who's Ann Wolfe?" Brianna asked.

"She's a professional boxer." Dixie waved a pickle in the air and then pretended to box for a moment. "You have to read the sports pages more often. She's pretty good. She even fought a man."

"A boxer. See, that's another problem, too. Women should not be allowed to box." Brianna was annoyed. She hated these kinds of conversations because, ultimately, she was always left out. No one was listening to her any longer.

"What do you think?" Jeanie directed everyone's attention to Joanna. "What does a refined Yankee woman like yourself find appealing in another woman?"

"I, uh," Joanna said.

"Probably someone like Audrey Hepburn. Someone who wouldn't leave crackers in your bed," Jeanie said.

"That was Barbara Mandrell." Brianna corrected Jeanie and smiled at her own joke. No one heard her.

"Oh, Emma Stone," Ruthie said and clapped her hands.

"No, Joanna would definitely go for someone older, someone who could take care of her." Dixie stopped chopping peppers and looked around for approval.

"Not since she got her tampon money. She doesn't need anyone but her Mexican workers and Suzette." Jeanie paused for a moment. "Suzette. Hmm."

"Oh! Now that is disgusting. Joanna is not thinking about having sex with Suzette!" Brianna yelled, and Jeanie howled with laughter, slapping her knee.

"I, uh," Joanna said. How could Joanna call these women friends? They were insane. Yet each time she met them, they brought her into the fold. They said outrageous things and left her speechless, but later, it would make her smile.

"A man is supposed to be rough and tough," Dixie said, eager to take her turn. "But not a woman. I think if I was to have a romance with a—"

"A romance," Ruthie said with a snicker.

"That's what Mormons call it." Jeanie pretended to whisper to her tablemate. "And when a man marries multiple wives, that's a whirlwind romance."

"Are you having fun? Do you want an answer or not?" Dixie asked playfully. But she was far too eager to take her turn to be deterred. "I would choose . . . hmm. Well, I guess she would be a lot like the woman I once had an affair with."

"What!" Both Jeanie and Ruthie surged forward, almost leaving their seats.

Dixie's smile grew as she looked over at Brianna, giving her a little wink. "In fact, she looked a little like you, peaches."

"That's disgusting!" Brianna batted away Dixie's hand, smiling all the same.

"Go on," Ruthie said, wanting more details, but Dixie began to laugh.

"Not really. Geez." She laughed at her audience. "You know, I do believe I should be offended. You're all a little too ready to accept anything I say. Believe it or not, I wasn't that wild!"

"Said the former stripper." Jeanie rolled her eyes.

"Probably an intellectual. An aggressive CEO. Someone with money and power," Dixie said.

"Wow, you think ya know a person," Ruthie said.

"So, let's have it, Jeanie." Dixie peered back at her friend. "Who's your ideal woman?"

"Hands down, I'm gonna have to go with Raquel Welch, in her day."

There was applause from both Ruthie and Dixie.

"Good choice," Dixie applauded.

"Although I must say, Joanna is rather fetching!" Jeanie said and wiggled a little finger at Joanna.

"Akkk," Ruthie covered her eyes.

*  *  *  *

Joanna reached into her purse, pulling out an envelope. It was thicker than usual, complete with a week's worth of pay—cash. As she did, she thought about the words of warning she'd received from Kelly McDonald, the resident well-meaning, but ever-nosey, bank teller.

"You can't pay 'em beaners outright," she'd said with a laugh. "You won't see 'em again. You got to pay day wages only. And nothing extra. You pay over scale, and they start to get sassy and start thinkin' they deserve more." She'd wagged a finger at Joanna. "I seen it over and over. Someone comes in, overpays and next thing you know, they's makin' demands from other people, saying they want more money."

Joanna had thanked her and left the bank with her brain humming. It was as if Kelly was talking about some subspecies of humans, as though you couldn't let *them* know that they might actually *deserve* more money for their hard work and that it was *our* responsibility to be sure they weren't clued into this.

The business of paying the men—men who had all demonstrated a great devotion to The Shady Land and the work needed—had seemed ridiculous to Joanna. Why should she continue to pay them daily when she knew they would return day after day? It was easier to pay them on a weekly basis.

She looked forward to handing the envelope to Manuel. It was a show of faith and gratitude. And it would be greatly appreciated, she knew. Just days before, she had traded in her Jeep for a sturdy, reliable, not-too-pretty truck. Then she'd turned the truck keys over to Manuel.

"You take care of the truck, use it to drive back and forth," she said, plopping the keys into his hands.

He'd been stunned.

Every morning, she'd driven out to the money tree to pick the men up, and she didn't like it. She didn't like seeing all the men out there and felt guilty that she couldn't give them all work.

"What about the ones who aren't picked up?" she'd asked Manuel one morning. He'd shrugged.

"They don't work."

As many as six men lived together in tiny hotel rooms to save money. Anything extra they had went back home to loved ones.

"How do you stand living so close together?" she'd asked another time, after seeing how they all lived. It was not a critical question, but one of interest, and Manuel understood that.

"We just do," he'd said.

As a courtesy to one another, they were neat. Joanna had seen inside their room on two separate occasions. Both times, all the bedding was rolled up and everything was very tidy. Hand-washed clothing hung on a clothesline just over a portable fan. They owned a small refrigerator, a coffee maker, and a microwave. There was no room for any personal knickknacks or home décor.

In the impersonal world of newspapers, she'd shared the frustrations of illegal aliens charging over the borders. She'd heard all the arguments lobbed back and forth about illegal immigrants and employment. *They're taking our jobs* versus *We're doing the work no one else wants to do,* and *They're sending our money back to Mexico* versus *Your workforce would shut down if we walked.*

In retrospect, she was sure she'd agreed with the argument that our resources were being sent across the border and that the Mexican government enjoyed watching its citizens cross the border rather than dealing with its own poverty. It was all—

A screech startled Joanna. She rushed to the back door and stood transfixed. Under the orange and red sun-streaked sky, Joanna watched as Manuel sprinted across the horizon. He was screaming. Hot on his tail was Eduardo.

The rest of the men were seated on the patio, hooting and hollering. No one moved to help Manuel as the giant emu sprinted behind him.

Choking back a laugh, Joanna stepped out on to the porch. Both Carlos and Andres folded over, nearly hysterical with laughter. Even the shy Marcos laughed out loud, albeit with his hand over his mouth.

Joanna saw the Costilla brothers watching with arms folded across their chests and wearing huge grins. Briefly, she caught Roberto's eye. She wanted to laugh with him for a moment, but she looked back at Manuel.

There was no telling how long the pot-bellied, cigar-smoking Manuel could hold out in a foot race with an emu. A lean, young emu.

"Manuel!" Joanna cupped her hands around her mouth and moved to the edge of the patio. She was not certain whether he could hear her over the howls of laughter.

"Manuel! Drop your beer! Your beer!" Joanna screamed. "He wants your beer! He just wants your beer! Drop the beer!"

Manuel sprinted by again, high stepping in such an exaggerated manner, Joanna almost believed Manuel was putting on a show to entertain the others. But when Eduardo pecked again at Manuel's backside, causing Manuel to shriek and high step with a little more gusto, Joanna recognized Manuel's fear.

*Stupid bird.* The little sucker had pecked her before as well. It hurt. It hurt a lot. What Suzette insisted on calling "love taps" from Eduardo left enormous welts. Joanna had learned very quickly to fight back, hitting Eduardo's knobby knees.

"Manuel, the beer!" Joanna yelled once more and then growled.

"Ooh!" She snapped up her weapon of choice against the beer-guzzling, back-pecking beast—a bamboo stick she kept against the back step.

Stick raised, Joanna charged forward after Eduardo. She ignored the roar of laughter behind her, and as she moved in, she began yelling Manuel's name, trying to get him to turn back and run toward the patio.

"Run, Manuel, run!" Andres yelled.

The men all jumped to their feet, waving their hats, and encouraging Manuel to continue on when Suzette pulled up in her golf cart. Her mouth dropped open.

Joanna was closing in on Eduardo when he changed directions, wings flapping, and turned back toward Joanna. She could have stood her ground and swung at the bird. But her problem was that she liked Eduardo. He was like a bizarre roommate, always hanging around and stealing her stuff, but was also pretty good company. More often than not, she found herself talking to him. He was very sweet, except when he was pecking her.

Realizing that Eduardo was no longer chasing him, Manuel stopped. Resting his hands on top of his knees, he could only shake his head and wheeze. He still held his beer by the neck of the bottle. He didn't know Joanna was on the run, having come to his rescue. He only knew he couldn't breathe.

Joanna turned. She'd been pecked enough times to know that while it hurt, it was not life threatening. She had a plan. Run! Specifically, run like hell toward the patio. But as she turned, she bumped into Roberto and stumbled back.

In a fluid movement, Roberto caught her with his left hand on her upper arm and pulled her to his side. With his right, he reached out, took hold of the bamboo stick, and waved it up. He barked at Eduardo, the way a rancher would move cattle, and Eduardo lurched to the side. The emu puffed up, flapping his wings, and briefly turned back toward Manuel.

"Manuel," someone yelled and the older man peeked up. His mouth hung open, his eyes were squinted in pain, and he groaned when he saw Eduardo coming.

"Throw the beer, man," someone else yelled. Manuel looked anguished. He looked at his bottle and back at the oncoming bird. Then, cursing under his breath, he took one final swig and threw the bottle away. Like a heat-seeking missile, Eduardo veered away from Manuel and followed the beverage.

Joanna and Roberto did not move. He still held her arm while Manuel stood, arched his back for a moment, and whistled.

"That bird is loco!" His accent was thick, his breathing still labored. "Aiyee," he grumbled, feeling his lower back. Finally, he responded to the jeers from the patio. It was something obscene and entertaining to the men.

"Thanks," Joanna said. She was keenly aware of the fact that Roberto had not released her. There was no longer any danger, as Eduardo was flipping the bottle around, trying to slurp out beer.

"I am happy to," Roberto said. His voice was deep.

"Oh," Joanna said and smiled. She'd never heard Roberto speak English before. Suddenly, she was nervous. He wasn't just someone to stare at. He could also be someone to talk to.

He released her arm and stepped back, smiling down at her.

*Man, but he is sexy.* Joanna's heart pounded. His eyes were dark and intense, yet kind and warm. His shoulders were broad, thick, and powerful. He was, in a word, yummy. The term "lost in his eyes" sprang to mind, and Joanna had to physically look away and step back to refocus her brain.

*This was ridiculous*, she thought. *Was she so hard up that she would start throwing herself at a stranger? At an employee? At someone who might not even be a legal resident?*

"Ms. Lucas," Suzette called and Joanna turned. Suzette was sitting in her golf cart next to the patio. It was as far as her cart would go.

"Oh, hi," Joanna called back.

"I'm gonna need for some of your men to bring Eduardo home," Suzette said, eyeballing the men. Suddenly, everyone stopped laughing. "I didn't realize you were all over here having a party!"

"We're not." Joanna walked back to Suzette, tempering herself. "We're not having a party, Suzette. It's the end of the day, and everyone was relaxing until . . ." she pointed back toward Eduardo. "Until he began to get a little more demanding than usual about his beer."

"Oh, that!" Suzette waved a hand, looking dismissive.

"I gotta tell ya, Suzette. He's starting to get a little out of hand. I mean, isn't there a way to keep him locked up?" Joanna asked, and Suzette looked hurt.

"I didn't realize he was such a problem."

"It's just that . . ." Joanna said.

Since Franklin's death, Suzette had been delicate. Not a word anyone would have ever assigned to Suzette Lee, yet she was.

"Your bird is loco!" Manuel stepped forward, still a bit unsteady on his feet.

"He's just—" Suzette furrowed her brow and turned back toward Joanna. "I came over to get you and put up Eduardo for the evening."

"Get me?" Joanna's eyebrows rose.

"For tonight! You know, the community meeting." She made little circle motions with her hand, limp at the wrist. "You said you would take me."

It was not a request. It was a statement. An order. Joanna sighed internally. She had the neighbor from hell.

She'd been so patient. She'd been so tolerant. She had drunk emus accosting her and wild cats roaring in the night. She had random drop-ins from townsfolk who had no other purpose to stop by other than to gather information on an outsider. She had a freaking electrician stalker who, she was quite sure, was not playing with a full deck. And now, since Franklin's death, she was playing babysitter to the whims and needs of Ms. Suzette Lee.

"You did say you would take me," Suzette said, staring at Joanna.

"Yes," Joanna said and managed a weak smile. "I did." She had no recollection of doing any such thing.

# 12

Had I known what was to come that evening, I would have done things a little differently. In hindsight, I reckon I should have been more forthcoming with Joanna about what was going on in this town. Maybe I could have prepared her for the lengths that the business types would stoop to protect their precious profits.

But I had no idea. I had no idea what would happen to my animals. I would have never imagined that my own neighbors would have done what they did. All for the sake of money. Had I known what was to come, I don't believe I would have gone to that community meeting. I'd have stayed home, shotgun in hand, and blown out the brains of every spineless bastard who came onto my land. Instead, I'd been too interested in the high art of manipulation.

Joanna had never promised to take me anywhere. I'd clean forgotten about the community meeting. After my precious Franklin died, I'd forgotten about a lot of things. It'd been hard to focus; it was as if I'd been plugged into a wall socket and charged up with pure rage.

The first night I came home to an empty house, I wasn't sad. I can honestly say that I was not sad. I'd been sad for so long as I watched my dear, sweet Franklin wither away. When I sat night after night, talking to a man whose mind just wasn't the same, I'd been so miserable. When he died, it was as though he gave me permission to move to the next phase. I was a certified pissed-off woman. You know what they say. Hell hath no fury like a woman scorned. Well, that night, I'd been scorched, and for that, those responsible would pay dearly.

Some folks might wonder how I could say I loved the tiger that ate my leg. I'd always said he didn't mean to. I mean, he had his eye on me, but I don't for a minute believe it was something he plotted. The opportunity arose. My idiot brother, Simon, forgot to latch the gate, thereby allowing Tony the Tiger to get out and do what came naturally to him. He mauled me. But at no time had he pretended to like me before. He'd always been real clear on the fact that if he ever got out, he would maul me. And so he did.

In some strange way, you have to respect that.

But when we started our high-dollar horse business in Marcus, no one said a word to us about possible pollution or toxic poisoning. When the appraiser came out to see our champion, a mare named Catalina, no one mentioned that she might not be able to have babies again, let alone die.

Instead, they pretended to be our friends—to be excited about the opportunities we would bring to Marcus. And the city councilmen, school superintendents, and local business leaders were all so proud and pleased when we began to appear in equestrian and business magazines.

At that time, I could pick up the phone and call anyone I wanted. They were, at all times, at our disposal. When our septic tank overflowed, spilling sewage into the backfields, we had neighbors from all around gather up our animals to take care of them. During the droughts in the eighties, friend after friend helped locate and haul trailers of hay. But when the animals started to get sick, the help stopped, and phone calls were no longer returned.

When the animals began to die, people ignored us, turned away, and acted as though we were outsiders.

Then, when Franklin began to get sick, it all fell back on me. *Oh, there she goes*, they'd said, *weird ol', one-legged Suzette Lee*. And they turned on me for my ingratitude about my prosthetic leg. But I'd played nice. At least, reasonably so. I'd had to deal with these people and rely on their help to take care of and transport Franklin. Our doctor was a Marcus resident. Our pharmacist was a Marcus resident. As I saw it, the state of Franklin's health had rested on my holding my tongue. So I did.

But now, as I maneuvered through my home, I saw reminders of a better life with Franklin and my horses, and I was angered. Enraged. And I did something I hadn't done in years. I picked up the phone and called a few people. I called John Simmons, the former owner of FFI. I called Randy Cross and Tim Davis, city councilmen. And I called Mary Ryan. I'd tried to call Mayor Whitmeyer, but Mary was being a sticky beak, so I just let her have it instead.

I told them all the same thing. Franklin was dead, and I blamed them. I was going to find a lawyer, and I was going to sue the town of Marcus for gross negligence. I told them all that I had proof of their negligence.

I did my research and learned that the particulate matter that comes from the manufacturing of cement was so microscopic, something like 2.5 microns and smaller, humans are not able to expel it from their lungs. It's so miniscule that the EPA labeled this the most dangerous kind of particulate. EPA scientists told FFI management that there is no safe level of exposure to PM 2.5 and any amount of exposure was capable of producing adverse health effects in the people inhaling it. In other words, it would explain all the illnesses in town. Yet, despite all that the scientists knew, we were bound by the laws of Texas. Business first. Don't ask too many questions.

I could only do what I could do. I would make sure that every media outlet got a hold of this story.

Admittedly, this was not a great strategy of attack. But in my defense, I was not thinking clearly. I wanted to see people squirm. I wanted to see them race around and cover their tracks. I had envisioned mass panic and some pathetic attempt to grovel at my feet.

I had not yet understood who, or what, I was dealing with.

I had even gone so far as to tell them that I would be attending the community meeting with friends, and that I would fight FFI's new permit application to burn an annual six million tires on top of all the other trash and filth they were exposing us to.

I had unlocked the gate and allowed the beast to come out. And as I've said before, this beast was the worst kind. This beast pretended to care about friends and neighbors. This beast pretended to be concerned about the community and the environment. As Jeanie said, it was the gorilla hovering in the corner, pretending to be picking its own fleas. All the while, it was watching us.

The evening of the community meeting, which I'd clean forgot about, Mary Ryan called me to confirm that I would be there. She said that Mayor Whitmeyer wished to speak to me privately beforehand. I'd agreed and then panicked. While I drove a mean golf cart, I hadn't driven a car in years. It went back to the whole prosthetic leg thing, which I didn't like talking about. Ironically enough, I had always relied upon the kindness of my neighbors.

I thought of Joanna. She was the closest and most convenient person. But there were other good reasons. First, I wanted to get to know her a little more. She had gone to great lengths to conceal her own personal information. I know because I had Googled her. Since Franklin had become bedridden, I'd become very dependent upon, and pretty savvy with, the Internet. To my way of thinking, if I couldn't find you online, you were hiding something.

Before she married into the tampon business, no one had ever heard of her. I checked school alumni, school and community organizations, and even various newspaper clippings for school awards. Her wedding, the opening of her studio, and a few socialite events in the Hamptons were all I could dig up on her. To my way of thinking, a person with little to no past is a person to hold with some regard.

Simply put, she was up to something. She had something to hide.

The second thing was that it was possible she was a spy planted by the FFI. I know. I'm not much of a conspiracy theorist. Leastways, I didn't used to be. But the more people who talked about pollution, the more major polluters of the world were getting a might jumpy. If she wasn't one of the bad guys, she needed to become one of the good guys.

She came from a long line of snooty, highbrow business execs. So, who better to saunter into the chamber of commerce and talk business? It had occurred to me that if Joanna was to learn all about the pollution, she might get pissed off enough to join the fight.

But first, I would have to decide what side of the fence she was on.

Telling her that she'd promised an old, legless woman a ride into town was just part of the plan. Sure enough, she couldn't say no.

But then, there came something else to ponder.

I'd seen the way she and that Mexican fella looked at each other. I'd seen it clear as day. Long after Eduardo got his beer and forgot everyone else, those two just stood there, looking all moon-eyed at each other.

If Joanna was on the up-and-up, she would be perfect for the cause. From the moment she came to town, there was an excited buzz about her. The local men were drooling. Women saw her as stylish and confident. She would be a spokesperson people would listen to. What I didn't need, however, was for her to begin some torrid affair with a migrant worker.

Joanna had no clue about the social faux pas of dating anything other than what you were. Lions stayed with lions. Tigers stayed with tigers. It wasn't personal. It just was.

* * * *

"What's she doing with him?" Dixie asked as they pulled into the parking lot.

Everyone leaned forward to see Suzette sitting in her portable wheelchair and talking to Mayor Bryant Whitmeyer near the side of the community center. Some twenty feet away was Joanna's canary yellow Volkswagen with Joanna sitting inside. She was about as indiscreet as a seven-foot-tall transvestite.

Mayor Whitmeyer was talking, using his hands to make grand gestures. But they were lost on Suzette, who was looking down at the ground. Those who did not know her might believe she was being chastised, but the girls could see the set of Suzette's jaw even from where they sat.

Dixie parked the car.

"Ten cars," Jeanie said, counting on her fingers. "Wow, it's a huge turnout. Hope we can find a seat."

"More will come. We're early." Brianna tapped her watch.

For a moment, they all sat back and watched Suzette.

"I wish I had the distinction of saying I was bit by a rattlesnake," Jeanie said, breaking the silence, and Ruthie cracked up.

"What?" Brianna turned in her seat to face Jeanie. "What is wrong with you?"

"Where do you come up with these . . . these ideas?" Ruthie asked with a laugh.

"Wouldn't that be a great story to tell, though?"

"Where do you come up with these insane ideas?" Brianna shook her head in disbelief.

"*Man vs. Beast*. It's a show on cable," Jeanie said. "It's this guy, and he goes out into the wild—"

"Is this where you got your 'unconscious mountain girl' routine?" Dixie asked and Jeanie gasped.

There was instant and intense curiosity among the women because Jeanie never gasped. But clearly, she had gasped.

"Hey!" She jabbed a finger at Dixie.

"Mountain girl?" Brianna turned to Dixie, who was laughing.

"Oh, her and her honeypot do this routine where . . ." she said, starting to giggle. "She's unconscious and—"

"Hey, hey!" Jeanie waved a hand from the backseat.

"Brad is like a ranger or mountaineer, and he comes across her while—" More giggles.

"You know, that was told in confidence," Jeanie said in a warning tone, but she was smiling. She was embarrassed, and Ruthie, in particular, was intrigued.

"You and Brad role-play?" Her eyes were wide.

"Yes," Jeanie said, folding her arms over her chest.

"You do?" she asked and burst out laughing.

"An unconscious mountain girl?" Brianna considered this out loud. Her tone was serious, which reduced Dixie and Ruthie to more giggles. "It sounds so dirty."

"Aw, geez." Jeanie looked out the window.

"I mean, dirty like . . . why on a mountain?"

"It's not just a mountain girl." Jeanie felt the need to explain. "I mean, we do other things."

"I can't believe you and Brad. I just wouldn't have thought you guys . . ." Ruthie said, stifling more laughter behind a hand.

"What? Do you think we don't have sex or something?"

"Well, I mean, you're the one always talking about sex with, you know, like animals and women and stuff." Ruthie attempted a more serious tactic as Jeanie looks horrified.

"I'm just playing. It's pretend! What?"

"I just thought you were sexually repressed," Ruthie said.

"Me?" Jeanie threw an accusatory glare at Ruthie that could not be missed. Ruthie cocked her head as though understanding the underlying implication.

"I'm not sexually repressed," Ruthie said. "Let me tell you

something, sister. I've come to the realization that the ones who talk the most about sex are most often the ones getting the least."

"Ha!" Jeanie yelled. "And what? The ones who never talk about it at all are getting the most? That true, Brianna?"

As soon as she said it, she regretted it. In that context, the relationship between Terry and Brianna was off limits to the girls. Jeanie knew better and looked at Ruthie.

Ruthie recovered quickly.

"We should call that Joanna Lucas over. See what Suzette's up to."

"You gonna tell Joanna that you think she's *fetching* again? Talk about scaring off the new girl." Brianna said, putting the word fetching in air quotes. Jeanie rolled her eyes, falling back against her seat. She'd hurt Brianna's feelings and would pay for it.

"Yes, I'm hoping to get her in the backseat with me and have wild, mountain girl sex."

Dixie rolled down her window and waved to Joanna until she looked up. Mayor Whitmeyer had shifted his stance, putting his entire backside to the parking lot. While it was most likely an attempt at having a more private conversation with Suzette, it also allowed Joanna to leave her Volkswagen and creep along the parking lot undetected.

She dipped her head a little as she walked toward them. She slowed as another car entered the small gravel parking lot, and she waved to it uncertainly. The girls all looked. It was a navy-blue Dodge Ram. Frank Wolan. Someone in the backseat grumbled at the sight of him.

"Hi," Joanna said, searching the car and the faces inside. She looked as though she were trying to remember names.

"Hey, girl!" Dixie said in her usual down-home voice. She patted the outside of the car. "Climb on in the back. We're stalling a few more minutes before we go inside."

"Uh," Joanna said hesitantly.

"Oh, come on. There's room." In truth, there wasn't. But both

Jeanie and Ruthie scrambled to make some, and Ruthie patted the now empty seat beside her. Joanna gave a little nod, looked back once more to see where Suzette was, and climbed into the backseat.

The invite had been welcomed.

There was something about the girls that made Joanna happy. Amid the chaos and uncertainty, the rumors and the infuriating lack of information about the safety of her new home, Joanna couldn't help but like these women and felt a growing kinship.

Within a few minutes, Joanna had briefed the women on the little bit of information she had about Suzette's meeting with the mayor. She was a bit confused how she'd promised to bring Suzette when she hadn't seen her since Franklin's death, except to wave to her when she was putting Eduardo back in his cage. She said as much to the women.

"It was kind of weird. I brought her to the funeral home, but she told me that I didn't need to stick around, that she had something else she had to do after the service," Joanna said.

"What?" Dixie and Brianna asked in unison. No one in the car could recall anything unusual, but then, they had been the first group to leave.

"I don't know, but she had Marcos, one of the workers I have, go over to her house and feed the . . . feed her animals. She was gone for several days after Franklin died. Just very private, you know?"

"She probably went to see family," Ruthie said.

"She doesn't have any family. Why do you think she never left here? They didn't have any place to go. And I know that because she told me so," Dixie said.

"Well, maybe she just went away, you know, just away," Brianna said, using a hand to illustrate some kind of floating motion.

Another car pulled into the parking lot, and everyone looked at their watches: six forty-eight. In silence, they watched Tim Davis step out of his car.

"Tim Davis," Dixie said, peering at Joanna in the rearview mirror. "He's a city councilman."

"He's a weasel," Jeanie said, wrinkling her nose.

"And he's a weasel."

"Where do you suppose everyone is?" Brianna asked again, surveying the parking lot. "I mean . . . where is everyone? We need people. We need outrage. We need numbers."

"Honey, we could have a hundred people show, and you and I both know that it wouldn't change things," Dixie said.

"Then why bother?" Joanna's question was sincere, but everyone in the car grew very quiet, and Joanna regretted the question.

"No, I just mean, if—"

"Naw, that's a fair question," Dixie said thoughtfully. "And a good one. Why bother if no one else does." She looked to her sisters in the car. "I guess my answer to that is because we know the truth. Our neighbors and friends here . . . they're not bad people. They're not dumb or uncaring. They just don't understand what's at stake. It's like they don't get what's happening. So, we just keep thinking that either we'll be able to make the bad guys listen and do what's right, or we'll make the good guys listen."

"Either way, someone's gotta listen, right?" Ruthie tried a smile.

When Jack Frawley pulled into the parking lot with several other employees from the city, Dixie let out a big sigh.

"Okay, well, I guess it's showtime. Everyone know what they're going to say?"

# 13

"Fire."

Suzette didn't scream the word. It came to Joanna's ears as a strangled whisper.

"Fire."

It was almost as though she'd half expected it. Suzette pressed her hand to her mouth. Joanna blinked. Suzette's entire barn, house, and back pasture were on fire.

The women had expected the meeting with the TCEQ and EPA would be pointless. They knew the deck was stacked. But they could not have anticipated disaster.

After the meeting, Suzette seemed more resigned than surprised, more defeated than horrified. "Oh, my God!" Joanna screamed as they reached the driveway. "No!" She shouted as she realized all the animal pens were on fire. "No! No!" She accelerated. She roared down the gravel driveway, spewing rocks and debris everywhere. But Suzette sat motionless. Frozen.

* * * *

They had been silent the entire drive home. Joanna had known from her conversation with the women in the car that they had not expected much. There were no great expectations for a high turnout. But they had been blindsided by what had taken place inside.

She thought it was like something out of a movie.

As soon as the six of them walked in, the entire room had gone silent. Joanna had recognized a few people: Mayor Whitmeyer; city council members, Tim Davis and Randy Cross; Eva Tobey and her daughter, Tiffany; the man from Eva's office, John Simmons; Jack Frawley and several men she didn't know. The men with Jack, she had later learned, were all city employees who held various positions with sewage, parks and recreation, and zoning. She'd also met two men from the FFI plant—Paul Cowell and Frank Wolan.

The Dallas EPA office had sent two representatives, Tom Bishop and Carl Fredricks, who, as far as anyone could tell, had nothing to say. Only the TCEQ representative, Angela Hunt, spoke.

In addition, there was Ian Jackson, a corporate lawyer representing the cement industry and at least seven or eight staff minions. It was dizzying, to say the least. There were so many new names and faces. Joanna had noted that everyone inside appeared to be familiar with the group of women she was with. While Joanna's face might be new to some, everyone knew "the girls." They had been quite vocal about their opinions of the cement plants and local pollution for years.

What was most interesting to Joanna was the reaction of the women. They'd looked surprised by the number of new faces at the meeting.

"Holy crap," Jeanie had muttered under her breath. "This is the Alamo. And I don't know about you, Jim Bowie, but I'm feeling a little outnumbered."

Dixie scanned the expensive legal team. They had notepads, recorders, and bound copies of various studies and research items.

"And outgunned," Dixie had whispered back.

Whatever it was they'd had to say about the pollution, about the rise in asthma among the young and very old, about the increase in birth defects—whatever issue they'd raised—the legal team of Ian Jackson had some study to support how the numbers in Marcus were no different than in other areas of the United States.

The deaths of Franklin Lee and other Marcus residents were all dismissed with the same patronizing dialogue: "While unfortunate, these deaths were no different from other deaths around the nation." And throughout it all, the EPA officials had sat silently while the TCEQ official made it clear that they were all complicit with FFI. It was stunning.

"Is it not true," Ian Jackson asked Suzette, his voice pumped too loudly for so small a group, "you're accustomed to being, shall we say, in the spotlight?"

Everyone looked at Suzette. It was true. She always seemed to be in the spotlight in one fashion or another. Ian Jackson strolled over to a table and took a notepad from one of his aides. He thumbed through it for dramatic effect.

"You had your leg chewed off by a tiger? How awful!"

No one spoke. They all let him take the floor, offering no new information but a new spin on old facts.

"Your town came together, held a huge fundraiser to buy you a new leg, which you"—Suzette squirmed in her seat, and both Dixie and Brianna shook their heads—"threw out into traffic, hitting the sheriff's cruiser and . . . I see here, you caused quite an accident with that leg."

Not one person raised a word in defense of Suzette.

"You're used to causing a commotion. Would that be fair to say?" the lawyer asked.

"Is this some kind of court case?" Suzette yelled back. "I thought this was a hearing about the tires." She had almost risen up from her chair, looking at Angela Hunt, who was supposed to be an impartial mediator. Instead, the woman watched the lawyer grill Suzette, looking a little amused.

Joanna took an instant dislike to Ms. Hunt. She was gaunt,

fortyish, and condescending. She was, to her credit, stylish. Everything about her screamed city girl. Her haircut, shoes, jewelry were all of the quality Joanna had come to know quite intimately, and instinctively, she felt as if she knew Angela Hunt. She'd met her fifty times over, and she never liked the type. Ms. Hunt believed she was dealing with a bunch of hicks who weren't worth her time or effort. She was annoyed that she'd had to leave the comforts of her city office to deal with some ridiculous tire-burning issue.

"I assure you," she'd said, smirking at Suzette, "that is why we are here." She turned to Ian Jackson. "Perhaps it would be best if we stick to the agenda."

He nodded but offered his own protest. "We're just trying to establish that—"

"I understand. But we need to stick to the agenda," she said, but there was no missing her expression.

When representatives from FFI stood to give their presentation about how burning tires was a cost-effective plan that would help reduce carbon dioxide in the atmosphere, the women became restless. But they'd been respectful. They waited out the entire nonsense to speak their piece.

When a slideshow presentation demonstrated how a large slingshot-type mechanism would catapult the tires into the cement kiln's furnace, no one laughed out loud.

"What a load of crap," Jeanie said, coughing into her hand.

It was FFI's position that by burning the tires, they would not have to burn so much coal, thereby reducing carbon monoxide emissions. But when Suzette cited research from other plants that burned tires, it was Ms. Hunt, not Ian Jackson, who cut her off. Because the TCEQ had not been notified of Suzette Lee's participation, she was not part of the agenda and, therefore, could not officially be recognized to speak.

For the next hour, FFI officials and Ian Jackson were given great discretion to offer reports that favored their position. Suzette was shut down. They had all been shut down.

Joanna had not been in Marcus long, but she knew that those women were firecrackers. They were outspoken and opinionated. But they'd been positively dismissed.

At one point, both Jeanie and Dixie began to shout in frustration. They threatened lawsuits, class action suits, gross negligence, and some other things that were almost incoherent. But the TCEQ representative, or as Dixie had later called her, the FFI whore, pointed out that they could only claim compensation status if they lived within two miles of the FFI plant.

"You're telling me that I have to live within two miles to claim it's affecting my lungs?" Dixie laughed.

"Please explain to me then," Suzette said, looking at Ian Jackson, "how it is that twenty years ago when you were burning far less toxic stuff, but no one knew anything about hazardous waste, you had to live within twenty miles of the plant; but now, all of a sudden, it's been dwindled down to two, and you're burning seven times the amount you once did? How is that? How does that work? And more importantly, Mr. Jackson, how do you sleep at night knowing how you're screwing with people's lives by screwing with the law? How does that—"

Once again, Suzette was not so politely told to shut up. She wasn't on the agenda, so she couldn't talk about anything.

"Is that true?" Joanna turned to Dixie, suddenly very interested. It didn't seem possible that any judge or politician would allow that to happen. If the cement plant was burning far more chemicals with far more damaging long-term effects to residents, and the emissions were traveling farther and farther into the atmosphere, which the EPA itself had concluded to be so, how could anyone reduce the area of affected citizens?

It was like a scene out of the Erin Brokovich movie, only this wasn't just about the water. It was also about the air. The air she was breathing at that very moment.

"Is that true?" Joanna realized she was standing. She was standing and asking that question out loud. Before she could stop herself, her hand was up and she stared at the TCEQ whore.

"How can that be right?" Joanna needed to know.

"I'm sorry. Who are you?"

There was a surreal silence with everyone staring at her, mouths gaping. For Joanna, it was an unhappy flashback to the church, to the tampon, and to Clayton.

"You must identify yourself," Angela Hunt said. But Joanna shook her head angrily.

"Why?" she asked. Why did anyone need to know that? As an American citizen, she should have been able to ask that question.

"That's Joanna Lucas," said Jack Frawley. "She's new to town. She's Suzette's neighbor, lives in the old Redmond house."

Jack Frawley folded his arms across his chest. He was leaning back in his chair, looking defiantly at the women. As he did, Ms. Hunt scribbled down Joanna's name. Joanna noticed that each member of the Ian Jackson's legal team did the same. It was an odd feeling.

"She's from the Lucas tampon empire," Jeanie shouted. "She's got serious connections, serious bucks. So the crap you've been giving us all these years ain't gonna fly anymore, boys!"
Joanna had been stunned into paralysis. She'd fallen back into her seat, unable to speak another word. But the girls had said enough for a lifetime. They'd argued every point of health, children, suspicious deaths, rare diseases, and quality of life. Their points had been loud, broad, and unheard. One by one, each woman had been dismissed for living too far away from the FFI plant. It was unbelievable and until they'd turned down Highway 875, Joanna would not have thought anything else could have been so disturbing.

* * * *

Joanna was out of the car in a flash. She did not stop to help

Suzette but ran to the lion's pen.

"No, please, no," she cried. Her vision blurred instantly because she already knew what she would find. "Please . . ."

She slid across the rocks as she skidded to a stop.

Joanna covered her eyes and cried out. Her scream was long and anguished.

Still ablaze within the pen, she could see the corpse of a lion. The figure of the cat looked more like a piece of art, a metal sculpture of a lion. It couldn't be real. But it was.

Joanna stepped back when she heard Suzette's voice call out behind her.

"Call 911!" Joanna yelled.

The heat was intense. As the wind shifted, Joanna was driven back, shielding her face against the sudden wave of heat. "Call 911!" she screamed and looked around. To her left, flames raged outside the windows of Suzette's home. To her right, the barn was also engulfed in flames. She made a desperate, frantic, worthless circle, searching for something constructive or helpful to do. There was nothing.

She turned back to the animal cages. Her shoulders slumped. All she could do was count the bodies. Suzette had four wild cats: Two lions, a snow leopard, and her personal favorite, Ms. Tilly, the tiger. Martha, the llama, and Eduardo were inside the barn. She stopped.

*Eduardo.*

Oh, God. She'd helped put Eduardo in the barn that evening.

He couldn't possibly have survived the fire in the barn. It was ablaze. There was no way in or out.

"Eduardo," she said out loud then gasped as one entire side of the lion's pen collapsed and fell forward.

She inched backwards. Already, her clothing, hair, and face were soaked with sweat. The stench of wood, metal, and other things Joanna didn't want to think about burning was in her nostrils.

"I can't believe this. I can't believe this," she said over and over. She could feel a frightening hysteria well up inside of her. When they'd left the community center, Suzette could not speak. Dixie, Brianna, Jeanie, and Ruthie had muttered something about calling Suzette later, but that was it. They were all deflated. All of them.

But now Suzette's animals were all dead.

It was the only thought drumming through her brain. Suzette's animals were dead. She didn't know how she would tell Suzette, and dread filled her heart.

"Are they?"

Joanna looked up as she dragged her feet to trudge toward the car.

Light from the house and barn shone over Suzette and the Volkswagen. The lines in Suzette's face hardened as she braced herself.

"Did you call 911?" Joanna asked rather than answer the question.

"Yeah . . . are they . . . did you check?" Suzette asked again.

"They're gone, Suzette." Joanna paused. "I mean, they didn't survive."

# 14

They were helpless. They could do nothing but watch as the fire slowed from a roar to glowing embers. With the new day came a light that showed the Lee property as it truly was. The house was but a partial structure, burned and gutted. It was gone. Everything was gone. Her animals, her furniture, her pictures, her home, her life. It was all gone.

The Lee home was just under five miles from the Marcus Fire Department, yet it took over twenty minutes for the fire truck to arrive after the first call to 911. With no fire hydrants anywhere in the vicinity, another fifteen minutes passed as the firefighters determined how they would pump water from Redmond Lake to the fire. In that time, the Lee homestead burned to the ground.

Joanna had not spoken for what seemed like hours. She just didn't know what to say. She'd said how sorry she was, berated the fire department, cursed the horridness of the fire, and bowed her head when Suzette prayed for the animals. There was nothing else to be said.

Only when she saw Manuel pull the truck into her driveway

did Joanna realize it was morning. She murmured to Suzette about talking to the men and ducked across the fence toward the back of her house. She was exhausted, filthy, and deeply saddened about the animals. And for reasons she did not understand, she burst into tears as soon as she saw Manuel coming toward her.

"Jo-anna," he said. He had a way in which he drawled her name. It was paternal and endearing. "What happened?" Without hesitation, he wrapped an arm around her.

"Suzette's house, barn . . ." She waved her hand across the horizon. "Burned down. It's all gone. The animals are dead. Eduardo . . ."

He nodded as he surveyed the damage. "But . . . how?"

Before Joanna could even shake her head, Manuel barked out orders in rapid Spanish. He waved Marcos and Gerardo over the fence. The men catapulted forward and within minutes brought Suzette back from the ruins of her home to the refuge of Joanna's property. Amid the devastation, Joanna smiled as she watched all one hundred twenty pounds of Marcos push and strain against Suzette's wheelchair. The golf cart was gone, burned in the fire. Suzette was stuck in the portable chair she'd used to attend the community meeting. But the combination of her weight, soft soil, and gravel made for a long trip back to Joanna's.

Marcos's expressions were priceless. For Suzette's benefit, he tried to be polite but behind her, he made faces at Gerardo. He tried not to giggle or grunt. Gerardo bent over, pulling up the front wheels of the chair, thus tipping Suzette back. And not very gracefully.

"I swear, if I fall out of this . . . leg or no leg, I'll beat you down like a dog," Suzette said. Both Marcos and Gerardo nodded, not understanding a word.

Again, Manuel fired off instructions to the men.

Joanna felt a gentle bump against her arm and looked back. Roberto had come up behind her, standing uncomfortably, marvelously close and for a moment, it was a wonderful distraction.

*He was so—*

A horn blared, and everyone looked toward the highway. For most of the morning, residents of Marcus had cruised up and down the road, peering at the smoldering mess. No one had entered the driveway except Manuel and his men.

Now Eva's car, followed by Dixie's Suburban, barreled down the driveway as though the house were still on fire. Both vehicles screeched to a halt, rocks flying.

"Oh my stars!" Brianna was the first to leap from the Suburban. "Oh my stars!" She clasped the sides of her face with her hands. She was horrified. "Oh my stars." It was all she could say.

All the women hurried from Joanna's driveway to the side of the house. Each woman turned, standing side by side, to stare at what had once been Suzette's home. There had been plenty of tongue clicking and declarations to God Almighty while Marcos and Gerardo struggled with Suzette.

Suzette watched as Gerardo kicked down the planks to the wooden fence, creating a space the width of her wheelchair. She'd become more agitated with every passing minute.

Marcos heaved the chair through the opening in the fence.

"Oh, Suzette—" Ruthie said, but Suzette didn't hear her.

"Don't you tell me you didn't know anything about this!" Suzette yelled at Eva.

"What?" Eva looked stunned.

"You knew about this." Suzette was insistent. She appeared hysterical—enraged beyond reason. "You knew I would be gone from the house. You knew when I was going to be home and when I wasn't!"

"What are you talking about?"

"You were sitting there with John Simmons! I saw you!"

"Suzette! Please. You're not making any sense," Eva said.

"Oh, I know exactly what I'm sayin', Eva Tobey. You're a

land whore!"

"A land . . ." Eva's face reddened as Jeanie snorted.

"Y'all think you can run me out. Well, you can't. I'm not goin' anywhere!"

Eva drew in a long, deep breath. The silence was deafening. It was as though no one was breathing. Not even Marcos. He'd stood completely still since the yelling began. Eva managed a cold dignified laugh.

"I don't need to take this," she said, turning on her heel. "I came as a neighbor, as a friend. But clearly, you're hysterical." As she turned, Dixie put out a hand, but Eva brushed it away and walked back to her car.

Dixie scowled at Suzette. "You know good and well she didn't have anything to do with this! You need to tell her you're sorry."

"I won't do any such thing." Suzette looked away, already pouting.

Everyone stared, unable to speak until Manuel's voice broke the silence. His instruction was to Marcos, and with a reluctant nod, Marcos was back to pushing the chair again.

Manuel looked at Joanna. "We should get her onto the back patio," he said. "The sun is really . . ." Manuel looked up. The combination of the rising sun and the smoldering fire promised an uncomfortable day.

The women parted, allowing Marcos and Suzette to pass first. Had it all not been so tragic, had it all not been so heartbreaking, the sight of skinny little Marcos pushing Suzette in her chair would have been funny. But when they arrived at the smooth surface of the patio floor and Marcos fell heavily against the stone wall, mopping his face and moaning, everyone smiled. Even Suzette had a flicker of a grin before she yelled at him.

"Oh, for shit's sake! It's not like you were pulling a freight train."

He didn't understand her words but knew enough to wave his hands, giving the international sign for "No, no. It's not you, it's me."

"Honey." Dixie's solemn voice interrupted them. "I'm so sorry about your animals."

"Oh, oh," Brianna murmured as though she'd just realized.

"I'm so sorry," Dixie said again.

Suzette seemed unable to speak, so she nodded.

"Well, you never needed all those animals anyway," Jeanie said. Everyone gasped. "What? I'm not being hateful. She didn't."

"Oh, Jeanie, shut up." Dixie hit Jeanie's arm hard and took a seat in one of the recliners Joanna had recently purchased.

Not that she would have ever imagined her first gathering of guests here for such horrific reasons, but this had been exactly how Joanna had envisioned her perfect patio. Dixie and Ruthie were both sitting in the recliners. Brianna was perched on one barstool, and Manuel was on another. Jeanie, Joanna, and Marcos sat on the wall. All that was missing was food and drink and an occasion far better than this one.

Manuel stood, situating the huge umbrella over Suzette.

"You can rebuild," Ruthie said, trying to be helpful.

"No, I can't. It'll never be the same," Suzette said unhappily.

"Sure you can," Ruthie said. "You can make it even better than before."

"I can't."

"You've always dreamed of having a better facility for the animals. You could build something even bigger." Brianna clapped her hands, showing both support and excitement for the future, but Suzette was unmoved.

Suzette had always abhorred the idea of wild animals in captivity. But she knew the reality was some jackass somewhere would always get one, abuse it, and then abandon it. For that reason, Suzette had believed her calling was to have some kind of sanctuary for big cats.

She'd never asked for the cats. In fact, when it was clear that toxic emissions from the cement plant had been harming the living community, Suzette had decided it was time to get out of the exotic animal rescue business. When she said as much to an animal control officer, he had shrugged his shoulders. "I guess that's it then. We'll have to euthanize 'em."

She remembered the most recent phone call. A man in Paris, Texas had owned a tiger for almost three years. The cat had been hand fed and brushed but then turned on the man's niece and bit her arm off. Who else but Suzette Lee of Marcus, Texas would take a tiger like that?

"I . . . can't," Suzette said and looked away, staring at Redmond Lake.

"Sure you can, honey," Dixie said. "Why, I bet if we all—"

"I won't do it!" Suzette yelled without warning.

"Oh, for hell's sake." Jeanie stood and faced Suzette. Her voice echoed against the walls. "Where else you gonna go, Suzette?"

Suzette's mouth fell open but almost immediately snapped shut again. Her face wrinkled for a moment, as though she were going to cry. Then she slammed her palms against the wheels of her chair, and she began jerking violently on them, trying to turn herself around. Marcos jumped up, looking first to Manuel. But Dixie was fast on her feet, shaking her head at the young man.

Manuel gestured at Marcos, poking his chin toward the kitchen door, and the two men slipped away as Dixie laid her hands on the wheelchair.

"Get your hands off my chair," Suzette said, slapping at her hands.

"No, I won't!" Dixie began to wrestle with Suzette. "Now you listen to me—"

The sudden emergence of Roberto rendered the other women speechless while Suzette crossed her arms and pouted.

Roberto came from the opposite end of the house, where the lumber had been stacked. He wore jeans, work boots, and a thin, worn T-shirt that stuck to his body in the intense humidity.

He had three boards balanced on his shoulder, and he appeared to be humming to himself. He slowed as he approached the group, preparing to swing wide for the narrow door and steps.

"Oh, my!" Dixie said, sounding more like a songbird.

Roberto smiled, nodded, but never lost stride. He managed to maneuver around Suzette and her chair.

"My, my, my, my, my." Dixie raised her eyebrows and turned toward Joanna.

"Oh." Suzette grunted, pulling on her wheels, but Dixie's grip was firm despite her momentary distraction.

"You know," Jeanie said and leaned in, eyeing Suzette. There was an undeniable smirk on her face. "You'd move a lot better if you had that leg of yours—"

"Oh, shut up, Jeanie!" Both Dixie and Suzette snapped at her in unison.

"Why did you throw your leg into traffic," Joanna asked, eager to distract Dixie from Roberto.

Suzette swung her head around to Joanna and glowered.

"Why did you move out here, all alone, with no family or friends?"

All eyes swung back to Joanna.

The queen of tampons was far more interesting than tiger-mauled, legless Suzette and Joanna was about to offer an answer just as a small man rounded the corner of the house. He was in his fifties with snow white hair. He was in excellent shape—neat and professional.

"Whatcha say, Bobby," Jeanie said.

"Fire Chief Slader," Dixie leaned over and whispered to Joanna.

"Jeanie." Bobby Slader gave her a nod. "Ladies."

Within the house, the men stopped working. Manuel had stopped first, looking toward the window and cocking his head. It was too quiet outside, and he was curious. He had been standing at the base of the staircase next to Andres and handing up tiles to

Carlos and Marcos. It was tedious work, but they wanted to be sure not one tile was dropped or chipped.

Carlos and Marcos were two and four steps up the staircase, passing tile up to Fernando, who was working his magic. He was laying the tile in beautiful, intricate patterns along the wall of the staircase. The pattern was his design, his idea, his masterpiece, and Joanna had given her full blessing. No questions asked.

It had all happened one day when Fernando had gone to Joanna's studio with a question about the staircase. Initially, the men were supposed to rebuild the existing staircase, but as they'd begun to work, they discovered just how rotted the wood was. So, Fernando had set out to find Joanna and bring her back to show her the problem.

Because they would have had to tear out the staircase and start from scratch, Fernando had proposed they split the staircase. Because of the enormous size of the house, it would only add to its grandeur to have a split staircase with one base nearest the front door and the other near the kitchen.

But when he'd walked into Joanna's studio, Fernando had been dumbstruck. Without one word of English, he'd told her everything she wanted to hear. He loved her work. She had been toiling with a piece, reworking it again and again, until he entered. His smile, the way he'd run his hands along the piece, nodded, and forced her to step back. Yes, it was good. And she'd laughed.

She had needed someone to walk in and do just that.

Then he had gestured to himself, patting his chest and speaking rapidly to her. She'd had no idea what he was saying. And she'd shaken her head at him. "You . . . like it? You . . . you want it?"

He'd picked up some of the clay and worked it with his hands.

"Oh! You're an artist, too," she'd said. It was a happy discovery.

She had floated back to the house, so flattered and relieved by his appraisal. In return, when Manuel explained the problem, she'd said, "It's up to Fernando." No interpretation was needed.

Fernando beamed.

Now Manuel raised his hand, and all conversation and work among the men stopped. One by one, they all turned toward the kitchen, listening to what was happening outside. And one by one, they all crept toward the back door.

"Lightning? Lightning?" They could hear Suzette's incredulous voice. "Lightning hit my house? That's funny, Bobby. I don't recall any kind of a storm last night."

Speaking in a whisper, Manuel translated to the men huddled in the kitchen.

The fire chief looked remorseful, his hat in hand. "That's the preliminary report, Ms. Lee. That's all I can tell you right now."

"Well, you can file this report, Bobby. Bullshit! I'm callin' it bullshit!"

"Aw, c'mon, Ms. Lee." Bobby shifted his feet.

"Don't 'aw, c'mon' me! You're tryin' to run me out!" Suzette was riled again.

"Now don't start with your conspiracy theories *again*, Ms. Lee. This—" Bobby said, but Suzette's fury was so great she started to rise from her chair, startling everyone.

"You know it's crap! You purposefully let that fire destroy my house!" she shrieked.

Bobby jerked his head up. "Now, hold on! You know good an' well that we didn't have the water capacity to put that thing out. It was an inferno. All we coulda done to put any kind of dent in that was to use the water pump on the lake. But it was just too much. It was too much. And it was too late. The house was fully engulfed."

"So you just stood there and let everything burn to the ground! My whole life, burned to the ground."

"We stood by to be sure it didn't turn into anything more. We just . . . I'm sorry to say it, Ms. Lee, but we just had to let it burn itself out. By the time we got there it was—"

"By the time you got there! Just why did it take you over twenty minutes to come four miles, Bobby?"

"It didn't take twenty minutes." He scowled at her.

"My arse! It took over twenty minutes, and we can consult the 911 call if you'd like. I'll take it to court. I'll take it to the US Supreme Court! It took you over—"

"Ms. Lee," he said and motioned his hands as though he were pressing all the tension down to the ground. "We were in the process of working on the trucks when your call came in. We were doing an annual—"

"I'm callin' another bullshit on that, too!"

"Ms. Lee, I promise you. We were working on the trucks when your call came in. Considering what we were doing, we got here real fast. And I don't think it was over twenty minutes."

"Bullshit!" Her voice was a roar. "You can't run me out!"

Bobby sighed and looked around the patio. "You can't stay on the property. Not right now." Although he addressed Suzette, he spoke to the group, looking at each of them.

"I'm not leaving!"

"Well," he said with a sigh. "You just can't stay there."

"You can't stop me." Suzette poked out her chin, not thinking anything through.

"Actually, I can." He lowered his gaze at her. His expression was kind but stern. There was no way he was going to let Suzette live in squalor on her property. It was a hazard and a violation of the health department.

"Fine. Then I'll stay here." Then, she looked at Joanna. "If you'll have me."

"Uhh," Joanna stammered.

"Ho, boy," both Dixie and Ruthie said at the same time.

"Ho, boy," Jeanie said, sitting back down on the wall.

Inside the house, Manuel ran his fingers through his hair and looked at his men.

"Ho, boy," he said.

# 15

It was just a feeling. Something was off.

They sat motionless for some time before anyone made a move. When they did, they moved in continued silence.

Everything was the same: the landscape, the territory, the darkness, and their route. Yet, it felt very different.

Newly-purchased night goggles allowed them to move forward without flashlights or any kind of light that would draw attention to their location. They moved swiftly, maneuvering around cacti and mesquite bushes.

Although the investment had been justified as a way to move undetected, it was a huge relief to know that they could now also spot snakes. There had been too many occasions when the initial snag, tug, and bite of a mesquite thorn was briefly and horrifyingly believed to be that of a snake. The dreaded cottonmouth was plentiful in the Marcus region and, in particular, on FFI land. And the irony had escaped none of them that the most vicious elements of life dwelled under the FFI umbrella.

But now they could watch for the snakes. Now they could use hand signals to communicate with each other. No more whispering or shoulder tapping. They could come and go with nary a word spoken.

"Shit!"

The others jumped.

"Where is it?"

The canister was gone.

They scattered, moving in small circles. This was the right place. This was where they'd left the canister just days before.

"Shit."

A foot kicked the stakes they had driven into the ground themselves.

"Someone got it. This is where it was . . ." The voice lingered in the air, almost floating while the others digested its full meaning. Then, a clank sounded.

Through the goggles, the image was vague.

"What the hell is this?" A strained whisper caused all to look. Each took a turn, peering closely at the object.

"It's a trap—an animal trap." The whisper was horrified.

"They know we're here," said another.

Not another word was spoken. They all moved at once with new worries, new panic. If there was one trap, would there be more? Who would set out animal traps for humans?

*Shit, shit, shit! They know we're here.*

* * * *

The curtains were drawn. Although it was well after hours, they did not wish to be seen.

"This is a private meeting," Mayor Whitmeyer said, scowling as John Simmons entered the office.

"That was my idea," said Frank Wolan, carrying an oversized bag, which he laid across the mayor's desk. It was a large burlap bag that clunked when he set it down, and he gave no indication of explaining its contents.

"Mayor," John said with a nod. "Hope you don't mind, but when Frank here called me and told me about this meeting, I thought I could help."

Mayor Whitmeyer said nothing. Ian Jackson, Randy Cross, and Tim Davis were already seated. Pleasantries were exchanged, though somberly.

"You said this was about the future of Marcus," the mayor said to Frank, eyeing John.

"Is this it? This all of us?" Frank looked around the room and then nodded. "All right then."

He stepped back toward the desk and unzipped the bag. All eyes were on Frank as he pulled out a metallic canister, looked around the room, and then set it upright.

"What is it?" the mayor asked.

"A pollution monitor." John stepped forward, his voice booming. Mayor Whitmeyer glowered. It was no coincidence that John had seated himself front and center at this meeting. Although he'd not yet officially entered his name in the US congressional representative's race, John Simmons was campaigning in the mayor's own office.

"A what?" Tim leaned forward, squinting at the canister.

John moved closer to the canister and tapped its side. "Basically, it traps or collects air samples. We've moved far beyond people complaining about smells or seeing smoke." He sighed, looking down at the canister. "They were able to sneak this onto private property."

"Who?" Tim's eyes shot up.

"Who? Who do you think," Frank retorted. "Those bitches."

"Wait. Exactly what does this thing do?" Randy asked. Like Tim, he slid forward in his chair, getting as close as possible to the canister without leaving his seat.

"It's a portable monitor that can collect air samples. Then it gets sent off to be analyzed for all kinds of toxic compounds," John said.

It was too perfect, too rehearsed for the mayor's liking.

"They measure different kinds of hazardous waste and how much of it there is in the air," Frank said, his face tight.

"Who? Who does that?" Tim asked.

"I'm tellin' ya, man, it's those bitches. Who do you think's always complaining about the self-regulations?" Frank's voice rose, but Tim shook his head.

"No, I get that. I mean . . . who does this . . . the analyzing?"

"Good question." Ian looked up from his notes. "The TCEQ does. The cost is about five hundred dollars per can to analyze." Everyone considered this for a moment.

"So, it's not a problem then." Randy tried his best to sound relieved. "We contact the TCEQ—"

Ian shook his head. "Not quite that easy. For one thing, if I was a gambling man, I would bet these people, whoever they are, have found a private company—probably out of state—to analyze the canisters. Anyone who has gone to this much trouble isn't going to trust a Texas governing body. Not now. "

"So, what?" The mayor wanted to cut to the chase. "What are we saying here?"

"This is a huge problem," Frank said.

"I don't think so," Ian said calmly. "We can change the data, incorporate more zip codes into the area to measure and report air quality." To date, Marcus and FFI had been allowed to self-regulate. It was a Texas loophole that entrusted cement plants and other big business to do the right thing and self-report what they burned. Sort of like asking professional athletes to self-report steroid use, Ian had mused to himself. "But what we need to know is who's behind this," Ian said.

"What we need," Mayor Whitmeyer said, pounding his fist against the tabletop, "is to do some aggressive public relations. We need to remind the people of this town how good FFI has been to us, how much we need it, and the last thing we need is for some bored housewives to dredge up negative information about Marcus!"

"Yeah," Frank said. "You work on that, Mayor. I'm gonna prove who's responsible for this."

* * * *

"What am I doing?" Joanna paced back and forth, cradling the phone between her ear and shoulder. "I mean, I need to get out of this place. I'm telling you, Marcus, everyone here is a little crazy. It's like . . . it's like there's something in the water and everyone's going batty."

As she spoke, she scrubbed off the clay on her hands.

She nodded as Marcus spoke. "Yes! She's here right now . . . in my house."

Marcus began to speak, but his words were garbled.

"Wait, you're breaking up." She moved toward the entrance of the studio, leaning on the door. "There. Say that again.

"I've been doing some research. It's not good. I wished we'd checked this out more before you left." His voice was deep, serious.

"What?" Her shoulders slumped. She was deflated.

"Well, it's messed up. Officially, of course, there's nothing concrete . . . No pun intended."

"Whatever."

"But . . . seriously, there's nothing official. The state of Texas has glossed over it so that it all looks good on paper and everything's fine, but then I searched online and found stories written by former residents of Marcus." There was another pause. "Joanna, it's not good."

"Like what?"

"A couple moved to Marcus and the wife got cancer, and then eight months later the husband got a different kind of cancer. There are numerous stories about different types of cancer popping up in one household. And there's a letter written by a schoolteacher. I guess a few years ago, FFI got busted for putting out too much toxic waste and that same year, there were a several cases of Down syndromebabies being born. I'm looking at stories from school nurses who say the number of children diagnosed with asthma has tripled, and the schools are on some kind of watchdog list because the buildings might be contaminated with high levels of toxic waste. Like I said, it's not good."

* * * *

He'd been watching her for some time. She'd been pacing back and forth, so he could only catch glimpses of her while she moved. But now she stood in the giant doorway of the old barn with the light illuminating her figure. She was gorgeous. He was transfixed.

There was something very raw about her. She had an edge that he couldn't quite articulate, but he knew one thing. She'd be a wild ride. She was edgy, angry, lonely, and desperate.

He'd imagined many times how she would fight him. But he'd felt the chemistry between them. He'd sensed it in how often they locked eyes. He'd felt the tension and her sexuality.

A woman like that doesn't want to be alone, he'd told himself.

He'd heard her voice when she was on the phone. She seemed agitated by something or someone. He watched her pace, and then when she settled herself down against the side of the barn, he tipped back his beer and watched some more.

She tilted her head back and stared at the stars. Then, moments after she flipped her phone closed, she disappeared into the barn and turned off the lights. He held his breath. If he didn't move, if he stayed right where he was, she would walk right by him to get to the house. All he would have to do is reach out and take her.

He imagined that for a moment.

She reappeared, her shadowy figure moving across the barn, closing the heavy doors. The moon shone brightly enough to see her, and he imagined that her eyes were only just adjusting to the darkness.

He smiled as she drew nearer.

She was talking to herself. Muttering.

She was wild. Strong.

She stopped. She stared at the ground for a moment, made a

funny noise, and leapt to the side. Something small and reptilian scampered away, sending Joanna in a different direction. She squealed and ran to the patio where she made a sound of relief and fell back into a chair.

He moved soundlessly up the path behind her as she dragged another chair closer and plopped her feet on to it. She showed no interest in moving indoors, enjoying instead the nice breeze that was a rarity, to be sure.

He drained the rest of his bottle as he reached the patio and stepped forward. He was so close to her, he could touch her, touch her hair. There was a scraping of gravel, a noise from his boot, and she turned around in her chair. There had been a smile on her face as though she were expecting a certain someone. She furrowed her brow when she saw him, and she jumped.

He moved, not wanting her to scream or alarm Suzette inside the house. He wasn't sure what happened. Did he pull her up or had she stood? Whatever happened, she was standing up against him, just a few inches shorter. Only her eyes showed as his hand covered her mouth, but they were expressive and beautiful.

"Hi," he said.

She panicked, thrashing and pushing wildly away from him. In the process, she head-butted his nose.

The bitch!

Blood gushed, and he grabbed his nose with one hand. But as she tried to move away, he grabbed her arm and jerked her violently toward the chair.

If it had been his intention to place her, however roughly, in the chair, he missed. He'd had one too many and that, combined with the throbbing pain and still-bleeding nose, made him unsteady on his feet. She crashed against the back of one chair, falling hard to the ground and whacking her head against the second chair. He towered above her, ranting and bleeding.

"Damn it!" He wiped his nose on his sleeve and then dove on

top of her.

* * * *

It was Doug Mitchell.

Joanna couldn't believe it!

He reeked of beer. He moved slowly and his speech was thick. He was talking gibberish. Terrifying gibberish—telling her that she wanted him. He knew she wanted him.

She tried to kick back against him to get him off her but couldn't. For a moment, he was so still she thought he'd passed out on top of her. Then came the slurred word.

"Bitch," he said.

Even as he called her names, she felt him move against her. He had no concern for her well-being. That was clear. Her head was forced up against the side of a fallen chair, the metal unrelenting against her cheek. Another iron leg was beneath her, and she arched up and away from it. But Doug's weight pressed her back down, causing electric pain in her lower back.

She tried to draw up her legs, but her left foot was wedged into the cross legs of the other chair. She seemed to be wrapped in iron. Pinned.

He spoke to her, calling her names and saying ridiculous and insane things. She panted for breath, fighting the steel in her back. Maybe she could find a way to communicate with him.

She blinked hard and stared up at the dark sky. Stars. The moon. Light upstairs.

Suzette!

She drew in a breath and tried to call out, but Doug kissed her hard, bruising her lips. She wanted to gag. To vomit. To scream.

With the back of her skull scraping the ground, she managed to turn her head and spit. She felt more warm blood trickling down her check, the fluid sliding down the back of her neck. She spit again.

Her back was throbbing.

His hand was under her shirt, clawing and grabbing her, and he was saying things that promised to be both hurtful and violent. He was insane.

She shifted again, fighting as much against the concrete as she was against Doug.

Then she saw it, a shadow. Something was there, and then it was gone. She blinked. Was she was seeing things?

Doug grabbed her between the legs, and she recoiled, losing ground against the chair. He squeezed, and she winced. But as she started to close her eyes and cry out, the shadow was there again. She froze. Ever so briefly, she didn't even feel Doug.

It was lightning fast, moving in so quickly she couldn't process what she saw.

Doug yelped. He released her, reared back, and glared at her. Joanna stared back, eyes wide. Doug scrunched up his face, readying to unleash a torrent of cuss words when it struck again. And again.

"Ow, shit!" This time, Doug reeled all the way up, falling over backward.

Eduardo pecked again.

"Ha!" Joanna laughed in disbelief. She scooted herself back against the stone wall as Eduardo hopped around Doug's body.

*Peck. Peck.*

"Eduardo!" Joanna screamed. "Eduardo!"

"Stop it!" Doug yelled.

From within the house, there was a noise, and Joanna looked at the window on the second floor.

"Eduardo!" She let her head fall back and screamed at the top of her lungs. She didn't care about Doug. She didn't care about anything at that moment. Eduardo was alive. He was alive. He was alive and pecking the shit out of Doug Mitchell!

There was a crash from within the house.

Doug staggered to his feet, arms flailing. Eduardo was a crazed bird. The combination of living in the wild after the fire and smelling beer all over Doug incited the bird to manic behavior. Half laughing, half crying, Joanna dragged herself to the bottle sitting on the patio floor and called to him, waving it. Eduardo halted and padded over to Joanna as she tipped the beer.

"Gonna kill that bird." Doug disappeared into the night.

In the distance, Joanna heard a motor catch. She looked at Eduardo.

"Good bird," she said, breathing heavily. "You're a good, good bird!"

# 16

God Almighty. The blood was back. But it wasn't just coming out the backdoor anymore. He stood staring into the toilet as droplets of blood fell and clouded the water. He was pissing blood now.

Something was wrong.

Somehow, he could convince himself bloody shit would fix itself or go away. But blood coming in his piss was something else altogether.

* * * *

A school bus stopped, the brakes giving a final squeak as it did so. Even before the door opened, he heard the children. They were excited. There was laughter, chatter, and an energy that he fed off.

They needed this. It was going to be perfect.

John Simmons stepped back as the bus door opened and Beth Hillsborough came down the steps.

"Beth," he said and extended a hand.

The formality seemed silly, but everything was a show. They had gone to grade school together and saw each other every Sunday at morning services, but today everything was a show.

He'd invited press and photographers. He'd invited parents and suggested they bring cameras as well.

Future Foundations Industries was giving a full-scale tour of the facility to the Marcus schoolchildren, complete with an ice cream party at the end of the tour. They would be given T-shirts, hats and pens, all with the FFI logo.

*  *  *  *

Manuel stopped short as he came around the corner. Roberto and Rolando bumped into him and then stepped to the side to see what the problem was. Like Manuel, they could only stare opened-mouthed, digesting the sight.

Suzette was perched on the edge of a barstool. The dead emu was alive and standing eye to eye with Suzette as she fed him grapes. And Joanna was curled up on a recliner. She looked sick.

"The bird," Manuel said, finding his composure. "He's not dead."

"No!" Suzette smiled triumphantly.

"Where has he . . . " Manuel said, looking from Suzette to Joanna. He paused, again studying Joanna. She seemed strange.

"I guess he was so traumatized, he hid in the woods or near the lake," Suzette said, speaking more to Eduardo than anyone else, "I am glad for you." Manuel gave a polite nod.

Both Roberto and Rolando stepped forward, careful not to get too close to Eduardo. Roberto stared down at Joanna, and she managed a smile.

"It's good that he did, too." Suzette continued to beam.

Joanna had never seen Suzette so happy. She'd never realized the value of Eduardo until last night. Suzette had hopped down the stairs. She was joyful—jubilant—for a beer guzzling emu. Go figure. But there she was—smiling.

"He saved Joanna's life," she said.

Manuel turned again, this time surveying Joanna a little more carefully. Frowning, he bent down and pulled Joanna's arm away from the pillow she clutched. As he did, she winced. The inside of her arm was showed a dark purple bruise. Roberto made a noise of disgust and turned toward the emu.

Suzette held up a hand. "No. It was that Doug Mitchell. He came here drunk last night. He jumped on Joanna. Right here on the patio. He knocked her down and was on top of her when Eduardo pecked him. To near death. He saved her life!" Suzette was elated, and Joanna had to laugh and then winced again.

"It wasn't quite like that." She smiled at Manuel.

"This is true?" Manuel asked, frowning.

Roberto gave an abrupt shove to the back of Manuel, speaking in Spanish. His tone was gruff, and while his English improved daily, he wanted to be sure he understood what was being said.

"You should see her back," Suzette said, and Joanna glared at her.

"Joanna, what is it?" Roberto asked.

"Let me see," Manuel said.

Joanna shook her head. "No, it's okay. I swear. It's not that bad."

"Let me see. Let me see," he demanded, and Joanna knew he would not let it rest until she sat forward. Deep down, she wanted him to be enraged. She wanted someone to care more about this than she did. However twisted and mentally crippled it was, she didn't care that much. It was wrong. She knew that. Doug Mitchell should be punished. She knew that, as well. But she'd been through it too many times. She knew the routine. Police, paperwork, accusations, denial. More paperwork. Rumors, gossip, crap. The fact was, she couldn't even muster up quiet indignation anymore.

She was okay. Saved by an emu. Wait until she told Marcus. Saved by an emu that liked the way her assailant had smelled.

"Let me see," Manuel said, his voice softer, and he pulled her forward.

Before she could stop herself, she let out a little whine. Her back ached.

Slowly, he pulled up the back of her shirt. When he'd seen only what she thought to be the very bottom of the bruise, he began cursing. Her entire back was one large bruise, already darkening to shades of purple and blue.

Then he turned and told the entire story to Roberto and Rolando. As he did, the other men came barreling around the corner. There was a quick succession of *whoas* as each jumped back at the sight of Eduardo. The giant bird was funny from a distance, especially when he was chasing Manuel. But not when he was standing so close on the patio.

Suzette flung the bowl to the side of the patio, sending the grapes flying onto the lawn, causing Eduardo to chase them. Cautiously, the men stepped forward, and Rolando filled them in. One by one, they stepped around to Joanna, giving her brotherly looks of concern.

Roberto was seething and muttering something that caused Manuel to shake his head.

"Suzette, see what's happening? Everyone's getting upset." Joanna ran her hand over her face and closed her eyes. *Geez, this is not happening.* "They're going to get mad, run off, do something stupid and—"

"No. I will not let that happen, but you cannot just let *this* happen. You must tell the police," Manuel said, gesturing to her injured body.

"I don't want you doing anything," she said to Roberto, who was still talking. He stopped. He understood. "I don't want you to get in trouble."

The truth was, Joanna was afraid that he'd kill Doug Mitchell and then be arrested or deported or both.

"He hurt you." Roberto's accent was thick. He enunciated each word.

"I was thinking," Joanna said to Manuel, but she and Roberto continued to stare at each other. "I would like it if maybe three of you moved into the house here at The Shady Land. Suzette's here now and we need help. Between her and . . . well, for safety reasons."

"That's what I said." Suzette's voice boomed across the patio. "That was my idea. I suggested that."

Joanna broke eye contact with Roberto and looked to Manuel. "Maybe you and—"

"Me," Roberto said, and Joanna smiled nervously. He understood much more than he let on.

Manuel was already nodding. "*Si,* and Marcos. He is good at looking after Miss Lee."

* * * *

I'd often been accused of being strange. I'd owned and loved a tiger that chewed off my leg. I'd once owned a cat that slept on a horse. I'd thrown my new leg into traffic, and I'd twice seen Lucille Ball since her death. But I could not compare to Jeanie Archer. As she began to talk again, I sat back and enjoyed the show.

"Who would you rather kiss? Vladimir Putin or Rush Limbaugh?" Jeanie asked the group, inciting a roar of protests.

I, for one, did not understand where she got her notions. On the outside, she appeared to be a normal person, but she was as weird as a three-legged duck.

"That is disgusting!" Dixie squealed.

But Ruthie pondered this. "I think Vladimir Putin's kind of sexy." There was another outcry.

"Sexy?" Jeanie laughed uproariously.

We'd agreed to meet at Quigley's Down Under to go through all the newspapers. Jeanie picked up the back copies from the last week of all the local and big city papers because there was a

150

question that needed to be answered.

Why didn't the people of Marcus turn out for the tire-burning permit meeting?

I knew of a dozen folks who were mighty unhappy about such a thing happening, and I found it more than a little curious that no one showed. So, when Dixie suggested we scour the papers to see if the public notice was ever published, it seemed as good a start as any.

I figured we'd find one or two teeny, tiny ads in the back of the local paper. Instead, we were forced to listen as Jeanie read almost every news item out loud, give social commentary, and express some pretty outrageous opinions.

For example, she'd decided that the cure to all the suicide bombings in Baghdad was to have low-flying aircraft spray pig fat throughout the city. The Muslim citizens would be so horrified at having pig fat touch them, they'd never go outside.

"And it's a little hard to blow people up if there's no one to blow up," she said.

But then she turned her attention to Ruthie. "You cannot find Vladimir Putin sexy." Jeanie waved a newspaper picture of the man in front of Ruthie. "This is not a sexy face. This is a face that does—"

"Easy," Dixie said with a tone of warning. "If Ruthie wants to think he's sexy, then she can think he's sexy."

"Man, that's as wrinkled as my grandmother's puss." Jeanie snorted, thumbing through more papers.

Brianna and Joanna worked, scouring the papers. Because I had promised Joanna to say nothing, no one knew anything about the Doug Mitchell business. But Joanna did not understand how small towns worked. I could all but guarantee that by the time we left Quigley's Down Under, most people would know about the assault.

Before we met the girls at the café, Marcos, Joanna and I had gone to the police station and met with Stan.

Right off, I could see we had a problem. Stan and Doug have always been drinkin' buddies, and the last thing Stan had wanted to hear was Joanna's version of the story. Course, me being with her hadn't helped matters. But we'd had pictures of her body, an eyewitness—me—and very credible evidence.

"Go check his body, Stan. He's gonna have pecker marks all over his body. You go check and see. He'll have pecker marks all over him," I'd said, and honestly, I don't know what in the hell was so funny that the other young police officers had gotten to giggling as they had, but I didn't have any trouble telling them to get lost.

Before we left, we'd filed a report, and Stan had promised to check Doug's body.

Course there had been a lot of promises made and broken of late.

As for the promise I'd made to Joanna . . . not sure how it happened that I broke it.

We'd been thumbing through the papers all morning long, finding—I might add—nothing. Besides Jeanie's constant comments about pig fat and some obsession with dropping child molesters into shark-infested waters, the process was mind numbing. Before I could stop myself, I had told the girls about Eduardo's return and his act of bravery.

Of course, this led to more details about Doug and before I knew it, the entire story was out. Including our visit to the police department.

Dixie sat at the coffee bar, grinning like a fool. "Oh, please, tell me about the pecker marks," she said, goading me.

"I just told him to look for 'em, is all," I said, getting a little irritated. "And I told 'em right before I left, too. Doug Mitchell will rue the day he messed with our guard emu. He's a giant pecker!" I just had to say it.

Everyone's head dropped, all looking at the newspapers. Only Joanna looked at me, though she didn't look mad.

"Suzette, I wish you'd stop saying that. Let's just say that Eduardo scared off Doug."

"Got it!" Brianna's voice rang out.

She'd been clicking away on the Internet, having given up on the papers we'd spread all over the tables. She jabbed a finger at the computer screen, all proud of herself.

"Right here. A small public notice for a tire-burning permit."

Someone asked her what paper it was, though I couldn't recall who. I just knew what happened next and I was angry. The small ad was placed in a paper one month prior to the meeting—a typical strategy to make sure most people would forget about the meeting. But what got me was the placement. Not inside the paper, but geographically. Technically following the law, FFI had placed an ad in the paper of an entirely different city.

Joanna was shocked. The rest of us, I'm sorry to say, just weren't all that surprised. Angry, but not surprised.

"Can they do that?" Joanna asked, and Dixie was fast on the phone.

"We're about to find out," she said.

That afternoon, I drank more coffee than is medically allowed, and truth be told, I felt sorry for Marcos, who insisted on pushing me back to the bathroom each time I had to go. I had to give him credit, though. Manuel had given him orders not to leave my side, and he never did. Even when I filled up the back bathroom with a little more air than I would have liked, if you know what I mean.

In the end, we got our answer.

Dixie called the mayor's office, the TCEQ, EPA, Eva Tobey, and the local papers. She either complained about or questioned the legality of that little move.

"It's legal," she said, getting off the phone with the TCEQ. "Supposedly, if they can prove that the paper has a wide enough circulation, it's all legal."

"Even if it's in another city?" someone complained.

"Even if it's in another city," she said with a sigh.

"Unbelievable!" Jeanie shook her head. "Who the hell is in charge around here?" It was one of those rhetorical questions. Truth was, there were people in charge but they weren't any good to us because instead of protecting the citizens they were supposed to protect, they were protecting business interests, like the good partisan political appointees they were or for whom they worked. There was a movement outside the window, and we all turned to see some high school kid putting up a sign.

John Simmons for US House of Representatives.

And *that* was as wrinkled as my grandmother's puss.

* * * *

Manuel stopped at the doorway to the kitchen and leaned on the frame, wiping his hands.

A man was poking around the grounds of Suzette's burned home. Periodically, he would stop and sift through the debris and ashes.

Manuel watched with interest.

The man did not wear a uniform. Instead, he was in jeans and a T-shirt. He used a Ball-Point to poke and prod the ground. As the man worked his way toward what was once the barn, Manuel moved down the steps and sat on the stone wall, watching.

"What is it?" Andres asked, coming out of the house. Manuel jutted out his chin, pointing toward Suzette's property. As he did so, the man stooped again, picking up an object and placed it in a plastic bag.

While Manuel very much wanted to ask the man what he was doing and, more specifically, who he was, he could not. Manuel was in no position to question anyone. So he watched.

# 17

Terry was in a rage. Brianna had no idea why, but there didn't have to be a reason. There rarely was—never one she could understand anyway. His moods generally had something to do with work; a bad conversation with someone else; or an event that took place two, five, or ten years ago.

Brianna had let herself go over the years. It was true. She knew it. But she also continued to make an attempt at good health by walking and watching what she ate and drank. Terry, however, subscribed to the Neanderthal notion that by being male, he could eat whatever, whenever, however he wanted.

He was enormous, unhealthy, and angry. And somehow it was all Brianna's fault.

Life was a roller coaster.

There were good days. For many years, she held on to such days when Terry was pleasant, even affectionate. But more often than not, he was volatile. So volatile, in fact, he'd lost his fierceness.

When she was in her thirties, he would threaten to take the children, to leave her, to turn the children against her. They were paralyzing threats, and she believed each one. But her late forties had been liberating. Her babies were grown, out of college, and making their own way in life. His threats of leaving her now were almost laughable. She wished. Oh, how she wished.

For the most part, it was embarrassing. It was embarrassing to her that he was such an ass, such a loser, that he had let himself go, and worse, that she continued to stay with him. But it was easier. She and Terry were a package deal. They were Mom and Dad. Grandma and Grandpa.

As embarrassing as he was, the idea of becoming a divorcee at her age was even more humiliating. It was easier to settle, to tolerate, and to endure. And this was where the girls came in. They made life worth living. They countered everything that Terry was and how he made her feel. When she was with the girls, they made her feel young, important, and free.

She was no Jeanie Archer or Dixie Quigley. But she didn't need to be. She loved being with them. As shocking as Jeanie could be, as wild as Dixie had once been, she could live vicariously through them. This, of course, would include their latest crusade.

"Them and your idiot friends," Terry would say, referring to the "saving the world" group. Environmentalists, tree huggers, do-gooders. Terry hated each label and each person who would stand behind such a label. No amount of reason, facts, or common sense would matter.

This would include the diagnosis of their only grandson's asthma. When Brianna had suggested it might be environmentally induced, he became enraged, blaming everyone from Democrats to liberals to college students and corporate sell-outs. He had nothing nice to say about anyone. It was exhausting, and Brianna had stopped listening long ago.

But every once in a while, she was afraid.

This was such a night.

They had been sitting together, eating dinner in front of the television, when a commercial came on. He had mentioned that someone they knew saw Brianna and her friends up at Quigley's Down Under, and he'd wondered what they were doing.

Terry didn't care what Brianna did with her time. This was just another way to let her know that he knew where she was most times. But she answered his question. Speaking before the commercials were over, she thought he might find interest in the fact that the public hearing notice was placed in a newspaper so far away from Marcus.

To her surprise, he was listening to her. Even when their show returned, he appeared riveted by what she was saying. For a moment, she lost her train of thought, peering both at Terry and the television set.

She reached the point where Dixie had made some inquiries when Terry jumped to his feet and threw his plate across the living room. Pasta, ham, and salad splattered everywhere.

"What the hell are you doing?" he roared, and he came at her.

It had been years since she'd physically recoiled from Terry.

Hours after the incident, she was still shaking. Not from fear, but disgust. Both with herself and her situation. She did this. This was her fault, and no one could or would be able to understand how an otherwise intelligent woman would stay.

She felt a self-loathing she'd not felt in years. The shame and hot tears were almost unbearable.

"You are not going to have anything else to do with those bitches!" he'd screamed, tossing her dinner tray to the side and towering over her like a madman. His lips had been so close to her ear, it still rang. She could still feel the spit spray from his mouth against her face. She could still feel and smell his breath, beating down on her while he screamed.

"Do you hear me? Do I make myself clear? Do you hear what I'm saying?"

He'd continued to scream at her, so close to her face, while she curled up into a fetal position on the couch.

He didn't stop screaming until she'd agreed, until she had nodded her head, crying out loud, "Yes, I promise not to see them anymore!"

"I'm not kidding. No more bitches!" He hadn't backed off until she'd pleaded with him to leave her alone. As he stormed out of the house and slammed the door behind him, she'd sobbed on the couch, hating herself more than she could hate him. And she did hate him.

* * * *

Jack Frawley, Frank Wolan, and Ian Jackson had been sitting in the back corner of the Dairy Queen for twenty minutes discussing local politics when John Simmons came in. He paused, waving to a few people, and sauntered back to the men. As he did, Ian slid out from the booth and put out his hand.

"John Simmons," he said with a smile. "Ian Jackson."

"Mr. Jackson. We've met. At the community center and . . . the other night in the mayor's office," John said, nodding.
"Ian, please."

"Ian." John gestured toward the booth and both men took a seat.

"I understand you're running for Congress," Ian said, aware of all Simmons' political aspirations.

"I can't think of a better man. John's ever' bit a part of this town, this state, its history . . . everything," Frank said.

Jack piped in. "It's time we get a little more support. We need someone who's not afraid of special interest groups or being politically incorrect. Bryant don't have the stomach for it."
Frank turned to Ian. "Bryant Whitmeyer. He's been mayor now for what? Six years? That right? Anyway, he's done all right. Don't get me wrong. He loves Marcus and its people, but he's trying to play both sides of the fence, and he's afraid of the tree huggers."

"He's in over his head," Jack said. "We need someone who

can look out for us, for our needs."

Ian glanced at John, who had poked out a lower lip as though he were listening and contemplating what was said. But every man at the table knew how things were. John Simmons and Bryant Whitmeyer had been butting heads for years, but things had escalated in the last year.

With the whole damned green movement, more and more people were starting to ask questions. It was almost more than John could tolerate. There were more complaints and more letters directed to the TCEQ and EPA for intervention. While the TCEQ had turned its head in the last decade, public debate from private citizens had turned up the heat, making it more difficult for them to do so.

John had always joked that if you wanted to make nice, move to Vermont, but if you wanted to show profit, settle in Texas. The Lone Star state was all about business and profit. He knew it. Politicians knew it. The governing bodies of the EPA and TCEQ knew it. And things had been working nicely.

Then some son-of-a-bitch Yankee lawyer came in with what was to be a landmark case in Texas history. The bastard was smart enough to know you can't sue a business in Texas over public health. It's business first, people second. So what he did was sue the EPA, stating the agency had been negligent in its duties to protect the citizens of Marcus and surrounding areas. With several hundred complainants and a long list of health issues, the EPA panicked and turned on the TCEQ.

It was a brilliant strategy that turned FFI's stepchildren against each other. The EPA coughed up vital documentation faster than anyone could have imagined possible for a government agency. There was the threat of federal involvement with the Dallas branch of the EPA in legal troubles, and it was clear that there was something much larger at stake.

It had always, always been business first. But with federal interference and the damned tree huggers looming around, there was a real threat of state legislation, specifically pollution regulation. Legal heads representing pollution-emitting industries around the nation had taken notice. If the industry regulations—specifically those of the cement industry—could be changed in Texas, industries were in jeopardy everywhere.

That was why Ian had been sent from Colorado. While Marcus was the "Cement Capital of Texas" and a major supplier around the world, Ian's company was the leading cement manufacturer in the world. Desmond Enterprises no longer viewed Future Foundation Industries as a competitor, but rather, a sibling in trouble. Big brother's lawyer was flown in to set things right.

Ian pushed an envelope across the table to John, who placed his hand on it and looked at Ian. He cocked his head.

As a woman clad in Dairy Queen attire approached and cleared a table next to theirs, the men silently looked at their menus. Ian let his arms fall forward, covering the envelope.

"Hey, John," the woman said, chomping on her gum.

She was short with uncommonly thin legs compared to her midsection. She had the look of a seasoned smoker; her skin was too rough and deeply lined for her actual age. In her early fifties, Tallulah was a celebrity in her own right in Marcus. Everyone knew who she was. Most avoided her, since there were too few hours in the day to spend listening to her long list of ailments. She was most likely to be in a good mood as she delivered the most horrible news. *I just came back from the doctor. He wants to take hair samples now because he can't figure why I can't breathe at night. I think he's afraid I might die in my sleep. That happens, you know. People die in their sleep.*

John gave a slight nod. "Good morning, Tallulah. How you holdin' up these days?"

"Oh, you know. Workin', always workin' . . . but I love it!" Her voice carried through the restaurant but drew no undue attention. The men were relieved when Tallulah saw another customer she knew and headed to the opposite end of the restaurant.

When she was gone, they all eyed each other for a moment. John looked at the envelope. "What is it?"

Ian smiled smugly. "Consider this a gift."

John pulled his hand back, his fingers twitching. "Do I want to touch this?" he asked and smiled at Frank. He chuckled, but the concern was real.

"Oh, yeah," Frank said and smiled back.

"Trust me, John. We want you to take it," Jack said.

"We both have a problem. Public perception or, more accurately, a small group of renegades were allowed to dictate to business. Am I right? And we both want to run a successful, uncomplicated business," Ian explained to John.

Every man at the table nodded.

"I think if we work together on this"—he leaned forward, pushing the envelope just a little more toward John—"we can control the game."

John nodded, taking a long look at the envelope.

"This is to help your bid for Congress." Ian leaned back. "And I assure you, it's all legal. This is a fair contribution and is documented as such. You've been a great friend to the Desmond family, and they want to support you in your personal endeavors."

His words hung over the table as each man took that in.

It was bullshit.

John wouldn't know a Desmond if he tripped over one.

He smiled. "Thank you. Please pass along that I am touched." He slipped the envelope into his shirt pocket.

Each man smiled, satisfied.

"I think we have an understanding," Ian said.

"But we still have a major problem, Frank." John looked at Frank, who nodded.

Frank was a pit bull, obsessed about the canister situation. As much as he loved his job, as disgusted as he was with continued rumors of health issues, this was a matter of territory. Some asshole had trespassed onto his territory, illegally placed a canister there, and was, until he had found the damned thing, laughing at him.

That game, he declared, was all but over. He knew who was responsible for it. He knew the name of each bitch. Now it was just a matter of proving it, and no mercy would follow.

"You let us work on that," Ian said, his voice deepening. He and his associates were aware of the trespassing situation. Even more so, they were investigating what other agencies might have received, analyzed, or communicated with residents of Marcus, Texas, in the last six months. It was slow going, but Ian was confident a name would be revealed.

Frank pursed his lips and grudgingly nodded.

# 18

"Honey," Tallulah whispered into the phone. "You wouldn't believe who was just in here."

She looked around for a moment, cupping her hand over the phone. "And you wouldn't believe what they were talking about . . ."

* * * *

They sat in silence for a long time, each man in his own world. When headlights came into view, they would perk up, and every time it turned out to be nothing.

"Just how long you figure on sittin' out here?" Paul asked.

"As long as it takes," Frank said.

He was glad to have Ian Jackson on board. No doubt Mr. Jackson had a fine mind and would win the legal battles ahead. But Frank wasn't going to sit idly by and allow pollution collection canisters on his property.

There hadn't been any activity since he found the last canister, but they would come back and attempt to gather evidence again. And he'd be ready for them. That knowledge brought Frank great satisfaction.

"I'm gonna catch 'em," he said, smiling to himself. It was a play on words. He'd either catch them in the act or they'd be caught by his traps.

*Bitches.*

* * * *

Ruthie stared up at the sky. "When I was eleven years old, I watched my babysitter and her boyfriend . . . you know, do it."

"I smoked at entire pack of cigarettes when I was ten. It took me a couple of days," Jeanie said, challenging her before taking a long pull from her drink. "I was sick as a dog, but I hung in there!"

"Good for you!" Dixie raised her drink.

Both Ruthie and Dixie were flat their backs on the recliners, and Jeanie was laid out on top of the bar on Joanna's patio. Suzette occupied the third recliner, and all balanced large margarita glasses on their bodies as they gazed at the stars. Joanna was still sitting up, but like the others, she was drunk. Only Dixie was sober, drinking her virgin margarita. For an extra kick, she'd added carbonated water.

"I stuffed my bra when I was in the eighth grade. Someone should make a note of this and tell Brianna. She always accused me of doing that, but I denied it." Ruthie rolled to one side, took a drag on her straw, and sighed with satisfaction. "But I did. I can admit it now. I stuffed."

"Well, hell, that's shocking news . . . Hey, news flash, Ruthie, everyone did that!" Jeanie laughed.

"I didn't," Dixie said.

"Well, of course you didn't," Jeanie said with a heavy drawl. "You were born with boobs. Right there in the baby ward of the hospital. You probably had perky little baby boobs, and all the little boy babies were already trying to—"

"As a matter of fact." Dixie was laughing and rolling around on the recliner, vying for a good position to take another drink.

"No! No! No!" Jeanie yelled and bolted upright. "No 'I was a stripper' stories and"—she wagged a finger at Suzette—"no 'I got my leg ripped off by a mad tiger' stories 'cause no one can beat those."

Joanna sat back, watching the show. They were like a comedy routine that never quit, they never seemed to run out of material, and they never tired of each other. They were infectious, and for the first time in the longest time, she felt a sense of belonging.

"I've been handcuffed before," Ruthie said.

"We've all been handcuffed before," both Dixie and Jeanie said at the same time, causing everyone to laugh.

"I've done the handcuffing before," Dixie said, causing Ruthie to snort her drink through her nose.

There was more laughter while Ruthie complained about the burning sensation.

"Now imagine that was pee coming out your nose," Jeanie said.

"What?" Suzette was astonished.

"Oh, forget her," Dixie said and waved a hand. "She wanted to know what was worse. Pee going out your nose or your mouth." Suzette mouthed a silent *oh*, not bothering to ask anything more about it.

"But tell the truth," Jeanie said as she rolled to one side of the bar, her eyebrows raised as high as they could possibly go. She looked twelve. "You can smell it, can't you?"

"Franklin wasn't the only man I've been with," Suzette said, ready to be part of the game. For a moment, there were genuine smiles.  Suzette was playing along, and it was enough, although no one was going to explore the statement. It was best for both Franklin and Suzette to leave that one alone.

The truth was, Suzette had been a bit loose in her days of rebellion. About the time she threw away her leg, she'd needed to prove to herself that she was still desirable. Sadly, by the time she'd realized that men would find a half-starved, mangy sheep desirable—given the proper circumstances—she'd already gone around about twice with the young men in her town. They'd all used her, but Franklin loved her. And from the time they'd said "I do" to one another, it was as if they were each first-time lovers. With Franklin dead and gone and Suzette half-drunk, it didn't seem right to speak of other lovers. It was a long time ago and best forgotten.

"Where is Brianna?" Joanna asked, wishing she were part of this.

"Hmm, not allowed to come out and play, I'm guessing," Ruthie said. She sat up, finished off the rest of her drink, and pushed her glass in Joanna's direction. Her expression was so comical Joanna couldn't help but laugh.

As Joanna came off the barstool, the patio spun a little too much. "Whoa, Sally," Joanna said, more to herself than anyone else.

"Uh-oh, Ms. Thang is unsteady on her feet!" Jeanie roared from the bar. In fact, she had wedged her feet into the creases of the leather on Joanna's new bar top to keep herself from rolling off.

Joanna pretended to gain her composure by doing a head roll and shoulder shrug. Cheers echoed around the patio as she strutted toward Ruthie, pitcher in hand.

"I've seen a *Playgirl,*" Ruthie said happily.

"I subscribed to *Playgirl!*" Jeanie shouted.

Joanna topped everyone off, giving herself the very last of the precious concoction while Dixie refilled her glass with more sparkling mineral water.

"You know," Ruthie said, pretending to be annoyed, "you can let me win this, Jeanie. You don't always have to be the most shocking."

"I'm not!" Jeanie defended herself. "Who's gonna have anything more shocking to offer up than Dixie Quigley, the mad Mormon stripper?"

Had she not been so intoxicated, Joanna might have been shocked when she realized that the voice she heard next was her own.

"One time, my bastard, asshole ex-husband wouldn't pull over when I needed to change my tampon, and he kept telling me to hold it. Like I could hold it. Jackass! So, when we got to the church—it was a wedding—and I finally could go to the bathroom, I saved the tampon in a Kleenex, walked out into the lobby of this beautiful, old church in front of all his rich friends, and put it in his hand. It was completely soaked in blood, and I said, 'Why don't *you* hold it for a while.' They told me later that someone fainted. It might have been him."

Utter and complete silence took hold of the patio. It took hold of that entire part of the universe. For just a moment, no one moved. Joanna threw back the rest of her drink, set down her glass with a little *clink*, and grinned.

"Holy crap!" Jeanie roared, and then what seemed like the entire Shady Land erupted with hysterical, raucous laughter.

* * * *

From inside, the men had been listening as the women whooped and carried on. It was amusing to them because they hadn't known women behaved like this.

In particular, Manuel had been raised in a traditional home. Of course, women would laugh and carry on when they got together, but it was most certainly a day affair. No alcohol involved.

His wife was very quiet and reserved, much like Joanna Lucas. But tonight Joanna had shown another side of herself. To her credit, she was not the loud one and for the most part, he'd never heard her voice. The others, however, were loud.

He and Roberto had been playing a game of chess while Marcos read in an overstuffed chair by the front window. Joanna had only begun to decorate the interior of the home as the men finished working inside. And so far, her taste was very nice. Manuel liked it very much; it was a Spanish style. She'd special-ordered a deep red oak wood floor and crossbeams for the living area. While the dining room still stood empty, she'd ordered overstuffed chairs and a couch for the living room. The colors were vibrant, matching the décor outside on the patio.

Another whoop and the men all looked up, exchanged smiles, and returned to their mental tasks.

Marcos would not go to bed until he'd seen to Ms. Lee. Roberto and Manuel would not go until their game was finished. Actually . . . Manuel had finished the game almost an hour earlier but was toying with Roberto, stalling for time.

It was the crashing noise that brought the men to their feet. By the time they'd reached the patio, Manuel could hear them.

"I'm sorry," someone said while Joanna murmured reassurances. Clearly, it was time for everyone to go home.

When Manuel got the doorway, Joanna was crouched on the ground, picking up pieces of glass. She almost fell back only to be caught by Jeanie and they all laughed.

"Ladies," Manuel said, projecting a very loud, deep voice. He was in no mood to be argued with. He was not going to let anyone drive home. Clearly, not one of them was capable. "I will drive you home."

It was another reason he liked women. In general, they were a peaceful bunch.

"Okay, *amigo*," Jeanie said and waved.

"Hurray for the cavalry." Ruthie scrambled for her purse.

"I can drive," Dixie said but Jeanie shook her head.

"You got your little sports car, and I can't leave my car."

"I drive you and Ruthie home. Marcos come get me after Ms. Suzette go to bed, yes?" Manuel said, nodding to everyone. Manuel turned to Roberto and Marcos, and gave instructions. No one argued about anything.

Marcos helped Suzette up the stairs and to her room, while Roberto picked up the broken glass before Joanna cut herself.

"Teach me some Spanish, Manuel," Jeanie said as he led her away. "I need to learn a few choice words for the lady who works the counter at the gas station."

As Jeanie walked away, she gave a backhanded wave to Joanna.

Joanna chuckled as they left then turned to watch Roberto for a few moments. When he finished picking up the glass, he stood.

She smiled at him. He smiled back. No one moved.

He broke eye contact first, moving toward the trashcan.

Before the girls had arrived, Joanna had been working in her studio. Their drop-by was a surprise—a fun surprise—but she'd left the light on and some clay unwrapped.

"I need to turn off the light," she said, very aware of how thick her tongue had become. The walk down to the barn would help clear her head a little. Without another word, she tottered down the narrow path.

It was a difficult walk, as she stumbled over the small weeds and sticks snagging her feet. Only when she made it to the open doors of the barn did she feel steady again. Everything was as she'd left it, and she wrapped the clay block that had already begun to crack.

Her studio was no more than a large workbench in the middle of a barn. But to Joanna, it was splendor. It was hers. Even in a near-drunken stupor, she loved it and felt the compulsion to straighten and tidy.

It had seemed to Roberto that she had been gone for too long. He'd not heard any noises to indicate a problem, but he also could not imagine that she could be working. So, what was she doing? Worried, a little curious, and most certainly not ready to say good night without seeing her again, he walked down the slight incline to the barn.

Joanna was a nice woman and his boss. She was someone Manuel said should be respected at all times. She was beautiful, sweet, soft, vulnerable, and sexy. She was also from a different world. Joanna was a woman who would never have anything to do with him. She was of money and culture. She was white.

Her giggles were infectious, her eyes were enchanting, and her body was inviting. He'd concluded long ago that it was hard to concentrate on anything when she was around.

She turned out the light, talking to herself, and stumbled forward.

He surprised her as much as she startled him, and they both jumped, grabbed each other's arm, and laughed nervously.

They both said "sorry" at the same time, and Roberto marveled that she was so close. As they leaned against the side of the barn, a lock of her hair caught on the wood, and he freed it. That was when it happened. She looked up with those eyes—those eyes that always seemed to be waiting for him to say or do something.

So, he did.

There was no hesitation as he moved forward. He'd seen her expression. Her eyes half closed as she reached up against him. She surprised him when she sought out his mouth. She was everything he imagined—soft, warm, hungry, and passionate. There was a sweetness, but the heavy taste of margarita on her tongue excited him as he roamed her body with his hands. She gave no indication of letting go as she tangled her fingers in his hair, almost clutching it.

He ached for her to let him go further but wanted her to tell him to stop. Where they were going would cause all kinds of problems. Later, he would say it was beyond his control. Later he would try to explain things to Manuel, and the old man would not hear a word of it. But it *was* beyond anything he could control. Her smell, her soft, full lips, the way she grabbed him. It was overwhelming and debilitating.

He caressed her waist, moving higher as they kissed. She

jerked his hair, moving his head to one side and allowing her to tug and nip his bottom lip. For a moment, she sucked on it, pulled it into her mouth, and he moved his hands up. As quickly as it had begun Joanna stopped and pulled away, staring into his eyes. For a moment, they both just looked at each other and then began to laugh.

# 19

At three forty-five, he walked out with the rest of the day crew. There was a new sense of camaraderie among the men. They were a unified front. And it was such a load of crap, it made his head hurt.

At approximately three, the evening shift had come in early and joined the day shift in the break room. John Simmons had stood on a table just as he'd done when he was an owner.

John couldn't stand to be out of the spotlight, so it wasn't a surprise to anyone that he was back, standing on a table. This time, however, there were "Simmons for US Congress" signs littered throughout the break room.

John's campaign began, starting where his roots were the deepest and strongest—with the workingman.

"I was part of the beginning," John said, his voice booming over the heads of FFI employees. They cheered and whistled as though he were offering some new information. "When we built Future Foundations in Marcus, we were the most technologically advanced plant in the United States. That was more than sixty years ago. But now, we're under attack. From liberals!"

Boos and hisses filled the room.

"From tree huggers and outsiders!"

More jeering.

"From people who don't know what the hell they're talking about!" John raised his voice a little higher.

"What's worse . . ." he said, lowering his voice for dramatic effect, "we have people right here in Marcus. Neighbors. Maybe friends." He shook his head. "And they are trying to destroy this plant, our vision, our jobs, our dreams."

A grumble swept the room like a wave.

"We all have a job to do that goes beyond our tasks here at the plant or my bid for US Congress. We have to protect our town, protect our jobs, and protect this plant from those who would tear it all away from us.

"We clean up other people's business. We recycle their tires and old cars. Isn't that the funny part of it? We recycle, and we're getting harassed for recycling. We're getting harassed for providing a public service. And I'll tell you why. Because nothin' we do will ever be good enough! There are just some people out there hell-bent on destruction. Greenies, leftists, liberals, socialists, communists! Find a word for it, I don't care! It comes down to people with their fruity little ideas about a utopia where old cars and tires and oil and hazardous waste magically disappear. They all want it to disappear, but they just don't want to know about it. Am I right? Am I right!

"I am! And I'm here to tell you this. If you don't stand up for your job right now, you could lose it. You have to fight for what you want. Right now, here in this town!" He pounded a fist in an open hand. "You have to speak out for what you believe in. Let your neighbors know that this is a great company, that we are good stewards of the earth, that we are providing a service . . . a needed service, and that Marcus *needs* FFI!"

When John was done, the men validated each other by back-patting and chest-thumping.

But *he* was pissing and shitting blood. It didn't matter how much John Simmons tried to pump everyone up. The fact remained, he was pissing blood.

He walked out to his truck among the chatter of co-workers and lifelong buddies as they talked excitedly about John and what a great state representative he would make. *Simmons won't stand for this kind of crap!* Some were saying. *He'll put a stop to it.*

But *he* was bleeding.

Internally.

A lot of men said they weren't going to listen to any more noise about how bad FFI was for the environment. They weren't sick, so how bad could it be? They were going to defend what was theirs. *But holy shit!* He was pissing blood.

But what had bothered him the most, even more than his own disturbing medical problem, was John's final statement. "Exciting things are in store for this town. And those of you who are loyal to us will be rewarded!" *What did that mean?*

* * * *


"You have got to be kidding me!" Jeanie yelled at the paper lying open on the table. Beside her, Joanna sipped a cup of coffee and tried not to look alarmed by the sudden outburst. Both Merilee and Dixie were behind the counter, filling a large luncheon order. Ruthie had volunteered to act as cashier for the few customers who had ambled in during the last hour, but Jeanie could not be torn away from the papers. Since the recent scandal over the FFI public hearing notice, Jeanie had been scouring all the big papers for any information on anything regarding the TCEQ, EPA, public hearings, tire burning, or cement.

"Look at this!" Jeanie continued to roar, holding the paper up. Dixie and Merilee only glanced up. Jeanie turned and shook the paper at Joanna.

"What?" Dixie continued with her sandwich making, irritated.

Her chicken salad croissants were legend in Marcus, and as happens with things of legendary status, Dixie had become obsessively concerned that each batch be better, tastier, and zestier.

She had a specific, magical number of alfalfa sprouts, spicy sweet pickles, and mustard seeds for each sandwich that Merilee had yet to grasp. This created the slightest bit of friction behind the counter. Merilee didn't dare look away for too long. Dixie couldn't look away.

"This! This!" Jeanie was pounding on the paper. Ruthie peered from behind the register, her shoulders slumping when she saw what had Jeanie so agitated. "It's an FFI advertisement." She looked at the girls behind the counter.

"Oh, for goodness' sake, Jeanie, not now," Dixie said with a sigh.

"No, really. You have to see this!" Jeanie picked up the paper, describing the advertisement out loud before she turned it around for them to see. "This," she pointed to Joanna, "is the kind of stuff that goes on around here. And what's scary is that people think this crap is normal. They buy it hook, line, and sinker."

"What?" Joanna asked. Merilee and Dixie both groaned. Dixie tried to wave Joanna off, but it was too late.

"What, you say? We've got a nice little shot of FFI in the background, and in the front . . . are you ready? Are you ready for this? Our cheerleaders from the high school doing some kind of little cheer stance in a bed of bluebonnets, and . . . and the caption reads 'Leaders in the Environment. Pioneers of Recycling. We are Your Future.' "

Jeanie circled the café as though she were trying to show everyone in the room the picture but stopped with Joanna. "This is why you need to hang with me, girlie. I'll show you what's what, and this"—she tapped the newspaper—"stinks.

"I think that's nice."

Dixie, Merilee, and Ruthie all looked up. Jeanie spun around, clutching the newspaper to her chest.

It was Rosa Schultz.

Jeanie's eyes narrowed. There was an on-going joke about Rosa that presumably even Rosa was aware of. She was called "the other white meat." She was short, brown, and round, but when Rosa looked in the mirror, she saw tall, white, and lean.

Before Rosa had become a Schultz, she'd been a Chavez. But Rosa did everything she could to alienate herself from her Latino roots. She was a loud opponent of anything that would enrich or empower the lives of minorities, the poor, or disenfranchised. She married Jerry Schultz, and they officially became the most nauseating couple Jeanie had ever known. Everything was about America, being American, standing up for America, but they were so damned dumb. They flew their Texas flag over the American flag on their fifty-foot-tall pole. And to the great irritation of veterans and other patriots, they also flew the flags day and night without lighting, allowing darkness to fall on the American flag. They were so wrapped up in their image of the stand-up American they didn't realize how many mistakes they were making.

Jeanie couldn't help herself and turned on Rosa. "You think this is nice?"

Rosa sat with a friend, and while her friend appeared uncertain under Jeanie's intense gaze, Rosa looked contrite. "Yes, I do. And if you weren't so hellfire bent on destroying the company, you'd see that they do a lot of good things for all of us." She gave a little nod of self-satisfaction.

"Look, Rosa. I know that Jerry works for the company, so you're too blind to see what's going on. But haven't you noticed all the problems we've had around here since they started burning hazardous waste? And now they want to burn tires on top of everything else, and you don't think that's a problem? Really?"

"They've done a ton of research studies, and nothing has been proven, Jeanie," Rosa said, stamping a foot. "You're just trying to—"

"So, you're telling me you haven't been to funerals of young people or children who've died with no explanation for why they just got sick so suddenly? You haven't noticed anything?" Jeanie asked.

She turned to Joanna and shook her head. "You haven't been here long enough to know this, Joanna, but it ain't right here. You heard the expression 'something stinks in Denmark?' Yeah. Well, something's toxic in Marcus, but no one wants to talk about it because it makes us uncomfortable."

Dixie muttered under her breath. She didn't like having this kind of conversation in her café. It wasn't that she disagreed, but it was just bad for business.

"Jeanie, you know good and well that happens all over the world, not just here in Marcus. You know death is just a sad, sad part of life. Even little kids die, too. Much as I don't like it, it's part of life. And it's disgusting to me that you're trying to capitalize on that just so you'll have something to scream about."

As soon as Rosa said it, Dixie's head whipped up. Ruthie gasped, Joanna covered her mouth, and Merilee groaned. But Jeanie laughed. It was a deep, hearty, dangerous laugh, and she shook her head as she moved toward Rosa's table.

"Oh, geez," Dixie said, wiping her hands.

"Look, short, brown, and round, I know that you like to pretend that you were born in a white, Republican home where your mama wore an apron and baked cookies while your dad did his Ward Cleaver routine. But here in the real world, we see things a little differently."

As Jeanie spoke, Joanna slowly covered her face, peeking through her fingers.

Jeanie leaned against Rosa's table and smiled unnervingly while Rosa looked aghast. "What I'm trying to capitalize on is the truth. It's disgusting to me—funny that you should use that phrase when it applies so nicely to you—but it's disgusting to me that you have turned your back on your heritage, your people, your own family because you want to live some gross little Republican wannabe dream. And, by the way, that's all you'll ever be—a wannabe.

"Because let me clue you in on a little conservative secret. They don't want you. They want your vote. That is, they want the Latino vote. They'll woo you, say whatever it is they think you want to hear, and use you up, laughing all the way to the voting booths. And when I say *you,* I mean a La-tin-ah."

With her hands in fists, Jeanie pressed her knuckles on the table, leaning so far forward that Rosa had to sit back in her chair. Although her demeanor was aggressive, her tone was so quiet, it was almost a whisper. Everyone held their breath, and slowly Joanna's hands slid down her face as her mouth fell open.

"Why don't you take a look in the mirror? You couldn't be more minority if you tried. A Mexican *and* a woman. I know, I know . . . perish the thought, right? But if you don't have it in you to do the right thing as a woman, as a human being, as an American or whatever else is important to you, then why don't you think like a mother. You're so frickin' worried about a business that pumps millions of pounds of hazardous waste into the air every year that you won't consider the possibility that, gee, maybe this crap is bad for us. It's hurting little kids. It's hurting small children and babies whose lungs are not fully developed yet and who have no chance to fight the effects of that cement kiln crap that settles like a film in their lungs."

Jeanie's voice began to rise. "You won't consider that each time a kid from this small town is rushed to the hospital because he can't breathe, it's because super microscopic particulates from the kilns are ingested into the human body. By the way, God didn't mean for microscopic particulates to infest the human body. But why don't you ever consider the children? And I don't mean some shit about not being able to catch their breath. I mean kids literally not being able to breathe, children who died in their loved ones arms because they got no oxygen. They could not breathe."

Tears formed in Jeanie's eyes as she recalled how her own sister had collapsed. For a moment, she squeezed her eyes shut before opening them and refocusing. Rosa had shrunk back into her chair, but her eyes were flashing, and Jeanie knew the woman wasn't even listening. She was already trying to come up with her pathetic rebuttal. Jeanie pushed on, still not done.

"Your idiot husband and his jackass co-workers who go to church and pray every Sunday about being good stewards of the earth have managed to convince themselves that they are doing us all a service by recycling. But listen up, Rosa. And this is the important part right here, so try, just for a moment, to dislodge your official 'I am a conservative voter' card from your ass and concentrate on these words. If we're taking the hazardous waste the Puerto Rican government doesn't want and can't properly dispose of . . . if we're taking hazardous waste from Kentucky, Louisiana, and Utah because they don't know what to do with it . . . and we're 'burning' it," Jeanie said, making little quote marks around the word *burning*. "Where is it going? If it's not going into our air and soil and water, then where is it going?"

"We take hazardous waste from Puerto Rico?" Rosa's friend asked.

The question surprised Jeanie, and she stepped back from the table, eyeing the friend. She was someone Jeanie had seen around but did not formally know. She was probably a transplant and, like a lot of recent residents, had moved to Marcus for country living but easy access to the city.

"Yeah!" Jeanie's voice softened. "They don't want it because it's . . . it's hazardous. Bad for people, bad for animals, bad for the air, bad for the environment." She shrugged. "And they were smart enough to find some suckers who would take it and make a profit off it."

The friend glanced at Rosa.

"FFI will brag that they are performing a service, but they get paid to take this nasty stuff off the hands of other states, which are more than happy to pay that price. It gets the dangerous stuff away from them and their people. It's our problem, literally. Not theirs." With that, Jeanie turned back to Rosa. "The answer is the cement." Rosa looked confused.

"The answer is that whatever dangerous stuff isn't burned off in the emissions, it's poured into the cement." Jeanie turned back to the friend. "The cement that the FFI makes from the fuel and heat burned from lethal hazardous compounds. It all goes into the cement that is used for hospitals, schools, businesses, churches . . . your home."

No one said a word. Rosa didn't seem to know what to say. Clearly, she had not gotten the memo about hazardous cement being used to build hospitals and schools.

Briefly, Jeanie believed she'd made an impact until Rosa opened her mouth. "If you did a little more research, I think you'd find that our air quality isn't any worse than anywhere else around here." She gathered her things and stood, driving Jeanie back a little, and turned to her friend.

"C'mon, Shelly." Rosa turned and walked off.
Shelly nodded, but she managed to offer a weak smile to Jeanie, who nodded. Rosa hadn't heard a thing, but Shelly had. Whoever this Shelly person was, she had most definitely been listening.

* * * *

Myra Thompson stood on Brianna's front porch.

"Well, hey, Myra," Brianna said, slightly confused. Myra was holding a plate of homemade brownies and had a huge welcome-to-the-neighborhood kind of smile on her face. It made Brianna laugh.

"What are you doing?"

"Well, I've come to see you, silly," Myra said. Her voice was too friendly, too chummy, and it caused Brianna's smile to fade.

"What?"

"Well, I heard about you and Terry getting into it and that you were pretty down. So," she said, drawing in a deep breath and pushing her way into the house, "here I am. I always say, nothing, but nothing, mends a broken heart like a plate full of brownies and cold milk." She turned once she was inside. "You do have milk, right?"

"I, uh . . ."

"Good. I can tell by the expression on your face we're gonna need a lot of milk." She laughed at her own joke. As Brianna stood at the door, Myra marched straight to the kitchen.

"Well, come on, girl!" Myra's voice rang out, snapping Brianna from her trance. She blinked, shut the door, and followed the voice. What else could she do? Myra was in her kitchen, waiting to get all the latest gossip on her fight. Could things get any worse?

"How did you . . . " Brianna turned to stare at Myra. Already, Myra had located the plates, forks, and glasses. For a large woman, she moved quickly. She was floating on a cloud.

"The other night." Brianna could only stare. Stunned. "When Terry came over to our place, he was mad as a hornet. It took Jeff hours to calm him down. But, well, they got to talkin', and Terry told some stuff. I hope you don't mind. Don't be mad at him. He was just so mad and so worried about you. You know . . ." As Myra spoke, she laid out the plates and forks. "He's a good man. He's got a right to worry about you. Those women, those girls . . . I know you've been friends all your life but honestly, Brianna . . ." Myra managed a motherly smile. "They just aren't good for you. I mean, have you heard them talk?"
Brianna stared.

"Jeanie Archer is . . . I know, she's funny and all, but she puts people off. She's shocking. Too shocking. And Dixie Quigley. Land sakes, Brianna. She's a stripper. And a Mormon!" She put a hand to her chest as though the latter far outweighed the former in terms of shock value.

"A Mormon." Myra began dishing out brownies, heaping three squares per plate. How long was she going to stay? Brianna wondered. "You do know they worship the devil." Myra sat down and patted the empty chair next to her.

"Well, no, they don't," Brianna said quietly.

"Oh, Lord. She's begun recruiting you, hasn't she?"

Brianna smiled. She recalled one of their most recent Mormon conversations. It was when Jeanie was giving Dixie a hard time about the story of the Book of Mormon being found in the woods. Jeanie had thrown up her hands in disgust. "If you're not willing to answer my questions, maybe I'll just come to your church and ask a few myself."

Dixie recoiled in mock terror. "No! I forbid you to come to my church."

"Well, hell, I'd think they'd want another body there. Aren't they all about recruitment? They're always riding around on their little bikes with their little nametags, knocking on people's doors right in the middle of important TV shows and asking people to come to church."

"That's different," Dixie said.

"How?" Jeanie asked. Ruthie and Brianna had to smile. As usual, Jeanie was getting herself all wound up about the Mormon Church because Dixie wasn't giving her the answers she wanted.

"We don't want you."

"What? Well, do you want Brianna? Or Ruthie?"

"Maybe."

"But you don't want me." She started to pout.

"No. We don't want you."

"Because my mind is too strong," Jeanie said triumphantly. "You can't bend my mind with all your brainwashing stuff. I won't worship seagulls."

"Why," Dixie asked with a sigh, "would you worship seagulls?" A patient smile played on her lips.

"I don't. You do!"

"I worship seagulls?"

"Yes. That's what Mormons do! You worship seagulls because a bunch of seagulls came and ate up all the locusts that were about to destroy the crops when the first Mormons moved to Utah. Ever since, you people have worshipped seagulls."

Brianna and Ruthie began to laugh.

"You pinhead. We don't worship seagulls. And before you start making stuff up or believing ridiculous stories, you should do better research," Dixie said.

"Then let me come to your church and ask questions."

"No."

"Why not? Are you ashamed of me?" Jeanie asked and feigned heartbreak.

"Yes!" Dixie sighed again. "I'm ashamed of you because you're a Methodist." And all the women had gasped.

The memory of it forced a chuckle from Brianna, causing sudden curiosity in Myra.

"The last thing Dixie Quigley is doing is recruiting. Trust me."

"Well, it's a good thing. I mean, I don't know how she could with her being who she is."

Brianna opened her mouth to challenge that but stopped. Terry had put Myra up to the home visit. Myra was going to report back the moment she was in her car, calling both Jeff and Terry.

*Was Brianna being a good girl?*

*Was she staying home?*

*Had she gone off to see the girls?*

For the next hour, Brianna turned off her brain, ate brownies, and pretended to listen to Myra drone about her recipe secrets.

# 20

One thing I know is sometimes outrage is necessary. You got to get the blood pumping in order to get off the pot. That's where Joanna was. Ever since she'd come to Marcus, let's face it, she'd been watching the world go by while sittin' on the pot. She'd been so worried about what other people thought of her and even more so about falling flat on her face because of what one man, who wasn't around, would think if she did fall.

I didn't know who this Clayton Lucas character was, but I did know that he'd done some kind of number on her mind. When we'd set out, I determined that I might impart a little of my own wisdom on the subject of being your own woman.

Joanna was very young. She was strong and creative and all kinds of positive things you might attribute to someone being successful and happy. To an outsider, it might have looked like she had it all. Funny thing was, she didn't seem that happy.
It reminded me of my leg.

Now, there would be those in town who have said that as soon as I got my leg ripped off, I was a changed person. I became less than agreeable most days, even ugly at times. And, of course, that would stand to reason with most folks. I got my leg torn off, so I became crabby. But that wasn't it.

Yes, I did become agitated when I lost my leg. I was annoyed by Simon's stupidity, but I never blamed Tony the Tiger. I was upset when I was in the hospital because there were rumors that Tony would be hunted down and killed. In the following months when I didn't know Tony's fate, I was anxious, to put it mildly. But once we secured my cat's safety, I relaxed and focused on my physical therapy and getting used to my new condition.

I'd been in the wheelchair three months when I was fitted for a new leg. The entire town was excited about it. In fact, the entire town was invested in the damned thing. And that was how it came to be that I became *agitated.*

I made the national news, and because I was a celebrity of sorts, the community and other neighboring towns had a big fund-raiser—a fish fry out at the Payne's place to raise money for my leg. They say about six hundred folks turned out. I don't remember much, except that all the people wanted to see the girl who'd had her leg ripped off by a tiger. So, I sat in the hot sun all day, shook hundreds of hands, smiled, and—at the end of the day—accepted a check for forty-six hundred dollars. It represented full payment on a brand new leg so that everyone in town could watch me learn to use the damned thing.

*"I saw Suzette using her leg today."*

*"Where was that?"*

*"Oh, 'round the post office. She was gettin' along pretty good."*

*"That right? I think that's where I saw her facedown on the pavement. 'Bout when did you see her? I wonder how long she'd been lyin' there on the pavement like that. I'd a helped her, but you know how she is about gettin' a hand up. Ever since she took the money for a new leg, she's been pissy."*

It was true. I was a bit pissy. People did a real nice thing, putting together that fish fry and raising the money for a new leg.

But then, something else happened. The community formed an attachment to the leg that had nothing to do with my health or my progress. It was always, *How's that new leg workin' out for ya, Suzette?* If I was feeling poorly, well it couldn't be because of the new leg. If I fell down, skinned up my old leg, well, it couldn't have been because of the new leg. If I was slow to get somewhere, it was just a matter of getting used to the new leg. And if I was early, well it was because of that new leg.

I was appreciative of everything folks had done for me, but the ownership people felt toward my leg had become too much. What finally tore it for me was the day Jack Frawley compared my new leg to his new truck. That was the day I lost my leg. For good. I was getting out of my car and heading to the pharmacy. Stan Berry, a rookie cop back then, saw me coming and jumped out of his cruiser to slow down traffic and let me pass. Well, all right then. I didn't particularly care for that, but I appreciated the gesture.

Then Jack coasted by in his daddy's new pickup truck. The damned fool had been driving around town for days, showing off the new toy. He rolled down his window and hollered, "Lookee here, Suzette. This here truck cost the same as that leg of yours, only I don't have a double-wide like you!"

That was it. I tore off my leg and flung it so hard it shattered the back window of Frawley's new truck. It was a beautiful sight. Of course, I never meant for Mrs. Charlotte to plow into the back of him or for the other cars to plow into them. But I never apologized. I said from that moment on that the only person who should be apologizing was that stupid ass Jack Frawley. Needless to say, me and Jack never have gotten on too well.

No sooner did I adopt a wheelchair than I learned to adopt the attitude of taking a back seat. It was a position I learned I liked very much. While in my wheelchair, I tended to settle at the back of rooms, church, schools, social functions, and parties and could quietly and happily observe things like how local politicians glad-handed their neighbors but drank and ate with the local business leaders, or how so many women—too many women—continued to play the role of soccer mom and fund-raiser, always leaving the heavy political issues to their male counterparts. It was painful to hear women say, *Oh, I don't read the newspapers. I'm not very political.* This laziness was their license for American stupidity. And it was the reason residents had accepted hazardous waste burning in their backyards.

I also saw how the teenagers were changing, how the town was growing, and how more city folks were coming in. 'Course, in hindsight, I realize that I'd misjudged Joanna.

I've always said there are three kinds of women: women who never take the lead, leaving it to men; women who succeed without men, and women who succeed in spite of men.

Joanna didn't know it yet, but she was a woman who would succeed despite it all. On the surface, she was upper crust—wealthy, educated, and snooty. People might have passed judgment on her for being pretty or wearing too little clothing, but in Marcus, she was considered conservatively acceptable.

It's a funny thing about small towns. We've been programmed to think that if you oppose a current business or political agenda or religious belief, then you're a radical, a rebel. But isn't that what the American ideal is all about? And the same folks who fly their American flags day and night, chest-thumping about being Americans, don't want anyone to make anything better if it goes against the status quo.

I don't know a whole lot about our nation's history. Truth be told, I slept through most of my history classes as a kid and today can't seem to keep up with all the new little countries popping up or who's in charge of what. My brain's gone idle. But I do know that our founding fathers and mothers were rebels, men and women who'd just had it with the taxation on tea and one day said, *To hell with it!*

As I recall, they got pretty fired up, stirred up the neighbors, and agreed to have one major disagreement with the king across the way. It was a rebellion against a monarch's abuse of his subjects. In many ways, it was how Ms. Joanna Lucas came to little ol' Marcus. She didn't like the way her abusive monarch was treating her and had herself a little rebellion with a bloody tampon. With that thought, I realized the citizens of Marcus were also much overdue for a local rebellion.

Like I said, I don't know much, but what I do know is this: When an American business can come into a town, stink up the air, pollute the water and soil, and tell you everything is okay when animals and children are getting sick, our founding fathers and mothers are rolling over in their graves. When our own politicians are more interested in talking to big business than the little man, we are in trouble. I know when the government takes the side of business over public health, remnants of old King George's view of the colonials provides a firm reminder of what we're all about. People around here will try to say it's downright un-American to fight city hall, but it's as American as apple pie. Or throwing tea. And just as those early Americans had to get mad enough to throw their tea into the harbor, just as I had to get mad enough to throw my leg at Jack Frawley's truck, Joanna had to get mad about her situation.

She had been mistaken when she thought buying The Shady Land would liberate her. She'd been wrong in thinking that moving away and making a life of her own would liberate her. What she had to do was learn to stand up for herself. She had to learn to stand up and speak out, and that lesson came in the form of John Simmons. He would never know how responsible he was for his own undoing.

The girls had taken to Joanna. That was a fact. And not just because they saw her as a new force to fight pollution and greed. She was a friend. Joanna had become a regular at Quigley's Down Under. At first, she would show up with the pretense of ordering sandwiches for the money tree men, but she would linger. She would smile at Jeanie's outrageous comments and empathize with Merilee's profuse sweat glands. Customers came to know her name, greet her, and—on a few occasions—assume she was of the same mindset as Jeanie as she appeared to be amused by stupid questions and inane comments.

So by the time Joanna was invited to go with us to meet with John Simmons at City Hall one afternoon, it was natural. Dixie had arranged a meeting between us to discuss the proposed permit to burn four million tires in addition to everything else. The permit was to be grandfathered into a new law because, you see, if it's grandfathered in, actual pollution could not harm the fair citizens of Marcus. Dixie called bullshit and wanted a sit-down. Without hesitation, Joanna agreed to attend. Dressed in jeans, a worn white T-shirt, and flip flops, she had not intended to speak but merely listen. But a few minutes into the conversation, she could not hold her tongue. John told us that our health would be perfectly fine as we were beyond the two-mile radius of the cement plant's emissions. Dixie said she thought that was bologna since the rule for public health and safety used to be focused on anyone who lived within a twenty-mile radius. John said the new law was two miles, and I saw Joanna raise her eyebrows.

"Let me ask you something," Jeanie said. "If we're burning more things than ever before, how can you reduce the miles of who's affected? Ain't that kinda ass backward, John? That just don't make any sense to anyone, and you know it. Why, there's Kindle Park right there less than a mile from the plant with little kids playing on the swings and slides. What about that, John?" Everyone nodded, and then he said it. As sure as we were all sitting there, he said it and sealed his own fate with the slightest shrug. "That's the general public, and we're talking about individual households."

Joanna choked.

The rest of the girls laughed. We had heard this before. It was another trick, another ruse, another way to get around what they wanted, but Joanna was stunned. I think before she even realized it, she shot to her feet. "What? What did you just say? Did you just say the general public didn't matter?"

John shook his head but Joanna didn't stop. "Yes, you did. You just said that little kids—children on a playground—were the general public and didn't matter. You just . . . you just said that." She looked as though she might stagger backward, and Jeanie had begun to stand up to catch her, but Joanna backed up against a wall and braced herself. She ran her fingers through her hair and laughed. I saw Dixie and Jeanie exchange glances while Joanna laughed and shook her head.

"What world am I living in? What place is this?" She began to pace but then stopped. She turned and looked at John Simmons in a way that Tony the Tiger had once looked at me and said, "I know you. My God, I know you. You're running for office, but you have no intention of representing the people who will put you there. You really don't care about the general public. You're in this for you. You're a poser, a liar, a fraud. Worse, you're a bully and—" John stood up and began to protest, but Joanna stepped forward with a voice so loud it surprised us all.

"You're nothing more than a giant figurehead for corporate greed and destruction! You really don't care about the general public because they—we—are completely insignificant to you! Yeah, I know exactly who you are!" And with that, she excused herself and left the room.

I'd set out that day to tell her about my leg because it was a liberating moment for me when I pitched it away. Instead, she got a much better message from our local figurehead, and it set her in motion in a way I my leg couldn't.


* * * *

The very next day we'd decided to go to town to see what was up. We left Marcos standing by the car as Joanna pushed my chair into Quigley's Down Under. I offered to buy him something to eat, but I think all the women made him nervous. Especially Jeanie. Every time she said something, she looked over to him and asked, "*¿Comprendo?*" She was convinced that he knew more English than he was lettin' on, and there was some kind of plot all the Latinos had, pretending not to understand us and then laughing behind our backs.

As soon as we entered the café, it was Jeanie as usual. She was playing her favorite game, "What would you rather eat?"

"I don't care," Dixie said. "I'd rather eat the head."

"That's disgusting," Jeanie said.

Another thing about Jeanie's games. She asked you which you would rather: eat a turtle's head or intestines, sleep with Dick Cheney or Richard Nixon in his day, or lick a toilet or a kitty litter box. But in the end, if your answer didn't match hers, it was wrong. It was wrong and disgusting.

"But you've already got intestines inside of you," Jeanie said while Merilee made faces behind the counter.

"So? Just because I have intestines doesn't mean I want to eat someone else's," Dixie said and scrunched up her face at Jeanie.

"Jeanie Archer!" I bellowed, causing everyone to jump. It was my customary way of saying hello without all the formalities. "You're dang near forty-seven years old, if you ain't already. When are you going to stop asking people if they'd eat a turtle's head?"

All heads swung around, all smiling.

"It's an important social question," Jeanie deadpanned and Joanna balked.

"Eating a turtle's head?"

"Sure. You can tell a lot about a person by whether they'd rather eat a turtle's head—eyes and snout and all—over intestines, which, by the way, you already possess." She looked at Dixie again as though sealing her argument. She pointed a finger to Joanna. "Which would you rather eat?"

"The head . . . there's less to eat," Joanna said seriously.

"An excellent point!" Jeanie thundered. Since Joanna's outburst with John Simmons, Joanna had done the near impossible. She had breached the inner circle of respect with Jeanie Archer, and almost every answer Joanna gave was excellent.

Jeanie stood over a table with several newspapers spread open. She looked as though she were reading them all at the same time. I recognized a few folks from town in the back corner, taking their lunch break. Most were ignoring Jeanie, although she did entertain people with her insane questions. I saw Della Wright smirking over her chicken salad croissant. She would stomp the turtle dead herself and eat both the head and intestines. She was a four-time rodeo champion and tougher than a coyote.

Dixie perched on the edge of her stool behind the cash register while Merilee continued to make sandwiches. As had become habit, Ruthie and Jeanie toiled over newspapers and were discussing pressing matters about turtle heads and intestines when we came in. The mood changed right away as John Simmons entered the building.

You can tell a lot about a person by the way a room changes when she enters. The room sort of sighs with contentment when Ruthie walks in. Jeanie and Dixie make everything electric, the way a bunch of kids get when they scuff their shoes over a shag carpet—giddy with the anticipation of shocking each other. Jeanie and Dixie have the same effect on a room of adults.

John Simmons walked in, and there was instant, uncomfortable silence. Della Wright continued to chew, but she was suddenly serious and very alert. She looked like she was watching a breaking news bulletin on television.

"Ladies," John said. His voice was deep.

"John." Dixie's voice was syrupy sweet. "It's been a while since you been in here. What can I do ya for?"

"I'll take a coffee." He looked around as though he figured he ought to order something to have a real reason to be inside

Quigley's. Dixie nodded and hopped off her stool.

"What are you doing there?" He ambled over toward Jeanie. His demeanor was pleasant and breezy, as though he had come in on a whim, as though we hadn't just been in his office confronting him on his politics. But this was his way. Out in public, he was a buddy to everyone.

Jeanie drew her eyebrows together and pursed her lips. "Well, John . . ." she said, doing her best imitation of a game show host. She had that "tell him what he's won!" voice and the girls settled in for the show. Ruthie cut eyes to Dixie and smiled.

"I'm checking the newspapers every day for any public notices or hearing dates for anything that concerns the public health in regards to FFI. Because I can't trust the TCEQ or EPA, as they appear to be either completely incompetent or in the pocket of local industry, I have to look on behalf of the public. I'm now part of a private citizens group that has taken up the charge."

"I take offense at that." He was not amused.

"Again? Well, now why on earth would you, John? This has nothing to do with you. You're no longer affiliated with Future Foundations. I didn't mean anything against you." She smiled sweetly.

If he'd come in to play nice, to pretend to be that congressional candidate who was concerned about our feelings and opinions, the charade was gone.

"I came in here to tell you to knock it off, Jeanie. Now, I mean it. This has all gone far enough." He stepped a little closer. "You're playing with a huge corporation with lawyers who will chew you up and spit you out. You don't know what you're up against, and you're causing too much trouble."

"I'm causing trouble?" Jeanie stood up straight and stared at John. "I'm causing trouble . . . because I'm invested in the health of the public? Or am I causing trouble because I care about how many different chemicals are pumped into my air? Or because I just don't want to get cancer while someone else gets richer?

Which is it?" Jeanie looked around the room. "I'm confused."
"Jeanie, you know good and well that you're just stirrin' the pot."
As his temper rose, so did his drawl, and I had to smile. Jeanie
could piss off a ladybug once she got going.

"John? Do you, by any chance, know Julie Perkins? You know
her kid, Joshua? He's about twelve years old and almost the same
size as Julie. Big kid. Problem with that is . . . Joshua is mentally
retarded, blind, deaf, he's got cerebral palsy. He's got lung issues,
kidney issues, hell . . . if there's an issue to have, he's got it.
Basically, he's a human vegetable. And I'm not tryin' to be mean
when I say that, I'm just layin' it out there. Am I right?" Jeanie
looked at the girls for a moment. Some nodded.

"Couple of weeks ago, ol' Tim Perkins just up and walked out
on 'em, said he couldn't handle it anymore. But here's the funny
part, John." There was an extra punch when Jeanie said his name.
"Just down the street from the Perkins are two other families with
kids with similar problems, all born around the same time as each
other, which would leave many to conclude that something was
indeed in the air at the time."

"Now, you may not know Julie Perkins but surely you've heard
of Tim. He works for you . . . or, at least, he did. He's an employee
of FFI. Hell, you can bet he brought home some of that arsenic and
lead, mercury, benzene, and dioxins on his clothing, but he can't
handle his son anymore. He can't handle the issues." Jeanie
stepped a little closer to John, and for a moment, I wasn't sure if
she was going to hit him or cry. We all held our breath.

"Here's the funny thing, John. Julie can't handle Joshua either.
Like . . . literally. He's too big, too heavy. The medical costs are
too much. So, she's taking money from the state. Now, I'm
thinking that's wrong. I'm thinking that it's pretty ironic that a
company man walks out on his kid; the company doesn't care
about the kid, any kid, for that matter. The state of Texas says big
business should be able to do as it pleases, but now all these
families are on welfare, takin' state money, and everything is

screwed up. People are getting sicker, no one seems to care as long as palms are gettin' greased, but"—she laughed out loud in a forced, barking sound—"I am causing trouble."

There was an awful silence that seemed to last for minutes as Jeanie and John stared at each other.

Dixie walked up behind him, a cup of coffee balanced in her hand. John looked at the coffee for another moment and drew in a long breath as though he was meditating. He exhaled and managed a perfect smile.

"You girls don't understand all that is at stake here."

"Please, explain it to us," Jeanie mirrored his smile and sat back down.

"I tried to tell you this earlier when you—" He stopped and looked around the room until he saw Joanna. "Marcus is fixin' to make major changes. We're going to build a big football stadium and—"

The quiet and always-reasonable Ruthie spoke up. "Why would we build a large and expensive football stadium when we can't even win a football game?"

Della snickered from the back of the room. "It's that good ol' boy mentality. Build it and they will come." Hers was a deep, ghostly voice.

There were some chuckles, and John scowled.

"You girls don't know what you're dealing with," he said in a threatening tone.

It was a funny thing about the term *girls*. The girls called themselves *the girls,* and no one batted an eyelash. It was said with affection and devotion to one another. John said *girls,* and there was a bite to it.

Dixie pulled back the coffee and cocked her head. "Is there something you want to come out and say, John?"

"Yeah. I'll tell you what I want to say. We have your canister, and if you trespass again, we'll prosecute." He looked down at Dixie and her cup of coffee. "I think I'll pass." He waved a hand

and strode out, leaving the women to stare after him.

"What the hell was that supposed to mean?" Jeanie asked and looked around the room at the confused women.

Ruthie shrugged.

"What canister? What's he talkin' about a canister?"

# 21

In the months that followed, several different, unhappy events occurred in rapid succession. It felt masterfully and tragically choreographed in a way I had never experienced before. One of our most popular schoolteachers died of a brain tumor. She was just forty-two years old. The TCEQ awarded the tire-burning permit to FFI despite a growing public protest. Brianna had become a near stranger to the girls, and despite all the noise we were making, John Simmons was an early frontrunner in the US Congress polls by a notable number and had already proclaimed how he would be focusing on enhancing business opportunities in the state. And in the midst of it all, I developed a cough.

At first, we all thought the cough had begun after the fire, and most everyone believed it was just a combination of stress and smoke inhalation. But after weeks of coughing, I had to admit it wasn't going away and agreed to see a specialist outside of Marcus. Joanna took it upon herself to shuttle me from appointment to appointment, and I will admit that I rather liked that. She found me a specialist in Waco and dragged me out for more detailed tests.

It seems that on top of bronchitis and emphysema, I need a new heart. Mine is failing. But in all reality, I don't know if I will ever get one. So, for now, my life will include the constant presence of an oxygen tank. It had made me think about my sweet darling, and I had felt sad. But this was just the beginning of my troubles.

I'd received this information just days after learning the results from the private investigator I'd hired regarding the cause of the fire. I put the town of Marcus on notice that I aimed to sue based on the presumption that it was not lightning, but man who started the fire.

Danged if I wasn't right. The investigator discovered a can with traces of gasoline, an igniter, and a timer that had been used to set the fire. With no one home to put it out, it spread quickly. Proving just who started the fire was another matter.

The city had countered. An animal activist organization no one had ever heard of had filed a lawsuit against me for cruel and inhumane treatment of exotic animals that ultimately led to their demise.

For his own protection, Eduardo had to be caged full time. Manuel and the other men had built a large pen for Eduardo to live in. While it was no secret that the men liked this plan so that they could finally drink beer on the patio in safety, they felt badly for Eduardo and were sometimes given to sneaking a few drinks to him.

Joanna seemed to withdraw. She spent more and more time in her studio, working entire days away without ever once stepping outside. Joanna's lawyer friend, Marcus Watkins, lobbied hard for her to leave her new home. But she refused.

She was the lone bright spot for me. Instead of running away, Joanna had appeared to dig in deeper. Never once had she suggested that I leave The Shady Land. In fact, as the house neared completion, Rolando and Andres moved in. The entire crew could have moved into the house for all Joanna would notice. She almost lived in the barn.

Little by little, I watched from my window as Roberto moved a miniature refrigerator, a microwave, and various pieces of furniture down to the barn. Day and night, I caught glimpses of Joanna working away. But as much as I wanted to see what she was doing, I could not. My chair would not go down the incline, and though I didn't want to admit it out loud, my physical condition had worsened. Physical activity became just about impossible.

But if I had a coughing spell, Joanna would hotfoot it up to the house to check on me. There were times when I wished my precious could see Joanna. If we had ever been able to have a daughter, she would be just like Joanna. I knew it.

But for this wonderful feeling, everything seemed to be drawing to a dark close. It seemed to be the end of almost everything. I could feel it. Hovering. Heavy.

Then, on a breezy and cool day, the phone rang.

"Girllll, are you okay?" I knew that voice. It was Tallulah Walker.

"Yes, why?" I braced myself for whatever madness Tallulah had to say next.

"All of you? All the girls, I mean. They all okay?" Tallulah was whispering. But clearly, she was calling from work at the Dairy Queen.

"Yes. I mean, I guess so. Why?" I wasn't in the mood for any of Tallulah's nonsense.

"Girl, you need to get down here. It's all anybody's talkin' about. They caught one of . . . well, I thought it was one of you girls." Even while she was talking, I could hear the lunch rush clatter in the background. "You sure everyone's okay?"

"For hell's sake, Tallulah. What are you talking about?"

"Frank Wolan and 'em are in here talkin' 'bout last night. One of those traps they got set up there at FFI . . . it went off. They caught 'em one of . . . well, one of you guys."

"What? Who caught what? What are you talkin' about?" I leaned forward in my chair, trying to get a better handle on what

Tallulah was going on about.

With Tallulah, it could be something or it could be nothing, but something in her voice and talk of a trap going off set the hairs on the back of my neck on end.

"The trap. One 'em traps Frank set out caught a human. Or parts of one. They're in here right now." Tallulah was breathing so hard, I could barely understand her. But I knew whatever she was saying was real enough. She sounded both scared and excited. "It has some little hunk of flesh and some jean material stuck in the teeth."

"A trap! A steel trap? Like a wild game trap?"

"Yes, and Frank's up here right now braggin' 'bout how he got hisself a human."

"Well, who? Who is it?"

"I don't know!" Her voice shot up. There was a pause as she caught herself and calmed down again. "That's why I'm callin' you," she whispered.

My mind reeled, and I knew I had to talk to the girls.

"I'm callin' to say be sure that no one goes to a doctor or anything. Not around here. Not even a vet. They're talkin' about how they've made calls to every nurse, doctor, vet, and midwife. You name it, they've called and are waitin' for someone up to show up with a leg wound."

She clicked off, leaving me to stare at the phone in my hand for a moment.

"Damn!" I bolted upright, stabbing the phone's keypad.

"Quigley's Down Under."

"Hey, Merilee! Is Dixie there?" I wheezed into the phone. The sudden excitement had made it hard to breathe.

"Nah. This Suzette?"

"Yeah, listen—"

"Well, hey, Suzette. You can't say hi no more?"

"Hi. Listen. Do you know where she is? It's real important."

"Nope. She said something came up. Her and Jeanie are

somewhere. What's wrong?"

"Nothing. I'll . . . um, I'll call you later." I hung up the phone and then dialed both Dixie's and Jeanie's cell phone numbers. There was no answer, so I called Ruthie's home phone number and then her cell. On its third ring, Ruthie answered.

"Hello?"

"Ruthie, oh, thank goodness. You okay?"

"Uh, yeah."

"What about Dixie and Jeanie. You know where they are?"

"Well, yeah, they're right here with—"

"Are they okay? Are they hurt or . . ." I swallowed hard. I could feel a lump in my stomach.

"No. What's the matter?" Ruthie spoke too slowly for my comfort.

"Where are you?"

"We're here with Brianna."

*Brianna.*

My heart fell. "Is she okay?"

There was a pause. A painful, worrisome pause.

"Hello? Ruthie?" My heart pounded in my chest.

"Not . . . really," Ruthie said quietly.

"Oh, no. Where are you?"

"We're at Springwood Park. We didn't want anyone to see us."

I slammed down the phone and called for Joanna.

* * * *

He traced his finger along her abdomen, and she smiled. For a moment, she watched the finger. She liked how it looked against her own skin. She liked the contrast, and she wondered about that. As an artist, she'd always been drawn to stark color contrast.

Roberto's hands were a deep brown and looked even darker against her pale stomach. Her gaze traveled up the length of his arm to his shoulder and then to his face, just inches from hers. She smiled.

"You don't go so far away." He teased her. He moved in, kissing her along her chin and jaw line, and she tilted her head and closed her eyes, taking in each kiss.

"I didn't." Her smile broadened. "I have no other place to go." She laughed as he began kissing her neck. "I've given you all my money!"

"But I am worth it?" His accent was so thick there were times she could not understand everything that he said to her. As always, she got the general idea, and that was enough.

"Hmm." She pretended to think that over, and he growled, climbing on top of her. She gagged and wheezed even though he'd not put five pounds of pressure on her. Hovering over her on his hands and knees, he flashed a huge grin, and she giggled.

Both Joanna and Roberto were dressed in jeans and T-shirts. Only their feet were bare. They were taking things slowly. For the first time in her life, Joanna had a boyfriend who treated her like a lady. There was kissing and touching but no more. Roberto was the perfect gentleman.

"Fine. My job is done. I will go."

She frowned at him. "Oh, no. You have to completely renovate this barn. This is . . ." She glanced around, trying to look disgusted. "This is unacceptable to me!"

As he crawled over her, she drew up her knees, laughing all the while.

"So bossy. Bossy, bossy lady," he murmured against her neck.

He felt so good against her body. It was so much more than his physical body. It was the way he growled and played with her. It was the way he looked at her and talked to her. The irony was, half the time she wasn't sure what he was saying, but she felt more connected to him than any person she could ever recall.

In the privacy of the barn, she and Roberto could be together. Roberto had carried in a futon for her to use when she worked late, and bit by bit, he'd created a place for her, complete with pillows and blankets.

She'd found paradise in a worn-down old barn.

She relaxed, letting her knees fall to each side so that he could nestle between her legs, lying so lightly yet so completely against her. With a sigh, she laid her head against the pillow and closed her eyes as he began to trace her again with his hand.

"Joanna!"

Both Roberto and Joanna jumped.

It was Marcos.

* * * *

Frank Wolan was a giant ass.

In my view, he was the worst kind of American imaginable. He lived up to every negative stereotype of the redneck Texan. He didn't read a newspaper. He held hard and fast to certain political views without understanding the whats and whys of any of them. He believed only the information that was spoon-fed to him by ultraconservative right-wingers. And he refused to hear anything negative about FFI.

This last characteristic was the most vexing.

If you loved something—be it your house, your town, your company, or your country—and there was something wrong with it, you fixed it. You fixed it because you loved it and believed that it was worth repairing or improving. That's where the love came in. But today's Americans were in denial. They subscribed to the notion that if you identified a problem, you were un-American, an alarmist, or a troublemaker.

It was a new side to conservatism that would have made Ronald Reagan sad. If something looked bad, cover it up, conceal the truth, and attack those who would try to right a wrong. Frank was a heavy subscriber to this way of thinking.

They knew this going in. They knew that bastard Frank had taken their canister. They knew they would never get it back and had gone to great lengths to alert their contacts about possible inquiries and investigations.

To their horror, they had discovered that Frank had set traps. Actual steel-toothed, spring-loaded, iron traps that would sever a leg if snapped in the right—or wrong—place.

Among themselves, they had nicknamed Frank "Little Karl." He was Little Karl Rove. If they said Little Karl's place, it meant the back property of FFI.

They went to Little Karl's.

The loss of the first canister was problematic. Not only was it expensive, not only was it not theirs to lose, but it had tipped off the enemy. But they were working on a schedule, and they needed more evidence, so without asking questions, another canister was sent to them with a note.

"Be careful. We need this one back. Ticktock."

Perhaps they would have been more careful had they not been moving so quickly. Perhaps the night goggles had given them false confidence. It was pointless, but very human, to sit back and analyze what had gone wrong.

After their first canister had been confiscated and they'd discovered the animal traps, they'd returned to Little Karl's four times. Each time, they were a little more nervous, aware of the growing danger. Statistically speaking, it was only a matter of time before they'd be caught. They just hadn't imagined it would be so literally.

In record time, they'd fanned out and located the new canister. Days before, they'd set out two canisters. One was disguised in a fake mesquite tree. It was, to say the least, brilliant. The other, a useless decoy, lay precariously on its side some fifty feet away with a few twigs against it to give the illusion of a pathetic attempt to camouflage it.

The decoy was gone, and the real canister was intact and ready.

There was a quiet sense of satisfaction among the group as they headed back. Perhaps this was why they were not paying as much attention to their route.

The focus at that point was to get back to the truck as soon as possible. Already, their minds were racing. *Get back to the truck. Get back to the house. Prepare for the road trip.* They would not send *this* canister by mail or courier. They would take this one to the laboratory personally.

The sound snapped them back to reality. It was brutal. The sickening sigh and click of a metal latch releasing. The anguished cry. It was even more horrific in that it was carried out in whispers, heavy panting, and gasps of gut-wrenching pain.

They moved quickly, amid the quiet sobs, getting a shoulder up and under each arm to hurry their pace back to the truck to see the extent of the damage and to get out before anyone else was hurt.

There was blood. There was fear. But there was also a new kind of anger. They weren't doing this out of boredom or vandalism. Children were getting sick, and politicians were not paying attention. Citizens were being hospitalized, and industry was profiting with a sense of entitlement rather than any sense of fellowship. People were dying, and the citizens were being lied to by those who were supposed to be looking out for them. And now, someone who cared about those friends and family and neighbors, about the welfare of the town, had been critically hurt by Frank Wolan. Someone was going to pay.

# 22

Paul Cowell stood at the helm of the conveyer belt, arms folded across his chest. His mouth was drawn around the toothpick he chewed on so diligently while staring at the machinery in front of him. Several men stood around him—all with their arms folded, all staring at the conveyer belt, all periodically looking at Paul to see what he wanted to do next.

"Shit!" Paul shook his head in disgust. This was not what he needed.

Ian Jackson was visiting later in the week. Everyone was well aware of Gustoff Mattias's "surprise visit" to the site. The Marcus News was coming out to do a piece on the million-dollar machinery that had been the star of the huge debate. Now this.

"Turn it off," he said. Only Rodney Strobel moved. Everyone stood as they had been, staring at the conveyor belt.

For two years, FFI had lobbied to burn tires. Environmentalists had cried foul, naming all the metals in tire treads as additional toxic poisoning, not to mention the emissions that came from their burning. Mercury levels would rise, as would benzene and styrene levels, a huge red flag in the national green community as the latter two pollutants were linked closely with cancer. But Ian and his associates had done nothing short of a spectacular snow job to convince the TCEQ that by using tires as an alternative fuel to heat the kilns, the levels of carbon dioxide could be drastically reduced by burning less coal.

It had placed the greenies in a very difficult corner. They were always crying about how dirty coal was, so to be able to reduce carbon dioxide emissions had been their number one cause. Which one was more important?

While they were busy chewing on that, Ian had gone to work on another alternative fuel. Glycerin. The beautiful, gloppy glycerin used in the pharmaceutical and food industries. The problem was that the sudden emergence and mass production of glycerin posed a serious challenge to industry worldwide because no one knew what to do with it when no longer needed. It was difficult to burn, and with the growing glut of this compound, corporations had taken to pumping it back into the earth. But in their never-ending quest for alternative and cheap fuels, cement plants had a solution. For a fee, they could dispose of the unwanted liquid waste and recycle it.

State legislators loved it; all they heard were the key words—recycle and profit. Crisis averted.

In turn, the cement plant industry could reasonably ask to add another solid fuel to its "test burn" inventory—for example, petroleum coke that could only be described as the very dirty coal-like material of carbon. It was no surprise the environmentalists didn't like it, but Ian had found a way to spin this as well. Like the liquid glycerin, the cement plants provided a public service by eliminating these hydrocarbons.

It was an effective legal one-two punch that would satisfy politicians and their claim to support recycling while generating huge profit margins and product. In turn, FFI touted an environmental friendly stance in its quarterly newsletter and promised its neighbors they were green and concerned.

Paul stared down at the machine. And it all rested on punch number one. The hopper. Tires were shredded in the chipper, a loud and large machine with rotating blades, and sent to the hopper that spread the tire chips on the conveyer belt. Everything was synchronized so that the chips could feed the fire in a large kiln. Everything was about feeding the fire.

People did not understand what it took to make fire. They could not conceptualize the heat and materials needed for the process. To generate twenty-seven hundred degrees Fahrenheit, the plant needed everything it could get. And yes, the demand for alternative fuels was on the rise.

In truth, Paul wasn't wild about some of the things they were burning, but they needed heat and heat required fuel. Bottom line—this was his job. He had a fancy title and all kinds of accolades on his office walls. In the end, he was the guy in charge of producing heat. Lots and lots of heat. Successful test cases with tire chips would lead to more ways to procure and burn off glycerin, which would ultimately open the door for the intake of petroleum coke.

But now the damned chipper was overheating and allowing large and uneven clumps of tire to fall into the kiln, causing irregular and uneven distribution of emissions. Huge plumes of heavy smoke puffed out anywhere from two to twenty minutes apart.

He ran his fingers through his hair. He couldn't have this, not with TCEQ air samplings on the line and not with Gustoff Mattias coming.

It would be hard to sell good public relations with great clouds of dark gray smoke billowing from the stacks outside.

"Just turn the damned thing off," he said again. Maintenance alone on the chipper would far outweigh its efficiency costs. And Paul knew from past history what was coming next. As soon as the company took a hit financially, they would start cutting corners. Again.

* * * *

Joanna took a few more shots from her digital camera, making sure she had several good angles to show the press. She wanted to make sure that everyone could see just how close the elementary school would be to the quarry site.

It was less than two football field lengths away.

And, astonishingly, when she called the FFI public relations department about this, she was told, "Well, I hardly think it's that close."

"I measured it," Joanna said to the man, and there was a long pause.

"We're in compliance," he said in an unemotional voice.

"Are you serious? You're honestly telling me that you're okay with putting a quarry next to an elementary school with children . . . some who are so young their little lungs are still developing or who already have asthma?"

There was another long, unhappy pause and then the man did something few people of late had been able to do. He shocked Joanna Lucas.

"Well, we were here first."

"What?" Joanna asked, not understanding.

"That land. We had it before the school was built. We were here first." This was his explanation, and to that, Joanna had nothing else to say.

Later, when she repeated the conversation to the stunned patrons of Quigley's Down Under, her blood began to boil. Only then did she begin to put the pieces together. Only then did it occur to her the Marcus school board would have agreed to knowingly purchase land next to a proposed quarry site and the city board members would have knowingly allowed it. And only then did it dawn on everyone that this was not just about the cement plant or pollution but about ownership and entitlement. This was about land and what you could do with it.

Pump it, drill it, strip it, rape it, poison it, and build a quarry site right next to an elementary school because the money was right.

The general public really did not matter.

At closing, Joanna walked out with Dixie to her car.

"Honey, this isn't new. It doesn't make it right, but it's not new," Dixie said, but suddenly frowned. Ruthie and Jeanie were sitting on the hood of her vehicle, both holding their breath.

"What are you two doing?" she asked when they reached her giant Suburban. They looked ridiculous. Neither one spoke, each eyeing the other one for a sign of weakness.

Dixie rolled her eyes, exhaling. She shifted her weight to one hip and checked her wristwatch, watching the second hand.

The idiots were having a breath-holding contest.

"No sense in talking anymore until someone gives in. It should only be a matter of seconds, though. Ruthie looks like she's going to fall off the car," Dixie stage-whispered to Joanna.

Ruthie rocked back and forth on the hood, making strange, gas-like noises. Despite herself, Joanna began to laugh.

When Ruthie began stomping her foot on the front bumper, Dixie checked her watch again.

"Five, four, three . . ."

Ruthie made a final noise and then gasped for air.

Jeanie consulted her watch, still holding her breath. Dixie just stared, suppressing a smile. "They're idiots, but they're entertaining," Dixie said to Joanna as more seconds ticked off.

"I had one minute and eighteen seconds," Ruthie bragged.

"That's very good," Dixie said as though she were talking to a small child. But Ruthie was in no condition to notice. She focused on taking long, steady breaths.

"Dang, Jeanie," she said, looking at her watch.

Jeanie exhaled with a cough and struggled for composure as she spoke, "One minute, forty seconds. That's better than last time."

Ruthie waved a hand in gratitude, still fighting for air.

"Why?" Joanna began.

"This is it? You two sit around having breath-holding contests?" Dixie asked.

"Hey, it's pertinent information," Jeanie said, and Ruthie grinned.

"Pertinent information." Dixie eyed her, then shooed them both off the hood.

As they climbed into the Suburban, Jeanie continued in all seriousness. "We could be driving down the road and accidentally drive into a lake. When rescuers come, you could say, 'Hey, they've been down there in the water for over a minute. Jeanie can hold her breath for one minute and forty seconds, but Ruthie can't!' "

Joanna laughed out loud.

"Ah," Dixie said and started the car. "So, should you guys ever drive into a lake and I'm standing around to see this, I should time how long you're down there?"

"I think you've missed the point entirely." Jeanie settled back into her seat.

"Oh, no. I think I've got it." Dixie winked at Joanna.

"So, you get good pictures?" Ruthie asked Joanna, struggling to sound even-keeled again.

"I think so."

"I guess we'll find out," Dixie said.

"You think maybe that's what Terry is talking about when he says we're bad for Brianna? You think stupid breathing contests are what he's talking about?" Dixie asked somberly.

"I think unless we stay home baking cookies, he's gonna have a problem with us," Ruthie said.

"So . . . how about standing on the side of the road taking pictures of a future quarry site to give to the media in an effort to expose our corrupt soon-to-be new congressional representative . . . What? Not so good?" Jeanie cocked her head, a look of innocence washed over her face.

"Ha. Not so much." Dixie tried to laugh.

"I miss Brianna," Ruthie said. "She just looked so . . . so sad." Despite her protests at the park, Brianna looked like a shell of her former self. She'd been quiet, withdrawn, and tired looking. In the words of Jeanie, Brianna was beat down. It had been difficult for her friends to see. Slowly, it seemed, Terry was winning. But not for long. Jeanie had promised this much. They would continue to reach out to her, call her, text her, sneak out to see her when Terry was away.

She had promised them that she wasn't mad, but she needed a break. She promised that Terry hadn't been any worse than usual, she was just tired of all the fighting and thought that if she gave domestic life a better shot, maybe her marriage would improve. She had told them with little passion and even less conviction that she loved Terry and wanted to make things work.

To that, there was little the girls could say. They'd hugged her, wished her well, and asked her to call or stop by Quigley's.

"You know," Ruthie said, interrupting everyone from their thoughts of Brianna. "Us giving a picture of the quarry to the paper isn't going to endear us anymore to Terry."

"Maybe he doesn't realize how bad things are," Joanna said, and the other women laughed.

"Oh, he knows." Jeanie growled.

"Why does he have to know it was us? Who says we can't just offer up the picture and a story idea to Ted and be done with it?" Dixie asked.

Ruthie glanced out the window. "Right. We're in, we're out . . . we can provide the picture as a scoop to Ted. He's a story hound; he'll love it."

It was, however brief, a perfect solution to the girls. Fight local politics and win Brianna back.

They had not counted on Myra Thompson.

Myra was wedged into a chair across from Ted McKee's desk. One hip was hitched up to the side so she would fit in the chair better, causing her skirt to be askew. She looked uncomfortable, though she was doing her damnedest to look comfortable.

She was in the middle of doing what the girls said she did best—gossiping.

According to Jeanie, Ted had long ago created a gossip column for Myra. It was his way of letting her be the town gossip and still dish the dirt in his paper. It only made the paper more of a town joke. He was a hack, printing only what he deemed to be news. He refused to write about or print anything about complicated issues that he could not understand, such as the Middle East or the inner workings of Congress, stating that his purpose was to report local news. What he wrote about or how he wrote was dictated by who advertised with him. No surprise, Future Foundations was a big client, so he never reported on the TCEQ or EPA hearings, public nuisance complaints of which there were many in regards to strange odors, or the dangers of cement kiln dust. He actively ignored medical studies on the disproportionably high numbers of children born with medical problems, and he refused to investigate local politicians and their relationships with the cement plant. But pictures of a proposed quarry next to an elementary school, the girls believed, was sure to spark enough controversy that even Ted would run it in his paper. They had to hope that this once, just this once, he would think about how many parents would be enraged by this and buy a copy of the paper.

Instead, he glanced at the picture in Joanna's camera, handed it to Myra for a peek, and chuckled. "That's not news. We've known about that site for years," he said, his tone condescending.

Dixie, Joanna, Ruth, and Jeanie all exchanged glances. Dixie stepped forward. "You knew about a future quarry site next to an elementary school and didn't think that was news?"

"Dixie," Ted said with a heavy sigh. "They've owned that

property for some twenty years now. This isn't news. It's just been sittin' there, and I expect it's gonna keep sittin' there for another twenty. Hell, you can ask Eva Tobey. She's the one who sold it to 'em. She brokered the deal." He glanced at Myra and rolled his eyes.

"What?" Joanna's voice sounded more like a gasp. "She brokered a deal to put an elementary school next to a quarry site? A toxic quarry site?"

"Why do you care all of a sudden?" Ted asked Dixie, ignoring Joanna.

"Yeah." Myra attempted to turn herself in her chair without success. "What's it got to do with you?"

Dixie shook her head. Joanna stood, motionless, speechless. Jeanie slowly turned to Myra. "What does little children's health have to do with us? Hmm. No, no . . ." she said and wagged a finger at Ruthie. "Don't tell me. Let me work this out on my own . . ." Jeanie tapped her finger against her chin, staring up at the ceiling. "What do children and their future here in Marcus . . . have to do . . . how are they any of my concern?"

Dixie pushed Jeanie to the side, giving a combined look of humor and irritation.

"C'mon, Ted. Even *you* can see that this is news."

"Even *I* can see? Well, now, what the hell kind of comment is that?" Ted bristled from behind his desk.

Myra continued to watch Jeanie with growing agitation.

"I cannot believe Eva Tobey brokered that deal," Joanna said.

"Children get sick in my neighborhood . . ." Jeanie said and continued to tap her chin and stare at the ceiling. Ruthie, ever the faithful audience for her buddy, cocked her head, pretending to wait for the answer. "Hmm. And . . . and I have a fair idea ahead of time that this could be a problem . . ."

"Oh, for hell's sake, Jeanie! You're not funny," Myra said, huffing.

"I think she's funny," Ruthie said, winking at Jeanie.

"No!" Dixie whirled on Myra, standing just inches from her chair and towering over her. Myra shrunk back. "You're right about that. None of this is funny! You all knew that there was land designated to be a quarry right next to an elementary school!"

"I'm funny," Jeanie said.

"What the hell is wrong with you people? Don't you have kids of your own? Don't you care about other children?" Dixie was on a tear, waving Joanna's digital camera around.

"Who builds a quarry next to an elementary school," Joanna said to no one in particular.

"They're probably not even going to do anything with it," Ted said, growing concerned by Dixie's outburst.

"Who approves *having* a quarry next to an elementary school," Joanna continued speaking to herself.

"It's a tricky kind of humor," Jeanie said to Ruthie, the only person listening.

"They just put out a sign saying it's a future quarry site, and when we asked FFI about it, they just said they were here first." Dixie slapped a hand on her hip and glowered.

"But you actually need to have a sense of humor to get mine. See, that's how it works," Jeanie said, giving Myra a little poke. Myra jumped as though she'd forgotten Jeanie was in the room. As soon as she looked at her, Jeanie gave a reassuring nod.

"You called," Myra said, furrowing her brows at Jeanie but turning to Dixie, "FFI to complain? Why'd you do that?"

"She didn't," Joanna stepped forward. "I did."

"Why'd she—" Dixie choked a laugh. She looked to both Jeanie and Ruthie for support.

Jeanie shrugged. "The woman has no humor."

"You're just tryin' to stir up trouble. That's all this is about, Dixie. You and your . . ." Myra draw an imaginary line between the three women with her finger. "And you." She pointed to Joanna. "Can't you see what they're doin'? They are dragging you into their little game!"

"You think putting an elementary school next to a quarry is a game?" Joanna asked incredulously.

"I want to know what you meant by *even I* could see that it was news." Ted was still fixated on Dixie.

"I made the huge mistake of thinking that you could, for once, get your head out of John Simmons's ass long enough to see news. But I was wrong." Dixie threw down the challenge, and he stiffened. "I forgot that you're an advertising whore and not a news hound. My mistake." Dixie gave a jerk of the head to the girls and started to turn. "I won't mistake this place for an actual newspaper again. Not that anyone ever does."

"It's no wonder Terry Smart can't stand you all," Myra said, and a little smile played on her lips. "It's good that he put a stop to—"

Jeanie moved like a cat. One moment, she had been preening her stand-up routine. The next, she was in Myra Thompson's face with nary an ounce of humor in her voice.

"Oh, that's right. You and Terry are best buds now, aren't you? How does that work? How does it work when a pathetic, fat warthog manages to become friends with a wife beater?" Myra's mouth fell open.

"Do you convince him that you need his wife for company since you got no one else? Or does he convince you he's husband of the year and has nothing but the best of intentions for his wife— the wife he likes to abuse . . . and abuse . . . and abuse!" With each sentence, Jeanie's voice grew louder and louder.

"Now, hold on! Terry beats his wife?" There was an air of excitement in Ted's voice.

"Yeah. He belittles her and demeans her and abuses her and screams at her and makes her feel like crap!" Jeanie couldn't stop herself. Dixie and Ruthie knew they couldn't stop her either. Joanna looked back and forth between the women, uncertain as to what she should do.

Jeanie was frantic. The crack and pitch of her voice told them all they needed to know. Jeanie couldn't stop herself.

"And the only people she's got in her life, that she's ever had in her life who make her happy and make her laugh and maybe, just for a few hours here and there, make her forget what a shithole life and a shitwad husband she has, he puts a stop to her seeing us because he wouldn't want to lose his abusive control over her!" Silence fell over the small office. No one moved.

Jeanie became very aware of how close her face was to Myra's. A tiny bit of spittle glistened on the right cheek of Myra's big face, but Myra didn't dare move to wipe it away. She merely blinked until Jeanie pulled back.

"But then," Jeanie said, straightening her shirt, "you bein' who are you, I reckon you already know all about that, now don't you?"

Myra swallowed hard.

Jeanie turned and walked out, and as she did, it hit her. "Oh, man, what have I done?"

# 23

"You sold land to FFI?" Dixie burst into Eva's real estate office. She had dropped off Jeanie, Ruthie, and Joanna before she'd doubled back. She didn't want interference when she talked to Eva.

This wasn't going to be businesswoman to businesswoman. Hell, she knew how much FFI had probably paid for that piece of land. She wasn't going to begrudge her a smart deal. This was personal. She and Eva had history, and she wanted to be alone to talk in peace. Over the years, they had shared a lover and then fought bitterly over him, unaware of his other infidelities. They then reached an agreement, an unusual kind of friendship based on a shared embarrassment and hurt. Eva had helped Dixie establish Quigley's Down Under and in turn, Dixie had always steered business to Eva. They understood each other.

Eva was sitting at her oversized desk, swamped with papers and file folders, holding a phone with one hand and a shoe in her other. She looked up, her facial expression frozen. A half second later, she turned in her chair, said something quietly into the phone, and hung up.

"Is there something you wanted, Dixie?" she asked as she turned back, slipping her shoe back on.

Ever-confident, ever-cool Eva Tobey. She was dressed to the
nines, having an air of confidence, of big cities, of higher
education, of world travel. Not of small towns. Not of Marcus. She
sized up Dixie, taking her time with her lukewarm reception.
Dixie either didn't notice or didn't care. She'd been stared down
by pros. Eva's effort was mediocre at best.

"You alone? Where are the kids?" Dixie looked toward the
back of the office.

"Out showing property." Eva was swiveling back and forth in
her chair, the legs crossed. "Have a seat." There was another long
pause between the women. "You look like you want to talk."

"I don't want to talk, Eva. I want answers." Dixie's voice was
almost a growl.

A perfect, pretty smile was set. Eva put on her best real estate
agent face and gestured toward the chair nearest her desk.

"You sold the property next to the elementary school." Dixie
didn't sit, and she didn't ask, either. It was a statement.
Eva nodded.

"Which was purchased first? The school property or the
property next to it?"

Eva raised her eyebrows slightly, and Dixie knew she
understood.

"Future Foundations purchased the land about two months
before the school board settled on that property."

Dixie stared at her, waiting for more, but nothing came. The
two women watched each other for a moment.

"And did the school board know FFI had purchased land before
them? Did they know that they were going to build a school next to
a quarry site?"

Eva nodded her head.

"Are you shittin' me? You knew? You knew and you—"

"Dixie! It was over twenty years ago. I . . ." Eva shrugged.
"Who knew what was really going to happen?"

"When FFI purchased the land, did they state or stipulate in the

deal that they were gonna use that land as a future quarry?"
Eva laced her fingers together and fell back in her chair. For a
moment, she seemed lost in her thoughts. But if she remembered
anything, she didn't say.

"But the school board knew? That's what I want to know. Did
the school board and city councilmen know it was next to a quarry
site when they used city money, taxpayers' dollars, money of
parents who would send their little kids to the school?"

"Yes."

Eva closed her eyes, running her fingers through her hair.

"And you did nothing to stop it. It just didn't occur to you that
that was a crappy idea—" Dixie was on a rant, but Eva held up a
hand.

"Look, I was just the broker. That's it. I didn't set up the deal. I
didn't even go on site. I only brokered the final paperwork. The
whole thing . . ." She paused again, rubbing her head. "The whole
thing was John Simmons's doing. I didn't even realize what was
going on until it was done. I swear."

* * * *

Word of Suzette's condition spread quickly, so Tallulah's
onslaught of phone calls and long messages left on Joanna's home
phone were no surprise. Not one to be outdone by an illness or
disease, she was quick to empathize with Suzette.

"Girlll, you need to call me. I stayed up most the night last
night. I couldn't breathe right. I got light-headed from lack of
oxygen. Call me!" Joanna erased all the messages without passing
along the content.

"Girlll, I talked to Dr. Hamil this morning and was telling him
about you. Your heart's probably enlarged now. I'm getting mine
tested. They say it could just blow while I'm at work. I could be
dead before I hit the floor. At least you're in a chair so if your heart
explodes, you won't crack your head on the ground."

It was because of her constant and ludicrous messages that Joanna almost didn't hear Tallulah's little bomb.

"Joanna, this is Tallulah. Thought you should know . . ."

* * * *

Quigley's Down Under was packed. I don't ever recall so many gathering at one time, not even at Dixie's grand opening when a rumor had circulated at the cement plant that Dixie was going to do a pole dance and bring in some of her stripper friends. It was a hard day for those fellas who'd all taken off work to see that. Instead, they'd gotten sandwiches and little fruity drinks with cute little umbrellas. Somehow the word "pole" got convoluted from "umbrella." It had been pretty entertaining to watch them try to hide their disappointment.

But the standing-room-only crowd gathered at Quigley's was there because of a different rumor. Dixie had called every mother and every schoolteacher she knew and said something so powerful that they could not avoid being there. She'd said, "Honey, did you know that they're building a rock quarry next to the elementary school? Now, I know you love your family . . . the question is, how much?"

It was a brilliant pitch because no mother ever wants her motherhood called into question. Just about every mother in town was in Quigley's Down Under—every mother but Brianna, that is. As woman after woman came in, Dixie, Jeanie, and Ruthie watched the door, and disappointment crossed their faces with each person who was not Brianna. Word had it that Terry had smacked her around again, and she was afraid to show herself. It was a crying shame, and the girls were sick about it. But soon enough Merilee distracted them, as she became more and more upset every time someone else came in the door. She'd never been good with big crowds.

"I can't serve this many people!" she said in a whine.

Even as the first wave of women had entered the café, she had begun to get testy with Ruthie and Jeanie, who were poised behind the counter ready to take orders. Ruthie had repeatedly promised Merilee that she was there to help make sandwiches.

"I can't do this," Merilee said as though it were her chant. "I can't do this, I can't do this."

"Oh, hush up, Merilee! We can do this. Hell, if I could raise three teenage boys and all their dingbat friends they brought around," Jeanie yelled and waved a hand at Merilee, "I can feed a bunch of mothers."

I had to smile at Jeanie's pronunciations of mothers—*muth-as*.

Ten minutes later, it was Jeanie who had backed up against the wall, hands on her head, wailing about one thing or another. The temperature in the café had jumped from a comfortable seventy-four degrees to about eighty-eight. Women were fanning themselves, chatting nonstop, and loudly waving down Dixie for drink orders. I was just about to ask Joanna, who had been arranging seats, to push me outdoors. Hell, I'd be better off outside with Marcos in the Texas heat than in that café. We'd tried to bring Marcos inside, but he preferred to stand outside next to the truck. The last thing he wanted was to stand inside a café filled with women.

"Ladies! Ladies!" Dixie shouted at last and climbed up onto a chair. "Thank you all for coming. Let's get a few ground rules out of the way, and then we'll get started. First, I want to thank you all very much for coming. This was something every mother would want to know about, and I just knew we had good mothers in this community."

There was a variety of cheers from the group.

"Now, we all know that this ain't the kind of crowd Merilee likes, so let's make this easy on her, shall we? Everyone's getting' fruit juice, chips, and either a chicken salad sandwich on a croissant or a BLT. Let's show a quick hand of chicken salads." She marked down the number of hands and signaled to Merilee.

"And BLTs?"

With a nod, Jeanie and Ruthie went to work.

"What if we don't want either one of those things?" Rosa Schultz's hand went up, and Dixie's shoulders fell. Leave it to Rosa to want something special or extra.

"Well, now Rosa, get with the spirit. We're here for the good of our community, and we're ordering easy items for the good of my cook who, if pushed too far, will either walk out or spit in your food. And I don't think we want either, so . . . just order what's offered, and make this easy on everyone."

There was an uncomfortable silence while everyone looked at Merilee to see if Dixie was kidding.

*Does Merilee really spit in food?*

Kelly McDonald turned to another woman. "She doesn't spit in your food, but she does sweat a lot. I've worried about that. She sweats profusely when she gets agitated. You ever noticed that? I wonder how she keeps her sweat from falling in your sandwich."

"I'll just have the fruit juice," several women called out. And so the meeting began.

Within minutes Dixie laid out the details. Nothing she said came as a shock or a surprise. After all, the city council of Marcus had been allowing too many things that were counterproductive to public health for too long. Still, it being our kids and all, it was distressing all the same.

She explained how the school board had known about possible future quarry plans and how FFI planned to build the quarry—kids or no kids.

"Imagine some of those little kids with asthma! Can you imagine Cormac Miller or Evan Smith out there? Or little Hanna Payne? " A voice from the back of the room called out, "Can you imagine them playing on the playground breathing in all that . . . that dust and—"

"Hazardous toxic waste?" Ruthie finished the sentence.

Renewed horrified glances were exchanged throughout the room.

*What did these women think?* For too many years, we'd all lived with it. They had all lived with it, and their perspective of what was normal and what was right was skewed.

"Well, what can we do about it?" someone asked, and there were nervous murmurs of agreement. They were mighty pissed, but at the same time, this was their hometown and they didn't cotton to stirring things up. Good Texas womenfolk did not do that. Fortunately for us, Dixie and the girls were not that kind of good Texas womenfolk.

"FFI is having a big shindig for John Simmons," she said.

Right off the bat, I could see a shift in the room. Just about every woman in the room had a man who thought John Simmons hung the moon. Maybe the women did, too. It was hard to tell. Texas women don't tend to separate their own political views from the views of their men.

Dixie caught the vibe right away. "John Simmons is a good man, I'm sure."

I smiled. She had to be choking on those words. John Simmons was a prickless wonder.

"But we've got to make him understand our concerns . . . as mothers." Her speech was polished and perfect, and the women began to relax a little. "We need to attend that meeting, make signs or pass out flyers expressing our concerns . . . because if we don't . . ." Dixie's tone was more of a promise. "Our children will be going to school next to a quarry. All the lead, mercury, arsenic, and benzene that we already know is being emitted into the air will now also land right next to our children. With each truckload that's dumped, the tiny, microscopic cement dust will make its way into the school, into the hallways and classrooms, and into their little developing lungs. Is that what you want? Is it?"
Silence. More shifting in the chairs.

I might have heard a speech like this ten times over while

living in Marcus. Hell, half the time the speech was coming from me. But on this day, the words struck home. My lungs had been invaded in a way this group of knuckleheads couldn't understand. I felt as though I was breathing through a straw all the time.

I'd once heard a doctor explain that to fully understand what it felt like for a kid to have asthma I ought to try to vacuum my house while only breathing through a straw. I did and about passed out.

At the time, I'd been healthy, and it was a challenge. Now I was living with that feeling all the time. Unlike my little vacuum experiment, I couldn't pull the straw out to get a big gulp of air.

I thought about that straw a lot.

What could any of these women know about that? For them, this new *dilemma* was a hard call. The health and welfare of their children or supporting their husbands' political views. My precious Franklin hadn't been that way. He knew better than to get in my way of thinking. He'd never, not once, told me how to think or vote, and I couldn't understand these women. But Dixie had pulled the kid card on them, and they were thoroughly confused.
When the last of the fruit juice had been drunk, the group dispersed with the agreement that everyone would meet outside the community center next Tuesday night to protest the quarry, and if I'd had to bet right then, I would have said less than half of those women were going to show.

But Dixie had bigger problems than trying to take on city hall or whatever or whoever she was taking on. She had bigger public relation problems than the fact that she was a former stripper turned Mormon in a small, conservative Texas town. She was friends with Joanna Lucas. Since Joanna's meeting with John Simmons, word had gotten out that she had been disrespectful and almost threatened him. The outsider had made disparaging remarks about the great state of Texas. With Myra Thompson wagging her big mouth about Joanna driving around taking pictures of FFI property, some suggested that Joanna was nothing more than an agitator.

I'd heard it building toward the back of the room, but as more and more women filed out of the café, a few lingered. It was a quiet kind of hissing, like a snake in your garage, slowly working up its courage or anger to lash out. It can be there all day and then just all of a sudden decide it's pissed.

"Bitch."

I heard the word and looked over to see Amy Mitchell. And wouldn't you just know it, Myra Thompson was standing right there with her, boring holes into the side of Joanna's face.

I never did like Amy Mitchell. She was one of those women I couldn't understand. Amy was the kind of woman who blamed another woman for her man's infidelity. She was the kind of woman who would allow a child to be mistreated or abused just so that she could keep her man. The value of a man, in her eyes, was more important than anything else. Amy Mitchell was the kind of woman who would say that a woman deserved to be raped if she dressed in a certain manner.

I had several schools of thought on that last matter. The first being no woman puts on an outfit, looks in the mirror and says, "Oh, yeah, baby. Tonight is the night that I get myself raped and possibly killed!" I've seen many a woman dress in a manner that made it clear she was looking to get attention but never to get physically hurt. But it seems to me that the kind of women who are most ardent in their theories about clothes and rape victims look like they've been beat repeatedly with an ugly stick.

Well, Amy Mitchell had been bludgeoned.

"Bitch!" Amy hissed again and again until other women began to focus in, and the whispers began.

*Oh, that's right. Joanna Lucas put Doug Mitchell in jail for hitting on her.*

*Joanna came on to Doug, and when he turned her down, she made up some lies about him attacking her.*

*Doug's getting out of county jail. What do you supposed he'll do when he sees her again?*

Whatever it was that Amy had planned to say to Joanna, Myra had herself a front row seat. I raised my hand to get Jeanie's attention. In this sort of situation, it was best to have Jeanie around. She was different from any other woman I knew. She was rough. Tough. She'd stomp on your head and spit in your face if you got in her way. Yeah, even in her late forties, she'd stomp on your head and spit in your face.

Maybe in my day, when I had both legs and could breathe, I woulda been the same way. I liked to think so.

But Jeanie stood behind the counter, mouth hanging open with a strange expression on her face. It was funny how she never said a word, never moved a muscle, but everyone in the room seemed to hear her thoughts. One by one we all turned to look out the window toward the parking lot, and my heart sank.

They had Marcos.

They had skinny, little Marcos pinned up against the side of a pickup truck, punching him. More than ever, I could not breathe. I was worthless and hated myself for it. I couldn't help him. I couldn't save him.

"No!" Joanna gasped, almost tipping my chair trying to get around me. She began to yell as she pushed her way through the café and out the door. It played out in slow motion, and I could see everything—the way they held Marcos up with his feet dangling, the way Joanna charged out the door and then skittered to a stop when Doug stepped out from the pack. I could see the way he stood, the way he held himself, and without hearing a word spoken, I knew he had threatened her. Again. And the men who surrounded him found humor in it. It was all a big joke.

I saw how he turned on his heel, and the men dropped Marcos. He collapsed in a heap. One by one, they all climbed into their trucks and pulled away, leaving Joanna hovering over Marcos. But I didn't see how it was that Amy managed to fall over a table and chair and hit her head. I didn't see any of that. Hell, I could barely breathe. I thought maybe I'd heard her cussing, saying something ugly about someone. But as I told the police, I didn't see her fall down and hit her head. Neither did Jeanie. Although it remains unclear why Myra thinks she saw Jeanie hit Amy, even though Merilee, Ruthie, and Dixie all insist that Amy was so busy cussing about something that she slipped and fell, hitting her head against the table and chair as she went down.

Amy has always been a little clumsy like that.

# 24

The door slammed with such ferocity that Brianna jumped in her chair.

"Brianna!"

She braced herself. She had been sitting in her favorite chair, reading a book. At first, this activity had driven her crazy. She'd had a routine—up early in the morning, making breakfast for Terry. But as soon as he was out the door, so was she. She would walk to the café with Ruthie, joined sometimes by Jeanie. They would drink coffee, talk, and discuss whatever was in the paper. By late afternoon, she'd be back home, cleaning house, and preparing dinner. It had been difficult to settle into the routine of no girls, no raucous discussions about pee coming out of your nose or having a breath-holding contest. Although Jeanie was appalling, Brianna missed her most of all. The sudden quietness of her life was deafening.

"Brianna!" Terry charged through the quiet house.

"Right here," she said, surprised by how tiny her voice sounded.

"What the hell?" He appeared in the entranceway of their small living room. His face was flushed, his chest heaving, and Brianna was alarmed; she knew that look. She knew it well, and her mind reeled. Unable to imagine what had happened or what she could have done, she tensed. She felt like she was underwater. The sound of her heartbeat pulsing violently echoed in her ears.

He gritted his teeth as he moved forward.

"You told your stupid bitch friends that I beat you?"

* * * *

Dave Sappenfield placed the phone call personally.

"Mr. Simmons," he said. "We got a hit."

John set his feet flat on the ground and bolted upright. He'd been sitting back in his chair, chewing on the issue of illegal immigrants. If Frank and some of the other men at the plant had their way, the money tree would be wiped out. But they weren't thinking clearly; they had secure jobs at the plant. But what about Nathaniel Blauncett, Randy Cross, or Tim Davis? They were ranchers who depended on cheap, strong labor without the hassle of taxes.

John was the first to admit there was a serious problem with illegal immigrants in this country, but not in his own town. Taking on that issue was a death sentence for his campaign. Frank and his buddies beating up a local Mexican was one thing, calling in immigration was quite another.

Besides, he was sure the message had been delivered to the local beaners. They needed to steer clear of the environmental bullshit. Paint, dig, build, whatever. But stay away from the bitches and their little cause because they were about to be squashed.

"Someone from your town brought in a canister," Dave Sappenfield said. John already knew who was responsible for it.

"One of my guys caught it."

*God bless Dave Sappenfield.* John leaned back in his chair and smiled to himself. He and Dave had a lucrative agreement they'd established many years ago when the two had met at a TCEQ hearing in Austin. Most of the officials in attendance were desk jockeys of some variety, and they had flocked to the golf course like moths to flame, leaving the good ol' boys behind. When John met Dave, he was nursing a beer in the hotel bar and in a most agreeable position to hear the long-term political plans of John Simmons.

"And?" John asked.

"And . . . we caught it. Let's just say, you're in the clear. The results have been sent out, and FFI is in compliance across the board."

There was another pause while John nodded to himself. He was pleased. He was very pleased.

"And I expect our deal to be honored."

John smiled. "You can count on it."

* * * *

"So, when you put the tampon in his hand," Jeanie said and leaned forward, a grin widening as she visualized the scene, "were you, like, carrying it in your own hand or did you have it wrapped in something?"

The girls were sitting on Joanna's back patio late one evening. It was days before the FFI luncheon for John Simmons's campaign, and Joanna had invited everyone over for a surprise. But first Jeanie was having some fun with her.

Suppressing a smile, Joanna said, "Well, I wrapped it in a Kleenex."

"Did he drop it once he realized what it was?" Ruthie asked with a snicker.

"What does he do in the tampon industry?" Dixie asked.

"Yeah, ya know, if he was really good at what he does, he should've been able to handle it!" Jeanie laughed at her own joke.

"Did you get free tampons with your divorce?" Ruthie asked,

causing everyone to look at her. "What?"

"Free tampons? She got money! Lots and lots of money!" Jeanie said gleefully.

They sat under the decorative hanging lights, sipping homemade lemon margaritas while Dixie nursed a frozen lemonade. It had not occurred to the women that Joanna had asked them to come for any reason other than to sit on her patio and socialize.

Joanna realized that for the moment, this was all she wanted. Not just for her, but for Suzette.

Suzette's health had declined rapidly. The loss of her husband followed by the sudden loss of her animals and house had taken its toll on Suzette. She'd been shaken when Doug Mitchell and his ape friends had accosted Marcos. For the most part, Marcos was just scared, but Suzette had been frantic for her newly adopted son.

The always outspoken and outrageous Suzette had become very quiet. Speaking, let alone breathing, was a chore, so she chose her words and actions carefully. Joanna watched Suzette, who was smiling at Jeanie, who was harassing Ruthie.

"Oh, yeah, this guy is worth millions, and you wanna know if Joanna got free tampons!" Jeanie was laughing. "Yes, I'd like a million dollars' worth of tampons please. It's for me and two hundred and fifty thousand of my very best friends." She thrust a fist into the air. "Stop all needless bleeding!"

"I was just wondering," Ruthie said and scowled at Jeanie.

"Ovulators unite!" Another first pump.

"It was more of property settlement," Joanna said in an attempt to stop Jeanie.

"On this house specifically?" Dixie's eyebrows shot up.

"Well, there were several properties, I picked this one because . . . I liked the name of the town." Joanna was embarrassed about that as the girls all chuckled.

"Little did you know." Jeanie raised her glass in a solemn toast. It was a sobering moment, and everyone fell silent, studying the drink in her hand.

"You just don't strike me as someone who would allow herself to be mistreated by a man," Ruthie said.

Joanna felt all eyes turn toward her.

"She isn't. She put a bloody tampon in the guy's hand!" Jeanie burst out laughing.

"But before that . . ." Ruthie said.

Joanna had already told them that Clayton Lucas had been an unfaithful, verbally abusive husband, and that she had long overstayed that relationship.

She shrugged. "It kind of sneaks up on you. Before you know it, you're being treated like crap."

As she spoke, Roberto stepped out from the kitchen, holding a pitcher of the margarita concoction in one hand and Dixie's frozen lemonade in the other. At once, everyone smiled at him.

His T-shirt and jeans were snug, nicely framing his body. He was lean, muscular, and perfectly proportioned. All eyes watched as he topped off each outstretched glass.

"How's Marcos?" Dixie asked, studying Roberto.

Joanna smiled as he filled her glass.

"Fine. Really, no worse for wear but . . . he's still shaken. I mean, just about what happened. I don't think he wants to go back into town any time soon."

Roberto filled up Jeanie's glass. She smiled, leaned back, and gave him a long look. "How's your English these days, Roberto?"

"Is pretty good."

"You understand things pretty good?" she asked, and he nodded. "Like how's the weather today or you have great hair or . . . your pants fit like an English castle."

Dixie snorted as she sipped her drink, and Roberto frowned, shaking his head.

"It doesn't matter, honey. This is yummy. Thanks," Dixie said and sent him away with a wave. She winced and touched her forehead. "Brain freeze!"

"So, when was the last time you and your ex talked?" Ruthie refocused on Joanna.

"So, how are you and Roberto, the Harlequin Romance cover boy doing?" Jeanie asked, eyes still following him into the kitchen.

Joanna rose, smiling. "It's time to show you guys what I've been working on." She motioned them to follow her. It was the best way to avoid the questions.

"You all go on. I've already seen it." Breathing was difficult for Suzette. As the girls stood, Roberto emerged to bring Suzette into the house.

"What was that supposed to mean about his pants fitting like an English castle?" Ruthie asked as they stumbled toward the barn by flashlight.

"No ballroom," Jeanie said.

Dixie opened her mouth to laugh when Joanna swung her flashlight around, leveling it on Jeanie's face.

"That's okay. I don't need a dance floor. I'm more interested in the castle's artillery," Joanna said.

"Oh, snap!" Dixie shouted.

* * * *

Marcos had opted to stay home. I couldn't blame him. Instead, I got Roberto to take me, and I could tell that there was a part of him that was hoping to get jumped by the gringos who'd jumped Marcos.

Roberto didn't have the fear that many of the men had. He and his brother had working green cards, but there was something else. Roberto had an edge to him; he was a fighter. The need to get revenge for Marcos was obvious. He was angry. He was very quiet, always pleasant, but he was very angry.

While Joanna parked the truck, Roberto agreed to push me into the mayor's office.

"You got an appointment?" Mary Ryan asked when she saw me. There was no love lost between us, and it was no secret.

"Don't need one." As I saw it, I didn't. As a citizen of Marcus, I should have access to my mayor at all times. Particularly when I had a ticking time bomb in my lap.

I had official results that *someone,* not lightning, had set my barn and house on fire. I'll never know how much my cats suffered. I'll never know if it was because of my cats or because of Franklin's illness that someone did what they did. But I had an official report from the investigative team I had hired. A time-activated device was used to start the fire, and the fire department didn't do shit to save my animals. That's what I did know. And I wanted answers.

I wanted answers because I knew just one more thing—I was dying.  It wasn't anything dramatic. It was gradual, slow, and unfair. When I learned that I had encephalitis in addition to my failing heart, I was scared. It just sounded scary. My brain was swelling, my muscles were deteriorating, my life was being sucked away from me, but before I left this world, there were a few things I was going to iron out, by damn. Stopping to talk about all this with Mary Ryan was not in the game plan, so I had Roberto push right by her. While she was busy yelling *hey*, Roberto pushed me right into Whitmeyer's office, only to find him and John Simmons having a little powwow.

I'll be damned if that John Simmons wasn't everywhere, all the time. So I left my report with Whitmeyer and made it clear that I was expecting full restitution for my home, barn, and animals. They were stunned by the time Roberto wheeled me out of there, and I felt good enough to smile—something I hadn't done for some time. But when we got outside, the good feeling faded.

Joanna was backed up against her truck with none other than that bastard Frank Wolan in her face.

"Ms. Suzette," Roberto leaned over and whispered in my ear. "You okay to sit here? I be right back."

As I said in my report to the responding officer, I don't know how it was that Frank fell and hit his head against the pavement.

His claims that he was assaulted are ridiculous and unfounded as Joanna Lucas, Roberto Costilla, and I all watched him trip and fall. I believed he was embarrassed. He'd always been a little clumsy like that.

# 25

Clayton Lucas disconnected his phone, tilted back his head, and laughed.

"What?" the young woman seated next to him asked.

They had been driving in his convertible arguing about her hair when his cell rang. He almost hadn't answered it because of the unfamiliar name and number. But Charity's incessant whining caused him to take the call.

"Hello?"

"Mr. Lucas, you don't know me," the caller had said and unleashed a story that caused Clayton to pull over. Once stopped, Charity had continued to mutter and complain about her hair. Funny how she'd liked the idea of how she would look in the sports car until the wind started blowing. Clayton had shot several dirty looks in her direction, indicating she'd better shut up. And fast.

He couldn't believe what he was hearing and wanted to use every brain cell, every fiber of his being, to absorb each and every detail. It was unbelievable.

He punched the headrest to Charity's seat at one point to startle her from her whining. She jerked to the side and looked doe-eyed at him, her feelings apparently hurt. But Clayton didn't care. He needed her to shut up for just a few damn minutes so that he could concentrate on the caller.

Apparently, his dearly divorced Joanna was causing problems. Big surprise. It wasn't enough that the little bitch was purposefully spending an exorbitant amount of money on the renovation of the Texas house. It wasn't enough that she had shamed the family name, making sure to create such a scandal that local papers had picked up the story of his infidelity and "abusive" manners.

He cringed. *Abusive.*

Of course, the papers failed to mention that she was an annoying little bitch. They neglected to highlight her love of spending money or the fact that perhaps if she'd had a personality in or out of bed he might not have been forced to wander.

The papers also failed to mention that she was all too eager to hop into his bed when he was worth money to her. She was hot and willing when she wanted his money. No sooner had they wed, she became cold and unresponsive. Shit, it was no wonder he looked elsewhere. She drove him to it. But apparently, that didn't make for a good story, and the people in his community and business never got to read about that.

Instead, everyone laughed about the damned tampon incident. He played along with it, trying to spin it in his favor—called her a crazy bitch. He told everyone he could how that little stunt of hers—that disgusting, revolting "act of defiance" as the papers put it—was proof positive that she was tacky trash.

But the damage had been done. The jokes, the constant whispers and murmurs behind his back. And his father was never going to let him live the Joanna incident down. It would not and had not mattered that he'd paraded hundreds of women through the Lucas estate. Joanna's name would burn forever in the brains of every living Lucas.

His feelings toward her before that fateful day were nothing compared to how he felt since. He'd dreamed and fantasized about running her over, hiring a hit man, or throttling her with his bare hands. The bitch not only took his money, she took his name and made a joke of it. She made a mockery of the Lucas legacy. She was the trash who put a bloody, used tampon in the hands of the heir to the tampon industry. She dragged his name through the press, had the sympathy of countless women's groups, made his family and him fodder for late night talk shows, and walked away the victor with his money in her pocket. He'd found legions of Joanna sympathizers on the Internet who made her out to be some kind of hero because of the tampon stunt. Then, in the wake of his destruction, she pulled up stakes and left.

His lawyers and accountants had handled the settlement of the divorce. By all accounts, he could wash his hands of her. And initially, he had. He'd turned the studio over to Charity, and no one ever mentioned Joanna's name. At least, not to his face. There was no reason to waste a moment's breath on her. Yet, he'd been burned. Clayton Lucas had been burned and *publicly* humiliated, and this horrible fact seared his brain. Joanna invaded his sleep, his daydreams, his every waking minute. He loathed her with every fiber of his being.

The phone call had been a reprieve from his torment. She would not have the last laugh. The stupid little cow had gone and messed with the wrong people in Texas, and it would be his undying pleasure to help expose her true nature.

* * * *

He limped in through the backdoor, hoping that no one would see him. Just in case, however, he walked as evenly as possible, gritting through the pain. Each step was a new exercise in agony.

Six more, four more, two more steps to the door. He made small grunting noises as he walked. When he was inside with the door pulled behind him, he exhaled, letting out an anguished moan.

"Oh, geez . . . oh, man." He groaned from the pain.

"Tommy?" a voice from behind said, and he froze for a moment.

The back of the office was dimly lit, and he'd believed he was alone.

"Yeah." He steadied his voice.

Tommy Tobey was in tremendous pain. All he needed was to sit down and rest his leg. The wound had been cleaned and stitched, and he was on antibiotics and painkillers, but the doctor on call had not been convinced Tommy was in the clear.

"God only knows how dirty that thing was," the on-call physician had said, shaking his head at Tommy's story about his injury. The injury was such that Tommy's explanation was plausible—he was changing a tire when the jack collapsed, grabbing and shredding his pant leg and catching his calf.

The meat of his calf was a mess. He cringed, thinking about the sickening sound as he sprang the trap. Had he been just a fraction of a second faster, the trap would have snapped on its own. His foot had cleared the trap, just nudging the outside frame. But it had been enough to set off the trigger, causing the trap to jump up and snap closed. It came high enough to grab hold of his calf. A bullet could not have been more painful.

The only thing working for Tommy and Tiffany Tobey was that the injury looked like any type of machinery could have caused it. A tire jack gone awry seemed to be the least interesting and least questionable injury.

And no one had questioned them. As Tommy regaled the attending nurse with his tire-changing story, Tiffany had stood by nodding. Still, they'd driven almost three hours before stopping at a hospital. The farther they were from Marcus, the better.

In the days that followed, it was easy to keep Tommy out of the office. Tiffany had lined up phantom real estate showings, and no one had seemed to notice he was gone. But that would only work for so long. Tommy needed to come into the office to keep up the appearance that it was business as usual. Even if all he did was sit behind the desk and return phone calls so that Tobey Realty would show up on caller ID.

"That you?"

"Yeah." He sighed as he eased back into a chair. His calf was throbbing. Tiffany appeared, pillow already in hand, as he lifted his leg onto another chair.

"You get the results?" she asked, wincing with him as his calf settled into the pillow. Since childhood, Tommy and Tiffany had always shared each other's pains and illnesses. They were the typical twins, starting and finishing each other's sentences and communicating on a level most people couldn't understand.

In fact, it was because of Tiffany that Tommy's injuries were not any worse. Somehow, she'd sensed something. They'd been walking back to the truck, maneuvering through the mesquite and keeping a watchful eye for any human activity.

Frank Wolan knew someone had been on FFI land, and he knew about the canisters. The man scared Tiffany. She knew that with each step they took on FFI property, there was the likelihood of being caught or even injured.

While Tommy had been focused on the canisters, Tiffany had scanned the area. She looked and listened, keeping one eye trained on her brother. Then, just as she'd moved ahead of Tommy, she had a funny feeling. She turned around and whispered to watch his step. Tommy frowned and looked around, lifting his left foot just as the trap snapped closed. It was that slight movement, that tiny stutter step that saved his foot.

"I got 'em," he said.

Tiffany raised her eyebrows. She knew that tone. "What?"

As he settled his leg, he pushed an envelope to his sister. She eyed him suspiciously and reached for the envelope.

"What is it?"

"The results." Tommy frowned, readjusting his leg. Tiffany stared at him for a moment. "Not what we wanted to hear."

"What?" Tiffany whined and dropped her shoulders. She tore the envelope open, scanning the report. *In compliance. In compliance. In compliance.* She dropped the report on Tommy's desk and fell back into a chair next to it.

"So, that's it?" She ran her hands through her hair. She could feel a tension headache coming on and tried not to think about the time, money, and energy devoted to their nighttime runs to FFI.

Tommy shrugged.

Only moments before Tommy had entered through the backdoor, Tiffany had come in the front. She hadn't even flipped on the lights to the office when she heard movement, guessing it was Tommy. She had been so full of hope, so ready for some kind of vindication, however small. She was ready, but it would not come. Once again, the monster had beaten her.

They sat in silence together. How could FFI be in compliance when people were getting sick? How could an industry be in compliance when everyone was developing asthma and people from out of town complained of burning lungs and eyes? How could the state of Texas allow an industry to hold the largest hazardous waste burning permit in the United States and still allow that same industry to self-regulate?

Tiffany could feel tears of frustration welling up in her eyes.

Do you let the kid who was repeatedly caught with his hands in the cookie jar monitor the cookie jar?

A small laugh escaped her lips as she shook her head.

Tommy looked up. "Don't." He knew what she was thinking, what she was feeling, and his throat thickened. "Don't," he whispered.

It had been two years, but the pain was still so raw. Tommy remembered the text message as though it were yesterday.

**The bunny died.**

And he had laughed. He had whooped out loud and laughed, shouting across the office to his mother. "I'm gonna be an uncle!

Tif is pregnant!"

Three months later, they learned that the baby was severely deformed. It had felt like a death sentence, but Tiffany and Peter insisted on keeping the baby. One month later, it *was* a death sentence. The baby was stillborn. One month after that, Peter left her. Six months later, an elementary school nurse shared information with Tiffany that would change their lives. The Texas Rehabilitation Commission reportedly sent out a record number of nurses and teacher's aides to the Marcus zip code to help classrooms and families with the growing number of children with severe disabilities, and more red flags were raised. In the time frame during which his sister had gotten pregnant, there had been a large number of babies born with Down syndrome and other severe physical impairments in Marcus. All fingers had pointed to one thing—unusually high levels of mercury, benzene, and lead emissions released into the air by the cement plant.

Tiffany had been consumed with rage, despair, and paranoia. Each time she saw another pregnant woman, she'd felt compelled to approach her, telling her nightmarish things that only made the poor woman want to run from her. Slowly, Tiffany was changing. She hadn't seen that she was driving people away and becoming almost militant in her stance. It was not until Tommy suggested something more proactive than approaching pregnant women that she'd stopped.

He'd had read several articles about a local environmental group in Houston taking on the air pollution there. Air canisters were used to bring forth convincing evidence to local politicians about the industry.

Even with the new tire-burning permit and the strong possibility that John Simmons would become a congressional representative, Tiffany was happier. She was doing something constructive and productive for her dead baby.

"We'll find another way," he said. But it was too late. Tiffany began to sob.

"I can't imagine what you are talking about!" Eva said from the front door. Both Tommy and Tiffany froze.

"There ain't that many Tobeys from Marcus, Texas, Eva," Tommy and Tiffany looked across the desk at each other, and Tommy brought his leg down to the floor.

"Well, maybe there's more than you think, John! But bulldoggin' your way into my face, calling me a liar, and all but accusing me of some crime doesn't make me the guilty party." Eva's voice was strained.

The door slammed shut and their mother stormed into the office with John Simmons on her heels. The twins stared at each other.

"It had the name Tobey on it, and it's just a matter of time 'fore we confirm it was you or Tommy or Tiffany. And when I do, Eva, so help me God—"

"Enough!" Eva made a slapping noise against a desk or tabletop. "Say what you've got to say and get out!"

"Don't think I don't see what's going on. I'm not surprised about Dixie Quigley or Jeanie Archer. They're trouble. They love to stir the cauldron just for the sake of causing trouble. What do you expect from a couple of whores? And this new gal, Joanna Lucas. She's no better, and I already got the wheels in motion to expose the kind of person she is. She's in this for money. I don't quite know her angle, but she's a money-grubbin' bitch, I guarantee it. But you have a lucrative business with a good name in this community."

There was a pause.

"Do you want to throw all that away?"

"Are you threatening me?"

"I'm warning you."

"You're threatening me, John, and I won't stand for it. You had better—"

"I am warning you to stay away from those women!" he said.

"Whoa! What are you talking about? What have I got to do with—"

"I'm going to bury them, and you know I can!" he roared. "I don't know what your connection is to them, but I know they've been running their mouths and trying to get the entire town riled up. And if it's the last thing I do, I'm going to bury them. You know I will. I'm going to bury them and anyone who stands with them."

There was a slam of a door, and the twins cringed at the sound of their mother's low growl.

# 26

Joanna stood back and laughed. It was a masterpiece—perhaps not one any gallery owner or art critic would appreciate, but to Joanna, this work represented so much more than art. It was a symbol of her newfound independence. For the first time in her life, she was going to publicly share her work with other people.  It was one thing to show the girls. It was quite another to show the world. She was making a bold statement among a few friends but also among many more adversaries. More than anything, she felt like she was staking a claim in the community. She was setting down roots and declaring war through her artwork.

She smiled. This was her battle cry. Her rebel yell, as Suzette called it.

At last, she had a rebel yell. Not a desperate act of defiance like with the bloody tampon. But a large, political statement made from her own sweat, her own hands.

Man, how she wished Clayton could see this! She was an artist. An artist with a statement.

"So," Roberto said from behind her. His hand snaked around her waist, pulling her against him. She happily conceded, leaning into him, lifting her arms up and backward, and slipping her hands behind his neck. She felt his soft hair as he bent down to kiss her neck.

"How are you going to move it?" he mumbled against her neck, and her smile faded.

*How was she going to move it?*

* * * *

John Simmons frowned. It was Dave Sappenfield on the phone. Again.

"We . . . you have another problem," Dave said.

"Another canister?" John could feel his jaw tighten.

"No, no . . . You got bigger problems than that."

* * * *

"What is this?" Dixie asked, inspecting a metal urn in the glove compartment of Jeanie's truck.

They had set out on another mission. That's what all this had become. A mission. But there had been a secret delight for Dixie, spending this time with the girls. She had never had girlfriends before. Her life was one exclusively of men. One brother, one father. A string of boyfriends. Some abusive, others just pathetic. But it was the final boyfriend who had introduced her to stripping. Despite the protests of her father and friends, Dixie had decided she had met the man she was going to marry. Instead of wedded bliss, she'd found herself in enormous credit card debt. Six cards in her name and no car with only a part-time job. Her dream man was gone, and she was in trouble. She'd been too proud and embarrassed to go home. A friend had told her she could make fast, easy money stripping. If she was willing to sell her soul, willing to mentally check out night after night, able to convince herself there was a plan to reclaim her life, she could strip. She'd been willing.

Not only had she been willing, she became quite adept at turning off all emotions. There was no fear. As many drunks as there were, the club had large, able men there to protect Dixie and the other dancers. There was no disgust. As drunk or pathetic as the men were, they were there with money in hand. They were there for a show, and she was the show. They didn't know her, and she didn't know or care about them. It was a straight up business venture. And there was no remorse. Why should there be remorse? She wasn't the one paying another person to strip. She wasn't the one getting drunk, cheating on a lover, or making an ass of herself. They were not allowed to touch her, and she never went home with anyone. She had no remorse because there was no need for remorse.

At least, that was how it seemed for a time. Then, it began to crawl under her skin. All of it. The smell of sweaty men with beer and gin oozing from their pores. The long, sagging expressions of pathetic men who were drunk, depressed, desperate, or deranged. It was what the dancers called the Ds of dancing—their hazardous duty.

The truth of it was, Dixie loved men. But dancing had hardened her. It had shown her the irrefutable ugly side of men. It was ironic then that she should join the Mormon Church, a historically male-dominated religion, when she was so thoroughly beaten down by the drunken, sweaty, disgusting world of men in which she dwelled night after night.

What she knew of the Mormon Church had not been pretty. Joseph Smith founded the church and took multiple wives. It was a divine calling from God that the more wives a man had, the more he would be rewarded in heaven. Brigham Young, the second in command, had done the same, but as ugly as all that was, polygamy had also existed in the Holy Bible. The mistreatment of women had occurred throughout the history of mankind. It was not just a Mormon thing.

In fact, what religion wasn't male dominated? She had hit the proverbial bottom of the barrel with religion, relationships, and life when the doorbell rang. She had been sitting on her couch, nursing a hangover and a fat lip. The drunkenness had come hours after the fat lip in an attempt to numb the pain.

It had been at the end of a long night when she'd questioned a man's sobriety. All she wanted to do was go home but she'd seen a customer falling all over the place, and Dixie had wondered about his ability to drive. As usual, the ass had believed he was going home with her.

It was so typical. Had it not been so pathetic and often dangerous, it would have been funny. Men would come to the club to watch women strip and dance for them. In exchange, they would pay. This was the agreed-upon relationship. Many came to look, gawk, and joke with buddies. But there were those who came, waiting to make eye contact with a dancer and believed themselves to be the one she connected with. They would believe themselves to be the one guy she had picked out from the crowd and would take home.

These were the same guys who could never imagine or accept that the real lives and the on-stage personas of the dancers were very different. The reality was most of the dancers were married and that all of them looked at the strip business as a means to pay their bills. The men were viewed as pathetic and disgusting. Sex with patrons was the last thing on anyone's mind, and going home with some drunk because he threw a couple of dollars her way was never an option for Dixie or any of the other girls.

Still, there were always those who expected some restitution. And Dixie always seemed to attract the aggressive drunks.

So, when she and her fat lip opened the door, Dixie almost laughed. Standing in front of her were two young women dressed in frilly little dresses and holding Bibles, as well as the Book of Mormon.

"Laura Ingalls?" Dixie smiled, and the women were momentarily confused.

"No, I'm Sister . . ." one of the prairie girls said as Dixie staggered back to her couch, leaving the door open. Tentatively, the girls followed her in. Almost four hours later, they left.

She didn't know why, but she spilled her guts to them. She told them everything. They came knocking on her door; the least they could do was listen to her woes. And they did. They listened with more interest and sympathy than Dixie could have imagined possible.

There was something called the Women's Relief Society in the Mormon Church, and the girls had invited Dixie to a meeting. They were making something. They were always making some kind of care packages for victims of tornadoes or hurricanes or fires. It wasn't so much what they were doing but that they were doing it together. The Mormon Church was universally regarded as the most proactive church for humanitarian aid, and Dixie liked the idea of a church being so plugged in to the woes of the world. Dixie felt a kind of kinship to the women. Her logic was twisted; she knew that. But knowing that the women of the Mormon Church had been historically mistreated had also intrigued her. Overall, women throughout history were not treated well but Mormon women endured further indignations, expected to be sister wives, as though it were divine intervention.

The fact that the Mormon Church had renounced its previous stance on polygamy, however, was a plus for Dixie. It was a church that was willing to fix its boo-boos, willing to change. When she told her family she was going to become a Mormon, they came unhinged. They couldn't understand. The Church of the Latter-day Saints had a suspicious and strange history, but it was trying to change.

So was she.

It was hard to explain to her friends now that she became a Mormon because of a fat lip and the Ingalls sisters, but that was the thrust of it. And as soon as she did, things began to click for her. She got help through the church in so many ways. Her finances, her car, and her living situation were completely turned around. It was how she'd found herself again.

She had to give up alcohol but that wasn't an issue as she had already quit. She had seen the evils of alcohol and didn't care if she never tasted it again. Giving up coffee was another issue, and she struggled with this from time to time. She hated the way the rest of the world viewed Mormons, often saying it was not a Christian faith. But people were often afraid of those things they didn't understand, and Dixie forgave them their ignorance. In fact, she had fun with it. For example, telling Jeanie that she'd been inducted into the Mormon Church by way of a Mormon client in her stripper days was just good entertainment. Jeanie wouldn't have enjoyed the Ingalls sisters story as much as a Mormon stripper client.

Still, as wonderful as the church had been for Dixie, the girls had empowered her. They sometimes teased her about her faith, but they were with her always, and she loved them. Finally, in her forties she had the sisterhood she had always dreamed about.

"It's Granny," Jeanie said, looking at the canister and flashing a smile.

Dixie jumped, nearly dropping the canister.

"What?"

"That's Granny . . . my grandmother," Jeanie, said and Dixie looked horrified.

"This is your grandmother? Your grandmother's ashes?" She turned the canister over and over in her hands.

"That's Granny."

"That's Granny," Dixie repeated, still digesting the information.

Jeanie looked around the cab of the truck. "What? Is there an echo in here?"

"You keep her grandmother's ashes in the glove compartment of your truck?"

"Yeah. She always liked being on the go." Jeanie shrugged. Dixie snorted.

"What? She did," Jeanie said and shrugged again. "I didn't know where to put her, and it didn't figure to just stick her in a closet so . . . I take her everywhere I go. She likes it."

"She likes it? How the hell do you know if she likes it?"

"Watch the language there, sister," Jeanie said, pointing at the canister.

"You're kidding me, right? You, Queen Potty Mouth, are telling me to watch my language."

"In this truck, we watch what we say. It upsets Granny."

Dixie stared at her, stunned. A slow smile crept across her lips. She wanted to say something but was speechless. Jeanie Archer was telling her to watch her language because her cremated grandmother who lived in a canister in the glove compartment of her truck might get offended. Dixie could only shake her head, looking at the canister cradled in her hands.

"After we got her, me and my brother weren't sure what to do with her. You know, do we split her up, sprinkle her over a garden or something? We weren't sure. So, we were standing in the kitchen at Bobby's house, right, and he suggests we split her up. Her baggie didn't really fit into the box Bobby got. It was this nice oak box for ashes, only she didn't all fit in."

As Jeanie spoke, Dixie found herself mesmerized by the fact that Jeanie was being serious. It was compelling, so oddly compelling.

"So, we were gonna split her up. I swear, Dixie, I had just said I didn't think we should because I didn't think Granny would like that, and Bobby just said 'Oh, don't worry about it' or something like that. So he starts to pour her ashes into another little box when all the power in the house went out. Just like that." Jeanie snapped her fingers. "And that fast"—she snapped again—"Bobby said, 'Okay, Granny!' He put her back in that there canister, and said I could take her."

She chuckled to herself. "I think it kinda spooked him."

"Soooo," Dixie said, slightly raising the canister, "You keep all of Granny in the glove compartment."

"Yeah, and the two times I let the f-bomb fly, my damn"—she winced a little—"truck broke down. So, don't cuss."

* * * *

"Where the hell have you been?" Marcus's voice startled Joanna.

"Right here," she said and looked around her barn as though Marcus could see her. She felt defensive.

"Look, I don't know what you're doing—"

"You won't believe what's going on, Marcus," she whispered. She was so excited about her project and what was going on, she wanted to share everything.

"I won't believe—Joanna, do you have any idea what's going on? I've been getting—"

"Marcus, listen. You know how I told you—"

"Wait, stop. Joanna, stop! Answer me this. Do you have illegal immigrants working for you?"

She had been smiling in anticipation of telling him about her project, about how she had connected with Suzette, Dixie, Jeanie, and Ruthie . . . even Brianna. She froze.

"Illegal immigrants?"

"Yeah. Those guys who work for you. Are they illegal?"

"I, uh . . . I don't really know. I mean, I never came straight out and asked. I know a few of them have working visas." She frowned.

"Okay, listen. I got a call. And let me tell you, sweetheart—"

"A call? From who?"

"It doesn't matter. You've pissed off some people in your town. I don't know what the hell you're doing but . . . what are *you* doing?"

"That's what I was trying to tell you," she said with a sigh. "Marcus, you wouldn't believe what's been going on. I know I told you about the local cement plant, but it's—"

"Joanna, sweetheart. I'm sorry. I want to hear about this. But right now, we've got to take care of some business fast. You have to fire, release, let go, whatever. You've got to send away anyone who might be an illegal immigrant right now. Like now!" His voice was almost urgent. "Clayton's lawyer is already on high alert and making noises about illegal activities on your end, using the Lucas family fortune. I'm telling you, Joanna, if you get caught with anyone on your property who doesn't have the proper paperwork, you'll lose it all."

"How did you . . . exactly who called you?" Joanna felt light-headed.

"Who called me? Clayton's ass wipe attorney. Hate that man." No secret there. Everyone hated Chad Evans III. "But it's who called *him* that matters. You got some higher-up there in your lovely little town who has it in for you. He tracked down Clayton and has been telling stories about you. You got a sexual harassment case against that Doug Mitchell, hired illegal immigrants, and now you're having an affair with an illegal immigrant. What are you doing?"

"What?" She almost laughed.

"I told you to get out of there. That place is crazy."

"But it's not! This is my home." She sounded desperate, and she wanted to cry. Part of her could not believe she said it herself—it was home.

"I know how stubborn you are. I know you can't stand losing, but you could lose everything. That place is . . . Joanna, why do you want to stay there? You need to come back home."

"This is home. I know it sounds crazy, but this is home," she said, and she meant it. For the first time in her life, she fit in. Doug Mitchell, his crazy wife, and all. In fact, it was because of the instability, because of the girls, because of this new quest to fight for what was right that she felt a tug of belonging.

"It's not healthy there. And I mean that in more ways than one. I'm not just talking about the air quality."

"You know what? Two months ago, I would have completely agreed with you. I was ready to bail, but now . . . I can't leave now. There are too many people who need me to stay here."

"Who? Your illegal aliens?" His voice was more of a growl. "Of all the times for you to settle down."

"Not funny. No . . . Suzette. She needs me. She's getting sicker by the day, and she has no family. She needs me here. And—" Joanna was ready to count off the emotional connections to the community.

"You think staying there is going to make a difference?" "Well, what changes if I leave? How does anything get better if I tuck tail and run?"

"How does anything get better if you piss off the wrong people and lose everything, or worse, get sick like some of those people you were telling me about?" Marcus was the voice of reason.

"Because I am making a difference." Until that moment, she had not realized how invested she had become in her home, in Suzette, in her friends, in Marcus. This was more than sticking it to Clayton. This was more than being on her own.

"Joanna, they've been doing this a long time. You think they're going to let some outsider come in, stir up trouble, and just roll over? This is Texas politics, baby. They're not going to play nice, and they're damned sure not going to just give up. These are some straight up, good old boys who'd just as soon ride up wearing white hoods and burn down your house."

"That's already been done." Joanna tried to joke. "I don't know about the white hood part. No one saw them do it, but they burned down Suzette's house."

"Exactly. How do you know you're not next?"

"That's just it, Marcus. I guess I don't and that pisses me off. This good-old-boy bullshit has got to stop, and the idea that I'm supposed to leave town rather than try to help people . . . I'm not going to do it, Marcus."

"Okay. I don't agree with you, but okay. I'm with you. But get rid of the illegals. Now."

* * * *

Brianna practically dove on the phone. Anything to distract Myra from her barrage of questions. Maybe if Brianna stayed on the phone long enough, she would get the hint and go away.

Brianna knew why Myra was coming around so often. In part, she'd delegated herself to be the person to save Brianna's soul. She would be the one to talk Brianna into coming back to church so she could sit beside her during the Sunday morning sermons and gossip about everyone who came through the doors. It was not lost on Brianna that Myra wanted to be seen with her, so later she could tell everyone about Terry's abuse and how she, Myra, was counseling Brianna.

While Myra was trying to get information from Brianna, she was also Brianna's watchdog. Terry had put her up to it to make sure that Brianna didn't spend her time with the girls. It was so typical. Once he learned of the abuse *rumor*, Terry decided it was best to have Myra around all the time to prove that there was no abuse.

"Hello," Brianna said.

"Hi, Brianna, it's Joanna Lucas."

Brianna's heart skipped a beat. She was surprisingly happy to hear from the young woman she'd been only just getting to know. She missed the girls.

"Hey, I was wondering . . ." Joanna began. Myra cocked her head, indicating to Brianna that she wondered who was on the phone. "You know, we're all meeting at Quigley's café tomorrow."

As Brianna listened, she was careful not to divulge too much information. But then she said, "Well, maybe I'll try to come."

256

Myra didn't even try to mask her intense interest.

"Where are ya going?" Myra asked when Brianna hung up the phone.

"Oh, I guess there's some kind of town hall meeting up at the café," Brianna said, trying to play it cool.

"Well, I hope you're not going, are you? That last one was a joke. They just want to stir up trouble. I can see why Terry doesn't want you around those girls. Brianna, they are trouble with a capital T."

It was asking for trouble, but Brianna couldn't help herself. "What about all the health issues? You don't think they're making up all of that, do you?"

"Honey, I am fine," Myra said and waved a hand at her. "I've lived here all my life with no problems. My parents and their parents are fine. Now I'm sorry about some of these people 'round here getting sick, but don't you think some of those people who got cancer or asthma mighta gotten sick no matter where they lived?"

Brianna said nothing. She was all too aware of Marcus residents like Myra. Unless she got sick herself, it was someone else's problem. Unless someone in her family faced a health issue, it couldn't have anything to do with where she lived. As long as she and her family were well, that was all that mattered. Marcus was littered with these fine, upstanding citizens.

"And besides," Myra said. "What about your husband?"

That caught Brianna's attention.

"What about him?"

"You are bound by duty to protect and serve him." Myra looked so pleased with herself as she spoke. She settled back against the couch, smiling and confident that she had settled any argument Brianna could have had.

Brianna wanted to scream. "Protect and serve?" Her voice dripped with sarcasm.

"That's right. It says so in the Bible."

* * * *

Ian Jackson sat back, examining the file he had on Joanna Lucas. He paused, looking at her picture once more. *Pretty woman. Appealing to most people.* She was reportedly kind, good-natured, moderately educated, well-groomed, and well-spoken. On the plus side, she had a suspect background—dysfunctional family, personal history filled with bad breakups, and a well-documented story of the bloody tampon.

Whoever her public relations manager was, Ian had to give credit where credit was due. Ian admired how they turned handing someone a bloody, used tampon into something to be proud of. But this wasn't the Hamptons. He was playing for keeps, and Joanna Lucas would not walk away unscathed this time.

It was already in the works. She would receive company soon. Very soon. Few people would look kindly upon a woman who chose to house and have sex with illegal aliens.

John Simmons wanted assurances that while the Lucas woman would be charged, the money tree would be left untouched. Of course, the irony was that the money tree sat on federal property— on the US postal service property, to be exact—right next to Simmons's own precious little park.

John talked a good game about building a huge Berlin Wall across the Texas border to stop the Mexicans from coming over, but he didn't want his own constituents to go without cheap labor. Ian couldn't have cared less. He wasn't concerned about the welfare of his fellow Texans or the state of Texas. He was a transplant from Colorado. What did he care. It was the Wild West out here, and the notion of political correctness meant nothing. Business was business at any cost. And Joanna Lucas would become an example. Going after some of the other residents posed a bigger problem. They had family, neighbors, connections, ties to the community, and ties to John Simmons.

Marcus, Texas, and Texans as a whole, had a long-standing tradition of following by the rules of the Lone Star state. Don't mess with Texas. Don't ask too many questions, don't question authority. As long as everyone stayed in check, stayed in their place, there'd be no problems. But things were changing.

Al Gore and his ridiculous *Inconvenient Truth.* That ass had no idea.

There was some hippie movement that had swept into Marcus, taking the feebleminded with it, including Suzette Lee and her idiot friends. While they flapped their gums over the cement plant, the industry was on the cusp of passing one of the biggest legislative rulings in US history. It was a deal that would be worth billions nationwide, and they didn't need a group of loudmouthed women screwing it all up.

He looked at her picture again.

No one needed a rebel.

# 27

Della Wright sat slack-jawed at her table and stared at Jeanie. The café was filling up, and Merilee was becoming increasingly agitated. But Della focused on Jeanie and her proposition. To Della's way of thinking, Jeanie was just making it worse, not better.

"I'm serious. If I offered you a hundred grand—cash, right now, the full amount, under the table, no taxes taken out, would you be willing to go grocery shopping wearing nothing but spike heels and a blond wig?" Jeanie's eyes were wide with anticipation.

"Hell, no," Della said with a laugh.

"For a hundred grand? You wouldn't do it for a hundred grand?"

"Grocery shop naked?" Della shook her head. "I don't think so."

"You're an idiot!"

"Well, how long is the wig?" Della asked.
"How long is the wig? Why do you care? I'm talking about giving you . . ."

A few women were standing at the counter, watching Merilee fall apart as she prepared sandwiches. They turned to watch Jeanie for a moment.

"What is with Jeanie today?" one asked.

"She's on a tangent today," another woman said with a chuckle.

Dixie leaned over the counter, a hand to her mouth in a mock whisper. "Apparently, this is kind of a reverse road rage deal. Actually, it's pretty interesting to watch." She smiled.

"Road rage?" someone asked.

"Kelly," Jeanie yelled across the café to Kelly McDonald. "What about you? If I gave you a quarter mil—two hundred and fifty thousand dollars cash—would you walk from the Dairy Queen to here, alongside the highway, buck naked?"

Kelly pretended to consider this.

"Yeah, it's the reverse of road rage. See, Jeanie can't get mad and cuss and carry on like the rest of us in her car because of her dead grandmother," Dixie said.

Their expressions were blank.

"Who are you kidding? Kelly, half the men in this town have already seen ya bare ass naked. You might as well get some cash for it!" Jeanie's voice roared in the background.

There were whoops of laughter.

"See, her dead grandmother doesn't like her cussing, and since her Granny is in the truck, she can't cuss." Dixie spread her hands and shrugged as though to say, *You see? This explains it all.* She smiled.

"Her dead granny is in her truck?" someone asked, and there were some looks of serious concern.

Dixie nodded, enjoying herself. If anyone were to be accused of having a dead body in their vehicle, it would be most believable that Jeanie Archer would be toting around the deceased.

"Hell, I'd do it for a hundred bucks, and none of the men in this town have seen this lovely human vessel unclothed before!" Jeanie's voice was rising as she gained an audience.

The women at the counter stared at her in disbelief.

"She's got her dead grandmother in her truck?" someone else whispered.

"Jeanie, I've got a hundred dollars right here and now. I'd like to see you walk from here to the gas station naked. That's just halfway." Rosa's challenge was met with a chorus of cheers.

"Dixie Quigley, you're lyin'," one of the women said, chastising her.

Dixie laughed and held up a hand. "I swear, but it's the truth. The gospel truth. Her dead granny is in her truck right now at this very minute."

"I can't do this," Merilee said, and Dixie turned.

"Here, honey, I'm comin'," Dixie said over her shoulder, and she turned to the women and winked. "I can prove it. I swear it's the truth."

". . . Five hundred dollars and I'll do it!" Jeanie's voice was growing louder still.

A number of voices rose, each offering to kick in a twenty. Everyone wanted to see this, and everyone believed she just might do it.

"Can I run?" Jeanie asked, playing with the buttons on her shirt.

"Honey, I would pay extra just to see that!" someone shouted. Joanna entered the café to a whoop of laughter and instantly smiled, not yet knowing why.

As Dixie helped Merilee, women wandered behind the counters, opening glass cases and helping themselves to whatever pastries, brownies, cakes, and pasta side dishes they wanted. Each woman then recorded what she'd taken on a pad of paper next to the register.

At last, Dixie and Merilee had worked out a suitable arrangement for Merilee's anxiety attacks. For this one special occasion, they'd come in hours beforehand, making and baking the entrées and desserts that the customers would then serve to themselves and pay for on the honor system. Everyone seemed to like this system, though to an outsider it might appear to be utter chaos. Everyone was everywhere. The café was loud, hot, and busy, and Jeanie was standing in the middle of the room with her shirt undone.

"Joanna!" Ruthie shouted, and she hurried across the crowded café. "Would you pay money to see Jeanie naked?"

"No, I don't believe I want to see that," Joanna said. Several women burst into laughter at Joanna's expression.

"I'm taking off my pants!" Jeanie called out.

"Why is she doing that?" Joanna asked Ruthie, who laughed and shrugged.

"I don't know. It has something to do with her dead granny and none of the men in this town seeing her naked before."

Before Joanna could ask, Dixie spied her and clapped her hands. Dixie had been waiting for that moment.

"Thank goodness, girl," Dixie said. "I was starting to get worried I'd have to see Jeanie's bare, white ass." Dixie turned to the crowd. "Jeanie, keep your clothes on. All right now, let's get to it—enough of this silly business."

"Aw, c'mon, Dixie. I was about to make some serious cold, hard cash." Jeanie played along.

"Jeanie, dear, no one wants to see you strip for—Don't even go there . . ." Dixie said when Jeanie's eyes lit up. She narrowed hers, dropping her voice.

There were some snickers, but the room quieted down. Within minutes, Dixie had managed to get everyone seated and explained what it was Joanna had been doing in her barn. There were a number of items on Dixie's list. It was important to have the women attend the FFI luncheon in a timely fashion with picket signs. If anyone could bring small children, that would be great because the press would be there, and they always liked to see children at protests.

As she spoke, Myra Thompson came in with a friend. The two women skulked to the back of the café with their arms folded across their chests.

Dixie gave a small nod as she spoke, keenly aware of the fact that whatever was said from that point on would most definitely be reported to FFI. In fact, there was a good chance one of the women already there was reporting information to her husband, but Myra cinched it.

While Dixie tried to convince the ladies to talk to the press, Ruthie and Merilee helped the last of the women get their food. By the time it was Joanna's turn to talk, Merilee was settling down, and her profuse sweating had subsided.

Jeanie drummed her fingers on the table without realizing it. Everything was happening so quickly. A few months ago, no one even cared about any of this. That is, no one but the girls. But within weeks, they had a genuine movement on their hands. It was all coming to a head. Jeanie smiled to herself. A big, giant head.

"Our biggest challenge is a trailer. We need a flatbed trailer," Joanna said.

It was a problem. Every woman said the same thing. "My husband would kill me if he found out I'd let it be used for this." Joanna faced failure after all her hard work and big dreams. Her great project, her artistic act of rebellion, was going to remain buried in the barn because it could not be moved due to a terrible oversight.

"A trailer?" Myra asked.

She had come with the intention of being a fly on the wall—to say nothing and take mental notes. But she would be damned if she was going to stand by and allow the other women from her town be recruited to ride on the back of a flatbed trailer like misfit homecoming queens to protest the cement plant. They would look like fools.

"A trailer," Joanna said and cleared her throat. "We . . ." She began to speak but stopped. She tried a smile, but it was weak, and she was forced to look at the floor for a moment of composure. This small gesture silenced the otherwise busy café. Suddenly, everyone was silent and expectant, and Joanna looked up. She had tears in her eyes.

"I . . . My name is Joanna Lucas. Most of you know me, but I guess I should make proper introductions to those who don't. I moved here more because I was running away than because I actually wanted to be here." She shrugged apologetically. "But I love it here now. I know I've only been here a short while, and you've all lived here most of your lives, but I already love it here.

"But, uh, there are a few things that I know are wrong. I ran away from a place that, believe me, had tons of problems, but every night I could sleep with the windows open and feel the cool breeze and listen to birds. But you can't do that here." Joanna paused for a moment, catching her breath, and glanced toward Dixie and Ruthie. Both nodded encouragingly.

"I've been doing a lot of research on exactly what comes out of the cement stacks, all the kinds of chemicals being burned and how it effects the human body, but I know a lot of people don't believe—or won't believe or whatever—that it's harming us. I know it's hard because you can't see it. But that's the other thing about living here in Marcus and another reason why I can't leave my windows open. I've heard some of you, well, most of you complain about this. The dust.

"Of all the places I have ever lived, I have never seen or felt this kind of thick silt before. You know what I'm talking about. It's the heavy coating on our ceiling fans and cars. I hear women say how you have to dust almost every day because it coats everything, and I have to wonder how much of it coats our insides when we breathe it. When small children are running around outside, and we already know how many have asthma, don't you wonder how much of that same stuff that coats our homes is inside of us?"

She stepped back and looked around the room. Again, she shrugged and looked embarrassed. "Now that this is my new home, I just want it to be as perfect as it can be. That's all."

"Listen to this!" Jeanie yelled, holding up a newspaper.

All heads turned to the corner where she sat.

"State lawmakers are considering shielding major oil companies from lawsuits that claim a fuel additive designed to improve air quality is actually a defective product that the industry knew would contaminate drinking water across Texas and the country.

"The focus of House Bill 1927 is MTBE, which has been found in hundreds of public drinking water supplies nationwide, including Thomasville, Waller, and Marcus, and could cost billions of dollars to clean up. MTBE, or methyl tertiary-butyl ether, has caused odor and taste problems in some water supplies, and the federal government has labeled it a possible human carcinogen.

"The bill would exempt oil companies from having to clean waterways contaminated with MTBE and other fuel additives. The full House is set to vote on the bill today." She looked up and met the blank expressions.

"Don't you get it? The poor babies are trying to say that it would be too expensive for them to clean up their own mess, their own crap that they make and dump into our water, and if we want to drink water, we should have to pay for cleaning up their shit!" There were some grumbles.

"What has that got to do with the trailer?" Myra stamped the floor. She hated Jeanie and her big mouth with a passion.

"Try to pay attention, Myra," Jeanie said, and Ruthie glanced at Dixie. Jeanie's voice had changed. It had deepened in the way it always did when she was about to tear into someone.
Dixie whispered from the corner of her mouth, "It's a good thing Granny's in the truck."

"We're all here today because we're worried about how the cement plant is spewing toxic crap into our air and doesn't care. You just heard Joanna say it . . . we can't even have our windows open and if we do, we got that dust crap all over everything. FFI doesn't give a rat's ass about your health, your lungs, your babies, or anything so long as they turn a profit. But that wasn't enough.

They made sure they got local politicians, local businesses, state politicians, everyone else on their side to get what they want. And if you cross them, especially in this Stepford Wives, bullshit town, you're the bad guy. But even that wasn't enough, so they decided to put a rock quarry next to our elementary school because"—she forced a laugh—"what the hell? Who gives a flying crap about our children?"

There was a gasp in the café.

"Granny's rollin' over," Dixie said to Ruthie.

Jeanie continued to rant. "Well, lookee here. It's working so damn well for them, look who else jumps in. The oil companies. And they are now saying that they can shit, piss, and vomit poison into our water supply and don't have to clean it up because . . . *they* aren't drinking it.

"Oh, hell no! They gotta figure that if we're dumb and ignorant enough to continue to live here in this toxic waste land of shit and not say a word because that's not what good Texans do, well, then to hell with us. If *we're* stupid enough to drink poisoned water and inhale toxic air, why should they care?"

Jeanie hopped off her stool and walked toward Myra. "And if you can't see that, if you can't see the very bad, very frightening trend that is occurring here, then you got way bigger problems than your supposed glandular issue."

Another gasp, this time from Myra as she fought to maintain her composure. "You're asking these women to go against their husbands."

"Oh, don't give me that line of brainwashed bullcrap." Jeanie put her hands on her hips and looked around the room. "Not once, *not once,* have you ever heard any of us say we wanted the production of cement to stop. Never. And I dare anyone to say otherwise! We've always said that if you're going to make cement, be right about it. Don't burn hazardous waste and then bury it right next to a school. You know?" She raised her arms and looked around the room.

"Shit fire," Jeanie said and looked back at Myra. "Be morally right about it. But don't sit there and say—"

"These are my friends—" Myra interrupted, but Jeanie charged forward.

"Friends, my ass! These women are your pigeons. You zip through them as fast as you can—only interested in what kind of gossip you can get."

Jeanie pointed to the woman standing next to Myra. "You ought to know better than anyone, Linda. Hell, how many times are you going to let her talk trash behind your back?"

Jeanie then redirected her tirade to the group. "I get that most of us in this room either have a relative or a friend who works at the plant. I don't wish anyone any less money or fewer benefits or any of the things FFI likes to say will disappear if they are forced to go pollution free. I get that! But that can't be the final argument!" She looked around at each woman.

No one was eating. Everyone was staring at her wide-eyed.

"I mean, this can't be the final word like . . . like with this oil company. It can't be okay to say 'Yeah, we're going to contaminate the water, but we don't want to pay to clean it up.' It's just not right. It's not right!"

Even Jeanie was surprised by her passion. She was yelling. Only when she stopped talking did she realize she'd been yelling. For a moment, no one moved. No one said a word.

Then from the back of the room, a hand raised.

Everyone turned to stare.

It was Cissy Brown, the preacher's wife. "But we'll conduct ourselves with dignity." It was not a question but rather, a statement. She was in. Cissy Brown was in, but only if they demonstrated with class and dignity.

"Absolutely," Ruthie and Joanna said at the same time.

The front door flew open, and Brianna burst into the café. For a moment, she looked wildly around until she saw both Jeanie and Dixie.

"I'm sorry! I'm so sorry . . . I shouldn't have . . . I just missed you . . . I should have told you what was going on. I'm so sorry."

"Oh," Dixie whispered, taking a step forward.

"I don't want to be shut out. I missed you all so much." Brianna's voice was suddenly quite loud, and she was almost crying. "I don't want to be away from you all . . . I've been so . . . miserable. I want to be with you, have fun . . . I want to be the fun gal, too."

She looked around until she found Jeanie. There was a look of desperation in her eyes. "I would rather pee come out of my mouth!" she blurted out.

Dixie's mouth dropped open as utterances of shock were expressed around the café.

"I can play, too! I would want pee to come out of my mouth. And I would have a breath-holding contest, too! And if I had to choose, I would choose Angelina Jolie or Sophia Loren when she was really hot. And—"

"Yes!" Jeanie pumped her fist into the air.

* * * *

The plans were set in motion. With Myra as a witness, Brianna had offered her flatbed trailer to protest the cement plant—the place of her husband's employment. It was her own act of rebellion, her warrior cry, and one that made the girls nervous, but Brianna had been insistent. She wanted the girls to use the trailer for this cause.

Throughout the café there were congratulatory pats on backs. Brianna's relationship with her husband was not a secret, and everyone knew this was a huge step for her. Although Joanna and Brianna were only getting to know each other, no one could appreciate Brianna's position better than Joanna. She smiled at

Brianna, both proud of her and afraid for her future at the same
time. But she'd resolved that she would be there for Brianna. And
if it came to it, Brianna could move in with her.
She rather liked that idea of Brianna moving to The Shady Land.
Joanna's home would always be open to anyone and everyone who
needed help.

Joanna had been standing next to the door, nearest the cash
register, taking in all the noise and activity. While women paid
Dixie on their way out, they discussed the following day's protest.

*It was happening. It was really happening.*

Then Myra and her friend walked by.
"Frank Wolan won't stand for this," Myra said under her breath,
but Joanna had heard it all the same. She watched them walk out
the door.

# 28

I'd once believed that I would die a happy woman if I could just see FFI pay the penalty for what they'd done to our community. I'd reached a point where I didn't want revenge anymore, something I had dreamed about when my precious Franklin was so sick. I'd mellowed as I'd gotten sick and decided that a nice apology would be equally satisfying. But I'd been wrong.

The evening had been difficult. Joanna had to ask two very important members of the household to leave because of the damned lawyers. And her damned ex-husband. And that damned John Simmons. And I meant damned. They were souls who should be damned if I had anything to say about it. You could bet when I went to see my sweet precious once more, we would pass on the message to those in charge as to who still on earth should be damned. He might not listen, but I wagered it was worth speaking up about.

Joanna had struggled with the decision. I'd seen it in her eyes all day but hadn't known what was happening. She was so sad. But together, she and Roberto talked to the men. Only Roberto, his brother Rolando, Andres, and Fernando had the proper paperwork to stay. Watching Marcos and Manuel go was pretty tough.

Joanna took it the hardest. While she cried and gave hugs, the men looked baffled by her reaction. For them, this was par for the course. This was part of their nomadic lifestyle. While they were thanking her for her kindness, she was losing part of her family. They had become her brothers.

I'd said my good-byes to Marcos and frankly, I just didn't feel well. I didn't want to be downstairs any longer, so one of the other men helped me up the stairs once more. They were capable, but I would miss Marcos. I'd come to rely on him the most.

"I am here," Roberto said again and again, reassuring me, but it wasn't the same. Marcos was gone.

So, I'd gone to my room and stared out the window.

Manuel and Fernando had agreed to load the flatbed trailer. Joanna's work had to be bolted to the flatbed. Then, just in case Terry Smart came looking for the trailer, they would move it to another, undisclosed location. I had to laugh at that. It was top secret information. Oh, how I wished that my sweet precious could have been here to see this.

From my window, I could see Joanna moping around, saddened that this would be the last night of the men working with her. The Shady Land would not be the same. But they were all in good spirits. Oddly enough, it had occurred to me that the men had something else going on. Their moods were almost festive. But I could've never guessed what was to come. I couldn't have known the hilarity, the sweet justice that was coming my way.


It was almost midnight.

The boys had taken the trailer away hours before. I'd already chuckled over all that business when I heard a noise. It sounded more like scuffling with a few grunts and laughter mixed in. It sounded like a lot of people trying very hard to be quiet.

I had been sitting up already since most sleeping positions were no longer an option. Breathing had become so difficult that sitting up was the only way to get good air.

It took me a moment to get the chair next to the window. I'd expected to see the men returning the trailer or something to that effect. Instead, I saw something that I can only partially describe. I'd like to say here and now that at no time did I actually see anyone's face. I never heard a name called, a word spoken, or any kind of distinguishing mark that would allow me to identify anyone.

What I saw was a man wearing some kind of headgear, but it was hard to see clearly as it was dark. The moonlight offered just enough light. It looked as though there was duct taped around his head and under his chin so that it couldn't move. His hands were taped down to his sides, forcing him to stand straight like a cattle prod. It looked as though rolls and rolls of duct tape had been used on him, binding him very tightly so he could not flail his arms or legs. Even so, he was thrashing about, struggling to get free. Other unidentified men carried him to Eduardo's pen which was situated on the back property.

As I watched the activities outside, I knew that I could die a happy woman now. It was one of the funniest things I'd ever seen in my life, and I had a front row seat. And no television show or movie was ever this hilarious. I can say it stirred emotions in me of humor, anger, and pure joy. It was justice served Marcus-style, and I loved it. Loved it!

In the moonlight, Eduardo appeared to be very interested. In his agitated state, he crooned, which caused the taped man to freeze and listen. For anyone who's never heard an emu croon, it's unnerving. At least, that's what I've been told. Emus make a deep, thumping noise that sounds like far away drums beating.
Just before Eduardo's pen, the men stopped and poured something over the taped man, exciting Eduardo beyond his wildest dreams. As I watched, I realized it had been a long time since Eduardo had had any beer.

He began scratching the ground, thumping, and running mad circles on his two skinny legs.

The taped man's head was doused and his clothes were soaked. Eduardo thumped and ran. There was just one thing drumming through his little bird brain. *Beer. Beer. Beer. Beer. Beer. Oh, boy, beer!*

If I was a gambling gal, I would say that it looked like the men carrying the taped man were laughing as they opened the pen and tossed him inside. But like I said, I couldn't see anyone clearly.

Eduardo pounced and I heard something like a groan, although I wasn't entirely certain. Eduardo leaped on and around the taped man, madly pecking at his clothing, trying to get a taste of the precious liquid. Each time he did, the taped man appeared to go rigid, and the men standing outside the pen doubled over.

The merriment of Eduardo and the men outside the pen was apparent, but when a light flipped on from within the house, the men outside the pen froze and turned to the house.

Joanna stumbled by my door. She paused, backed up, and peeked into my room.

"What are you doing?" she asked, blinking in the dimly lit hallway.

"Couldn't sleep," I said.

She rubbed her eyes. "Well, I thought I heard something outside."

"Joanna, I need to ask you to do me a favor."

She stared at me.

"Just go on back to bed."

"Yeah, but I thought I heard something outside." She pointed halfheartedly to the window and made another move. "I was going to check—"

"Just go to bed. I'm watching."

She frowned, taking a step forward. "What? Is there something out there?"

"Please, Joanna, just go back to bed. I'll tell you about it tomorrow."

For a moment, she studied my face. Then, she nodded and turned on her heel, going back to bed. By the time the light in the hall turned off and I looked back out the window, they were gone. The men outside the pen and the taped man—the pecked, taped man—were all gone.

Under the pale light of the moon, Eduardo appeared to be very happy.

* * * *

Someone was shouting. Joanna rolled over to look at the clock. It wasn't even six-thirty in the morning. Roberto had been sleeping beside her, and she paused for a moment, staring at his perfect features before he stirred.

It was their first night together in her bed, in her room. It was still all so high school as they slept together, fully clothed. There was no sex, yet it was the best, most wonderful, most intense relationship of her life.

*"¡Policía!"* Carlos shouted, and Roberto was up before Joanna could roll out of bed.

To Joanna's surprise, Suzette was already downstairs, having been carried down by Rolando and Fernando. Joanna felt a flush of embarrassment. Presumably, the entire household knew where Roberto had spent the night.

Four police cars, three of which were unmarked, rolled up the driveway and stopped in front of the house.

Dressed in jeans and a white T-shirt, Joanna stood beside Roberto. She was barefoot and bleary eyed as Stan Berry marched up the front porch. *What was the Chief of Police doing on her doorstep?*

Fernando stood with the door open, inviting them inside, but he was not smiling. Joanna looked at Roberto, whose eyes never left Stan.

"We have reports that you have hired and have been housing

illegal immigrants," Stan said directly to Joanna, not bothering to look at anyone else.

"I have my papers," said Roberto. His voice was deep.

Stan didn't acknowledge Roberto's comment and continued to speak only to Joanna. "We need to check to see if everything is in order, and, of course, your permission to inspect the property." It was a bluff and Joanna knew it, but she would play along. The sooner she could make them walk away, the better. She had watched enough television to know they needed a warrant. Suzette started to speak out, but Joanna shushed her. She shrugged. "Sure. I have nothing to hide." She didn't. There was nothing to be found. No extra men. No trailer. Nothing.

Suzette, Andres, Fernando, the Costilla brothers, and Joanna moved to the kitchen. No one spoke while Joanna made coffee. They sat around the table, drank, and peered over the rims of their mugs while uniformed men searched the property.

This was the day, and nothing was going to mess it up.

* * * *

"You look like hell." Paul almost laughed when Doug walked into the Dairy Queen. Paul and Frank sat in the booth while Paul absentmindedly played with the salt and pepper shakers.

Doug looked like he'd been beaten with a baseball bat. Large bruises covered his arms. Visible just above the collar of his shirt was what looked like another large bruise.

"What happened to you?" Paul asked.

Doug grimaced as he slowly slid into the booth. Every muscle in his body ached. He felt like he'd been hit by a truck and for all he knew, he had.

"Couldn't say," Doug said. "I was jumped."

"Jumped?" Frank whispered and leaned forward in his seat. "You kiddin' me? You got jumped? Here? In Marcus?"

"Yup. And I'll give you three guesses who's responsible for

it." Doug's eyes narrowed at the men as they shook his heads.

"You're not suggesting that it was 'em women," Paul said with a laugh.

Doug shrugged, wincing a little as he slid farther into the booth.

"You can't seriously think it was a group of women who did that to you," Frank said and pointed at Doug's bruised body.

"All I know is I was jumped, probably by men." He thought about this for a moment. "Yeah, by men." He nodded. *Most definitely men. Who else?* "But then I was duct taped, thrown in the back of a truck, taken out to the country or someplace in the middle of nowhere, and beaten with something kind of sharp."

"Something kind of sharp? Like what?" Paul asked.

"I don't know. Look at this." Doug pulled his shirt collar to the side, showing the men part of the purplish-green bruise on his chest.

Paul let out a low whistle. "You report this?"

He readjusted his collar and looked around the diner. "Hell, no. I'm not reportin' nothin'. So, when I get my revenge—and I will—there won't be any record of any of this, and no one can call it revenge. It'll just be some kind of freak accident."

"I don't know, man," Paul said and shook his head again. "Seems like we're pissin' off a lot of people. Maybe it's time to back off, you know?"

Frank studied his friend for a moment. He let out a deep sigh, reached for a menu, and scanned it before waving it at Tallulah.

"You ready to order?" he asked Paul.

"I ain't hungry." Paul hadn't been hungry for weeks.

"Something wrong with you?" Frank eyed him after he'd placed his order. He made sure to wait until Tallulah had taken Doug's order and was a good distance away. Paul shrugged. The three men eyed each other for a moment as Tallulah brought over three large Dr. Peppers and smiled. As she began to speak, Frank dismissed her. He was in no mood for Tallulah and her nonsense. He watched her scuttle away and focused back on Paul and Doug.

"So, what is it you want?" Frank asked Doug.

"Revenge."

"I understand that, but . . ." Frank chuckled as he looked at Doug's battered body. "Why call us?"

"I heard you been having problems with those women," he said in low tones, and Frank nodded. "I want to help."

Throughout lunch, the men discussed how to handle the women, always careful never to share too much. At last, when Doug stood and reached for his wallet, Frank waved a hand at him.

"It's on me, Buddy. I'll be calling you pretty soon." Only when Doug Mitchell was out in the parking lot did Frank turn to Paul.

"How come you didn't come to me first?" Frank asked.

"What are you talkin' about?" Paul frowned, but he knew.

"You been sick. Blood work comes back, and you got some stream in your load," Frank said with a laugh.

Paul put a straw in his drink. "That's one way of puttin' it . . . Yeah, it's been going on for a while, and I haven't been feeling real good for a while, either. But when I noticed blood in my uh . . . when you start crappin' blood, you get a little worried, you know? I didn't say nothing at first, hoping it would just kind of go away. And it did for a little bit. But I knew when it came back, I had to say something."

"Well, you shoulda told me instead of going up top." Frank was pissed. He didn't like anyone, especially a friend, going over his head.

"What? You think I did it on the sly? I don't particularly like talking about the fact that I got blood in my shit. And I dang sure don't want to walk around talkin' about it with my friends."

"Yeah, well, now we got paperwork on this." Frank shook his head, frustrated that Paul hadn't thought this through. He was losing it over some blood. Everybody knew that from time to time, it was normal that blood could show up in your urine or feces. It was just how it was. And the last thing they needed with everything going on was for someone to leave a paper trail to some bad blood work.

"We're sending you—" Frank said, then stopped himself. "You need to take a vacation."

"A vacation?" Paul raised his eyebrows. This could be the beginning of the end for him, and Frank read his face.

"No. The Family and Medical Leave Act. It's all good. We send you off, get you clean, bring you back in about three weeks, and retest you. Everything looks good, you're back in." Frank sat back in the booth.

Paul managed a smile. "But why am I bleeding?"

"How y'all doin'?" Tallulah asked, surprising both men. Suddenly, she was there, listening to their conversation. "You goin' to that big rally today?"

"Rally?" Frank asked.

The luncheon for Gustoff Mathias and John Simmons was a luncheon. *A luncheon.* It was supposed to be a tribute to John Simmons in his bid for US Congressional representative and a welcome to Gustoff. Frank didn't like the word *rally.*

"Yeah, boy. It's a big ol' rally up at the convention center for what's his face. That new owner of FFI," she said.
Frank and Paul exchanged glances.

"Oh, yeah . . . well, what's happening at the rally? You gonna sing or something?" Frank forced a smile at Tallulah, and she lapsed into a chorus of giggles.

"Me? Oh, not me. Oh, my . . . not me."

Frank was already on the phone as she walked away. He hissed, speaking in such low tones Paul couldn't understand what he said. Frank slid out from the booth, pulled his wallet from his back pocket, and slapped some money down on the table. He pointed a finger at Paul.

"We need to get you out of here for a while. Effective immediately, you're off the job until further notice."

Before Paul could say another word, Frank was gone. Just like that. Paul looked at Frank's basket of fries. Still no appetite.

"Looks like he stuck you out." Tallulah sidled up to the table. "You got no idea."

* * * *

Gustoff Mattias closed his book as the voice on the overhead speaker notified passengers of their impending landing. He had been preparing for this trip for some time. The setup was perfect. The entire area was limestone, the key ingredient for cement. The land was unused and perfect. John Simmons appeared to be the only man invested in the land, and he was nothing more than a puppet.

But he would work nicely because the people of Marcus, Texas appeared to like and respect the man. And with the backing of the industry, there was no reason why Simmons would not do well with constituents in other counties.

Gustoff had to admit that of all his companies, this had been the easiest takeover. Texas was ripe for the picking. Land was cheap, and politicians were even cheaper. While the green movement had made a global sweep, Texans seemed unconcerned or unconvinced. He was not sure which, but it had hardly mattered. The bottom line was, industry ruled in Texas.

Early predictions were that FFI would be a top producer with little resistance regarding regulations or compliance. What was considered highly toxic in his homeland was labeled "in compliance" by Texas politicians and politically appointed EPA officials. Having Simmons in the US Congress would be a help, too.

He smiled. It was beautiful. Just beautiful.

280

# 29

*Ticktock.*
It drummed in my ears.
*Ticktock.*
I'd never heard it before, the ticking of time drumming through my head, telling me that something important was coming, but I didn't know what.
*Ticktock.*
The boys brought me down to the landing in the foyer. Fernando had done such a marvelous job with the ceramic tiles along the staircase. They were so beautiful, so colorful, so lively that they awakened my ears once more to the sounds.
*Ticktock.*
I looked at Joanna. "Well, I guess this is your big day." She looked drawn, nervous, but pleased as she nodded and looked at Roberto.
"Ticktock," I said to her and she nodded again, thinking she knew what I meant.

* * * *

Terry Smart stood at the end of The Shady Land driveway. Leaning against his pickup with his arms folded over his chest and one leg kicked out in front of the other, he looked like an ad for cigarettes. His cowboy hat was shoved back on his head, and he looked just as cool and calm as any man could.

"Where's my damned trailer?" he asked as soon as Joanna drove up.

As she rolled to stop, she muttered under her breath to Roberto and Andres. Both men were ready for whatever Terry might bring. But Terry made no movement.

"I know you have it." Arms still folded, he motioned toward the back of the property with his chin. "I want it back."

"I don't have your trailer," Joanna said. The trailer had already been moved. If all had gone according to plan, Dixie and Jeanie were in Jeanie's truck, hauling the trailer to the community center as she spoke.

"Where's Brianna?" Suzette leaned forward. Her voice was so hoarse and breathy, Joanna wasn't sure Terry understood the question.

"Where's Brianna?" Joanna asked, trying to sound a little friendlier.

"I want my trailer," Terry said. He pushed away from his truck with his shoulder, gave Roberto a lingering look, and opened his truck door. "And I'm gonna get it."

* * * *

"You think anyone'll notice us?" Jeanie looked at Dixie with a huge grin on her face.

Dixie looked back toward the trailer and broke up. "Gol dang, I still can't get over that! That's a frickin' riot."

Jeanie gunned the engine. Both women were grinning in mental preparation for what was to come.

"Be sure to take Main Street," Dixie said.

As they eased forward, Jeanie leaned over toward the glove compartment and patted the top of it. "Here we go, Granny. Prepare for the ride of your life!"

* * * *

Officer Kyle Granger was in the perfect position. He'd backed the cruiser up against the back fence of the Dairy Queen with the nose facing Main Street. With a hot cup of coffee in his right hand, and an egg, bacon, and cheese sandwich in his left, he munched away as the late-morning traffic rolled by.

He was one of four police officers who had transferred to Marcus for its more rural and peaceful setting. It was thirty minutes outside of Dallas and yet a world away.

He smiled. His position was perfect. Marcus residents knew this was his spot. Most people slowed down as they passed the DQ, and sometimes they waved while he enjoyed his meal. This suited him, as he had no desire to write up tickets to neighbors. But out-of-towners and new drivers were a different story. Should they roar by, which they seldom did, he could pull them over before they reached the café near the highway.

But at this time of day, Marcus was pretty dead. Today, even more so. Most residents were over at the community center.

Although he and the other officers had heard some talk of a big meeting, they'd had no idea how big until the briefing this morning. Some foreign hotshot was landing a private charter on Simmons's private airstrip. The chief and four other officers were to be on hand to escort the guy in. That left two officers on the beat and the chief was having stress attacks.

"If anything goes wrong . . ." He'd run through every worst-case scenario he could think of until no one was listening anymore. Each officer promised that nothing would go wrong. It was simply a luncheon that held no importance, no meaning, and no significance—as far as Officer Granger could tell—to anyone on the force or anyone he knew personally. It was just FFI giving a luncheon for John Simmons, which Simmons already knew about, so it wasn't as if it were a surprise.

Officer Granger took a huge bite of his sandwich and chewed. He was in mid-chew when he saw it and his jaw froze open, food hanging in his mouth.

The beep, beep from Jeanie's truck jolted him and reminded him to swallow. Dixie leaned out and waved enthusiastically at him. And for the first time in his life, he could honestly say it was what was behind her, not what was in front, that nearly choked him. The low-cut shirt she wore didn't catch his attention either. She could have been wearing a potato sack for all he noticed. There was no missing that trailer. And there was no missing what was on the trailer.

"Holy shit." He jumped, hearing his own voice. "Damn!" he yelled, feeling the burn of the coffee against his skin. He jerked and twisted, reaching for napkins, and tried to wrestle the coffee cup into a cup holder. When he looked up, the truck and trailer were gone.

"Ho, boy." He reached for the radio.

* * * *

"Honey, he's leavin' town."

I squinted at my cell.

"What is it?" Joanna asked.

"I don't know. I hate these damned things. I can never

hear anyone," I whispered into the phone, bringing it back to my ear in time to hear the rest of Tallulah's sentence.

". . . with all the blood in the poop. That's what you need . . ."

"Tallulah," I said again, a little more impatiently. "I can't—"

". . . otherwise it'll be too late. But he's the one you wanna talk to, girl. He's the one who knows all that stuff."

"Tallulah, we don't have time for this now. We're going to the luncheon to see John Simmons," I said impatiently.

"Well, why would you want to do something like that? We don't like him, remember?"

"I know that. Don't you think I know that? We're going to—Tallulah, let me catch you later." I hung up before Tallulah could say another word.

I gave Joanna a huff. "I swear, I think the chemicals in the air have about rotted her brain."

"What did she want?"

"Oh, hell, I don't know. Something about her poop."

* * * *

I had been more tense than usual. I couldn't really explain why; I had just had a bad feeling, like worrying I'd left the stove on when I'd gone out for a movie. I guessed it was the guilt I still felt about my animals. If I hadn't threatened to sue the city over Franklin's death and made people mad, maybe my house and my animals might be still safe.

I had a feeling of doom. A ticktock feeling that I couldn't shake.

In fact, that ticktock sound had been growing louder for a few weeks now. I could hear it in my ears, in my brain, in my sleep, in my every waking thought. And that constant ticktocking had overtaken the notion that I might live to see justice in Marcus—justice for my precious Franklin, for my animals, for all the families who'd been sick or were hurting. To be honest, I'd begun to give up on the idea of justice.

Instead, I tried to focus on just being happy. Despite the fact that I was dying, I was happy. I was terminally ill. That was what the doctor said. Terminally ill. But I was happy. Besides our honeymoon, I couldn't recall a period in my life when I'd been this happy. I loved Joanna. I could say that and mean it. She was like the daughter I never had. I loved the house and the men who lived there. Roberto, I knew, was there for the long haul.

I loved all the girls. They made me laugh and helped me forget my troubles. But Joanna had been a wonderful surprise. Who could have foreseen that she would create such delicious, hilarious trouble? Who would have guessed that she would be my voice for justice?

But when Gustoff Mattias stepped out of his big-city limousine and saw Jeanie and Dixie drive by, my ticktocking went away. It was the most beautiful sight I had ever seen, and at no time had I enjoyed greater satisfaction.

A few of the ladies from our meeting had showed up for a pathetic protest, but it was okay. I never really expected anyone to show anyway. It hadn't mattered. Only the girls mattered.

Mr. Mattias had stepped out, turning toward the outstretched hand of John Simmons. John was more puffed up than usual, eager for the luncheon in his honor to begin.

From where we sat, we could see John's face perfectly. Joanna had parked the truck under a tree, adjacent to the community center, and she was nervously chewing a hangnail.

"There." Roberto pointed toward Jeanie's truck barreling down the road.

I swear, I felt like a kid again. I just sat back and clapped my hands. Roberto turned and smiled at me. It was a happy day.

As the truck rounded the corner, Jeanie laid on the horn. Beep, beep!

All heads turned, and John's mouth dropped open.

Riding on the flatbed trailer behind Jeanie's massive two-ton pickup was a sculpture so large it equaled the size of five refrigerators, two stacked atop of three on the bottom. The sculpture was handcrafted by the loving hands of Joanna Lucas, local artist and renegade. Made of Styrofoam and encased in painted modeling clay was an enormous, lifelike bust of John Simmons's head, roaring through the town of Marcus.

The Big John Head had pursed, oversized lips smooching a cement stack. And on the side of the truck was a hand-painted sign that read *Who is John Simmons in Bed With?*

Standing in front of the community center, the real John Simmons went ashen as Gustoff Mattias turned to look at him, frowning.

* * * *

Pictures of the Big John Head went out over the wire to newspapers and television stations around the state. Ordinarily, small town politics did little to pique the interest of readers and viewers. But editor after editor, reporter after reporter had laughed out loud. The visual was excellent. It was ingenious, outrageous, entertaining. Suddenly, the Big John Head and Marcus, Texas were tonight's news and tomorrow's headlines, and John Simmons saw red.

"Bitches!" John roared. "Do they think this is a game? Do they think they can get away with this? Do they think that I'm just going to roll over and take this? I haven't even gotten started!"

* * * *

Paul Cowell turned and looked down into the toilet. The blood was gone. But, he had to wonder, would it come back? Would it? Even more troubling was the question of why it had begun in the first place. He didn't like the FFI answer: take a vacation. That didn't resolve the issue, and Paul's imagination was active enough that he'd begun to think very bad thoughts.

Cancer. Mercury poisoning. Blood poisoning.

He and Stephanie had been trying to start a family for years. Maybe this was why they couldn't. Even if he could, did he want to now? He'd heard the stories, and he certainly knew of enough families who'd had a baby born with something wrong with it. He walked into the bedroom, sat down on the bed, and buried his head in his hands. What was he supposed to do? No one gave him any reasons, any explanations, any reassurances to consider. Was he supposed to just accept this condition, whatever it was, for the good of the company?

He looked at his wedding picture. Stephanie had framed it and placed it on his bedside table. She had done so playfully, telling him that his wife would be forever watching him. He looked at her beautiful face.

*For better or for worse.*

It was time to tell Stephanie.

# 30

Merilee looked stricken, and Dixie laughed at the sight of her.

"Oh, Merl, honey, relax!" Dixie said as she moved in to give her a reassuring hug.

No doubt, word had spread throughout the town of the Big John Head and the girls' involvement. Most certainly, it would only be a matter of time before people were pouring into the café to get the scoop.

Dixie knew this because she'd been the one who repeatedly leaned out the truck window, screaming, "C'mon down to Quigley's Down Under and get the full lowdown!"

They had laughed so hard, their sides hurt. Jeanie had driven through every side street, main street, and parking lot. They'd honked, yelled, and even had fun with Officer Granger when he'd tried to pull them over. Brianna had anticipated Terry's attempt to retrieve his trailer and had supplied the girls with a handwritten note stating that as half owner of the trailer, she'd given full permission for its usage. The tags were legal, and everything was in order.

"So, what are you going to do, Officer Granger?" Dixie had asked, teasing him with a thick drawl. "I haven't been cuffed in a while."

"Aw, now, Dixie, quit it."

"Are you going to get rough with me?"

"C'mon, Dixie, knock that off."

"I'm a screamer."

With that, he'd blushed and walked away, sending the girls into more peals of laughter. But it had all been a bit much for Suzette. As much fun as she'd had, she was tired and needed to go home. Roberto and Andres saw to it that Suzette got her rest while Joanna, Ruthie, Dixie, and Jeanie went to the café.

"Did you see all the people looking at it, taking pictures? Joanna, you are officially an artist. By tomorrow, everyone is going to know your name!" Ruthie said.

Jeanie had made a wide circle in the parking lot and parked the Big John Head in the middle of the shopping square. Even as they'd walked toward the café, all four women continued to marvel at the giant sculpture, shaking their heads and laughing.

"Too frickin' funny," Jeanie said.

It had all been too funny until they walked into the café. Dixie had misread Merilee's expression. She had slung an arm over her manager as she told her to relax. But no sooner had she said the words than she froze.

John Simmons, Frank Wolan, that Ian Jackson bastard, Doug Mitchell, and three goons she'd never seen before sat inside. The seven men were doing the "big man" sit, spread out between four tables. Each man had his chair pushed just a few inches too far from the table and had his legs stretched out wide in front of his body. The posturing worked. They looked large and menacing. "Ladies," John Simmons said with a smile. It was unnerving. Jeanie moved toward the front of the female pack while Merilee slipped behind the counter.

Like an animal sensing her fear, John called to Merilee.

"Merl, babe, can you bring me another cup of coffee?" His voice was disgustingly sweet.

Merilee made some unintelligible noise, and Dixie held up her hand, indicating that "Merl" wouldn't do it. It was a cat and mouse game for John, but Dixie was not going to allow Merilee to be intimidated.

"Oh, my," Joanna whispered from behind Jeanie. Her voice was anguished, and Ruthie took her hand. "That's . . ." Joanna croaked. "That's my . . ."

"What is it you want, John?" Jeanie asked, standing in a way that her friends recognized from all the way back to their days on the school yard playground; Jeanie Archer was posturing. Trouble was coming. Big trouble. The kind of *oh, shit* trouble that no one could control was coming, and Jeanie had taken her stance. Joanna squeezed Ruthie's hand.

"Now, that's a funny question, Ms. Archer." John's voice was smooth as silk. "I want what's best for this town and for the people who live here. Apparently . . ." he said, giving the Big John Head in the parking lot an exaggerated glance, "you just don't see it that way."

"Ever' body's entitled to their own opinion." Jeanie placed her hands on her hips and leaned on one leg. It was her "Don't Mess with Me" stance.

Dixie brought out the cup of coffee for John, but as she turned, Doug reached out and took hold of her wrist.

He smiled up at her. "Aren't you gonna ask me what I want?"

The girls could see a change in Joanna's breathing. It was rapid and distressed.

Several things sprang to Dixie's mind, but she played nice and said, "Okay, Doug. What would you like?"

His pause was too long. As a pathetic, obvious power play, he let his eyes roam over her body.

"You have the right to refuse service," Jeanie said loudly to Dixie.

"I don't think that's necessary," Ian said. "We don't intend to stay long. We just wanted to pay a little visit. Chat. See what it was you girls wanted."

Again, the word *girls* was said with design. Dixie settled her hands on her hips, and Jeanie opened her mouth to protest it.

"That's a cute little trick you got out there." John wagged a finger toward the window and the Big John Head beyond. "Quite an imagination you got." With that, he leaned to one side, making it known that he was looking around Jeanie toward Joanna. Joanna made a small sound and the girls circled closer, instinctually trying to protect her. "That would be your work, isn't that right, Ms. Lucas?" John asked. He was smiling.

Joanna licked her lips in an attempt to answer.

"And you better not touch it!" Jeanie took a step forward. "If one scratch or dent gets on that big head, we'll sue. We'll make sure of that."

"I wouldn't dream of it," he said, adding a small chuckle. "You've done more for my campaign than I could have ever imagined, and I thank you."

"You're so full of crap," Jeanie said with a hiss.

"Hello, Joanna," one of the goons said.

Both Dixie and Jeanie looked him over. Ruthie stepped to the side for a better look.

There was something about his voice, his manner. He wasn't from   Marcus. In fact, he was light years from Marcus. He was stiff, uptight, and snotty. He was, Dixie noted, soft.

"He's a nancy boy." Jeanie's voice was a growl.

"He's the ex," Dixie said.

Joanna released Ruthie from her grip and smoothed her hand over her shirt.

"Clayton," she said, her voice shaking.

Dixie hoped the other men didn't notice the trembling in Joanna's voice.

Jeanie folded her arms, taking a step closer to the man, and then a smile crept over her face.

"So you're the one who held a bloody tampon." She laughed. "You know, I don't think I even know any women who can say that. You just palmed the whole thing."

A few of the men gave Clayton a curious look. He blinked, turning from Jeanie back to Joanna. His face was a mask of complete boredom.

"Still letting other people talk for you?" he asked and then smiled at Joanna, and she stiffened.

But Jeanie didn't let that throw her. "She can do that." Jeanie leaned toward Clayton, offering a challenging look. "She's famous 'round here. She's famous for putting a bloody tampon in your hand. Ha!" Jeanie slapped her leg, and Clayton frowned.

"Do you still feel it sometimes? I mean, does it burn in your hand? Or maybe you liked it. Did you like it? I mean, now when you say you handle tampons, you can really mean it." She laughed at her own joke and looked around the room. "Huh? You know? Am I right?" Her voice grew louder.

Ian liked Jeanie. He'd become familiar with the woman and her antics. She was abrasive, heedless, fearless, and often tactless. She said what she wanted and took pleasure in shocking people. Had she not been such a pain in his ass, he would have found her entertaining. Jeanie effectively shut Clayton Lucas down. Whatever clever thing he'd planned to say, he had no shot with Jeanie in the room. Ian thought she would have made an excellent lawyer.

However entertaining, though, she had to be stopped. It was time for them to follow the plan, do what they'd planned to do. Tag team Joanna. For whatever reasons, she appeared to be the thread of this new anti-John Simmons movement. While the women of the Quigley's Down Under café had a history of complaining, no one had ever done anything until Joanna moved to town. They were also quite protective of the young woman. But fortunately for Ian, the young woman had a sordid history that could be exposed, and she also had a habit of running when things got ugly.

"I'm a little concerned about your employment records, Ms. Lucas," he said. Joanna turned to the lawyer. Her look of confusion was priceless.

"I'm sorry. I should say records as an employer." Ian, nodded to Clayton. *You're up.*

"My lawyers are looking into our arrangement over the house. At no time did I agree to pay for illegal immigrants or to you housing them," Clayton said.

"I know the men you have with you right now are legal, but we've taken statements from neighbors who have seen others working for you . . ." Ian raised his eyebrows.

"I'm not paying another dime until this is all sorted out." Clayton pointed one finger up. It was his declaration.

"I've taken the liberty of setting up council for Mr. Mitchell and his legal troubles. A sexual harassment charge, I believe?" John asked, turning to Doug as though he were uncertain.

Doug trained his eyes hard on Joanna. "Sexual battery. I got a good lawyer now." He nodded to Clayton. "So I can beat this bullshit, trumped-up charge."

"Really, Joanna." Clayton clucked his tongue and shook his head in a patronizing manner. "Do you really want to bring your past into a courtroom?"

Joanna's mouth fell open. "I . . ."

Clayton's smile was smug. "Yeah, me and Doug here have become good friends. I'm paying for his lawyer. Top-notch guy. He's gonna kick your lyin', pathetic ass in court."

Clayton turned toward the girls. "Your little friend's a whore. Her parents were drunks—the whole family was—and poor little Joanna here used her body to pay the bills. What a good daughter you were." His smile was pure evil.

Joanna found her voice. "That's not true!" She turned to her friends. "That's not true!"

"Oh, sweetheart, don't forget . . . I know things. In fact," he said, leaning back in his chair and crossing one leg over the other, "that's how we met. The man she was screwing, Geoff Hoffman, remember? What was it? He didn't give you what you wanted?"

"Shut up, Clayton. That's not true, and you know it!" Tears welled up in her eyes.

It was true that she'd been seeing Geoff when she met Clayton. He'd practically thrown himself at her when she was tending bar. Every night he'd been there, giving her outrageous tips. He was exciting, wealthy, and good-looking. What wasn't there to like? And he did pay to get her brother out of jail. He'd helped Joanna with some of her parents' bills, too. He'd been there during the worst period of her life. But she hadn't had sex with him for money. Clayton knew that.

Geoff was married, and Clayton had been at the same party when Joanna discovered she was the mistress. It had been Clayton who played the role of boyfriend, saving his good buddy Hoffman. Only later did Joanna learn how often the boys from Clayton's club played this little charade. And it was later still when she understood why Clayton had asked her to marry him. It wasn't out of love, but spite. It had been no secret that Geoff was obsessed with Joanna. Marrying her had been an act of triumph for Clayton, Geoff's longtime rival and drinking buddy.

She'd been his ultimate trophy wife. He'd paraded her in front of Geoff at parties, always taking private joy at her discomfort and Geoff's wistful glances. At one particular party when he'd had too much to drink, he'd grabbed Joanna's crotch in front Geoff and a group of men. "This is mine. All mine, gentlemen." But behind closed doors, when he was angry, drunk, or both, he loved to insinuate that Joanna had been nothing more than a whore for her parents' addictions.

"You're damaged goods," he'd loved to say, and it was his license to go out and screw whatever female he could.
"Who paid to get your brother out of jail?"

Joanna knew what was coming.

"A married man you were screwing at the time and now . . ." he said with a laugh, "now you're screwing some farmhand that I'm paying for. A Mexican farmhand." He looked around the room.

Doug said, "She wanted me to do her. It was only when that Mexican came outside that—"

Jeanie hurled a saltshaker at Doug, narrowly missing his head. Every man was on his feet.

"Did you see that? Assault with a deadly weapon! Assault with a deadly weapon!" Doug shouted.

Dixie lunged at Jeanie, driving her back against the register and whispering in her ear.

Clayton laughed out loud. "You've aligned yourselves with a loser, *girls!*"

He turned to Joanna. "You're damaged goods, Joanna. You've always been damaged goods."

John stepped forward, motioning the others to follow as Joanna fell back into a chair and stared down at the ground.

John leaned over her. "Sometimes a fight just isn't worth it." His lips were so close to her ear, it sent chills of revulsion down her spine. "You stand to lose everything. You need to ask yourself if it's worth it."

"We'll be in touch," Ian said, moving past the women.

No one spoke another word.

*Damaged goods.*

The words rang in her ears, and Joanna buried her face in her hands. She'd almost forgotten those words, that feeling, her past. She'd almost forgotten that Clayton Lucas even existed.
Just moments before, she'd been on top of the world. She'd been having so much fun. She'd expressed herself artistically and had, however briefly, truly believed it was going to make a difference. Now she was humiliated. Devastated.

*Damaged goods.*

What would happen now? Her mind reeled. Clayton still owned her. That's what it came down to. He could get on a plane, come into her world, and still own her. There were still conditions to the divorce settlement.

He knew about the big head, he knew about Roberto. He would take everything away from her, humiliate her in court, drive away her friends, take away The Shady Land, and ruin her. Again. Tears streamed down her face. She could tear down the giant head and drop the charges against Doug. She could sell the house and get the hell out. Marcus wasn't a healthy place to live anyway. Texas politics were never going to change. She could move to Wyoming or someplace where Clayton could never find her. For a moment, the café was silent. No one knew what to say. The girls all exchanged glances between them.

"Assault with a deadly weapon." Jeanie mimicked Doug and laughed. "Get it. *A salt.*" She picked up a saltshaker and wiggled it at the girls.

Joanna wiped her eyes, trying to smile.

"Look, Joanna. Whatever he was talking about, we don't care. We just don't care. You're a good person, and we love you." Dixie shrugged.

"That's right, sugar." Ruthie slid into a seat next to Joanna. "Don't underestimate the power of us girls. For whatever they try to say in defense of Doug Mitchell, I'll find you ten more women who can prove he hit on them. Doug Mitchell is a snake."

"Right. And there's no way they can prove anything about illegal workers or anything like that. Honey, I can name you about ten farmers who'll have John's head if he messes with their labor," Dixie said.

"We've grown up with John, all of us have. He's nothin' but a bully and always has been, and for the first time, that Big John Head has him scared. For the first time, he's dealing with a group of people—a group of women, no less—who can't be scared off, bought out, blackmailed, or bullied. John and his stupid little friends are a bunch of pissants, and you got 'em on the run," Ruthie said with a defiant nod.

"The people of Marcus ain't gonna let you get run out, Joanna." Slowly, each woman turned with mouths open to look at Merilee. "You're good people. You deserve better, and I don't know what the hell the problem is with your ex-husband or how much money he's got, but it ain't gonna stop you girls! You're gonna change history, right here in Texas. You're gonna make things right again, and the women and mothers of this county will support you. We're sick of our babies gettin' sick, and we're tired of the dumb-ass men tellin' us it's nothing to worry about!" Merilee's voice rang out, echoing off the walls, and when she finished, she gave a little nod and turned back to the kitchen. At once, they all burst into laughter.

"Well, look at you, Miss Thang," Dixie smiled at Merilee.

"Assault with a deadly weapon." Jeanie mimicked him again and rolled her eyes. "What a wuss."

# 31

Numb. That was the word for it. As Joanna walked back into her house, she still felt numb. More than that, she felt abused in the same way she had when she still lived with Clayton. There were days when he'd made so many remarks about her family, her past, and Geoff Hoffman, both privately and publicly, that her humiliation was a heavy, wet coat, weighing her down. He was killing her.

All of that flooded back, and she could barely think.

Dimly, she heard Fernando say something to her, and she nodded, not knowing what he'd said. She plopped her keys on the kitchen counter and trudged up the stairs, passing Andres and Rolando. If they said something to her, she didn't hear.

It wasn't until she felt Suzette's hands that she realized someone was speaking to her and that she was lying on her bed with tears streaming down her face.

"What is it, precious?" Suzette asked, stroking Joanna's hair.

Suzette had rolled into the room and without leaving her chair, had managed to place Joanna's head in her lap.

It was a difficult task for Suzette since breathing was a constant challenge for her. The way she held her head and the way she sat had a direct impact on her quality of breath. Still, she stroked Joanna's head with hands that were soft and soothing. She whispered comforting things that Joanna didn't even understand as words, just noises.

For a long time, Joanna didn't speak. She let Suzette comfort her, and she imagined how nice it would have been to have had Suzette as her mother.

"Why didn't you ever have kids?" Joanna asked.

"Couldn't. I'd a liked to. Couldn't."

"You would have made a great mom," Joanna said after a quiet moment, her head still in Suzette's lap.

"I know it. That's what I told my cats all the time," Suzette said with a soft chuckle.

Joanna found the sound of Suzette's oxygen machine oddly soothing. Neither woman moved for almost an hour. No man came up the stairs. Joanna told Suzette about Clayton and his sudden appearance, about her past, about her family, and about Geoff Hoffman. It was a cleansing experience. She let it all out, and she didn't hold anything back as she described Clayton's horrible abuse. She was damaged goods.

When it was all out of her, she closed her eyes, feeling the loving hands of Suzette.

It was Suzette's turn to talk.

* * * *

Tommy was not surprised to see Frank and John enter the office. In fact, he'd been expecting them. He knew when he'd seen the report that something was off. He'd examined FFI's self-reported records, using the Freedom of Information Act to demand them from the EPA and TCEQ. FFI grudgingly acknowledged releasing thousands of pounds per hour of benzene, toluene, xylenes, styrene, and total hydrocarbons into the atmosphere.

Experts had all agreed that the numbers were low.

The numbers that Tommy got back from the air canister report, however, were even lower than FFI's self-reported admission. That raised a red flag. Both he and his sister knew something was up. Someone was working on the inside. And that meant this would all get back to John, who had deep pockets and even deeper connections.

Tommy smiled and contemplated how to play it. Act surprised. Indifferent. He opted for the latter.

"Don't bother gettin' up," Frank said.

"It's nuthin'" Tommy said with a sniff, doing his best John Wayne impersonation. Frank frowned and Tommy shrugged. "What's up?"

John surveyed the office. "Tiffany around? No? I just thought she ought to be here, too, since she was part of all this."

Tommy showed no expression.

"Let's not play games," John said.

"I don't play games." Tommy's tone was flat and emotionless.

"Good. I haven't quite decided what to do about your mother."

He'd meant to show no facial expression, but the mention of his mother was unexpected, and he widened his eyes.

"But you're finished." John folded his arms.

The two men stared at each other while Frank, smiling, made himself comfortable in a nearby chair.

"Frank has agreed not to press charges on behalf of FFI for trespassing," John said.

"Where would I have trespassed?"

"And I've smoothed over ruffled feathers at corporate regarding your air canisters." John continued, not missing a beat.

"What air canisters?"

"So you and your sister won't have to worry about the hassle of lawyers or an arrest record—embarrassing."

"I don't know what you're talking about." Tommy's voice remained flat and neutral.

"But I'm sure you realize that your business is over."

"What are you talking about?" Tommy tried to laugh, though there was no humor. He knew that if any man could make good on a threat like that, it was John. Inwardly, he cringed.

"Come now, Tommy. Let's not insult each other. We all know what's been going on, what's wrong with your leg, your late night activities with your sister."

"I don't know—"

"And I don't want this. I don't want to make this public . . . not so much for you but for your sister. Don't you think Tiffany's been through enough already?" There was something in his tone that made Tommy's heart ache.

Frank shook his head, making tsk-ing noises. "Poor Tiffany."

"Imagine what a public scandal would do to her." John added.

Tommy looked between the two men. It was so clear that they had rehearsed this little skit, only Frank couldn't even pretend to contain his glee. Even his sympathetic head shakes were riddled with humor.

"She never recovered after she lost the baby. You might say she hasn't been exactly . . . right." John allowed Tommy to stew over that for a moment.

"That happens sometimes to women when they lose their babies."

Tommy shot to his feet and instantly regretted it. Pain coursed through his body, and he clenched his teeth, trying to sit down and maintain a modicum of composure.

Frank bared teeth with his widening smile. "What's the matter there, Tom? Something wrong with your leg?"

John, however, was not smiling. "Don't fight me on this, boy, or it'll get real ugly, real fast, and I'll have no choice but to drag your poor, despondent sister right into the middle of it. Step down quietly. You're done." He gave a head jerk to Frank.

"In regard to your mother . . . I haven't quite made up my mind yet. She's a good woman. I'm sure she would be both disgusted and embarrassed by what you've done."

As he reached the door, Frank turned back toward Tommy.

"This goes without saying, but next time you trespass, you might just lose the whole leg. I wouldn't advise going back."

* * * *

Brianna's suitcases were packed and sitting by the front door when Terry came home. She'd planned it all out. She'd had this fantasy for a long time and had finally set everything in motion.

For almost six years, she'd been secretly saving money. For the first couple of years, she hadn't been reliable. She would begin to save, secretly returning items to get the cash back and pretending to buy birthday or anniversary presents for people but pocketing the money. Instead, she would make them homemade desserts or a silk floral arrangement. But eventually, she'd get discouraged or convince herself that life with Terry wasn't so bad, and she would stop saving. It had only been about a year and half ago that she'd become dedicated to the cause—Brianna's Freedom! It was easy enough to squeeze out a hundred a month without anyone realizing it. She'd opened a savings account in a neighboring town and had all the account information sent to her cousin's address in Nevada. No one knew about this account. Not Dixie, not Ruthie, not Jeanie. Only her cousin Sandra knew and guarded that information with her life. Sandra had a special box in which she placed the mostly unopened envelopes, periodically calling Brianna with updates. She never asked why, and Brianna never said. They were as close as sisters, and no explanations were necessary. But Sandra knew. And like so many, she was hopeful. So hopeful, in fact, that she donated to the fund herself. In the past year, Sandra had put three hundred dollars into Brianna's freedom fund, bringing the grand total to nearly five thousand dollars.

And now Joanna had asked Brianna to come live at The Shady Land. Rolando, Roberto, Andres, and Fernando would never allow

Terry to drag her away. She would be safe there. With the children grown and out of the house, there were no more excuses.

In her fantasy, she would sneak away in the middle of the night and disappear. But the reality was her children needed to know where she was, and the entire town would know of her new address at The Shady Land. She was excited about the prospect of living there.

But there was a part of Brianna that was not yet ready to ask for help from others. She was embarrassed her cousin was involved. She was embarrassed the girls knew as much as they did. She wanted to handle this herself.

"You think you're cute," Terry said as soon as he came in the door, but he stopped when he saw the suitcases. He studied them for a moment.

"What the hell are these?" he yelled, and Brianna flinched. From the study, she'd heard his key in the lock and his initial rant over the trailer. At the sight of her suitcases, things just went from bad to worse.

She hoisted herself from the couch, ready to square off. As she walked to the foyer, she talked to herself. *You're going to be all right. He can't hurt you. Be strong. You have friends. You're going to do this. You're going to leave. He's seen the suitcases. There is no turning back. Don't show fear. Don't look scared. Look him in the eye. You can do this. You can do this.*

"Where do you think you're going?" he yelled at her as soon as she appeared. Before she could answer, he laughed in her face. "You think you're going somewhere?"

"I—"

"Where do you think you could go and sit on your fat ass all day and do nothing? I got news for you . . . They don't pay top dollar for someone to make cakes and flower arrangements."

"I have it all worked out." Brianna's voice was small and meek sounding, and she cleared her throat, hoping to sound stronger. "I . . ."

With one step he was in her face, glaring down at her and driving her back into the wall. She felt herself swallow hard and regretted that Terry saw it.

He leered. "You have it all worked out?" he asked, tilting his head to one side and then the other, laughing at her. "Not with my money. You're not going anywhere with my money."

"I have my own money." *Big mistake.* She swallowed again as his eyes narrowed, and he took another step forward. She heard the bang before she even felt it. She was flat against the door to the coat closet, her back smashed against it, staring up at him. She averted her eyes, screaming at herself as she did so. *Look him in the eye. Look back at him. Don't be afraid. He can't stop you. You have friends. You can do this. You can do this.*

"You have money?" He studied her up and down and smiled again. "Well, now . . . do tell." He folded his arms. It was a posture she knew well. From that innocent pose, he could backhand her faster than a rattler. She winced. Then she panicked.

"A little." He glared. "Not much." She was looking at his folded arms. Tears welled up, and her chest was ready to explode. She tried to sidestep him, slide along the wall toward the front door, but he shifted with her. His arms remained folded. She watched him. At any moment, a powerful, spring-loaded arm would lash out and knock her silly.

"Where do you think you're going?" he asked. His voice was a low growl.

"My suitcases . . ." she said, but it sounded more like babble. She could hear it but couldn't stop it. It was that or cry. "I . . . they . . . sitting there. I should . . ."

"You're not going anywhere."

* * * *

"Your gum line is not receding because of the chemicals in the air," Dixie said into the phone, rolling her eyes at Ruthie and Jeanie. "Your gum line is receding because . . . well, hell, I don't know whatcha got going on there, but it's not because of the pollution, Tallulah."

Jeanie scowled. "Nut."

Dixie frowned and covered the mouthpiece to the phone.

"No, I don't know why your gum line and your hairline would be receding at that same time, but I don't . . ."

Jeanie and Ruthie looked at each other and rolled their eyes.

"Well, yeah, I guess maybe a receding hairline on a female is a little unusual, although maybe not as much as you think."

"Nut!" Jeanie cupped her hands, calling out a little louder.

"But you just can't go blaming every little thing on the pollution around here."

Merilee came from around the counter and placed a plate of apricot turnovers before Jeanie, her best guinea pig. "Try these."

"Are they peach? I can't stand peaches."

"No. Just try 'em," Merilee said, then shook her head at Dixie.

"Every time people get riled up about the cement plant around here, it stirs Tallulah into a frenzy. You watch," she said, walking back to the kitchen, "when this all dies down again, so will Tallulah."

Jeanie froze with her turnover still poised for a big bite and looked at Merilee. "What makes you think this is going to die down?"

" 'Cause it always does. Every three or four years, everyone goes nuts over something to do with all the pollution and sick people, and then it all gets smoothed over one way or another."

Jeanie looked at Ruthie.

Merilee was right. It always did.

"You don't think there's anything to all this?" Ruthie asked, surprised to hear Merilee speak this way.

"Oh, I know there is. Too many sick kids and animals and such. I know there's something to it all," she said with a helpless shrug. "But no one can ever prove anything, and it always gets covered up one way or another. You just watch, couple of months and no one will even be talkin' about this anymore." She chuckled with a sudden thought. "You're gonna need something even bigger than that Big John Head."

"Just because your dog is losing all his hair don't mean he's dyin', Tallulah," Dixie said. She was pacing. "We're all dyin'. It's like four hundred degrees outside. It's Texas. He's losing his hair 'cause he's sheddin'."

"That's our problem right there." Jeanie motioned to Dixie. "We got people like Tallulah claiming to be every kind of sick, and it just hurts our cause. I wish she'd hurry up and get seriously sick."

"You don't mean that!" Ruthie slapped Jeanie's arm.

"Oh, yeah, I do. Why does someone like Suzette Lee have to go and get so sick when someone like Tallulah Walker would love nothing better?"

Dixie sighed. "Okay, yeah, that might explain your hair, but it doesn't explain your gum line."

"She's got nothing better to do all day but gossip and make up illnesses for herself," Jeanie said, biting into the turnover. As she was chewing, she gave an enthusiastic thumbs-up sign to Merilee.

"But don't you think that's sad? I mean, it's sad she's that lonely. She just wants attention," Ruthie said.

"I don't think it works like that. I don't think your teeth actually get hot, Tallulah." Dixie shook her head at the girls. Merilee snorted with laughter.

"Do you floss? You should floss." Dixie was remarkably patient.

"That's crap," Jeanie said with a full mouth.

"It's sad." Ruthie sighed.

"Nut!" Jeanie called out to Dixie, who waved her off.

"Your gums are bleeding because you never floss. The more you floss, the less they'll bleed."

"Jeanie Archer, if you believe in a higher power, if you believe there is a place for you in heaven, you better knock that off. I keep telling you—" Ruthie stopped mid-sentence when she saw Jeanie use her hand as a shadow puppet, mimicking Ruthie. Merilee shook her head, smiling.

"You don't have to be so mean all the time, Jeanie," Ruthie said.

"I don't know about that." Dixie stopped pacing. "Out the other end?"

"If Tallulah actually had something real, then I'd be nice to her. How about this? God?" Jeanie looked heavenward. "Could you please give Tallulah Walker something besides a receding gum line? In exchange, I promise to—"

"What do you mean, blood in a bowel movement?" Dixie's voice rang out above Jeanie's, and everyone looked at her.

*Blood in the bowels?*

# 32

"You must think we're a bunch of idiots," a voice from behind her said. Joanna spun around to face the three men standing behind her in the grocery aisle.

"What?" She wasn't sure if she had understood them, so she smiled, hoping they were kidding or that she knew one of them.

"You must think we're just a bunch of dumb-ass hicks," the first man said.

"You think I'd work in a place if I thought it was poisoning me? You think I'm that dumb?" the second asked.

"She must." The third man nodded.

"No, I—" She shook her head, feeling embarrassed.

"You think I'd expose my kids to that?" the first man asked.

Joanna stood in the cereal aisle, public enemy number one.

"I don't think you're dumb, I just think . . . I just don't think you . . . I think you're listening to the wrong people." Joanna struggled to keep her composure.

"Ah, like the experts," the first one said sarcastically.

"No. I think you're listening to your bosses, which I understand, but they're not being honest with you."

"But *you* have a vested interest in our lives?" The second man cocked his head to the side, eyebrows raised. "Like getting Doug Mitchell fired from his job, trying to break up his marriage, and spreading rumors about him?"

Joanna gaped at the men.

"Like that? No thanks."

"Tell you what, sugar britches, if you're so hot for action, you don't have to go after married men or Mexicans. I'm right here." The third man spread his arms, making a suggestive gesture.

Joanna walked away, pushing her cart as fast as she could. She could feel her face flush, and she had to remind herself that what she was doing was a good thing. There was nothing to feel embarrassed about. She was right. She was doing the right thing. Still, it would be so easy to just run away and leave all this behind. But she couldn't.

* * * *

When Eva walked into Quigley's Down Under, the girls stopped talking. She wore a bright yellow summer jacket with a turquoise scarf and jewelry. Soft leather sandals and belt complemented a peasant skirt.

Jeanie pretended to shield her eyes. "What is it? What is it? I can't see! Is it a bus? An inferno? A meteor hurdling toward Quigley's?"

Dressed in shorts and T-shirts, and covered in sweat, the girls had just finished a four-mile walk. For once, Merilee, who had been in the kitchen, was the least sweaty of the group. Of course, the lunch crowd had yet to show. Her profuse sweating would begin momentarily.

Eva could not have been more different from the girls. They were opposite in every way.

"I need your help," Eva said.

Jeanie laughed. "Why the heck would we help you? You've screwed us at every turn."

Eva frowned, shaking her head.

"That's not true." She looked at Dixie first. "That's not true. I care very much about—" She stopped herself.

No one spoke as she pulled out a chair and sat across from Ruthie.

"You must understand." She looked as though she was going to cry. "When I sold that land to FFI for the quarry and the school board, I didn't really . . . Well, at first, I didn't know. But then, I didn't think about it. My business was growing and I was so determined to meet quotas that I didn't think about anything else." She shook her head "All I can say is . . . I knew something wasn't right, but deep down I didn't think anything was that bad. You know? You can't believe it could happen, and so I ignored it or pretended like it wasn't really happening.

"Then when Tiffany and the baby . . . when Tif lost her baby, well, that just . . ." She began to cry.

In an instant, Dixie was up and around the table, consoling her. As soon as Dixie's hand touched Eva's shoulder, everything came tumbling out. The late night runs with her children onto FFI property, their night vision goggles, the air canisters, and John Simmons's threats to ruin her business.

As she spoke, the girls looked at each other.

Eva Tobey, a nighttime environmental warrior. With night goggles, no less. Who knew?

* * * *

Merilee had been right about one thing. Within one month, most people had given up and moved on from the environmental concerns in Marcus. For a full week, the Big John Head made both local and state news. But soon the Big John Head was no longer news. The residents had settled down and were once again siding with the voice of big industry. And there had been some other local issues to distract the concerned citizens.

The "trial of the century" had played out in the local courtroom, The People of the State of Texas versus Douglas Mitchell. If the town had seemed divided over the cement plant, it was nothing compared to the Mitchell trial. The good news for Joanna was that Clayton had left town. However much he professed to hate his ex-wife, he hated small-town life more. By day three, Clayton was gone, but not before he'd funded the anti-Joanna crusade. She was painted as a frustrated, wannabe artist who would do anything for attention, including handing out tampons and throwing herself at married men.

But Amy Mitchell also learned more about her husband than she wanted. By the end of the trial, women she'd considered friends and others she barely knew had come forward with stories about Doug's philandering ways. The trial ended with lots of ill feelings, rumors of a Mitchell divorce, and community service for Doug. And like the Big John Head, the interest in the Doug Mitchell trial fizzled out.

There had been a very high profile funeral and the continuing romance between Joanna and Roberto. With the renovation of Shady Land almost complete, Andres had moved on, finding work somewhere north. Joanna's lawyer, Marcus Watkins, finalized a deal with the Lucas family, who severed ties with Joanna and provided her with a large financial settlement. One of the first things Joanna did was get word to Manuel and Marcos. She wanted them to come back but they, too, had moved north, taking jobs with a working ranch.

"They'll be back." Roberto was sure of this. "Every season changes every job, and every job changes every season." It was the motto of the money tree.

Only Brianna hadn't changed. It was hard to dissolve a thirty-four-year marriage, no matter how awful. As patient as they'd tried to be, it frustrated the girls to watch Brianna hang on to something so destructive. More than ever, Joanna hoped Brianna would move to The Shady Land. She'd grown fond of having a full house, something she had never had growing up.

John Simmons had been true to his word. Tommy had called his bluff, continuing his real estate business, and found himself being investigated for some trumped-up charge of fraudulent contracts and claims. John had every intention of picking away at the Tobey twins.

Fearing that he would discover their mother's involvement, Tommy and Tiffany had conceded defeat. John seemed poised for the greatest victory of his life. He owned Marcus and started his march to Washington D.C. Who could stop him?

When the EPA announced it would hold hearings at city hall on the acceptable level of mercury emissions, few cared. Too much had happened. Too little had been done.

Even when the girls met at the café to go over their depositions, they had little hope. John had paid them a special visit to name drop. He was having a power lunch with the state EPA representatives, Carl Fredricks and Tom Bishop. And he had given a special message to Joanna. He had told her, in no uncertain terms, that the next time he saw her he expected an apology. He'd also issued a thinly veiled threat that her actions would have a direct effect on the successes or failures of her friends' businesses. This would include Quigley's, the money tree, and the Tobeys.

"I'm a man of my word. You come to me and extend that olive branch, and I'll accept. Case closed. No hard feelings."

But there were hard feelings. John didn't care who he destroyed in his path to political power. There were very hard feelings.

"You know they're going to allow it anyway," Ruthie said of the upcoming hearing. "I mean, there's nothing we could say that's going to change anyone's mind."

The café was full of Marcus's renegades—Tommy and Tiffany, Eva, and all the girls, including Brianna. Brianna would not stay long, but it was a beginning. She was coming out more often, even walking with Ruthie and Jeanie on occasion. She wasn't planning to attend the EPA hearing, but at least she was reconnecting with the girls.

They had gone over the reports from their air canister as opposed to reports supplied by FFI. Nothing matched up. Nothing was right. Yet no one else seemed interested in the disparities. Joanna ran her index finger down the itemized lists of toxic chemicals.

Tommy grimaced. "The TRIs don't change. I wish they did but . . ." he said with a shrug.

"TRIs?" Brianna asked.

"Toxic Release Inventory." Tiffany leaned across the table, poking a finger at the graphs. "It's the annual self-accounting reports by FFI and other industries of total releases, such as air, land, surface water, and underground injection of all the listed EPA chemicals by all point sources." After her baby, Daniel, was stillborn, she seemed to live and breathe this stuff.

"What?" Brianna asked.

"It's a breakdown of the shit they pump out into our water, air, and soil and how all that shit is broken down—like how much shit do we breathe; how much of that shit is benzene, a biggie for cancer; or how much styrene we get in our water supply, another biggie for cancer," Jeanie said, translating for Brianna.

Eva nodded, still watching Joanna scouring the TRIs. "And, sweetheart, it doesn't matter how much you look at them, the numbers don't match up to what we know they are pumping out." Joanna sighed. "I know."

"But until we can prove they're fudging the numbers, we've got nothing." Eva stated a fact.

"Oh, Lordy." Jeanie groaned as the café door opened.

In walked Tallulah.

"Be nice," Dixie whispered.

A couple followed Tallulah in. The woman was unfamiliar to Joanna, but the man seemed vaguely familiar.

"Y'all know Paul and Stephanie Cowell." Tallulah waved a hand over them as though she were performing a magic trick. Tallulah bubbled over with joy, having been invited to the café get-together by Dixie.

"I'm so happy you could come." Dixie hugged each person, hollering over her shoulder for Merilee to get them something to drink.

Tallulah giggled. "No coffee for me. If I drink coffee now, I'll be on the pot all night."

"Oh!" Jeanie covered her face. "No visuals!"

Dixie moved quickly, separating Tallulah from Jeanie while putting the Cowells in the center of the group. Paul represented exciting, new information. To date, he was an employee of FFI. He knew things. What, they just weren't sure of. Yet.

Both Joanna and Ruthie began tapping the TRIs, hoping for new information before Paul was even in his seat. At once, the women pounced, and Paul was overwhelmed. As Merilee leaned over and handed him an iced tea, Jeanie asked questions about FFI, the new owner, and how John Simmons was still connected. Joanna pushed the papers at him, hoping he might see something the others had missed. But it was Dixie who redirected everyone.

"Paul. Tell us about what is going on with you medically." He looked pained.

"He's got blood in his poop," Tallulah said, almost too happily. Everyone stopped talking.

"Say what?" Jeanie asked, her voice going up an octave.

"Blood. He's got blood in his poop."

Again, Paul winced.

"Well . . ." Jeanie looked around the room, and Dixie frowned at her. There was a joke on the tip of Jeanie's tongue.

"Don't."

"And you're telling us this because?" Ruthie raised one eyebrow.

"We think," Stephanie said in a monotone voice, "it might have something to do with where he works, with all the chemicals he's been exposed to."

"You sure you're not just constipated? You could be constipated," Jeanie said.

Merilee nodded at that thought. "I get anxious." She looked around the room as the women peered at her. "Well, sometimes it gets me, you know . . . I get stoved up ."

Both Brianna and Ruthie made faces and looked away.

Jeanie laughed. "You stoved up, there, Paul? How do you know you're just not stressed out from work?"

"They know about it—FFI does. John Simmons, he knows, too. And he arranged to have Paul go away for a while until his blood work looks clean again, and he stops passing blood," Stephanie said with a frown.

Although Paul frowned, he nodded.

*It was true. It was all true.*

"They sent my blood work off. Can't figure out what's wrong with me, but they wanted me to go away." He laced his fingers, placing his hands on the table and covering the papers. His hands were large and callused from years of hard labor. His face, Joanna had decided, couldn't have belonged to a man any older than thirty or thirty-two years old, but his hands were older. They were torn up, scarred, and hardened, and she stared at his hands while he spoke.

"We're scared. I mean, me and Stephanie, we're all each other's got. We've been trying and trying to have a baby—to start a family—but we can't. And I gotta wonder if it's because of this." Tiffany went rigid and gasped. Several people looked over as Eva wrapped her arm around her baby girl.

"But they couldn't tell us anything. They can't give any reason or any explanation for . . ." Stephanie paused and looked at her husband.

"For what's happening to me." Paul finished her thought. "I just don't know what else to do. But"—he shook his head—"I know it's not right not sayin' anything. I gotta think that it's got somethin' to do with where I work."

He didn't look up but continued to study his hands.

"We know of some others. Just a few, but they sort of had the same problems. They still work at FFI, and everything is okay, I guess. But . . ." Stephanie stopped and looked at her husband. She brushed his hair with her fingers. Her caress was delicate, scared. "We thought after they did all that blood work and stuff that we'd know something . . . anything." Stephanie's shoulder's sagged as she shook her head.

"Where'd you get the blood work done?" Ruthie asked.

"Oh, we have an in-house medical staff. You know, they look after us for stuff like this. But they send the blood, you know, all the lab work out," Paul said.

"To?" Tommy sounded very curious.

"Albright Laboratories." Tommy and Joanna looked at each other.

Without speaking, Joanna traced her finger along the paperwork, bumping Paul's hands to the side and causing him to watch what she was doing. Her finger stopped on the signature at the bottom of the paper—Dave Sappenfield.

Joanna waited, holding her breath.

At first, there was no reaction. Paul was in his own world as waves of emotions crossed his face. Then he tilted his head to the side to look at the name, and he looked at his wife. "That's the guy . . . from Albright Laboratories. That's the guy who signed off on all my paperwork."

Tommy and Joanna exchanged looks. It was the link. Suzette had always said there was a link.

# 33

EPA HEARING, MARCUS, TEXAS

## City Hall

I'd like to tell you a little about my town. Our local cement plant doesn't just hold the largest hazardous waste burning permit in the United States. It also burns tires and crushed cars. On any given day, you can sit out on the highway and watch the semis and 18-wheelers come into town, carrying the hundreds of crushed cars that are burned daily. Millions of tires and hazardous materials that other states don't want, we get. And we burn it all.

We burn it all day and throughout the night. People who are allergic to sulfur can't even come here to visit because their skin and throats burn. If you walk outside at night, you get can't escape the smell of rotten eggs. That would be our beloved cement plant. FFI likes to burn at night under the guise of darkness.

And what most people don't know is that the hospitals that house the children and the elderly, who are very sick and who require a germ-free, sterile environment, are built of cement made from hazardous waste.

But even the people who know don't care.

I don't get it. I don't understand how we've come to a point where otherwise intelligent people like you could be contemplating whether we should pump more mercury into the environment.

How have we gotten to the point where we're debating how many cancer-causing chemicals are acceptable to pump into the air? Not whether we should, but how many we can?

How crazy must we be to know what this is doing to our land, to our children, to our animals, and to our environment, but because we can make money from it, we wait and see how much our infants and elderly can tolerate before it's just . . . well, it's just too much toxic pollution.

If you look at our numbers, you'll see how many babies we have who are born with Down syndrome. And yes, I know that other zip codes have been included to pad the numbers and make it not seem so bad.

What if I told you, Mr. Bishop, that in your family there is a fifty percent chance that the next baby will be born with a physical handicap? But to make other members in your family feel better, you and I agreed to include all Bishops in the state of Texas to lower that statistic. That would make it look much better on paper and make all the other family members feel much better about themselves, but you and I would know better, wouldn't we, Mr. Bishop? And it wouldn't feel so great when you came home from work and your wife announced that she was pregnant, would it?

I wonder how you'd sleep at night.

You can spread out the numbers and the zip codes to make it look like it's not so bad here. But it's bad. We lead the nation with rare cancers, birth defects, skin ailments, and asthma. But you want to push the numbers around, include all the Bishops you can, and make it not seem so bad so FFI can spew more benzene, styrene, and mercury into the atmosphere.

But we know, don't we, Mr. Bishop? We know.

I love this little town and the people in it. There are some great people here. But the problem is, they don't believe in their own voices anymore. They don't believe in you, and forgive me for saying so, but I don't think *you* believe in you anymore, either. The proof of that is in the very fact that we're talking about how much more mercury is acceptable in our air so that a cement plant can make a heftier profit.

And when you put it in those terms, that doesn't sound very nice, does it? It isn't nice for the people or the environment that you're even contemplating this.

We hear people from the cement industry say that because we question the amount of hazardous waste emitted into our air, we're fanatics. People charge that we cry about all the dangers but don't offer solutions. They say that we're trying to destroy the cement plant.

That's not true. We don't want the plant to close. We don't want people to lose their jobs. We understand there is a need for cement. Of course there is.

We've offered solutions. We've asked that the cement plant put scrubbers on the cement kilns to reduce the amount of pollution that makes people sick, but the cement plant has refused because—big surprise—they don't want to have to spend any money. And you've let them get away with this. But don't you see? If you made the cement plants responsible, everyone would win. The air, the water, the citizens, our nation, this earth, you, me, everyone. It's so simple. Don't burn things that make people sick. And use modern technology to prevent people from getting sick in the future.

One of the greatest women I've ever known lived here in this town. She died five weeks ago today. But not before she suffered and not before she watched her own husband die of complications resulting from your bad decisions.

Her name was Suzette Lee, and if you ask anyone in this town, she was kind of a legend. She wasn't afraid of anyone or anything. She was brave, strong, and fearless—almost reckless, some might say. But she didn't have a chance against the poison that comes from burning hazardous waste.

You might wonder, well, if it's so bad here, why not leave? I guess there are a couple of ways to answer that. Yes, I could leave . . . but go where? Where will I be safe if you don't make the right decision here? If you don't stop this now, where does it end? So, does it matter where I move?

Suzette once told me something about damaged goods. We've been . . . I've been called this before.

Damaged goods are something you don't want. They are something to be discarded or thrown away, like broken eggs in an egg carton at the grocery store. Do you shop for groceries, Mr. Bishop? You know how you open the carton, see broken eggs, and reach as far away from that carton as you can because you suspect the cartons close by are damaged as well?

I could move away. But how far do I go? And why should I? I'm not damaged goods. The people of this town are not damaged goods to be abandoned, poisoned by more mercury and hazardous waste. Our babies are not so unimportant that our zip code is any less important than yours. You can incorporate as many zip codes as you want, Mr. Bishop, but eventually, you're going to run out.

Suzette Lee died in my house after she lost her husband, her horse-breeding farm, her cat sanctuary, her animals, and her home. She died with her eyes wide open, choking, and we couldn't save her.

I bought a beautiful house and moved here, not knowing anything about the cement plant or the air quality. I just saw a great house with lots of potential, and I had dreams of making it my very own. I had workers come in, knock out walls, and make it bright and airy and open, and with all that air in my house, with all the air in this great open country of ours, Suzette Lee died because she couldn't get good air into her lungs.

We're not damaged goods. We're people with hopes and dreams, friends and family. But we're not damaged goods, Mr.

Bishop. Don't give up on us. Don't give up on what's important in this world because I assure you, Mr. Bishop, it's not about money in the end.

* * * *

"I like how you kept saying Mr. Bishop's name over and over again," Dixie said as they sipped drinks on Joanna's patio.

Joanna smiled. "I figure he forgot who he was. I wanted him to connect himself to the EPA, thought maybe it might jar some memories of why he was really there."

"You figured wrong." Jeanie took a long pull from her drink.

"Yeah, well." Joanna sighed. "It was worth a shot." She leaned back in her chair, lifting her crossed legs and propping them on top of the bar. She sipped her margarita.

"I liked the part about damaged goods," Brianna said, a slow smile lighting her face.

Everyone contemplated this for a moment until an orange tabby leapt up onto Joanna's lap.

"Yuck!" Jeanie yelled, sticking her tongue out at the cat and wrinkling her nose.

"What? He's a good cat. Aren't you?" She cupped the purring animal's face in her hands. "Fernando brought him home. He's a good mouser for the barn."

"The same Fernando who brought home a goat," Jeanie said with a laugh, and Joanna nodded, smiling happily.

". . . to eat."

"We're not going to eat her. Muffin lives with Eduardo and keeps the area mowed." Joanna shrugged. It was all perfectly reasonable.

". . . to fatten her up so he can eat her."

"We're not going to eat her!" Joanna rolled her eyes.

"You're going to walk outside one day, and she's going to be on the grill. Mexicans love goat. You mark my words." Jeanie took

322

another swig of her drink.

"Why do you say things like that?" Ruthie was disgusted.

"You show me a Mexican who doesn't like goat and I'll show you a German who doesn't like strudel."

As if fearing the men could hear Jeanie, the women looked guiltily at Roberto, Rolando, and Fernando as they dug postholes on the back property and finished the new fencing.

Joanna groaned, causing the other women to laugh. Dixie crossed her arms and looked back at Brianna, who was smiling with a faraway look in her eyes. She was somewhere else. It was nice to have Brianna back again. It would be nicer when she was back with them emotionally, as well.

"What's next for you?" Dixie asked Brianna.

"Speaking of damaged goods?" Brianna asked, but it was posed in the form of a joke. At least, this was her attempt.

"You're not damaged goods," Dixie said, smiling at her friend. "Didn't you listen to what Suzette said about that? You have baggage."

"We all have baggage." Ruthie shrugged at her friend.

"But you're far from damaged."

"Neither are you, Simon!" Joanna shouted toward the back of the property. As if on cue, Simon roared, and the women laughed when Roberto jumped back and cursed in Spanish.
Roberto had been working on a connecting pen as per Suzette's instructions. She'd been very clear about the need for connecting pens with drop gates when housing large cats.

Six days before her death, the call from animal control had come in for the Cat Lady of Marcus. A half-starved, abused lion had been rescued, and there was no place for it to go.

Suzette died before the cat arrived, but she had known he was coming and had taken delight in naming the cat Simon after her now-deceased brother.

Simon, the African lion, had arrived agitated and angry. Joanna and Roberto were not ready for him. Despite all the bits of advice and information Suzette had given them, despite the double linked fenced enclosure Roberto and Rolando had created for him, they were not ready for the enormous, cranky feline.

"So, you're actually going to do this," Ruthie said.

"What?"

"You're going to keep this lion? A lion, Joanna. You have a lion in your backyard." Dixie stated the obvious. They all watched for a moment while Roberto continued driving stakes into the ground, jumping each time Simon swatted the fence, causing the links to stretch and creak.

"Why not? I've got an emu who likes to drink beer, who is now best friends with a goat—who we're not going to eat, by the way. Ever. And," she said, smiling down at her cat, "a tabby cat who likes to sleep on the Big John Head at night. Why not take in a lion?"

"Um, I don't know. Maybe because he's a lion." Jeanie looked around to her friends to see if anyone else was in agreement with her.

"He was treated like damaged goods," Joanna said and winked at Brianna. "What was I going to do? Turn him away?"
"Who owns a lion?" Jeanie asked incredulously. "I mean, who buys a lion for a pet?"

"As Suzette liked to say, someone with a little wee-wee."

Two weeks before she died, Suzette rewrote her will. The almost seventeen-acre Lee estate had been willed to Joanna Lucas with a special request that it be used as an animal sanctuary. Simon swiped the fence again, rocking Roberto back. As Roberto fell and landed on his backside, he yelled again, and the women laughed.

"What did Suzette say about the men who take care of lions?" Jeanie leaned forward, a huge grin on her face.

"So, I guess it's safe to say you're not going anywhere anytime soon. Not if you're building an animal sanctuary," Brianna said.

"Not anytime soon," Joanna said. "And I'm going to need help if you're still looking for a non-paying job."

"Sounds good." Brianna sat back and smiled.

"To Suzette!" Dixie lifted her lemonade glass, and the margarita glasses followed.

"To Suzette," they all said in unison and shifted their attention to the urn placed upon the bar.

* * * *

Four days later, the EPA ruled that it was permissible for the mercury levels to be raised. FFI forged ahead with its plan to burn more alternative fuels for cheaper costs and greater profit.

Two local environmental groups filed an historic lawsuit in Texas, suing the EPA for failing to protect the environment and the American people.

John Simmons stepped up his campaign for Congress. With campaign funds, the Simmons group rented a tour bus and mapped out their route around the tri-county area.

Early predictions had Simmons winning as the new US House member in a landslide.

Dave Sappenfield was charged with four counts of falsifying information on in-house laboratory results. As a reward for his efforts, he was fired by Albright Laboratories and John Simmons no longer returned his phone calls. So, in a final act of desperation, Sappenfield placed a phone call to Tobey Real Estate.

* * * *

Dixie was in the middle of the lunch hour rush when the phone call came in. With the overriding sense that the whole cement scandal had been swept under the rug again and that John Simmons was on his way to a certain victory, there was an unspoken forgiveness of the girls' environmental involvement. Old customers were filtering back in, and the lunch crowd was as busy as ever.

Merilee was sweating. Profusely.

Ruthie had perched herself on the edge of the stool, ringing up orders and taking money. For the girls, there was a renewed sense of calmness. However bittersweet, things were returning to normal.

"You can't fight city hall," Ruthie had said with a shrug on more than one occasion. Especially when city hall has a stake in local business.

"Quigley's Down Under," Dixie said into the phone, cradling it between her shoulder and ear. She was elbow deep in her famous chicken salad croissant sandwiches.

It was Eva, and she sounded uncharacteristically excited.

"We have to get out the Big John Head!"

"What?" Dixie almost laughed but was too busy and too stressed to play along.

In less than two minutes, Eva dropped the bomb. She had absolute evidence of John Simmons's involvement in FFI's falsification of information on the TRIs to the TCEQ and EPA.

"You want to know what's at the end of this rainbow?" Eva murmured into the phone. "At the end of each trail, it's not Gustoff Mattias or his people; it's John Simmons. I have the papers, Dixie. An actual, honest-to-goodness paper trail."

Everything slowed around Dixie.

The clatter and chatter of the lunch crowd faded in the distance.

"Where is Simmons now?" she asked.

"Austin. Our very own state capital," Eva whispered.

"So," she said, "We're taking the Big John Head on a road trip."

* * * *

"Crazy women!" Roberto laughed. He and his brother watched as Joanna slowly pulled the enormous head down the long driveway of The Shady Land. There had been a time when he had wondered about where his place was with Joanna and at The Shady Land. But no longer.

He loved Joanna, and she loved him.

For the first time in his life, he knew he had found a home and he had a purpose. It was insane. If someone had told him six months ago that he would be living with a woman like Joanna Lucas and taking care of exotic animals, he would have laughed. He knew nothing about animals. He and his brother had not had a secure home since they were children. Yet, somehow, through it all, they'd managed to stay together.

After Roberto had moved in with Joanna, Joanna took Rolando in as her brother, never batting an eyelash. She was the most amazing, warm human being he'd ever met, and she was his. All she wanted of him was his love. He could give her that. For eternity.

He'd grown up thinking that white women cared about money more than anything else in the world. They were about material items and social status. Not Joanna. She got dirty. She worked with her hands. She stood for hours in a hot barn, never complaining as she molded the clay.

She was learning Spanish. He was learning English. But they never had a communication problem. And one day, he told himself, he would tell their story to their grandchildren.

* * * *

Jeanie had called shotgun, relegating Eva and Tiffany to the back seat with Dixie and Ruthie. It was tight, but no one wanted to miss out. Each time Eva or Tiffany turned to the see the giant John Simmons head kissing a cement stack behind the truck, they burst into laughter.

"This is going to be so great," Tiffany said, and Eva patted her leg. It was wonderful to see her baby smiling again.

Eva had made phone calls alerting the media that they would arrive with huge, scandalous news.

"How will we find you?" one editor had asked, and she'd

laughed.

"Trust me, when we pull up to the capital, you won't be able to miss us."

It was their moment. Their moment of justice and revenge. And it was a long time coming . . . and about damned time.

"Ground rules," Jeanie said and turned in her seat, leaning over the back toward her new victims. "You can ask any question in this car, and it has to be answered."

Eva furrowed her brow, not sure if she liked the rules.

"What kinds of things do you intend on asking?" Eva asked.

"What kinds of things do you intend on asking," Jeanie asked, imitating Eva with a British accent, and the others laughed. It was going to be a ride to remember. Jeanie was keyed up.

"At some point," Ruthie said, leaning forward and making eye contact with both Tiffany and Eva, "she's going to need to know if you'd like urine to come out of your nose, if you'd eat from a kitty litter box, and if you'd walk naked through a parking lot for money."

Both Eva and Tiffany looked at Jeanie. As soon as they did, Jeanie raised her eyebrows and smiled triumphantly.

Joanna drove down the bumpy driveway, squinting ahead at something near the end of the lane.

"And I brought Granny!" Jeanie lifted a small canister, showing it to everyone in the vehicle.

"You brought Granny?" Ruthie asked and smiled approvingly.

"Does this mean we can't cuss now?" Dixie asked, though it was not a question. Both Eva and Tiffany looked confused. Dixie turned to the women to explain until Joanna's words caught her attention.

"That's okay," Joanna said with a laugh. "I brought Suzette," and she patted a foam-padded bag next to her. "She would have wanted to see this."

For a moment, both Jeanie and Joanna smiled. It was perfectly normal that they would each bring their maternal loved one.

"Look at that!" Dixie leaned forward, pointing ahead through the seats.

Standing at the edge of The Shady Land driveway was Brianna, saddled with two large suitcases. Joanna came to a complete stop, and for a moment, no one moved. Brianna seemed to look beyond the truck at the giant John Simmons head and laughed. Joanna eased forward, rolling down her window.

"How could I miss this?" Brianna gestured to the giant head.

"What's with the suitcases?" Joanna asked.

"Well, you seem to be picking up strays these days." Brianna looked uneasy, perhaps embarrassed.

"Not strays." Joanna put the truck in park and opened her door. "Wild, beautiful animals who weren't meant to be abused or caged up." She picked up the suitcases and hefted them into the back of the truck.

"Thanks, Joanna," Brianna whispered, pausing before the truck.

"You can sit up in front." Joanna put her arm around her friend. "Always room for one more." But that wasn't why Brianna hesitated, and Joanna knew it. She'd been there. She knew all about that first step to a new life. It was both exhilarating and terrifying. There was no way Brianna could know if she was making the right decision. She needed something familiar to cling to.

"Oh, good, Brianna! Tell me you don't agree with this," Jeanie yelled from the cab of the truck. "If we know that child molesters will molest again because . . . well, we do and because they always do . . . why would we have a system that lets them out? You talk about your damaged goods. Those people are damaged. We let 'em out so that they can damage other people. Why not make it mandatory that we do medical experiments on them? You know, make 'em worth something to us. We can test all kinds of medications and drugs and chemicals on them. If they die, who cares? They're no good to us anyway. If they live, they finally did something that contributes to our society.

"We could use them in car crash tests, too. You know, how well do those dummies work? Let's use real people. Let's use child molesters!"

Brianna smiled and climbed into the truck pulling the Big John Head.

* * * *

It was the showstopper of all showstoppers. The governor had promised a "monumental occasion," and Joanna had delivered. In fact, it was the most outrageous, most disgusting thing Joanna had ever done. And she couldn't help but feel a certain *déjà vu* all over again. But this time, she wasn't alone.

Throughout the ride to Austin, Jeanie held fast to the small cooler. It was their secret weapon. Wild elephants couldn't tear it from her; a nuclear meltdown would not take the cooler from her grip, Jeanie had said.

"I'm holding this until the very last minute. And then I'm handing it off to you, sister. It's all yours," Jeanie said.

They had all agreed that the final act would belong to Joanna. She would do it for Suzette.

Eva held the paper trail of evidence in a brown, expandable folder. The girls had the proof that FFI had been doctoring its TRIs to hide how many toxic chemicals the plant was spewing into the air, water, and soil.

In addition, the girls had the names and signatures of angry citizens and their toxicology reports. They also had the autopsy report of Tiffany's baby. Tiffany was a powerful living witness to the deadly effects of the cement plant's toxic emissions.
Still, the girls knew what they were up against. All the testimonies and evidence didn't mean a hill of beans to the TCEQ and EPA in the state of Texas. It would only get worse once John Simmons was elected and in a position of power to make even more deadly decisions in the name of business and profit. For the moment, he

had two things going for him. Strong financial backing from Gustoff Mattias Enterprises and the "Golden Boy" reputation of bringing international businesses to small-town Texas. He promised greater economic growth and better education and other platitudes. But he spent most of his time in denial. He denied any wrongdoing. He denied evidence of global warming. He denied the ill effects of burning hazardous waste. He denied any connection to Albright Laboratories, and he denied any knowledge of bloody stools.

That was going to change, and it was going to change in a most public manner.

The governor of Texas had invited John Simmons and Gustoff Mattias to the capital building, along with the press corps for what the governor called a *monumental occasion*. The Austrian government was joining forces with the state of Texas. Together, their venture would be global.

The *venture* disgusted the girls. They knew exactly what this arrangement was. The state of Texas had been declared the most polluted in the US, and if Texas were a country unto itself, it would be ranked seventh in the world.

Understanding the ramifications, the governor's office spun this, joining forces with Gustoff Mattias's government to declare a "global effort to help citizens in the US and abroad." For so many Americans who read only headlines to get their news, this was perfect.

TEXAS JOINS GLOBAL EFFORTS, and John Simmons was to be named as one of the leaders.

"Blech," Jeanie had said, making a face at the mere thought of it.

"You still got it?" Dixie asked Jeanie as they pulled up to the capitol building. People were everywhere—reporters, camera crews, and citizens were strewn across the green lawn.

"I got it. You don't worry about me. You worry about you. You know what you're supposed to say?" Jeanie licked her lips. Joanna smiled. They were all whispering. As their truck rolled forward with the gigantic Styrofoam John Simmons head trailing behind them, hundreds of people were turning, pointing, and smiling. One after another, cameras were lifted and pointed toward the head. Yet the women whispered amongst themselves, as though they still had some chance of sneaking up on the crowd. A scowling police officer was in instant pursuit, headed toward them. No doubt, local police had already been briefed on how to handle any negative publicity.

"Okay," Ruthie said, nudging Joanna. "It's now or never. Scoot!"

With that command, Operation PayBack was set in motion. Ruthie slid behind the wheel, already waving an apology to the police officer as Joanna hopped out from the driver's side. Dixie, Jeanie, Eva, and Tiffany were right behind her, leaving Brianna riding shotgun with Ruthie.

"Hey!" Brianna yelled, and the truck slowed once more, despite the furious gesturing of the police officer.

"Take Suzette!" she called out, handing a navy blue bag out the window. Eva trotted back to retrieve it.

"Keep moving! Keep moving!" the officer yelled.

Ruthie gave the horn a few taps as the girls slipped into the crowd. Dixie, Eva, and Tiffany moved toward the stage, positioning themselves near a CNN team, as Jeanie and Joanna moved toward the stairs leading to the stage.

Jeanie checked her watch. "We got about two more minutes."

The governor had not yet arrived but bodyguards had already taken their positions on and around the stage. John Simmons, Gustoff Mattias, and a handful of FFI officials waited on stage. Joanna could imagine the kind of self-congratulatory chatter going on up there.

There was a sudden hush of the crowd, and Joanna's heart lurched as she heard the whisper. "Here he comes."

*This was it.*

Polite applause. Cameras readjusted. Then the governor was standing before a lectern.

Joanna scanned the crowd, catching a glimpse of Suzette's urn as Eva was waving it back and forth over the heads of the crowd. Joanna smiled.

She turned back to Jeanie.

"You ready?" Jeanie grinned. It was a classic Jeanie Archer grin—broad, daring, mischievous. She lifted the small cooler and snickered. Her eyebrows were raised so high, she looked ten years old.

Joanna was aware of the governor's speech, of his introduction of a new leader in the business world and in the political arena—the lead in to John Simmons—when Dixie's voice rang out.

"Can you please ask John Simmons what he plans to do about the terrible health problem in his own hometown?"

The governor paused mid-sentence. He tried just a little too hard to look pleasant.

"I'm sorry? Who . . ." He stopped and looked around for an assistant or security guard to shut Dixie down, but she'd already turned to the camera audience. Within seconds, she'd reeled off statistics about asthma, cancers, brain tumors, and birth defects in Marcus, Texas. Eva joined in, shouting about quarries next to elementary schools and endangered cement plant workers.

As expected, John Simmons could not stand it and stepped forward.

Jeanie smiled, and whispered, "Atta boy." She lifted the lid to the cooler and pulled out the secret weapon. She glowed with anticipation.

John wagged a finger at the audience, cautioning them against believing either rumors or activists. As he said the word activists, there was a sneer.

Dixie did not back off.

"Are you denying any knowledge of health problems, Mr. Simmons?"

Tiffany was talking to a reporter, and John could see things spiraling away from his control. Dixie persisted, and Jeanie gave Joanna her nudge.

"This is it," Jeanie said to her, handing Joanna the baggie. Joanna could feel her legs moving. She could hear Dixie badgering John on stage. Dixie's setup was perfect. She was backing John into a corner, making him say he had no knowledge of any health problems and that, yes, he would look into any evidence suggesting anyone was sick as a result of the cement plant.

All eyes were on Dixie, making Joanna's approach to the steps easy. It was too easy. It was all coming back to her.

*The olive branch. He wanted the olive branch.*
John Simmons had nodded to the security guards when he saw Joanna. So smug, so sure of himself, he was sure she'd come to concede defeat. In turn, the security guards had assumed that because Simmons invited her to come forward, she was friend, not foe and did not check what she held in her hand.

One step up.

"I've seen nothing . . ." John said but stopped. The expression on his face was priceless as he realized Joanna Lucas was on stage and walking toward him, hand extended. So confident, he'd smiled.

Later, on the way home, on the patio at The Shady Land, and for years to come, the girls would howl with laughter at how he'd dropped his jaw and numbly, robotically extended his own hand to receive whatever it was Joanna had to give him.

It was no olive branch.

Before an Austin crowd; before the cameras of local, state, national, and international media outlets; before the entire world, Joanna passed a zip lock baggie to John. And he took it. He frowned down at it and uttered the line that would feed late-night

talk show hosts for a week: "What's this . . . oh, shit!"
It was Paul Cowell's latest bloody stool.

Joanna turned and walked away. It was the most outrageous, most appalling thing Joanna had ever done in her life. It was so beneath her, yet so absolutely appropriate, that she would wince and smile at the memory of it for the rest of her life. It was so shocking, so scandalous, and so undeniably disgusting that her single action of rebellion would reach legendary status before the ink had dried on John Simmons' indictment papers.

No longer would she be known as the queen of tampons.

On behalf of environmental heroes everywhere.

This story is far from over.

# ABOUT THE AUTHOR

Alexandra Allred holds her Masters in Kinesiology, with special interest in functional movement as she works with the special needs and senior populations. An advocate for all things healthy, Allred writes fiction, "for my own health. It makes me happy!"

This former national and professional athlete also teaches kickbox and bootcamp classes when not spending time with her family (both two- and four-legged) in Texas. She is an award-winning author for both her fiction and non-fiction works.